THE TRUTH
in HOPE

The TRUTH in HOPE

R.A. SIMPSON

gatekeeper press

Columbus, Ohio

The Truth in Hope

Published by Gatekeeper Press
2167 Stringtown Rd, Suite 109
Columbus, OH 43123-2989
www.GatekeeperPress.com

ISBN (hardcover): 9781662903540
ISBN (paperback): 9781662903557
eISBN: 9781662903564

With loving gratitude, to my parents,
Craig and Maryann Simpson
whose spirit and inspiration continue
to mold who I am and what I write.

"To live without hope is to cease to live."
—*Fyodor Dostoyevsky*

CHAPTER ONE

Northwoods, Wisconsin

JUNE 4, 2018

I t was an idyllic morning, a solitary and tranquil beginning of the day. Light was peeking through from the eastern horizon, slowing but surely melting the mist that had nestled on and concealed the pristine waters of Lake Gresham, just one of a thousand freshwater lakes buried so deeply in the woods of God's country. The resident loon began his serenade in perfect pitch. It was literally the only sound audible to human ears; not even a slight babble of water hitting rocks or receding from the small sand beach could be detected. The lake was glass.

The scene, so placid and comforting and peaceful, so soothing to the senses, so spiritual . . . totally belied the invasion of violence that was mere moments away.

A knotty pine Northwoods cabin completed the immediate surroundings with a pickup truck parked about fifty feet from the back door. The only occupant of the rustic and secluded dwelling had awakened concurrently with the first ray of light hitting his swollen noggin. He was not well. Never one to take responsibility, if given a chance to explain, being "overserved" would have been his feeble excuse.

Life is so often, as it should be, measured in "firsts." First kiss, train ride, winning hit, graduation, funeral, marriage, first child, child's first steps, first house, first divorce, first sexual experience, first fish caught, first beer, first job, roller coaster ride, airplane ride, child's first winning basket, child's first vocal solo. And the list goes on. Cannot it be said that a fulfilling life never tires of firsts with the enjoyment being amplified by sharing the same with loved ones?

Since yesterday morning, the liquor-infused slug in the cabin had stopped experiencing firsts. His last one had been about six months ago. It was an acquittal, or that's how he would describe it.

Although unknown to him, his final twenty-four hours had been filled with a series of "lasts." His last breakfast, lunch, and dinner. His last fish caught. His last smoke. His last game of pool. His last stare at a local. His last flirt. His last night out with the guys. His last beer. His last lie. His last time driving drunk. His last puke, which had failed to even register in his brain until he stepped in it the next morning when he rose from the couch where he'd crashed the previous evening.

He stumbled to the nearest bathroom to remedy his cotton mouth. There was no cup so he leaned under the faucet and slushed in a few gulps, enhancing the pain in his temples. Last drink of water.

He needed some fresh air. He walked towards the back door, passing the kitchen sink along the way. It was overflowing with a week's worth of dirty dishes. He rarely cleaned up his messes, typically leaving the burden to someone else. His parents were high on the list.

He reached the outside considerably earlier than his predator had anticipated. He relieved himself. His last piss. He reentered the cabin. Thank God for Keurig coffee makers. Put the K-cup in, pull the lever down, press the button. He could not have handled anything more complicated for his last cup of coffee. After his last swig, he felt a rumbling down under. He thought of looking for yesterday's sports page for some pot reading material but soon realized that even elemental reading was not yet on his radar. He finished his business. Last flush.

He sat down on the couch, shaded his eyes from the rising sun, spotted the vomit that he had deposited the previous evening, and exclaimed, "Shit!" He thought of cleaning it up, and actually intended to do so, but felt he would be better equipped for the task if he had a smoke first. Last good intention.

He staggered back out of the cabin and headed for his truck in search of a Marlboro Red. This time the predator was prepared, sight directly on his left temple. That was not, however, his preferred target. Thus, the dead fish and the photograph.

With about a minute remaining in his life, as he was inching towards the truck, the slug eyed an object on the ground in front of the driver's side door. His drunken, impaired vision prevented him from identifying the object until he was standing directly over it. It was a dead fish. A walleye. It was looking directly at him. Underneath the fish was an envelope. He picked it up, opened it, and removed the contents. It was a photograph. Of Hope and her parents, smiling directly into his bloodshot eyes. He recognized them, of course.

He turned to take his last look at the lake. He turned back to take his last look at the woods. It was then that he took his last breath. The bullet struck him directly between the eyes, splattering blood, brain, and bone against the driver's side window of his late model pickup. He crumpled over and landed in a semi-fetal position with Walter, the fish, still staring him down and the family photo still clutched in his right hand.

Nearly two days elapsed before the body was discovered. It would have been longer but for a visitor to the area taking a wrong turn down the lane leading to the lakeside retreat. By that time, it was a "dead heat" as to who smelled worse . . . Walter or the slug.

A funeral service would be held on the North Shore of Chicago. The casket would be closed. In the coming days, a number of people living about 350 miles south would be celebrating or suffering new "firsts."

The predator removed himself from his perch. He knew without checking vital signs that his target had expired. The residue on the truck window was self-explanatory. There were just three details to attend to before his exit from the scene.

He gently removed the photo from the decedent's hand, placed it back in the envelope, and secured it under the decedent's head. He removed two knitting needles from his breast pocket and strategically inserted one in the eye of the fish and the other just above the tail—to secure it from scavengers. Now, where was his phone?

The previous night, while being watched at one of the local watering holes, the now deceased had consistently replaced his phone in the left rear pocket of his jeans. He was currently wearing boxers, wool socks, and a Hooters t-shirt.

The predator did a quick perusal of the cab of the truck. Nothing there. He would have to breach the cabin. Not a problem. He walked in, dragging mud on the entrance and the vomit-soaked braided rug. He spotted a belt looped into a pair of jeans that were partially underneath the couch. He removed them with his gloved left hand. It was there. Left rear pocket. It was, of course, the latest model iPhone. Only two percent of juice remained. He didn't have much time. "Be quick, but don't be in a hurry." He heeded the words of a legendary coach.

He went back to the corpse and the fish, the latter having been placed at the scene about thirty minutes earlier. It had been netted the previous morning at a lake about an hour away. An ice chest had kept it fresh until his appearance this morning. A shame he had to sacrifice his favorite freshwater friend, best prepared broiled and served with drawn garlic butter. It was a couple inches short of being legal. The authorities would not notice.

Gravity was allowing blood and other fluids to flow from the mortal wound on the decedent's still recognizable face. The marksman took a brief five-second video with the dead man's phone, depicting his fate and, more importantly, memorializing the time of his death with considerably more accuracy than any potential forensic guess.

He searched the contacts on the phone, located whom he believed was his intended recipient—someone named "Pops"—attached the video to a text and pushed send. Within a matter of seconds, the battery expired and the phone went dead. He placed it in the right hand of the dead man.

He visually retraced his route from the woods, into the house, and back outside. A perfect trail had been left due to the heavy dew on the grass and mud outside. Boot prints would continue the trail on the floor of the interior of the cabin.

He walked to the shoreline of the lake, about a hundred feet away, where a small sand beach accepted his boot prints with more accuracy and detail; his return route to the body was parallel and similarly revealing.

Hours would be spent photographing the prints. Molds would be made of the size twelve Cabela's. Labor intensive investigation would follow to determine where and when they had been manufactured and sold. And hopefully to whom.

No worries, thought the predator. He briskly returned to his vehicle, which had been strategically parked on a curved portion of the lane leading to the cabin, secluded from the sight of anyone on the entry road or lakeside. He paused to take a final assessment of his morning's labor. The deceased predator, of a different subset, was taking his final sleep with a fish. Random families would be spared a lifetime of agony.

He opened the trunk, broke down his weapon, discarded his muddy boots, slipped into his size nine penny loafers, and checked his watch. It was 7:00 a.m. Time for breakfast.

Finding a remote cabin in northern Wisconsin can be a bit tricky, more so if your cell phone is dead and your car lacks GPS. All too well, Wayne Crawford now knew this.

Wayne, a sales rep for a power tools manufacturer in Iowa, was at the end of his workday, having just secured a handsome order from a local hardware store, the bulk of which was for chainsaws. Within the previous week, a couple of severe storms had passed through the Pinesap County area, causing considerable tree damage. An uptick in chain-saw sales would naturally follow. Wayne was familiar with the financial benefits flowing from acts of God.

A little celebration was in order. A nice dinner—salad, beer cheese soup, steak, loaded baked potato, a couple Point Specials, maybe more. He was not interested in eating alone and was really not that familiar with the restaurants in the area. But he knew someone who was.

Wayne and Jed Tucker had gone to school at UW-Stevens Point, where they had both played on the school's club hockey team. He had been to Jed's cabin once, but it was about five years before. No clear recollection of the route. He sat in his car, racking his brain trying to remember the name of the lake where Jed lived. Waste of time. This was a small town. Everybody knew everybody. He got out of his car and walked back to the hardware store.

"Forget something, Wayne?" asked George, the owner of the store.

"No, no, I'm good. I was just wondering if you know someone by the name of Jed Tucker."

"Jedediah! Absolutely. I was one of his hockey coaches in high school." That was not quite true. George had sponsored the Hodags when Jed starred there as a goalie. He'd donated sticks to the team. The jerseys had borne a patch that said, "Stick with George's Hardware." One was pinned to the wall behind the register. "He has an account here." That made sense. Jed did remodeling work, as Wayne recalled.

"Do you know where he lives?" asked Wayne.

"You betcha. Up there on Gresham."

Bingo, that was it. Gresham Lake.

"Directions, George?"

"Easy peasy, Wayne. Just take the slab north about three miles. Turn right on K. Go about another two miles

13

and turn south on North Birch Trail. From there, just follow the arrows."

"Thanks, George."

Wayne had traveled the area long enough to be able to translate George's directions. The "slab" referred to the main concrete road that ran through the village of Oneida Falls; in this case, Route 45. "K" was a county road. In Wisconsin, county roads were designated by letters. "Arrows"? Because of the density of the woods, it had been the tradition of property owners to nail wooden signs in the shape of arrows on trees which, if visible, would lead one to the intended destination.

Such was the case on North Birch Trail. "Just follow the arrows," George had said. Interesting. The number of arrow signs on trees could roughly vary from one to fifteen. Not all of them pointed in the same direction. Not all of them had the name of the owner on the sign. Some of them had the name that the owners, current or past, had given to their cabins, such as "Pine Needle Hideaway" or "Hidden Waters Retreat" and the like. Some signs bore the names of long-lost ancestors whose surnames had no connection to present day ownership. Some residents, not wanting to be found, had no signs at all.

It was getting late. It was overcast and dusk was settling in. The road was winding and there was a local tailgating him in a hurry to get home. He was getting frustrated trying to read the fucking arrow signs and hoping to get a glimpse of the name Tucker or Gresham. An oncoming car flashed its high beams at Wayne, who swerved to the right to avoid a collision. He was beginning to wonder whether this was such a good idea; he thought about turning around and enjoying the steak alone. In a few minutes, his uncertainty about the wisdom of the plan would evaporate. But it would be too late.

Alas, he caught glimpse of the type of name he was looking for: "Gresham Gathering," a white sign with green lettering pointing to the left. Without signaling, he turned left abruptly, resulting in the tailgater laying on his horn for an extended time. "Fuck you, cheesehead," he vented.

A darker and narrower road ensued. On the next lane there were two signs, but Wayne's attention was only drawn to one. It was the same white sign with green lettering with the arrow pointing to the right. The other one had a different shape with faded black lettering.

Wayne turned right—an unfortunate choice. The towering pines on each side of the road were claustrophobic, especially for the Iowan who had always lived on open, sprawling farms. Unknown to him, the tires of his car were now supplanting any tracks that may have been made the previous morning by the predator. Upon switching to high beams, two dark-colored birds with generous wing spans lifting off the ground could be observed. *Probably a dead rabbit or raccoon*, Wayne thought. The pickup truck came into view next. Good sign. Jed remodeled. That would be his vehicle of choice. Then a well-lit cabin appeared and Wayne exclaimed out loud, "Awesome!" Jed was home. It turned out the trip had been worth it.

His spirits buoyed, he stopped the car and turned off the engine. His intention was to walk to the back door and knock. Something, however, stopped him. It didn't feel right. This cabin was considerably larger than the one he had visited five years ago. And Jed's entry door was lakeside. He had the wrong place.

Now the intruder, Wayne stealthily began his walk back to his car, which was blocking the lane. Could he make it back in time before being noticed and perceived as a burglar? Or worse? Could he navigate the narrow lane that he had just traversed, except this time in reverse? He would never know.

About three steps into his journey, a clicking noise broke the silence of the night and light flooded the area. Security lights. On a timer. On motion. Or both. Instinctively, Wayne halted, raised his hands, and pleaded, "I'm lost, honestly." Silence. He slowly turned towards the back door of the cabin. No sound. No movement. He exhaled a long sigh of relief and continued his journey.

Buzzing. He heard a buzzing sound. He cautiously inched his way towards the source of this eerie, audible, and noxious smelling lure . . . to the place where yesterday's kill of human and fish lay in repose. Immediate regurgitation followed his briefest of glances. He dropped to his knees and attempted to crawl away from the carnage where a convention of flies, ants, and millipedes were feasting upon Walter and the slug. It was, after all, their turn, as the larger neighborhood varmints had previously had their fill.

Wayne continued his purging as he laboriously crawled toward the cabin door, further contaminating the crime scene in more ways than one. He reached the back stoop and struggled to stand and enter. He was finally able to do so, but having lost all systemic control, promptly defecated in his recently dry-cleaned khakis. It didn't register.

Entering the cabin, he did a visual search for a phone. Leaning against a granite kitchen counter for balance and support, he spied one ten to twelve feet away. As he headed in the direction of the phone, still grasping the granite, deposits of his feces cascaded along the way onto the newly installed kitchen ceramic tile. He was not aware.

He lifted the phone and then slumped down to the tile, as he had no strength to stand, landing in the corner where the wall met the lower cabinets beneath the counter. He dialed 911.

"911, who is calling?"

"Gathering. No, Gresham Gathering."

"Is this Mr. Wilkerson?"

"No, Wayne Crawford. Send cops." He dropped the phone. He began to sob. When the police arrived, he was in the same position and still sobbing.

Welcome to GRESHAM GATHERING.

Located about 150 feet to the east of Gresham Gathering, at the end of the lane, was a modest cabin built in the thirties. It had been passed down the family chain to its current owner who, at the moment, was relaxing from a hard day's work of hanging drywall. He was on his second Point Special and was about finished with the sausage-and-pepperoni deep dish that he had picked up coming home from work. He was satisfied and content watching his widescreen TV with newly ordered high-def satellite service. Especially now. Stanley Cup Playoffs. Western Conference finals. Minnesota Wild versus Chicago Blackhawks.

He heard sirens in the distance. As they drew closer, he could see that the cops were headed to his neighbor's place, the "Gathering." He wondered what the Illinois fucks were up to this time.

He went back to his game. Wild scored and won in overtime. Sudden death loss for the Hawks. Oh yeah.

Had Wayne Crawford been more diligent and obser-vant when examining the last set of signs, he could have avoided the misery that befell him that night and haunted him for years to come. The sign he'd been looking for was actually nailed considerably higher than the Wilkerson sign. An old wooden hockey stick. Netminder's. The paddle pointed towards the home of the drywaller and had two stickers affixed. One was quite old and read "George's Hardware" with a picture of a Hodag; the newer of the two was round and depicted the logo of the Minnesota Wild.

On the handle, in legible but somewhat faded handwritten letters, was the name that Jed Tucker had given to his humble abode on the shores of Gresham Lake, Wisconsin: "THE PUCK STOPS HERE."

Although unknown to him at the time, the Iowa chainsaw salesman had been the victim of another stroke of misfortune.

Cabins in the Northwoods use wells for water and septic tanks and fields for waste. Annual inspections are advised. Gresham Gathering's had been scheduled for 10:00 a.m. on the same day Bryce Wilkerson, the youngest of the clan, had entered his darkness. Aces Wild Septic Service, owned by local Native American Bud Roughwaters, a member of the Oneida tribe, had been providing this service for years. "Aces," as it was known in the area, had a very colorful fleet of trucks and tanks. On the side of each tank were the words "Aces Wild Septic"; underneath the business name were four playing cards, all aces with the four different suits. Under the playing cards, the company slogan read, in quotes and script: "Where a good flush always beats a full house."

Bud had assigned the job to his typically dependable son-in-law, Larry Beckhart. Larry called in sick the morning of the appointment. It seemed young Bryce wasn't the only one who had been overserved the previous evening.

Larry was captain and starting pitcher on his local slow-pitch softball team. The night before the shooting, his team played an away game against the first-place team in Sayner, Wisconsin.

The combatants on these teams were spirited guys of all ages. Most were blue collar, and many were strong, overweight, or both. The games tended to be high-scoring affairs. Lots of home runs hit, lots of beer consumed.

Larry's team, the "Aces," was sponsored by his father-in-law. Going into the bottom of the seventh, they were leading twenty to sixteen. One pitch later, the lead was cut to three. The next two batters popped up, both a little too anxious with their uppercut swings. One more out and the Aces would pull off the upset of the summer.

Next batter singled. The following drew a walk. Larry vehemently argued the call, suggesting the ump clean his glasses. A well-placed swinging bunt loaded the bases.

Butch Eliason strolled to the plate. He worked at a local lumberyard. He was very strong. And he hit lots of dingers.

The infield had a powwow on the mound. All were in agreement that Butch should be walked. Except Larry. He argued that Eliason had not had a solid at bat all night. He wouldn't throw him a strike. He'd coax him to swing at a bad pitch.

And that's exactly what he did. The first pitch he threw to the right-handed slugger was just shy of a foot outside. Butch reached across the plate and sent the twelve-inch sphere over the fence. It hit the light standard and bounced back onto the field, settling about ten feet in front of Larry as he was already exiting.

The players emptied the dugout. The fans, relatives and friends of the players, emptied the bleachers. Both groups would greet the hero of the day at home plate. Butch was slowly jogging around the bases, triumphantly pounding his fists in the air. Upon reaching home plate, he was mobbed in celebration by his teammates and fandom. Multiple beers were poured over his head. Everybody jumped up and down. It was a story that would be retold in years to come by the people of this small Northwoods hamlet.

Meanwhile, the losing pitcher took one last look at the celebration and headed straight to the Sayner Pub. Many of his fellow Aces followed suit. In time, most of the Sayner players joined in the frivolity. Two hours later, you couldn't tell the winners from the losers. The magic tonic of alcohol.

Captain Larry got home around 2:30 a.m. He knew as his head hit the pillow that sleep would not come easily, given the level of his blood alcohol and his mental postmortem of the game. He also knew that the shit inspection of the FIBs (Fucking Illinois Bastards) septic would be delayed.

The next day, Bud Roughwaters made the call to the baron of the property, Harold Wilkerson, at his law office in Chicago to reschedule the septic procedure. He was out town, but his trusty secretary answered and told Bud a reschedule would not be a problem. The appointment was made for a week later. No one would remember.

Deputy Sheriff Hallie Hogan had been on the job for approximately three months. She was assigned to the northern half of Pinesap County, Wisconsin. Shifts had been dull, to say the least. Most of the action was in the southern part of the county where Oneida Falls was located. It was the hub of the social activity. Bars, supper clubs, bowling alleys, more bars. Oh, she had written the occasional speeding ticket, investigated deer-related accidents, quelled a few domestic incidents. Life was about to change.

She was about three miles from the Wilkerson cabin when she received the dispatch to investigate the happenings at Gresham Gathering. Probably another domestic. Fortunately, she had GPS in her squad car. She punched in the address and followed the prompts. It was dark when she arrived.

"What is that putrid smell?" she asked herself as she walked to the back door, knocked, and announced her presence. She could hear a faint noise from the interior that sounded like someone weeping. She drew her service handgun, opened the door, and scanned the room in the ready position. She then spotted the Iowan, Mr. Crawford.

She rushed to his side and asked him if there was anyone else in the cabin. He shook his head no. Then he pointed outside. She satisfied herself that the remainder of the cabin was vacant and then contacted dispatch to order an ambulance while heading outdoors to further her inspection. Dispatch control could hear her regurgitation over the radio. "Send the Sheriff. Send Detective Spurlock and the fire department. There's a dead person here."

CHAPTER TWO

Doc and the Nurse

H e was not a doctor, and she was not a nurse. They were the names they had given each other when they'd first met, an event occasioned mostly by chance. The nicknames would stick for years to come.

Doc's flight to Chicago O'Hare had been cancelled. Not because of conditions in Pittsburgh but by blizzard-like elements in the Windy City. It was of no particular concern to him; he had been to "the 'Burgh" on many occasions and knew all the best restaurants. And he was off work the next day.

He'd headed to one of his favorite haunts, Grandy's, on Mount Washington, which overlooked the three rivers city. He sat down at the bar, ordered a drink, and picked up an abandoned *Post-Gazette*. He scanned the sports section. A small ad on the next-to-last page drew his attention. "Every Saturday at 10:00 a.m. Shared Stories." There was a website address, which he accessed when he got back to his downtown hotel. The next morning, he'd gone to the meeting at a small conference room in the venerable William Penn Hotel. His life would change.

Doc had gone to great lengths to both hide and suppress his past. People hide things from others; they suppress them from themselves. They try, anyway. It is considerably easier to execute the former. A snowstorm in Chicago led to a shitstorm of memories that were about to be shared with six strangers from Pennsylvania who all had one thing in common: each had been sexually abused as a child by an adult, one who was revered and respected more than anyone in their respective communities—a Catholic priest.

Doc grew up in a medium-sized town in north central Indiana. His family had been staunch Catholics for generations. The church was the predominant force in the community: socially, educationally, and spiritually. The school's athletic teams were annual state contenders in football and basketball. They recruited jocks away from the public schools. Many graduates of St. Joe High attended prestigious colleges out East or small private schools in the Midwest; but most who were college material longed for the campus where "Touchdown Jesus" reigned: Notre Dame. It was where Doc had aspired to be. He had watched Joe Montana as a kid. He had wanted to "play like a champion today." He had watched *Rudy* at least once a year. But it would not happen. His dream had died when he was ten years old. Shortly thereafter, his duties as altar boy ended without explanation.

The Nurse had been attending her second support group meeting that morning. She smiled when she heard the newcomer indicate his nickname as "Doc." He reciprocated when she stated hers. It was the beginning of a bond that would grow for years to come. They were always there for each other. A relationship that would continue to reach new levels.

The Nurse's dream of becoming one had ended when she was nine.

Her grandmother had been the nurse for her childhood doctor. She was old-fashioned, wearing the all-white uniform, stockings, and cap. She always smiled. She always helped. The Nurse adored her, wanted to follow in her footsteps. It wasn't to be.

Her whole family was proud when she'd been chosen for the elite girls' choir at Our Lady of the Missions church in the Bloomfield area of Pittsburgh. There had been a feast at their home, with all the cousins there. Casseroles of lasagna were brought. Wine flowed.

Two years later, to everyone's shock, the Nurse quit the choir. She quit trying at school. She began having nightmares. She became afraid, whereas before she'd been bold. Her angelic voice had been quieted. Her parents had no answers. They suffered daily. Counselors were not trusted. Friends gave support but had no remedies. They turned to the Church, unaware that they were staring the enemy in the face.

Thirty years had passed since Doc had been abused. He no longer lived in Indiana but still got his hometown paper. His abuser, Father Thomas Shields, had been killed by a drunk driver who was coming home from a post-funeral drinking binge. The whole town mourned. Doc wrote a letter to the newspaper, anonymously disclosing his abusive history with the deceased priest. They, of course, did not print it. It was passed on to the police, who passed it on to the county prosecutor. Difficult to charge a dead man. More difficult to disparage a local icon. It was eighty-sixed.

The relationship between Doc and the Nurse grew substantially after that first winter meeting in Pittsburgh. They became confidants. The Nurse eventually moved to the Chicago area where Doc lived. As a result, they grew closer. The Nurse shared.

> The room is very dark and massive. There is no apparent ceiling. The young girl wants to leave but she is paralyzed by her fear. There are distant noises. A choir, perhaps? Doors open and shut. Light creeps into the inescapable gorge. Benches appear, lots of them, all filled with people staring at her. Many are smiling at her. They want her to sing. She can barely breathe. Her fear augments. A door opens and a man in a robe enters. In unison, all in the benches kneel, close their eyes, and bow their heads. The man in the robe approaches the girl with a smile. She can smell his cologne and breath; she can see his wrinkly hands and his silver hair. She wants to scream.

> Her ability to scream returns as she awakens from the nightmare. She is mortified. She has soiled her bed. Her mother comes to comfort her. Had

she been in the dream? On one of the benches, smiling at her and urging her to sing? Yes, it was her! She must know what has happened. "What is it, my dear? What is wrong?" The young girl buries her head in her mother's bosom, realizing again that she does not know. And perhaps never will.

And Doc shared.

It is fall. The air is clear and crisp, and the trees are bleeding red, gold, and orange. Footballs fill the air in South Bend and in backyards dotted across northern Indiana. It is four on four, and the blond-haired lad of ten is playing quarterback. He is diagramming plays in the dirt. He throws a perfect spiral to his left end, who runs into the end zone. He keeps on running until he disappears. The other boys walk away in eerie silence. The young QB is alone. He drops to his knees as the leaves wilt and turn to brown, falling to the ground. The sun sets as he begins to weep.

The tears continue to flow as he awakes from his recurring dream. It's late August of his junior year in high school. St. Joseph High's football team has its opening game tonight. He is not on the team and he won't be attending the game. His parents do not understand; Father Shields does.

The meeting with strangers in Pittsburgh was Doc's first disclosure. It was a huge event for him, personally. Thirty years, three quarters of his life, had passed since the most respected man in town had perpetrated his monstrous and deviant behavior on this innocent and defenseless child of just ten years old. Dreams had been shattered. Self-esteem had been displaced with guilt; equilibrium had yielded to chaos; direction had been supplanted by aimlessness. And the shame of it all, the misplaced and undeserved shame.

> "Why can't I tell my parents, or my brother, or my friends, or my teachers, or my Sunday school teacher, or fucking anybody? Okay, I'll tell you why. Because it's dirty. I'm dirty. If I talk about it, I relive it. And if I relive it, I feel dirtier. So, I keep it inside. Buried deep inside. Besides, if I tell anybody what happened, where he put his hands and mouth and where he directed my hands and mouth . . . who will believe me? Oh, do you want me to tell you what he said: 'Oh, it's little Michael Duff. Your initials are M.D. Is that why they call you DOC?' And if you do believe me, then what? Is he going away? Hell no. He will continue to be the guiding fucking light of the community, and I will be looked upon as the troubled young boy who is doomed for failure. Either way I lose. So, if it's okay with

all of you, I believe I prefer to fail in silence."

Until Pittsburgh and the conference room at the William Penn Hotel and . . . the Nurse.

★   ★   ★

The Nurse. Real name: Kelle Russo. A girl, once destined for vocal fame, faded into relative obscurity in her hometown bordered by the three rivers. Her close-knit Italian family would never know what had caused her transformation from budding singer to computer geek.

Her father, Enzo, was four when he came to America. Old school. Roman Catholic. Family was everything. If he'd known the truth, it would have been the biggest story in Pittsburgh. *Italian butcher slays Father Rossini.* But he never knew. It was so painful to see his *bella figlia* lose her musical passion to be substituted by a cyber world that was beyond his comprehension.

It was infinitely more painful for Kelle. Her abuse was omnipresent. At school, for sure; at church, beyond measure. With her friends . . . excruciating. But the worst was at home. She had an inquisitive older sister and two protective younger brothers. Her grandparents lived in her neighborhood and still spoke mostly Italian.

> "What is wrong, my *bella nipotina*? Sing.
> Sing for me please. What is wrong? Please,
> sing for me."

And her parents. Oh, her parents. They lacked the ability to understand or believe that their beautiful daughter could be violated by the man they respected most in the world. Kelle had sensed this early on. There would be no disclosure. In her mind, it was not even a close decision.

> Mamma, Papà. Just love me. Forgive me. Trust me. I cannot tell you the truth. It is too painful. It was my fault. Oh, Papà. Please, just hold me. I will never shame you like I have shamed myself. Please, Papà, just end my pain without knowing its cause. Please, Papà.

She immersed herself into the computer age, at school and at home. It was lonely but seemingly safe. She became extremely proficient, so much so that she had been awarded a scholarship to the highly reputed Carnegie Mellon University in her hometown of Pittsburgh.

She'd graduated with honors. She'd met her future husband, who had been one of her grad assistants her senior year. They'd married and moved to New York City and took jobs with a rising software firm. It had seemed like the perfect move—new city, new job, new relationship. Within a year, Kelle discovered he was having an affair with a coworker who happened to be a friend of hers. She divorced him and moved back to Pitt.

At the insistence of her parents, she'd petitioned the Church for an annulment. Painful process.

Anything related to the Church was always occasioned by pain. Driving by it, entering it, attending mass, hearing a choir, listening to the priest chanting Latin. *Let me out of here*, her inner voices screamed. On occasion, she would get up and leave, telling her family that she was ill. And it was so true.

Eventually, she'd moved from home, secured a place in Mount Washington and a job setting up software programs for a national accounting firm. At an office Christmas party at the William Penn Hotel, she ran across a discarded flyer advertising "Shared Stories." In mid-January, she'd attended her first meeting. It had lasted two hours. Fifteen minutes into the meeting, she'd begun sobbing—and still was when the session closed. It had taken twenty years to break her silence.

A month later, a man from Chicago introduced himself as "Doc." Another shared story. More tears. And the dawn of healing.

CHAPTER THREE

Private Duff

M ichael Duff's graduation from St. Joe High was not a celebrated event, at least not by him. Oh, there had been the usual parties attended by friends and relatives, local and from afar. Congratulations were offered with enthusiasm, some of them genuine, some feigned. The people who really knew Michael were aware that he had underachieved and that his future would suffer from indecision and superficiality, both symptoms of a malady that had festered within him, an illness known to no one but himself. The knots in his stomach grew larger and tighter with each passing mediocre stage of his life.

So, for lack of a better plan, he'd enrolled in the area junior college, taking basic core classes and living at home. School lasted for two and a half semesters. The drive to campus took him past the church he used to attend, the literal scene of the crime and a daily reminder of the quagmire that continued to grow internally.

One day, in the spring of 2001, he'd just kept driving. He dropped out of school and, on impulse, enlisted in the United States Marine Corps, committing four years of his life to the service of his country. It had seemed like a laud-able plan. He could return to Main Street in his uniform. His hometown would be proud. He'd be a hero, perhaps. At last, M.D. had righted the ship. He could squelch the memory of his past and reinvent himself from college foot-ball star to decorated soldier.

Duff knew it was a fake, but he had become quite adept at denial. It was an escape made to look like a glo-rious rebound in life. Another secret that would serve to fertilize the cancerous one that continued to reside in his being, from which there was no apparent escape.

Within thirty days, he'd said goodbye to his parents, to a childhood sweetheart named Kate, and to the town of St. Joe, Indiana. He landed in San Diego, California, on yellow footprints. Seeming madmen with shaved heads in Smokey Bear hats were in his face, shouting orders at him and using obscenities that would curl the hair of a Mafia hitman. *Welcome to the Marines, maggot. I'm Mac Marine. Play ball with me or I'll cram the bat up your ass.*

For a short while, Michael Duff wondered to himself: *Am I creating more negative memories, ones that will dwarf those I have been concealing for the last seven years?*

It was the summer of 2001. Within three months, hijacked jet airliners would penetrate the twin towers in Manhattan and the security of a nation. Another layer of trauma was being hatched.

In many ways, Marine Corps Basic Training, or "boot camp" as it is commonly known, was the perfect remedy for Michael, at least on a temporary basis. It provided enor-mous structure. Every day was planned out to the minute.

5:30 a.m. reveille. Make your bunk, shave, shower, shine boots, shine brass belt buckle, press fatigues, align all clothing, wear a starched cover (cap), go to formation, stand at attention, no talking, march or run to mess hall in formation, wait for permission to enter mess hall, enter the mess hall. Read sign on the wall: "Take all you want, eat all you take." Not a suggestion but an order. Go through chow line and stand at attention behind your chair, awaiting the next step. In unison, "Sir, Platoon 1099 requests permission to eat, sir." *Eat, maggots.*

Sit down, eat, no talking. Finish all your food. Some of the privates had eyes bigger than their stomachs. Very unfortunate. If that occurred, the entire platoon would stand at attention. The Drill Instructor (DI) would stand behind the private who had not finished his plate and repeatedly yell, "Eat, private!" A smorgasbord of obscenities was sprinkled into his command. The entire mess hall would be drawn to the scene. After shoveling in the rest of the food, the DI would order the private to lick his plate. "Sir, yes, sir." Typically, following one of these occasions, the platoon would be ordered to run back to the barracks. Within the first three hundred meters, the offending private would stop and hurl all that he had just consumed. The remaining privates, standing at attention, would be ordered to watch him puke. "Sir, yes, sir." Upon arriving back at the barracks, the private who had failed to clean his plate would be given a bucket of soapy water and a sponge and ordered to return to the hurling site and clean up his mess.

Needless to say, this only happened one time during basic training.

No one could talk to the DIs without first gaining permission. It would go something like this:

"Sir, Private Duff requests permission to speak to the Drill Instructor, sir." The first and last word out of his mouth had to be "sir."

The DI would usually respond by saying something like, "Speak, private" or "Speak, maggot" or "Speak, Sally."

"Sir, Private Duff requests permission to make a head call, sir."

"Is it an emergency, private?"

"Yes, sir."

"Excuse me?"

"Yes, sir."

"What did you say?"

"Oh! SIR, YES, SIR!"

"Okay, Private Duff. I want you to run to the head, and the entire way I want to be able to hear your loudest and best siren sound. Do you understand?"

"Sir, yes, sir."

"Get out of here."

"Sir, yes, sir."

Duff, or whichever private it happened to be, would then race to the latrine while making his best imitation of an emergency siren. Very funny. Except no one could laugh. Or even ask permission to do so.

The rest of the day was filled with a myriad of activity. Physical training, or PT, was paramount, especially during the first four weeks. Long runs, calisthenics consisting of push-ups, sit-ups, jumping jacks, running in place, leg lifts, pull-ups, toe touchers, arm circles, mountain climbers, rope climbing, and everyone's favorite—squat thrusts, also known as burpees. The DIs would bark and swear and belittle during the entire workout. Fat guys suffered most. Duff was in fairly good shape and, despite not participating in sports in high school, was a good athlete. That's not to say that he didn't struggle, but it was nothing compared to the overweight recruits.

Close order drill, commonly referred to as marching, also occupied a good chunk of the daily routine. Four squads, usually about fifteen in number, would line up in a "column of fours" with a guide out front leading the group and carrying the flagstaff displaying the platoon number. Initially, the privates would interlock arms and respond to the commands of the DI, such as "left, right, left." Left foot always led. By the end of boot camp, the sixty-some-odd privates would be in sync and sound like one giant boot hitting the pavement. It built unity, discipline, and as the Marines called it, *esprit de corps*.

The platoon went to classes. *History of the Corps.* Founded November 10, 1775, in Philadelphia in a bar known as Tun Tavern. Always a big selling point for recruiters. *History of Battles.* Tripoli, Montezuma, Belleau Wood, Guadalcanal, Iwo Jima, Inchon, Chosin Reservoir, Khe Sanh, Hue City—all Marine battles were studied. The slogans were learned. "*Semper fidelis.*" "First to Fight." "Once a Marine, Always a Marine." Nicknames: "Devil Dogs." "Leathernecks." "Gyrenes." "Jarheads."

More teamwork. More unity. More structure. And more faux memory loss for Michael Duff.

There were three Drill Instructors assigned to Duff's Platoon 1099. They worked twenty-four-hour shifts. Staff

Sergeant Timmons was the Head DI. He was short in stature, about five-foot-seven, but high on the intimidation scale. If you incurred his wrath, his glare alone would scare the crap out of you. Literally.

Staff Sergeant McMannis was next in seniority. Tall, lean, athletic, and mean when he had to be. Which was often.

And then there was Sergeant Pinckney. Black, built like a brick shithouse, he had a green star, trimmed in gold, inlaid into his right front tooth. This guy was all Marine. On his first day of duty with the platoon, his opening statement had been, "Good morning, privates. My name is Sergeant Pinckney. Do not piss me off. Let me repeat. Do not, under any circumstances, piss me off." *Sir, yes, sir.*

They all had the same things in common. They were lifers. The military was their occupation, Marines were their stripes. They were in great physical shape. They ranged in age from mid-twenties to early forties, and there wasn't a private who could outrun any of them. And they were mean, or more accurately, they possessed the very convincing appearance of being mean. With a strong proclivity for creative profanity. They made Sergeant Hulka look like a camp counselor.

They had all been to DI school. They knew their job. Get the privates in shape physically. Break them down psychologically and emotionally. If they crack, fine. They're gone. You've done your job. If they don't, build them back up, individually and collectively, so that when the call is made to "send in the Marines," the tradition of "the few and the proud" will be perpetuated.

About a week into training, the DIs selected a marching guide, a secretary, and four squad leaders. Duff was appointed one of the four squad leaders. He was one of the older recruits, was athletic, and had completed some college. He became the peer leader of fifteen prospective marines.

The composition of the platoon was diverse. Hispanics, blacks, some Asians, and WASPs. Rednecks, country and city alike, were part of the group. Most of the states from Indiana to the West Coast were represented. Many were young. Just out of high school or dropouts. Some had drug problems or were delinquent or both. They had discovered and benefitted from very liberal recruiters who were more interested in quantity than quality.

Lots of Protestants. Baptists, Methodists, Lutherans, Episcopalians, Nazarenes, Presbyterians, a few Jews, and, drumroll . . . a handful of Catholics. Many claimed to be of a certain religion but very few practiced their beliefs. Similar to the rest of society.

Duff soon learned that Sundays were toughest. After a full schedule of activity for the week, Sunday mornings were free time for privates. They could go to church services if they so chose. They could read, write letters to family or girlfriends back home, shine their boots, press their uniforms, or do nothing. It became the only time, and for that matter—opportunity—for the kid from the north central Hoosier state to delve back into his still dark past.

Matt Hogan, a member of his squad from Denver, asked Duff one Sunday morning if he would care to join him at mass. Michael managed a weak smile, as if to say "thank you," shook his head, and simply said "no." *If only Matt knew, or my squad members, or the whole platoon, or my DIs, then . . . then what, Michael? They would know that you weren't worthy of being a recruit, or a squad leader, or a Marine, or a member of "the few and the proud"?*

He wrote a long letter to his girlfriend, not knowing if she still was, and yearned for Monday and a five-mile run.

There were some humorous moments during an otherwise grueling ten weeks of boot camp. It became an art to determine if one could laugh when such occasions arose.

Private Edward Hooks was in Duff's squad. He was seventeen, from a small town in western Texas, quiet and very afraid of the DIs. He was most compliant and never a problem for his squad leader.

At chow one evening, Duff noticed that Hooks was not in attendance. He remembered seeing him during a relay competition with another platoon during the afternoon schedule. Worried, he asked around to see if anyone knew his whereabouts. No one did. He approached Sergeant Pinckney, asked permission to speak, which was granted, and inquired about his missing squad member. Pinckney told him that Hooks was at the infirmary. Nothing more was said.

About 3:00 in the morning, all squads were awakened from their bunks and ordered to formation. Standing at attention in their white t-shirts and skivvies, Sergeant Pinckney addressed them.

"Privates, I have some bad news concerning Private Hooks. He was taken to the infirmary this afternoon and it seems he has come down with a case of spiral meningitis." Actually, it was a case of "spinal" meningitis. Sergeant Pinckney had put his own unique pronunciation to the very serious and contagious bacterial infection.

At attention and standing directly to the left of Private Duff was Private Phillip Benowitz. Phillip was Jewish and from Rogers Park, a far northeast neighborhood in Chicago. He was extremely bright but not very athletic and was having a difficult time adjusting to the personas of the Drill Instructors. In any event, upon hearing the regrettable news regarding Private Hooks, he fainted. At attention. No slumping of shoulders, no buckling of the knees. Straight down, like a tree falling in the forest after being severed by a chainsaw at ground level. Broke his black, horned-rimmed glasses and his already prominent proboscis.

Sergeant Pinckney, obviously misinterpreting Phillip's fall, said, "Oh my God. There goes another one. They're dropping like flies." Duff shook his head and guffawed internally. Benowitz showed up for the morning chow line with a bandaged schnoz and a new pair of specs. The platoon was placed on quarantine for a week and given light duty. Private Duff missed his physical workouts and structured daily routine.

More time to think.

"All ready on the left. All ready on the right. All ready on the firing range."

The seventh week of training saw the platoon travel to Camp Pendleton, a Marine base north of San Diego, for weapons training. Long and short arms. Duff was one of four recruits in the platoon who made expert. A pin would be placed above his shirt pocket at graduation about a month later. He was proud of his achievement and couldn't wait to write Kate back home and tell her the good news. There was no response. Damn.

A little darkness filtered through the California sunshine.

Graduation day at Marine Corps Recruit Depot, San Diego, California was huge. Many of the recruits had not made it through high school. Others had been budding

41

criminals. Still others were there because their futures were not yet defined. Michael Duff fell into this last category.

His home was two thousand miles away. No one would be making the trip to see his pass and review of the Commanding Officer. He would call home and talk to Mom and Dad. He would call Kate but there was no answer. He left a message with a feeble attempt at enthusiasm for his accomplishments during boot camp. Expert marksman and meritorious promotion to the rank of Private First Class. One of four. No return call from Kate. Celebration would be lukewarm.

The phone calls were the first allowed since the recruits were ordered to stand on the yellow footsteps ten weeks earlier. Letters only. Duff returned to his barracks, packed his C-bag with all of his current possessions, and sought out Lanny Kuharick, the platoon's secretary and Duff's buddy since the two had boarded the flight to San Diego at O'Hare Airport in Chicago.

Michael and Lanny had hit it off immediately since their first encounter. Chicago had been the last stop before boot camp. A final physical and then a bus to the airport. Both had done research prior to enlisting, which indicated that the "buddy system" would greatly diminish the stress that could occur during the basic training process. A few drinks prior to the boarding process cemented the relationship. A few more on the flight and they carried on like fraternity brothers.

Duff's "buddy" had been selected by the DIs as secretary for Platoon 1099, which proved to be very valuable to the Hoosier squad leader. Lanny had made it his habit to keep Duff apprised of the agenda, allowing him to prepare for the day's activity. It was not uncommon for the DIs to make random inspections of the barracks, checking for contraband among other infractions. Duff's squad was rarely reprimanded for violations, having been forewarned by Kuharick.

During long-distance runs, they stayed together, encouraging each other to complete the task one step after another. They were always in eye contact with each other, as sometimes that was the only way to communicate. Although many times suppressed from outward expression, they shared the lighter moments. Phillip Benowitz's fainting at attention would be relived often. The DIs would be remembered, mocked, and respected. It was Marine boot camp. They had made it.

Their first liberty had been in downtown San Diego. Neither was familiar with city. They went to bars and drank like marines in their new uniforms, both adorned with a single stripe on their respective shirt sleeves, signifying their meritorious promotion from boot camp. They also stood out like sore thumbs.

They were hustled by a couple of provocatively dressed locals. The naïve kid from Indiana was drawn to one of them. Lanny, a city slicker from Chicago, knew what would follow. After sufficient flirting from the girls, they disappeared and their pimp appeared, suggesting that a hundred bucks from each would lead to an hour of entertainment with the frisky fillies. Duff had been shocked; his buddy's suspicions, confirmed. They declined, kept on drinking, closed the bar, and made it back to base for their final night at MCRD. Camp Pendleton beckoned. AIT—Advanced Infantry Training. War games.

The date was September 9, 2001. In two days, the upcoming training would reach its peak in relevancy.

Recruits are given a job when they are admitted into the service. It's their MOS, or Military Occupation Specialty. Michael Duff was a Radio Relay Operator, numerical designation 2532. His buddy Lanny chose Motor Pool Specialist, 1533. No matter one's job when they reached Advanced Infantry Training at Camp Pendleton, everyone was a "grunt," slang for infantryman. It has been the philosophy of the Marines since its inception that "Every Marine is a rifleman." And so it was for the Midwest boys from Platoon 1099.

On September 11, 2001, reveille at Camp Pendleton was at 0600. Formation was at 0630. Four platoons were in formation, at attention, when a Captain John Worthington made this announcement in front of his troops.

"Marines. At about 0545 this morning, our country was attacked. Commercial airliners have been hijacked and flown into the World Trade Center in New York City. The number of fatalities at this time is unknown. If any of you have the firm belief that your family members may be in danger, please report the same to your squad leaders and command will follow up. Our training today will proceed as planned. But know this. There must be extra energy in your step, more urgency in your agenda, and a prayer from your heart for our fellow citizens on the opposite shore. Platoon Sergeants, take charge."

Gasps came from the gathering. Heads were involuntarily bowed. Everyone would remember this moment. Duff and Kuharick looked at each other and shook their heads. Duff said, "We're at war." Lanny nodded in the affirmative.

They prepared for their day. It included a three-mile run. Full gear with rifles. There were over two hundred marines in his company. Duff's platoon was last to take off into the terrain of the California base. As his grouping reached the crest of one of the many hills, he saw a sea of green helmets below. No faces. Just green helmets moving at the same pace to a destination unknown. He wondered how many would die in the next year. Or sooner.

★   ★   ★

One of the toughest realities of being a Marine in Southern California is just that. It's Southern California. Situated between San Diego and Los Angeles, Camp Pendleton is a perfect viewing place for planes arriving and departing from the two cities. Sooner or later, the marine in training longs to be on one of those planes, regardless of its destination.

And then there is the Pacific Ocean and its beaches, a tantalizing draw while humping the hills of San Onofre beach, with sunsets that defy comparison and competition. Why did they have to put this grueling and painful military base on such a majestic piece of real estate?

Read your history books, boys, and blame it on the Japanese.

The bombing of Pearl Harbor by Japan in December of 1941 triggered United States military involvement in World War II. Prior to that fateful day, the nation's involvement was limited to providing military aid and supplies, mainly to Great Britain, to fight the Nazis. After the bombing in Hawaii, the search for a West Coast training base by the Marines was galvanized and accelerated, leading to the condemnation of the ground that became Camp Pendleton, named for General Joseph Henry Pendleton, who had already been responsible for creating MCRD in San Diego. Needless to say, the real estate developers in Southern California did not think highly of General Joe for robbing from them seventeen miles of undeveloped shoreline on the Pacific Coast, worth billions of dollars.

The General died in February of 1942, unable to savor the finished product of his labors. Camp Pendleton would grow to become the largest populated Marine base in the nation. Thirty days following the 9/11 attacks in New York City, it would become the site of more trauma in the life of the young marine from north central Indiana.

★ ★ ★

It was October 11, 2001. Thirty days had elapsed since the devastating attack on the slender island of Manhattan three thousand miles away. Human remains were still being pulled from the chaotic rubble. It was a cool, dry, and clear autumn evening in Southern California. The sun had set on the grand Pacific Ocean, leaving a residue of lavender and pink streaks in its wake. People to the north and south of the base were having barbecues on the beach, drinking wine and beer, smoking pot, and making love.

Platoon 1099 and the rest of Company B were preparing for war games and campouts.

By design, the physical activity of the day had been light. Classes in the morning, a short run prior to lunch, and some light calisthenics in the afternoon. The remainder of the day was devoted to the preparation of the unit's first bivouac.

Many of the marines were in for an inaugural experience. They had never slept outside. Always inside in a bed at home, or on a couch, or in a sleeping bag during a weekend sleepover at a friend's house. Or at a hotel or motel.

Food had been prepared by Mom or a fast food cook or in a bag or can kept edible by preservatives. Not C-rations.

Digestive waste had been deposited in toilets, out-houses, port-a-potties, and—in emergency situations—the woods with the use of TP (toilet paper) or its distant cousin PT (paper towel) or, barring either, some broad maple, oak, or sycamore leaves. Not in a field latrine, sometimes referred to as "the straddler."

Duff and Kuharick remained squad leaders at AIT and were charged with the responsibility of preparing their marines for the bivouac exercise. Unlike boot camp, the squad leaders wore red armbands so they could be spotted by their squad members as well as the higher-ranking sergeants.

Marines were assigned to digging foxholes and field latrines, rationing water, managing ammo supply, distributing food supplies, setting up sleeping areas with and without tents, communication detail, medical supply; and all of it had to be accomplished covertly with no power and small flashlights, used sparingly. Plus, everybody was in full combat gear from head to toe with rifles and ammunition.

Platoons were trucked from their billets to an unknown area, where they were left to fend for themselves. It was dark. There was no civilization in sight. Hills, sand, rock, and critters. Another company had been delivered to an unknown location on the other side of the "playing field." For the next thirty-six hours, they were the enemy. *Let the games begin.*

Except on this day, the games were postponed. A transportation snafu. One fatality, four seriously injured. A rollover.

The platoons were delivered in shifts of eight using M1123 HMMWV, commonly known as Humvees. Duff's squad arrived first and began preparation for the bivouac. The three other squads were due to arrive at fifteen-minute intervals. Squads two and three did.

For purposes of transport, the Humvee roughly resembles a pickup truck. There is a driver and shotgun in the cab. The bed of the truck is equipped with slatted, wooden benches along the sides. There is just enough room for four soldiers in full gear per side. The squad leader is the last to enter and situates himself on the passenger side. He is also the first to disembark. A canvas cover is arched over the bed, supported by a metal structure. The back of the bed is open, save for an end gate that is secured when all are aboard and in place.

"All secure, Sergeant," said Lanny. This was the cue for the driver to take off. It was now very dark. It was clear. A new moon shed very little light on the rough terrain. Dirt roads kicked up clouds of dust, severely diminishing already low visibility like a thick fog on a narrow country road. Not a problem for Staff Sergeant Pitchford, a ten-year veteran of the Corps who had made this trek over a hundred times. With Corporal Simon riding shotgun, it was just another day at work. Actually, not quite.

The night before, Doug Pitchford had had some buddies over to watch a Lakers-Clippers game. Beer flowed as usual but nothing really out of the ordinary had occurred until around midnight, long after the game had concluded, when Doug's live-in girlfriend, Patty, confronted the group to keep the noise down with a bit of an edge in her voice. Feeling no pain and wanting to show his Marine buddies the proper bravado, Doug responded with, "Hey, who do you think pays the fucking bills around here?"

Well, that did it. Things had deteriorated from there. Some beer got spilled, profanities were exchanged, the visiting marines abandoned their posts, and Doug and Patty verbally duked it out for about an hour, at which point he'd retired to the couch and she to the bedroom. He was still feeling the effects of the episode when he reported to work the next day at 1700 hours for his twenty-four-hour shift with Company B and their first bivouac.

The subsequent investigation of the rollover accident would include a finding that the driver's "BAC" (blood alcohol concentration) was 0.00. Not mentioned in the report was the dull ache that persisted at the temples of Staff Sergeant Pitchford, or his fatigue occasioned by the events of the previous night, or his preoccupation with the volatility and future of his relationship with Patty.

Perhaps it was the combination of these conditions that caused him to fail to see and subsequently strike a protruding rock at the top of a rise in the rugged terrain as he was turning left on ground already slanted in the same direction. The Humvee rolled over two-and-a-quarter times before coming to rest on its driver's side. Pitchford and Corporal Simon were belted in and only suffered superficial injuries. Seven of the marines in the bed were tangled together like a bag of pretzels. They suffered injuries, some severe. Broken necks. Fractured arms and legs. Major lacerations with uncontrollable bleeding. Bullet wounds to the abdomen. All survived, some barely.

The eighth marine was not part of the chaotic human entanglement inside the bed of the truck. Following the first revolution of the truck on the craggy ground, his body catapulted outside of the vehicle through the back opening. His helmet was separated from his head as he exited. His gun went flying. His body became an unguided missile. All control was lost. There was no time to prepare for landing. There, in fact, would be no landing.

Facing upward, the marine's body was halted by a sharp ridge on a boulder about twenty feet from the truck. There was no give to the immoveable granite. It shattered the c1 vertebra and the lifeline which it was designed by nature to protect. Death was instantaneous as the spinal cord was severed. No pain. No warning. No life.

★ ★ ★

Word of the fatal accident travelled quickly. Humvees were dispatched to bring the marines, who were preparing for the bivouac, back to their billets. An eerie feeling invaded Private First Class Duff. He knew which squad had not made it to the camping site. He knew who the squad leader was to that group.

Within minutes, Duff's truck approached the scene of the rollover. From his viewpoint in the rear of the Humvee, he could see the overturned vehicle. He could see medics treating the wounded. Out of the corner of his eye, he spotted a fallen marine being carried by stretcher to a medical vehicle. He was completely covered by a makeshift shroud of unknown material. His left arm was dangling lifelessly from the stretcher.

There was a band of red cloth wrapped around his bicep.

CHAPTER FOUR

Hoosier Homecoming

Whatever progress Michael Duff had occasioned by his Marine Corps experience in an effort to overcome the effects of his sexual abuse by Father Shields evaporated immediately with the death of his marine "buddy" out in the middle of nowhere in Southern California. Through some miracle, he completed Advanced Infantry Training, although he was stripped of his duties as a squad leader, which he considered a blessing. He was no longer fit to lead. In all fairness, it became a burden for him to follow.

Following an unceremonious conclusion to the war games at Camp Pendleton, the marines were granted their first leave. Duff had nowhere to go but back home to Indiana. He took a flight out of LAX to Chicago. There were four or five other marines on the flight who were headed back to the Midwest as well. They were ecstatic about tasting their first breath of freedom since arriving for boot camp five months earlier. They were buying rounds for each other during the flight, flirting with the female flight attendants, and generally whooping it up. Michael attempted to join in the celebration, however lacking in authenticity. A deep-depression crater loomed on his horizon. Nonetheless, he did partake in the downing of six or seven beers, a foreshadowing of things to come. It got him through the four-and-a-half-hour flight.

The soothing of the alcohol began to wear off while waiting for his bags. As he watched the luggage travel in seemingly endless circles on the carousel, he thought, *that's my life*. Going around in circles. No direction. No goals. No pleasure.

It was approaching dusk when he boarded the bus outside of O'Hare Airport. But his world was growing darker than the skies. He was headed to St. Joe, Indiana. It was the Saturday after Thanksgiving. He was back where it all started. He sat in the back of the bus, hung his head, and wept.

It did not take long before things began to drastically deteriorate. Michael's parents attributed his worsening alcohol intake and mental health to the death of his fellow marine and, of course, to some degree, that was true. Unfortunately, they were unaware of the true source of their son's darkness.

Michael spent most of his time in bed. When he was awake, he sat idly, watching TV and drinking beer. Lots of it. He rarely made conversation. He was not rude, but his aloofness sent that message. His father began to scold him for his cold behavior. One day, he remarked that he didn't have what it took to be a Marine. The only response by Michael was to withdraw even more. It was becoming apparent that returning to California to finish his training would not occur.

Three days before he was to return to Camp Pendleton, Michael was driving home from a bar out in the country. He'd been visiting a high school friend. And getting hammered. It was dark and windy. Snow started to fall. It became blizzardly. The severe conditions outside, coupled with the level of alcohol inside his bloodstream, made a perfect recipe for disaster. He rolled the car into a ditch. He broke his femur, collapsed a lung, and lost a pint and a half of blood. He was in the hospital for two weeks. His career in the Marine Corps was over. There would be no hero's homecoming.

While in the hospital, his mother came to visit him every day. His dad came once to tell him that the military had given him a medical discharge. One day, a young priest came to offer him solace. Michael lied and told him he had to take a nap. When the priest left, he gave his nurse a list of approved visitors. At the bottom of the list he wrote, "NO PRIESTS."

One evening two days prior to his discharge from the hospital, there was a knock on his door. It was his nurse. She came in with the list of visitors that Michael had prepared earlier in his stay. She said there was someone there to see him whose name was not on the list. He gulped and nodded that the person could enter.

Thirty seconds later, there was a soft knock on the door. It was partially opened, and the smiling face of Katie Brumfield appeared. Duff put his face in his hands. He was overwhelmed to see her and equally overwhelmed with shame. He could not speak. She came to him and touched the back of his head, sat and waited for him to regain his composure.

Eventually, he did, and they talked. She had a shame of her own. She had not written to Michael. She had gotten involved in another relationship, which had turned dysfunctional and was now over. She lacked the courage at the time to tell him. She looked him in the eye and apologized. It was genuine.

Katie listened to Michael recounting his Marine Corps experience. She wept with him upon hearing of Lanny's death. Michael told her that he wished it had been him. His survivor's guilt was palpable.

He openly admitted his rampant drinking issues. It was, in his eyes, the only way to survive. He did not tell her about his boyhood experiences. His abuse, literally at the hands of Father Shields. He could never tell her that. In a way, his military trauma, his drinking, and his accident with serious injuries would always stand guard over his deep-seated secret of sexual abuse.

They visited for over an hour. Katie was a great listener. No judgment. But now it was her turn to get serious with Michael Duff.

"Michael, I'm so glad I came tonight. It has been great to see you. I pray that you will heal. Physically and emotionally. But you can't do it alone. You've been through too much. You lost your best friend. Your hopes of a military career are over. You almost lost your life. You're probably going to lose your license. And your drinking is obviously out of control. I understand that you will be out of here soon. Promise me that when you leave this place, the first thing you'll do is get connected with a counselor. You have to start to process this mess so that you can get your life back on track. Will you do that, Michael? Will you do that for yourself?"

Duff was touched by her genuine concern. He knew she was right. His eyes again welled up. He looked directly into her soft brown eyes and smiled with a short nod that said, 'I will.' She leaned over and kissed him softly on his forehead and said, "I'll be back."

Shortly after he was discharged from the hospital, Michael went to court. He was charged with DUI and, because of his high blood alcohol concentration of 0.27, he was subject to a maximum fine of $5,000 and up to a year in jail. Plus, a revocation of his driver's license. He received probation, a weekend in jail, a $1,000 fine, and mandatory alcohol counseling. The court duly considered his military experience and specifically the death of his fellow marine.

He was assessed by an alcohol professional who determined that Duff's drinking was mostly situational. He became depressed over the death of his friend and used the alcohol to temporarily relieve his pain. Deal with the depression and the alcohol problem will subside. Certainly a fair diagnosis. One problem. The assessor did not have all the facts. As always, Duff omitted his history as an altar boy at the local Catholic parish.

In time, Michael graduated into a recovery mode with his drinking problem. He worked on his guilt, not really knowing from which set of traumas it sprang. Most of all, he took action.

Six months after he returned home, he located Lanny's parents, who lived in Oak Park, Illinois, just west of Chicago. He rode three hours by train to meet with them. He talked about their friendship and how he loved and respected their son. He shared the challenges he'd had to overcome as a result of the tragedy. They appreciated his visit. He gave them his contact information . . . and his expert rifle badge. Tears were shed when the group embraced before he departed.

Michael Duff was well on his way to conquering his alcohol abuse. Intense counseling, both group and individual, ameliorated the healing process. The most beneficial tonic no doubt came from the love and compassion of Katie.

His victimization from childhood sexual abuse, however, remained unvanquished, a secret now buried more deeply with a Marine sentry fortifying its safekeeping.

Michael and Katie began to date during his recovery period. She had been his first love in high school. Her presence kept him on the straight and narrow, especially with respect to any residual drinking issues. Duff's failure to join her at mass became an issue. A delicate and long-standing one.

Duff went back to the community college in St. Joe. He received his associate's degree and became a pharmacy tech at a local drugstore. He received high marks from his boss and was eventually promoted to assistant manager of the business. This dual experience proved to be a successful apprenticeship. His combination of pharmacy and business acumen would pay dividends down the line.

Katie studied elementary education at a small four-year Catholic school not far from home. She commuted, preventing any interruptions in the progress of their courtship. Following graduation, she experienced two high moments in her young life. She landed a teaching job at a public school in a small town near St. Joe, and she landed a husband.

Katie and Michael were wed at Tippecanoe State Park in the fall of 2007. He had been very insistent on an outdoor wedding. Katie much preferred the church. They compromised. A Catholic priest was the officiant. One unknown to the past altar boy. The young Doc would not have survived a wedding in the same church where, over a decade ago, he had been violated sexually.

Fortunately for Michael, the weather on their wedding day was perfect. Full sunshine, brilliant fall color, a gentle breeze. Michael tolerated the officiant's involvement in the nuptials. He maintained his focus on Katie, his first and only love. The beauty of the day paled in comparison to hers. She had believed in his worth at a time when he had abandoned belief. She had rescued him from the throes of budding alcoholism. He owed her his life.

Two beautiful daughters graced their family in the next five years. Hannah and Gabby. The seemingly happy young couple and their kids moved to Chicago when Michael was offered a huge promotion to manage a down-town store. The iconic "Chicago" sign was his business neighbor. He was exhilarated by the new city, leaving his hometown and all its ugly reminders. It didn't last.

Duff eventually learned that moving from the birth-place of a virus did not guarantee that the virus would stay at home. One cannot escape a dark secret. It remains adhered to the fiber of one's being. It continues to rear its ugly head regardless of locality. And it did within a year of the move, leaving in its destructive wake the marriage of Michael and Katie.

Katie and the girls became lost living in Chicago on their own. Returning to Indiana was the practical option. Michael visited the girls every other weekend and on holi-days. It broke his heart.

He soon learned how deep loneliness can grow in the big city. The irony of feeling alone in a town with nearly three million people.

Worse yet, his secrets festered to a deeper shade of black.

CHAPTER FIVE

Chicago

December 2018

Three years had passed since Doc's cancelled flight in Pittsburgh. The process of healing was a never-ending one.

Some demons had been expelled and some guilt had been shed, but each day brought new challenges. Reading the daily newspaper, for instance. A day didn't go by when some new exposé didn't uncover a wider scope of abuse by priests somewhere in the world, not to mention the effort that "the Church" exerted to cover it up. These were the worst crimes imaginable. Over the last three years, Duff's guilt may have subsided, but not his anger. It would need a check.

Thank God Kelle had moved to Chicago. She kept him grounded and his anger intact. Or so she thought.

To some degree, however, Michael Duff, aka Doc, was a transformed man. He'd discovered routine, regimen actually, a behavior that had been absent since his Marine Corps days. He was seeing his life through a new lens, reassessing past decisions, most notably his divorce of five years earlier. He still loved Katie, his hometown sweetheart and former wife, and adored their two daughters, now ages four and seven. They still lived in Indiana. But for reasons unknown to Kate and the girls and not understood by him at the time, he had sabotaged his family, not because there was another woman, or a drug or booze issue (that had come much earlier), but simply out of fear, his own fear of himself and his unleashed anger. Perhaps someday they would be reunited. Perhaps someday they would understand. He could only hope.

He awoke every morning at 6:00 a.m. sharp, weekends included. He prepared himself for the day fastidiously. Clothes were now neatly pressed, shoes shined to a bright gloss, not a hair out of place, never a stubble.

7:30 a.m. was his departure time for work from his comfortable, two-bedroom condo in the trendy Chicago neighborhood of Roscoe Village. There was a hop to his step. He headed for the CTA Brown Line stop at Addison Street on this clear, brisk, and sunny December morning.

He didn't own a car, as long ago he had learned to navigate Chicago through its elaborate system of trains, buses, limos, taxis (land and water), Ubers, etc. Cars were a liability—expensive, immediate and continuing loss of value upon purchase, insurance, parking permits, repairs, fuel, stickers, tags; not to mention the incalculable hassle of traffic jams, stop lights, bikers, horn honking, road rage, diagonal streets, and the ultimate oxymoronic passageway . . . the expressways, which the majority of time resembled football arena parking lots.

So, Duff, a manager of a Loop Walgreens, took public transportation to work for a whopping $2.25. It wasn't that he was tight financially. In fact, before passing through the turnstiles, he would typically purchase a cappuccino at a local coffee shop for $3.95 to give him a little boost for the ride into the city. Actually, he loved the ride and the opportunity it gave him to study the people, reexplore the buildings and neighborhoods, and feel the pulse of the city that he had called home for the last seven years.

During the warmer months, Michael enjoyed getting off at the Merchandise Mart, covering the remaining distance to his shop on foot. It still thrilled him to the bone. Strolling across the Chicago River on the Wells Street bridge, taking a left on Wacker, and admiring the Mart, Marina Towers, Wrigley Building, and Tribune Tower. Trump Tower was there also. Beautiful building, troubling brand, or so he thought.

A right on State Street and a short two-and-a-half blocks south, and he was at work. The last stretch led him under the Lake Street L, home of the Green Line and northern border for the Loop and the iconic Chicago Theatre sign.

During inclement weather, of which Chicago had its fair share, he would remain on the Wells Street elevated and disembark at the Quincy stop, a diminutive street of just two blocks on the southwest side of the Loop. The Sears Tower, as Duff still called it, stood tall to the west as he left the platform. A five-block walk to his workplace remained. Who was the genius who well over a hundred years ago came up with the plan to raise the trains above the streets? He marveled at the steel trestles, the cars and pedestrians beneath, the stations, platforms, stairs, turnstiles, tracks, and, of course, the trains themselves weaving in and out of this architectural wonder of a city.

Its flaws, its violence, its hassle notwithstanding, this had become his city. And he loved it. It had given him great protection. It had been easy to conceal his secrets. Although, not anymore, or so he hoped.

Kelle Russo's arrival had occurred about a year earlier when her computer firm had offered her an opportunity to jumpstart a branch office in Chicago. Her cyber wizardry was opening new eyes from competitors and new vistas within her current employ. It was not a difficult decision for her to move.

An upgrade in salary was part of the incentive. Leaving Pittsburgh, although her home since birth, was also a plus. Too many reminders. Weddings, funerals, holiday masses, parades, graduations, and confirmations all physically reconnected her to the local parish church, causing a spike in the indelible memories of her abuse as a child. She was healing, but the process was slow and subject to backslides. A change of scenery was in order, financially and emotionally.

And, of course, she had a friend in the Windy City.

It wasn't long after her arrival that Doc and the Nurse connected at a local Italian restaurant and discussed initiating the "Pittsburgh Plan" for abuse victims in the Chicago area. Within a couple months, they found a meeting place in a Loop hotel, developed a web page describing the mission of their project, and placed ads in the local dailies. They decided to include all victims of sexual abuse, not just those who were the objects of Catholic priests.

Eight people showed up at the first meeting, way beyond expectations. Each had been advised to come in with their own nickname. Real names were on a volunteer basis, but in time were usually shared.

The ages of the victims ranged from nineteen to sixty-two. Their ages at the time of their victimization ranged from seven to fourteen. Four women and four men. It was the initial disclosure for all of them. Three were African

American, two were Hispanic, and three were white. Two were in an elite socioeconomic level, two were impoverished, and the other four were struggling in the middle class. All of them had or were still experiencing abuse of drugs or alcohol or both. Shattered relationships provided another common denominator.

The perpetrators were from various backgrounds and vocations. The element that abided in each was that they occupied a position of trust with respect to their victims. Two were Catholic priests, one was a Boy Scout leader, two were teachers, one was a wrestling coach, one was a stepfather, and the lone female was a volleyball coach. All were respected in the community. No reports had been lodged, so none had been prosecuted. The names of other victims would never be known. The extent and impact of emotional slaughter was left only to the imagination.

The anger in the group was palpable. "I feel so guilty that I didn't do something. I'm so fucking mad at myself. I could have saved so many other people if I had just spoken up. I don't sleep. It absolutely consumes me."

Within a short time, the size of the groups became unmanageable. Another meeting was established to meet the demand. They met once a month. Doc headed one; the Nurse, the other. Sometimes they both attended. It was a success. But it wasn't enough.

The groups were providing a service to the victims. But no accountability to the abusers. In time, that would change, prompted by a case where the abuse was reported. *People v. Bryce M. Wilkerson*, Circuit Court of Cook County, Illinois.

63

Duff got off the Brown Line at the Loop Quincy stop. He checked out the cold but bright blue sky that provided an exacting contrast to the black, majestic Sears Tower. He followed the trestles along Van Buren and turned north on State Street. Within minutes, he reached the corner of State and Madison, the absolute center of the Loop and geographical dividing lines for north and south (Madison) and east and west (State).

On the east side of State, for the next block stood Macy's Department store, formerly and more affectionately known as Marshall Fields. He marveled, as he always had, at the Christmas decorations on the store and the windows that depicted holidays scenes which mesmerized children and parents alike. Giant trumpets, adorned with garland and assorted ornaments, angled skyward from the third floor of the store, forming a canopy over the pedestrians below and extending the full length of the block and ending at the famous landmark, the Marshall Fields' clock.

There was a hum in the city, a pulse, an expectancy. Christmas was on the way.

There was no such joy a mere block away.

Daley Center. Courtroom 1807. Circuit Court of Cook County. *People v. Bryce M. Wilkerson*, Docket Number 16-CF-1411. Charge: Aggravated Criminal Sexual Abuse, a Class 2 Felony. Judge Drew Porter, presiding.

Victim: Jane Doe, barely age ten when violated, eleven-and-a-half at the time of her testimony at trial.

Jane Doe was actually Hope Emery-Wright, the daughter of Amaya Emery, a black woman who had grown up in the crime and poverty infested area on the west side of the city. She had an associate's degree from a city college (the first to do so in her family) and was self-employed as a website designer for real estate brokers. She was married to Joshua Wright, who worked construction. He was white and had grown up in a blue-collar family in Wheeling, a northwest suburb. They'd met twelve years ago when Amaya was running a food truck at a construction site where Josh was working.

They'd dated and withstood the attacks from both sides' families and friends, who'd discouraged and disapproved of the union because of their pigmentation difference. They'd married, rented an apartment on the northwest side, and begun their family. Hope had been born about a year later.

She flourished in her biracial home, fueled by the love and commitment of her parents. She was beautiful, talented, lovable, humble, and intelligent. And she was a gifted singer.

She'd started singing at an early age in church. It had continued during her elementary school years. She sang the national anthem at local sporting events. She was on YouTube. She won singing contests. Her recitals were well attended. She was a talent on the horizon. She dreamed.

She had a voice coach by the name of Bryce Wilkerson, a part-time faculty member of the Music Institute of Chicago, a private school on the north side near Hope's home. Their mission was to train young and gifted musicians and singers.

Bryce had grown up in Sycamore Pointe, an affluent North Shore suburb. As the crow flies, it was not that far from Hope's neighborhood. Their respective worlds, however, were separated by light years.

CHAPTER SIX

The Wilkersons

I f wealth is an important thing in the American culture, and to some it is the *only* milestone, then Bryce Miles Wilkerson had made an extremely wise choice of parents. Born with a silver spoon in his mouth, he never spit it out, nor really tried to, nor were his parents able to extract it, to their detriment as well as his.

"Beamer," an early moniker granted him by his North Shore childhood friends, based on his initials, had never fit the mold his parents had crafted for him. Not so with his older sibs.

Charles, ten years his senior, had been the pride and joy of Harold and Beatrice, one of the many beautiful couples of Sycamore Pointe, Illinois. New Trier High School, long considered one of the best public high schools in Illinois, if not the country, was not good enough for Charles. Just up the road was North Shore Academy (NSA for short), to which Hal was a contributing alum. High school reunions for Hal were still well-attended, beer-swigging events that would put Brett Kavanaugh's shenanigans to shame.

Never a strong traditional athlete, Charlie played squash for NSA and his senior year made Honorable Mention all-conference. Sounds good until one realizes that there are a whopping four schools in Illinois that offer the sport. Anyway, it was a great filler for his admission application to Yale. Maybe it worked, for Charlie got to be an Eli; or perhaps his class of '76 dad's generous annual alumni gifts were a factor. Place your bets.

In any event, "#1 son" had graduated with New Haven ivy at the top of his resume (no squash entry this go-round) and headed to Wall Street. He was doing very well as an account manager for a top brokerage firm in Manhattan. Although still commuting from New Jersey, he hoped before long his address would have a Greenwich, Connecticut zip code. His folks beamed while embellishing his achievements, especially at country club cocktail parties.

Charles rarely came home, however, and didn't seem to have a steady girlfriend.

Three years after Charles, the jewel of the family had been born and, appropriately, was named Jewel. From birth, she was adored. Gorgeous, bright, athletic (tennis whiz), gregarious, caring, seemingly flawless, especially in her dad's eyes. He'd pushed her . . . academically, athletically, and his favorite, socially. Not that Bea objected to his over-enthusiastic encouragement; she just thought it was a bit over the top. Perhaps, she thought, he was diverting some of the rays of limelight away from the Jewel's mom. If that were the case, she made certain her opinion and feelings remained unarticulated. No sense pissing off her daughter and husband with some off-hand comment about her bruised ego. Domestic tranquility would reign as it usually did in the Wilkerson household.

So where should Jewel go to college? She could have walked on and played tennis anywhere. She wanted to stay in the Midwest, which was pleasing to Dad. She had visited Indiana, Wisconsin, and Iowa—too far away. She'd also checked out smaller schools in the area: North Central in suburban Naperville; DePauw in Greencastle, Indiana; and Lawrence College in Appleton, Wisconsin. All great schools but suffering from lack of name recognition. Dad won out. Northwestern University, just down the block from Sycamore Pointe, in Evanston, would be her home for the next four years. She thought it had been her choice. She was wrong. It had been Hal's. He was a lawyer; he was shrewd. He had spent an entire career convincing people (clients, partners, wife, lovers, children) to see things his way, while leaving them with the impression that it wasn't his idea at all.

Dad perpetuated his adoration of his Jewel during her college days (never missed a tennis match, home or away), all the time regaling her achievements at myriad social gatherings. Bea experienced four more years of limelight neglect. There was no love in tennis. Or Hal.

Beatrice Ann Miles was from Galesburg, Illinois, a town of about thirty thousand, located forty-five miles northwest of Peoria. It had grown up as a railroad town, serving as a connection between Quincy and Chicago. It even changed its high school nickname to the Silver Streaks in 1935 because of the American Royal Zephyr, a passenger train line that ran through town. Carl Sandburg had been born there, author of the line "Hog Butcher for the World." The North Shore elite had surely heard of Carl and the poem he wrote to describe Chicago. His hometown was merely a correct answer to a high school quiz question. Probably just a nice town to be from.

Bea, as she came to be known, had grown up poor. Her dad worked for the railroad but was drafted during the Vietnam War and had died overseas defending his country from domino theories of the Red Scare, not that he had any idea what that was or meant. He was a hero, or so Bea was told. A sacred flag, his name etched on a wall, and a lot of movies were his legacy to her.

Her mom met a new man and they moved to Chicago. The only thing Bea knew about Chicago was gangsters, Al Capone (the most famous of them all), and tall buildings. Stepdad had a good job and they eventually migrated to the burbs—Glenview, close to Sycamore Pointe geographically, but a bit further down on the median income scale. Compared to her Galesburg digs, however, she was in tall cotton. And the New Trier school district.

She first met Hal Wilkerson her sophomore year. He, unfortunately, was a freshman. For whatever reason, during that time period it was not "cool" for a gal to date an underclassman. Bea didn't care. She went after him like a greyhound chasing a hare. There was some initial interest from Harold but it soon evaporated. She was older, she was from Glenview, and she used to live in Galesburg, wherever the hell that was. Later.

The next school year, Bea had been heartbroken to discover that Harold, at his father's insistence, had transferred to the hallowed grounds of North Shore Academy. He made the hockey team. She found out, went to his games, and yelled when he scored a goal and cringed when he absorbed a check into the boards. Mattered not. He never noticed. He had a girlfriend—more than one, actually. Bea did not give up. The summer following her high school graduation, she got a job. She didn't know it at the time, but it was the only job she would ever need. Cart girl. Hampshire Hills Country Club. Gamechanger.

Hampshire Hills was founded in 1914 but was still somewhat of a newcomer to the country club scene of Chicago's North Shore. Onwentsia, 1895. Old. Old school. Needed eight to ten references to join. No scandals in your history. Or none that could be found. Exmoor in Highland Park, 1896. Also had curling. Skokie Country Club, 1897. Members knew it was not named after the town of Skokie but rather the Native American word that means "swamp," upon which the course once sat.

But if you were fortunate to live in this elite area of the country, Hampshire Hills was the shit. Initiation fees were high, giving membership the false security that no riffraff would enter the gates. Old school rules. Must take caddies. Dinner in the clubhouse—coat and tie required. No cash needed. Remember your account number. No gratuities allowed. Place cell phones on silent mode when entering the grounds. No cargo shorts, caps worn with bills forward, and NO DENIM. Blah, blah, blah.

Fortunately for Bea, the residency requirement did not apply to employees. And the dress code for cart girls was very liberal.

It was a Sunday morning in June of 1972 when the bell had finally rung. Hal and his dad, Joseph Wilkerson, were on the fourth hole at Hampshire Hills. It was a par three and there was a bit of a lull in the play. Bea bounded up in the beverage cart, bounced out, and asked if anyone was thirsty. Hal and Dad got beers; sodas for the caddies. Joe gave Bea his account number and told her to add a fiver for a tip. She spontaneously gave him a huge hug and gushed, "Thank you, Mr. Wilkerson!" Then she drove to the next hole, never acknowledging Hal.

Bea had a solid figure, shapely legs, and was well-endowed. She had a bubbly downstate personality. Her tight white shorts and sleeveless Hampshire Hills red logoed shirt (with collar, of course) made her attractive, to say the least. The dangling earrings and well-applied makeup rounded things out, with just the right level of allurement. The caddies were rubbernecking stares, old man Wilkerson was gawking, and Hal felt a certain, sudden warmth burgeoning in his whitey tighties.

Papa Wilkerson was the first to mention what the four were fantasizing over. Turning to Hal, he queried, "Who the hell was that?" Hal pretended not to know much about her, mumbling that he had met her a few times when he was a freshman at New Trier. "Looks like a fun summer activity to me," Joe said. The caddies nodded in agreement. Hal said nothing and proceeded to shank his tee shot into the woods.

It would have been an upset indeed if Harold Eastman Wilkerson had failed to carry on the blueblood tradition of his ancestors. He had been born into mega wealth, elite social status, a flawless reputation, the appearance of propriety, altruism, and the absence of scandal. True, the Wilkerson clan was not thrilled with Hal's choice for a spouse. From their viewpoint, she was just not worthy to assume the family name, a no one from Galesburg—no money, no status, nothing close to the North Shore way of life. Hal never forgot when Papa Joe scolded him following the announcement of his engagement. "Jesus, Harold, I just thought you could bang her for the summer. Not marry her." Sorry, Dad.

The truth is that the relationship with the "cart girl from Galesburg" had immediately grown into a sexual whirlwind for both parties. Early on, they had a goal to have sex in every sand trap on the golf course and damn near succeeded. Before their relationship went sour, they always shared a chuckle when they drove past a golf course or played a round together at Hampshire Hills and spotted a bunker where they had done the dirty deed.

But alas, their desire for each other waned and it became obvious to both that they had little to talk about. Bea settled into her new-found wealth in Sycamore Pointe, presupposing that she would never experience poverty again. She spent her time volunteering for good causes, played in the ladies' golf league at the country club, bridge on Wednesdays, the symphony, the ballet. Blah blah blah. She suffered through Wilkerson family gatherings, both in Illinois and up north at Gresham Gathering, pretending to be interested and liking people whom she despised. She rarely missed the opportunity to share her background as the "cart girl from Galesburg" to friends of the family, knowing the discomfort it would cause her in-laws, and more so for Hal. She genuinely immersed herself in her children and their activities. In short, Beatrice Miles Wilkerson loved her new life: her status, her wealth and her children. Carl Sandburg would be proud.

Harold regretted the marriage after the thrill was gone. He came to share the opinion of his parents, that Bea could not measure up. He put up a good front at the club and other social events. His wife maintained her attractiveness and so with her on his arm, they left the impression of being the adorable couple. And after all, in their circle, it was the impression that counted. But there was no substance to their relationship. It morphed into a marriage of convenience and obligatory expression.

Not surprisingly, his libido didn't die with his lack of sexual desire for his wife. And with ease, he was able to meet his demand. Working late at his Loop law office, out of town depositions, and the like provided the opportunities for secret trysts for his carnal satisfaction. Bea was no dummy. She probably knew but was also aware who buttered her bread. Plus, she came to know her daughter's tennis coach fairly well.

And then came Bryce. Bryce Miles Wilkerson, the baby of the family, born ten years after Charlie and an accidental conception by his parents. Mom had been thrilled; Dad, not so much.

It had not been an easy pregnancy for Bea. She'd been bedridden for the final three months and the delivery was difficult. Bryce failed to thrive early and actually had to have surgery to open up a valve leading from his stomach to intestine . . . a pyloric stenosis. This stopped the projectile vomiting. Bea would never forget seeing her little baby being wheeled into surgery on the giant gurney. His tummy was scarred forever.

Mom spoiled little Bryce. Dad allowed it, having neither the time nor the desire to parent this child, whom he hadn't even wanted. He'd tolerated his toddler misbehavior. He'd yelled uncontrollably at him during his early formative years and transferred blame to Bea during his high school antics, telling her his actions were unbecoming a Wilkerson. *Fuck you, Hal! Take a real interest in your son.*

Dad made a special trip to North Shore Academy and, at the same time, made a substantial increase to his annual monetary gift. They agreed to take on Bryce. Hal was relieved. Anything to get the brat out of the house. NSA tolerated one semester, after which the call came to pick him up.

Back home, Mom continued to enable Beamer and Dad continued to ignore him. It became quite a challenge to minimize his son's behavior, especially to his coterie of social friends. Bryce had become the white elephant in the room.

Pot had been Bryce's drug of choice since eighth grade, but he was always willing to try other ways to escape who he was—or was not. Cocaine, meth, Xanax. He had not been stupid enough to try heroin. Oh . . . he drank too.

His first DUI never made it to court, as the cop who'd made the stop knew Bea. His mom was a bridge partner of Mrs. Wilkerson. Pass.

His second DUI was in the City of Chicago. An associate in Hal's law firm was a golfing buddy of the prosecutor handling the case for Cook County. He was given a diversion program which he barely completed. Two DUI arrests, no convictions, no loss of license.

Bryce had barely graduated from New Trier, and the school breathed a sigh of relief when he walked across the stage to receive his diploma. College was not a viable option, and Dad certainly didn't want to fork over any money for wasted tuition and fees.

There was, however, one thing that Bryce had learned to do. Sing.

He had played in garage bands during high school, an activity tolerated by Dad and encouraged by Mom. He'd always been the lead singer and he was very good. Country, rock, ballads, oldies. No rap. He was the local "rock star."

Oh, and he had lots of girlfriends. Of all ages.

Bryce was eventually hired as an "adjunct" instructor at the Music Institute of Chicago. He lived in the Andersonville neighborhood, where his fulltime job was a bartender at an Irish pub.

His father, Harold, was ecstatic that he was away from Sycamore Pointe. Out of sight, out of mind. Bea on the other hand, missed her youngest child. She shied away from driving in city traffic and, as a result, her visits with Bryce were few, occurring at home when Dad was away on business.

On those infrequent occasions, she would do his laundry, make his meals for a week in advance, buy him a new outfit or two, and listen to his lies about how good he was doing. She was eager to share at bridge club that he was an "adjunct voice instructor" at a private school for gifted musicians and vocalists. It sounded very impressive.

She omitted his ability to draw a Guinness.

CHAPTER SEVEN

The Groom

Hope Emery-Wright was an all-around good kid. And although she was becoming an exceptional vocalist, she never used her burgeoning talent to set herself above her peers. To her, she was just one of the gang, both at school and in the neighborhood. She was genuinely sweet and never braggadocious. Her teachers loved her. "A joy to teach. Couldn't ask for a better student," were typical remarks on her report cards.

And her singing was quickly turning heads. "And to think, she's only ten years old" was a common refrain following any of her live performances. One certainly could not assess blame to Hope's parents for wanting to cultivate her talent by investing in lessons at the Music Institute of Chicago, an esteemed school with a history of successes. Of course, that's exactly what they did upon realizing the catastrophe that had invaded their family.

★ ★ ★

Bryce Wilkerson's grooming of Hope was calculated, albeit time-consuming. Initially, after a lesson, he would give her a hug; during a lesson, a pat on the back; instructing her on the guitar, a wrap around the back, shoulders, arms, and hands to show her the frets. Tickets to a Billy Joel concert at Wrigley Field . . . how could her parents say no? Photos of Hope and Bryce at the concert would be found later at his apartment.

Her voice was maturing, and her parents were impressed. There was no apparent reason to be concerned. As time went by, Hope's trust in Bryce grew. The hugs grew longer, too, and a kiss on the cheek was added. Hope eagerly talked to her friends about her instructor, how much he was helping her, how much she enjoyed her lessons, and how cute he was.

A half year into the lessons, his touching became more ambiguous and frequent. His hand brushed against her newly developing breasts, a similar touch to her buttocks, a kiss on her cheek closer to her lips and lasting longer than appropriate. During one lesson, he offered her a sip of red wine, indicating it would calm her nerves and allow a more mature presentation of her voice. She accepted, of course. This was her coach. He had already done so much for her. She trusted him.

Kisses ripened to the lips, and pecks grew longer with growing hints of intimacy. Bryce was weakening in his infatuation and desire for Hope. He could hold out no longer. His hands groped Hope's small breasts and then lowered to her genital area, accompanied by passionate kisses on her neck. He attempted to invade her tights. She reflexively tightened and refused. He forcefully guided her hand to his erect penis. She ripped it from his grasp.

He backed off. He apologized. And told her it would never happen again, a hollow promise that went unfulfilled.

And there was no reason to tell her parents or anyone else for that matter, so he said. After all, she was so close to an audition for *The Voice*, the ultra-popular TV show.

She did not tell her parents. She did not tell anyone for months. She could not process what had happened. She was beyond confused. She felt filthy. She began losing sleep. She lost interest in her singing.

The lessons eventually stopped, not because she had so requested but for money reasons. Hope's parents had incurred unexpected medical expenses relating to her younger brother's food allergies. The mentoring stopped. Hope feigned disappointment when they asked if the lessons could temporarily cease. She hid her relief when they did.

But she was torn. For months, her feelings had gyrated and her thoughts had raced; her moods had been quiet and dark. Honestly, she missed her lessons, blaming herself for what had happened. She was so young, so immature, and so unable to understand that she was never the cause and never to be blamed.

She was pressed by her parents, teachers, and friends to open up, to tell them the untellable. Naturally, she refused. Almost daily, she was forced to lie to protect herself from the dirt that the truth would reveal. Her stomach ached, constantly in knots. Her guard, however, was weakening.

Hope's best friend was Emma. They often talked on school nights. Emma knew something traumatic had occurred to her friend. And further, that it was just a matter of time before she got the details. It happened one night over the phone.

Hope had bunkered herself under the covers of her bed. The door to her room was shut. She called Emma sobbing uncontrollably. It had been three months since her mentor's last unwanted grope. Her voice was muffled through the blankets and tears.

"I can't take it anymore. I can't take it anymore. Do you hear me, Emma? I can't take it."

"Can't take what, Emma? You have to tell me."

And she did. Hope finally succumbed to the truth, the most crucial of steps that would begin her healing. A step that some never take.

Emma listened with the compassion and the intuitive empathy only a child could muster. She was deeply saddened by the pain of her friend.

She promised Hope that she would tell no one. About a week later, however, her promise was inadvertently broken.

Emma was late for school one day. She'd hurriedly gotten dressed, eaten breakfast, gathered her schoolbooks, and then run to the bus stop. She left her phone behind on the breakfast table. Emma's mom, Sheryl, picked up the phone, which revealed the last text Hope had sent to her trusted friend. It read: "Thank you for everything. You've been a life saver." Sheryl scrolled down and soon discovered why her daughter was being thanked.

She called Amaya, Hope's mother.

Amaya Emery-Wright worked out of her family home in the Ravenswood neighborhood of Chicago. She was a very level-headed woman, organized, structured, and calm. Her life was headed in the right direction. She had steady work. Her husband earned a favorable wage. They had two beautiful children. She was in a good place; she had beaten some overwhelming odds coming from the west side of the city.

Then came the phone call from Emma's mom.

Growing up, she had experienced the shooting death of an older brother. This was worse. Considerably. She immediately collapsed on her computer desk. Her heart fell, her lungs heaved, and she screamed silently. Sheryl was patient but remorseful, wishing she had gone to Amaya's home to relate the horrific news in person.

"I'm so sorry, Amaya. I should have come over. I can now," she said.

With partial composure, Amaya replied, "Thank you, Sheryl. My husband is coming home for lunch. I'll be okay." It was a lie.

Amaya got as much information from Sheryl as her condition would allow her to. Her husband, Josh, would be home in about half an hour. She was supposed to pick her son up in an hour at his preschool for a doctor's appointment. At 3:00, Hope would be home from school. She had an appointment at 3:30 with a prospective client and a hair appointment at 5:00 p.m. Tonight, they were visiting friends in the neighborhood for a meal and cards. The kids would have a babysitter.

None of it mattered. Her thoughts ran wild. The avalanche of chaos in her being was beyond palpable. Alone in her own house, she literally screamed. She ran to the bathroom and threw up. She began to talk out loud to herself, at the same time pulling out her hair.

"My daughter has been molested. How did this happen? Oh my God. And I have to tell her father. Oh my God, help me! What am I going to do? He will kill him. I know he will. Why didn't I know sooner? My poor baby. My poor Hope."

Amaya dropped to her knees and sobbed until she could no longer.

She was able to reach a point of temporary recovery. On autopilot, she cancelled all appointments so she could devote her attention and energy to her husband and daughter. She had just completed her last call when Josh walked through the door, brimming with enthusiasm. "You're not going to believe this. I just won tickets to this Sunday's Bears-Packers game. All four of us can go. Unfreakingbelievable!"

"Josh, please sit down. I have something to tell you," said Amaya.

"I know, you think it will be too cold. Already checked the weather. Forty-five, sunny, light breeze. It's the Packers, babe."

"Please, Josh, just sit down. Please . . ." She broke down. She wailed. This was not Amaya. Typically, she was calm and in control. What was going on?

"It's Hope . . . she, she has been molested." More wailing, stronger.

Josh comforted his wife as best he could, while at the same time wanting to know all that she knew. As she reached a level of calm relating the contents of the call from Emma's mom, Josh's rage rose abruptly to a volcanic level.

"Where does he live?" asked Josh.

"Who?"

"Bryce Wilkerson. Where the fuck does he live, Amaya?"

Amaya had correctly anticipated her husband's reaction to the news. She clutched the keys to the family vehicle in her hand. "You're not going anywhere," she said. "I am not going to live without my husband. And our children are not going to live without their father."

CHAPTER EIGHT

Lunch at The Berghoff

J ack Strohl was an Assistant State's Attorney in Cook County, handling mostly drug-related prosecutions. He had known Michael Duff for about seven years. They were casual, social friends. They played an occasional round of golf together, had lunch from time to time in the Loop, and shared some brews after work, usually during the summer. They had met prior to Duff's divorce through their respective wives, who'd volunteered as aides at a Catholic grammar school on the north side of the city. Their contact had been less after Duff and Katie split.

In mid-December, they were having lunch at The Berghoff, an iconic restaurant on West Adams Street in the Loop. Strohl was handling a case involving opiate-based prescription drugs, labeling, refills, dosage, etc., and needed some clarification on drug protocol from Duff. He obliged. And as was his practice, he made inquiry to his lawyer acquaintance.

"So, anything juicy going on at the courthouse these days?" asked Duff.

"Well, the usual menu of violence, dysfunction, and creepiness," replied Strohl. "Nothing shocks me anymore. There is a really messy one going on right now at 26th and Cal. Defendant charged with the attempted murder and rape of his live-in girlfriend. Among other methods, he tried killing her by injecting a syringe full of toilet cleaner into her neck. It gave her a helluva burn but didn't kill her."

"I could have testified as to the effects of hydrochloric acid on human tissue," Duff chimed in.

"Yeah. Right. Actually, they had the doc who treated her at the emergency room testify. It would have taken considerably more of the cleaner to kill her. The defense attorney brought that out. I can hear his final argument now. 'Ladies and gentlemen, how can this be attempted murder? The amount was infinitesimal.' It's been dubbed the 'Mr. Clean' case."

"Anything else?" asked Duff.

Strohl thought. "Actually, there is a trial that is due to start next Monday that will draw some attention. Sexual abuse. Fondling case. Defendant is North Shore royalty. It's going to be heard at the Daley Center downtown rather than Leighton. It's strictly a victim credibility case. No witnesses, as usual. No confession. But the word I get is the young female victim is mature and quite credible. Eleven years old."

Eleven years old. Duff tried to mask his internal reaction and resulting flushed countenance, a skill perfected through years of practice. He inquired further.

"What's the defendant's relationship to the victim?"

"I'm not sure. I believe she is a gifted singer. And he is a coach or mentor of some kind at a music school on the north side."

Christ, Duff thought, *another singing career aborted.* He would share with Kelle, or maybe not.

"Why was the trial moved downtown?" asked Duff.

"I don't know. Perhaps the defense attorney didn't want to risk smudging his Italian tailor-made suit on the southwest side. Nicer digs by the Picasso and closer to his Loop office. They hired a biggie, Quinn Cooper. Smooth, polished, expensive, with an ego the size of the United Center. Doesn't lose many. And when he does, it's inevitably someone else's fault. Overreaching prosecutor. Erroneous rulings from the trial judge. Pretrial publicity. If not something specific like that, the general and over-used catchphrase 'miscarriage of justice' sounds good to the press and more so to his convicted client."

"Any clue as to how long it will last?"

"Probably the better part of a week. I'm pretty sure the *Trib* is going to cover it. It's got some interesting aspects. Defendant's father is a senior partner at a big firm atop the Standard Oil building. Lots of connections. Gobs of dough."

"Do you know the defendant's name?"

"Yeah. Wilkerson."

The Daley Center was a block from the Walgreen's at State and Washington. Michael Duff had never witnessed a trial, much less one in which he could identify with the victim. He would go. He would take his friend, if she was available. Actually, he was quite certain she would decline.

The criminal charges against Bryce Wilkerson had been filed in the fall of 2016. He faced five counts of Aggravated Criminal Sexual Abuse. Under Illinois law, each count was a Class 2 felony and could result in a sentence to the Illinois Department of Corrections, commonly known as the penitentiary or "slammer," for anywhere between three and seven years. The charges alleged that the abuse had occurred on two different occasions. Therefore, if convicted of all, he would face consecutive sentencing. Simply put, he was in a world of shit.

Quinn Cooper, Bryce's attorney, knew his exposure. He also was well aware of the wealth and, more importantly, the elite status of his client's North Shore family. Those facts worked to his advantage, allowing him to demand a retainer fee somewhere in the six-figure range. It was paid with dispatch. No questions asked. "Just get him off, Quinn. The fact that he has been charged is a nightmare. A conviction could fucking ruin us." These were Harold Wilkerson's words as he handed Quinn the check for his retainer.

Cooper unleashed his investigators on the case. No stone went unturned. As part of the discovery process, the State was required to turn over all material relevant to the case, including that information which could benefit the defense. Text and email messages from Hope to her friends assuring them that nothing was wrong were plentiful. She often expressed praise about her "wonderful teacher" before and after the abuse had allegedly occurred. Numerous adults had expressed concern to her about her quiet and withdrawn mood, among them her parents, teachers, school social workers, friends, and parents of her friends. She had told all of them that there was nothing to worry about.

The defense attorney would tally all of her lies, hoping that just one juror in the group of twelve would develop a reasonable doubt about the guilt of Cooper's client, the spoiled brat from the North Shore. Yes, just one. A hung jury usually spelled victory for the defendant, especially in a case of this nature.

She was, of course, lying to protect herself from the shame, the guilt, and the ugliness that almost without exception resides within the child victim of sexual abuse. Just ask Michael Duff or Kelle Russo or any of the members of their groups in Pittsburgh or Chicago or across the country. It was the silent killer that haunted its victims for a lifetime, defeating their ability to enjoy and grow and love and fulfill and experience peace in their own beings.

Over a year had elapsed since the filing of formal charges and the arrest of Wilkerson. Delay in bringing a case to trial typically benefits the defense. Witnesses die. Or move. Or forget. Or are intimidated. The stress on families spirals out of control. They become consumed by the case. It takes on a life of its own.

It's the worst, of course, on the eleven-year-old victim who must now face the perpetrator in open court, a pressure cooker of a venue, relating the worst experience of her life, in public and in front of twelve strangers comprising the jury. And then there is the remaining court staff who are present: the security bailiff, jury bailiff, clerk, court reporter, and, of course, the judge. The prosecutors, defense attorneys, counselors, victim advocates, and cops have all become part of the life of an eleven-year-old child. Many experts believe the whole trial process can be as traumatic as the violation itself, if not more so.

Prior to trial, the State had discovered that the young voice teacher had left additional victims in the wake of his sexual perversion. They'd come forward. One was another student at the Music Institute. Another was a freshman at New Trier High School who had seen Bryce perform at a street festival in Chicago. After the show, with alcohol as an aider and abettor, she'd been violated by his unbridled hands.

These other incidents of abuse were crucial for the strength of the State's case. They showed a pattern of misconduct. And although not formally charged in a specific criminal prosecution, they were relevant to the proof of the case involving Hope. Unfortunately, it failed to materialize. The parents of the other child victims did not want to subject their loved ones to the emotional distress attendant to testifying in open court. No one blamed them.

That left Hope alone. It was, after all, a one witness case, "occurrence witnesses" as they were called in the legal biz. The prosecution would also call a forensic expert witness who would describe the dynamics of sexual abuse—the denial, the shame, and the reality of the problem. This would counter arguments made by the defense based upon Hope's initial and many denials that anything was "wrong." It would also seek to educate those jurors who still lived in the dark ages with the belief that these types of the things just don't happen in the good ol' USA. Anyone involved in these painful proceedings knew all too well that they happened all too often.

Enormous support was provided to Hope to prepare her for the intimidating task that she was to undertake. Shortly after her abuse was disclosed, her parents had engaged Hope in counseling, which proved to be beneficial. Amaya and Josh participated also. There was a mountain of guilt that they had to overcome. Forgiving themselves for not protecting their precious daughter would be a lifetime process.

Hope was assigned a victim advocate by the name of Ann Benson, from the State's Attorney's office. Her job was to guide Hope through the judicial process, physically be with her during the trial, and generally prepare her for her testimony. "Hope, the truth is on your side. It is with you. Trust it. Remember, answer the question and tell the truth. You will be fine."

In preparation for the trial, Hope was taken to the courtroom where the proceedings were to be held. She sat in the witness chair, learned where the attorneys and judge would be situated, and most importantly, saw the location of the jury box.

Elaine Dunning was the lead prosecutor for the State. She was a veteran in the Cook County State's Attorney's office with a reputation for her relentless advocacy for children who had suffered sexual abuse. She was being assisted, or second chaired, by Drew Babcock, a relative newcomer to the process. This was his first jury trial and first sex case.

The preparation had been thorough. But it was over. It was now up to an eleven-year-old child relating her horrific abuse in a room full of adults, twelve of whom would judge her credibility. Some experts opined that such was tantamount to a further abusive episode of equal measure.

No one could have predicted the ensuing outcome.

CHAPTER NINE

The Truth in Hope

The day had finally arrived. Hope Emery-Wright was taking the witness stand. Nearly fifteen months had expired since Bryce Wilkerson, believed to be her trusted voice mentor, had obliterated that trust when he had kissed her passionately on the neck, cupped his hands around her newly developing breasts, and with those same hands attempted to invade her underwear and vaginal area before finally forcing her hand to touch his erect penis.

Although the victim from the outset, she had done her level best to hide the hideous acts that generated her shame and guilt and endless pain and confusion. She had lied to everyone. But now the truth would be spoken, not in the safety of her home, or the security of a counselor's office, or in a park while discussing the events with a trusted friend. But in open court. *Open.* This young, vulnerable eleven-year-old child on a witness stand, all alone with everyone in the room staring at her, listening to her every word relating to human behavior of the vilest nature.

The preparation for this day had been enormous and painstaking.

An assistant in the prosecutor's office conducted a mock cross-examination of Hope. She familiarized herself with the surroundings of the Daley Center, the entrance-ways, elevators, hallways, courtrooms, and other offices that she might occupy. Nothing would be strange to her on the day of her testimony.

Hope was a good student, a quick study, and, over the years, because of her public vocal performances, had developed a high level of poise and confidence. Everyone hoped it would carry over to the witness stand.

It did.

"The People call Hope Emery-Wright to the stand," announced Ms. Dunning.

Hope entered with her parents, who took their seats in the front row of the spectators' section. She walked directly to the clerk, who administered the oath to tell the truth, and without hesitation took the witness stand. She was dressed conservatively, wearing navy slacks, a white, long-sleeved blouse, and a navy sweater vest with small pine trees evenly distributed thereon. They resembled Christmas trees. The date was December 15. She wore no jewelry and no makeup. Her natural beauty required no enhancement.

She viewed her voice teacher for the first time since her withdrawal from the Music Institute. And he observed his former pupil. Each experienced increased voltage to their nervous systems.

The initial direct examination was predictable. Name, age, address, name of parents and sibling. School attended, grade, report card, activities, special interests which segued to the Music Institute and her teacher there by the name of Bryce Wilkerson.

At this point, Hope identified him for the record. She looked at him. Pointed him out to the jury and described his apparel for further identification purposes. The judge stated the identification of the defendant for the record.

Beatrice Wilkerson was sitting with her husband Harold behind their son in the second row of the gallery. Her expression turned indignant when Hope pointed to her son; her husband lowered his head.

The meat of Hope's testimony obviously was her recounting of the acts of violation, his unwanted kissing and fondling. Prior to her testimony in this regard, Ms. Dunning asked her to describe what had happened "for the ladies and gentlemen of the jury." This was a cue.

Hope paused and moved about a quarter turn in her witness chair so that she had full view of each juror. She took a full breath and held eye contact with key members of the jury, a tactic previously discussed with the veteran prosecutor.

Her testimony rang true. Her voice cracked with emotion at one point when she recounted the first kiss on her neck. It was real. She composed herself, took another deep breath, and continued. It enhanced her believability as a witness. Some jurors were literally on the edge of their seats. Her eyes penetrated the eyes of the people who would assess her story. She was believed. The truth was in her.

By design, the veteran prosecutor did not inquire of Hope as to the many lies she had told in an effort to conceal her abuse. She banked on defense counsel to do so. It was all part of the chess game strategy that trial lawyers engaged in. Quinn Cooper did not disappoint.

Through the discovery process and his own extensive investigation, Cooper had compiled a list of individuals who had questioned Hope about what was "wrong." Why had she become so withdrawn? So quiet? So sad? So "not Hope"?

Every encounter when asked, Hope had given essentially the same answer. "Nothing." A lie.

So, the parade of questions began. Actually, there was just one question that was used to apply to everyone to whom Hope had told the same lie. Parents. Teachers. School counselors. Friends. Parents of friends. Fill in the blank. *You lied to* _____.

And with respect to each question, Hope responded in the same way with calm and resolve. "Yes, I lied."

"And yet after all those past lies," the veteran defense counsel asked, "you expect this jury to believe you today?"

"Yes. Of course, I do. Because it is the truth."

Prosecutor Dunning asked one question on redirect examination. "Why, Hope? Why did you lie to all those people?"

Once again, Hope turned and spoke directly to the jurors. They were waiting for her explanation.

"I'm sure attorney Mr. Quinn was not sexually molested as a child." (No one will ever know whether she misspoke his name on purpose or otherwise.) "Because if he had been, he would know the answer to all his questions about why I lied. When Mr. Wilkerson, the man sitting over there, kissed me, and then touched my breasts, and then tried to put his hands down my pants, I felt something that I had never felt before.

"I had trusted him. I really liked him a lot. He was helping me with my singing. I thought he liked me. And then this happened. I felt dirty. Confused. Ugly. I am only eleven years old. Ten when this happened. Why did he do this? I blamed myself. It was not easy to lie. But telling the truth was impossible. Every time I was asked what was wrong, my heart raced, my body shook, and I got dizzy. Saying nothing was the quickest way to end the misery.

"I have only begun to heal. I relive this every day. I have horrible nightmares. A lot of them. It's with me everywhere.

Sometimes on the radio, I hear a song that he helped me sing. I burst into tears when that happens. My life is often very dark. Like I'm swimming in mud."

You could hear a pin drop in the courtroom. Every word sunk in with the jury. They could not hide their empathy for the young girl facing them. Two of the women wiped tears away. Many of the jurors were nodding their respective heads, signaling not only their belief but their support for this courageous young girl.

Judge Taylor broke the silence, turned to Quinn Cooper, and asked, "Any re-cross, counsel?"

"No further questions, your Honor."

Ms. Dunning told Hope that her testimony was captivating. She could not have done a better job. She also told her that there was no real way to predict what the jury would do. Portentous.

The State followed Hope's testimony with an expert forensic witness who testified about the dynamics of the child victims of sexual abuse. It dovetailed perfectly to what Hope had experienced.

Surprising no one, the defense opted not to put the young Wilkerson on the stand. The jury would be instructed that they could not consider that fact during its deliberation. Final arguments by the lawyers were scheduled for the following morning. The jury began deliberations after being instructed as to the law by Judge Porter.

Their first vote was nine-three for conviction. Two hours elapsed, filled with some animated discussion, and another vote was taken. Eleven to one. The first day of deliberation ended that way.

The jury was excused and ordered to come back the following day to continue its deliberations. The jurors were further ordered not to discuss the case with anyone. No newspapers, TV, or internet. All indicated that they understood. One understood but could not resist the temptation to surf the 'net.

The deadlocked vote lasted the entire morning of the next day. The foreperson of the jury informed the Court that they were hopelessly deadlocked. The judge read them a further instruction that applied to the situation and directed them to continue with their deliberations. It didn't help. At 4:30 p.m., the judge declared a mistrial. He scheduled a second trial in about three months.

The press cornered the foreperson of the jury after Court was adjourned. He willingly gave up the name of the lone dissenter. Raymond Hopkins, an insurance agent from the south suburbs. A *Tribune* reporter caught him before he boarded his commuter train and asked him about his vote. He was caught off guard. "Just didn't believe the girl. Had a nephew who was wrongly accused of molestation. A lot of this stuff is made up. The internet is full of it."

There was more drama outside the Daley Center within earshot of the Picasso statue. Hope's father, Josh Wright, lost it. Ran into the Wilkerson entourage and in no uncertain terms indicated to Bryce Wilkerson that he would get his. His language was more colorful than a marine at a bar on combat leave. Fortunately, security defused the situation before it got physical. It was, however, a major part of the story the next day, with photos. And TV footage.

What did not make the papers the next day was the identity of a courtroom spectator with seemingly no connection to the case. His name was Michael Duff. He had witnessed the testimony of Hope Emery-Wright. He empathized with her pain. And he was forming a plan to mitigate that pain, a plan that would hold the responsible parties accountable for it. The justice system had failed in that pursuit. With the help of the Nurse, he would not.

CHAPTER TEN

Vino Rosso

Two months had passed since the Wilkerson trial had ended in a mistrial, a "non-result" occasioned by the rogue behavior of a dissenting juror. At first blush, it appeared to be a tie. Wrong. A hung jury is a victory for the defense in most cases and especially where the State's key witness is a child. The emotional toll on Hope and her family was immeasurable. To summon further energy to engage in a retrial was pretty much against all odds and too much to ask. The State was left with no alternative but to dismiss the case.

The end of the criminal proceeding marked the beginning of a scheme to provide extrajudicial justice for Hope and her family. Michael Duff, aka "Doc," and Kelle Russo, aka "the Nurse" would lead the way. The Wilkersons were their target. The starting point was occasioned by a bottle of Tuscan wine. Vino Rosso.

La Scarola was a cozy Italian restaurant on Chicago's near west side. It had been a go-to spot for Doc and the Nurse since her move to Chicago. With her Italian background, she was attempting to teach him the finer points of Italian culture.

"Hey, before we order wine, I've been meaning to ask you a question," said Michael.

"Fire away. I've already told you my ugliest secrets."

"Your parents are Enzo and Maria, correct?"

"That is true."

"And your brothers . . . Pauli and Mario?"

She nodded affirmatively.

"Your sister's name is Rosa."

"Yes."

"So here is my question. 'Kelle' is an Irish name. Although I've never seen it spelled that way. How did you happen to end up with the most Irish of names when you're Italian?"

"Actually, I'm surprised it's taken so long for you to ask. I will gladly tell you. My mother had an extremely difficult time during my birth. There was a fibrous growth on her uterus that shifted during labor and blocked the birthing canal during delivery. An emergency Caesarean had to be performed. Both our lives were at risk.

"Obviously, we both made it, but it was extremely traumatic for my parents. My father made a promise to our doctor that, if all went well, he would name the baby after him. The doctor's name was Herman Keller. Had I been a boy, Keller would have been my name. Herman wasn't really an option. So, my dad lopped off the R and voila, Kelle."

"Wow. That's quite a story. What's your middle name?"

"Marie. My parents gave me the option when I got older as to what I wanted to be called. I stuck with Kelle."

"So, what kind of wine should we order?" asked Michael.

"I'll tell you what," Kelle responded. "I'll let you choose. I am curious to see what, if anything, you have learned."

The server brought some fresh bread, bottled water, and asked if the couple wanted a beverage to start the meal.

Doc studied the wine list, or pretended to, as he had already done so earlier and had made his decision. "Yes, we'll take a bottle of the Mazzoni Super Tuscan."

The Nurse smiled without making eye contact while buttering a slice of her *pane*. The server arrived and displayed the bottle to Doc, who nodded affirmatively as if he had been raised in Florence. Actually, growing up in the small Indiana town of St. Joseph, his exposure to wine had been limited to Boone's Farm Apple, a favorite for providing a weekend night of cheap drunkenness.

Nick, the waiter, deftly opened the bottle, placed the cork by Duff, and then poured a taster into his goblet. He swirled it around the glass, nosed it, took a sip, sloshed it around his mouth, swallowed, and then nodded again at the server, indicating his approval. Nick poured about four ounces into Kelle's glass as they exchanged subtle smiles, acknowledging Duff's amateur status in winetasting.

"Very good, Michael. Now, what is the major grape in that wine?"

"Sangiovese," he snapped back.

"Wow! You have been paying attention."

They clinked their goblets and settled in with light conversation until Duff saw an opening to introduce his agenda for the dinner.

"Do you remember that case I told you about a couple of months ago? The one that ended in a hung jury?"

Of course, she had. The similarities between the case and her own background were haunting. Ten-year-old girl. Gifted singer. *Why bring it up, Duff? You've just ruined an otherwise delicious plate of lasagna.*

"Yes."

"Well, the State has dismissed the case. Understandably, the family could not go through another trial. More pain and frustration. There was only one holdout. All that upheaval, and one asshole blocks closure."

"Can they sue the perp?" asked Kelle.

"Sure. I talked to my buddy, Jack Strohl, in the State's Attorney's office about that precise matter. He told me that she could sue but it would not be the practical thing to do. The civil courts take much longer to get to trial. And she would have to submit to depositions and other intrusive discovery procedures. The main reason, however, is that the defendant has no real funds of his own. His family is loaded but he's a bartender. It's called being judgment proof. Can't buy insurance that covers sexual abuse."

"Probably best for her. The longer she stays in the court system, the more she delays her healing process," said Kelle.

Michael took a sip of his wine. "I agree with you one hundred percent. But at the very least, these people deserve some compensation for what they have gone through. They're not rich, and good counseling doesn't come cheap. And not just for the girl. Think of what the parents have endured. Try to imagine their guilt."

Actually, Kelle had always thought about what her parents had *not* endured as they remained unaware of her abuse. And always would.

"So, it looks as if they have no options."

"Actually, I have been contemplating one, but I can't do it alone. Do you know anything about hacking?'

"Well, that came out of left field. What do you mean?"

"I've been doing a little research. The Wilkersons are royalty. Live in Sycamore Pointe. House is worth north of two mil. I'm sure that the annual interest on their investments is more than my annual income. I think they owe the girl."

"Agreed," said Kelle. "What do you propose? Giving them a call for a donation to an anonymous charity?"

Duff chuckled. "No. But I was considering a call after we obtained some leverage."

"What do you mean?" she asked.

"Leverage. An advantage. Such as some sensitive information that they would want to keep out of the public eye."

"You mean blackmail, Michael. Go ahead and say it."

"Well, technically yes. But for a good cause. To help a victim. You know, like us."

Russo looked at him without expression. She was processing his suggestion.

"I would need your help, Kelle. I know that you can hack. That you're quite good at it, actually. But not for our personal gain—for victims who have endured abuse similar to ours. I don't want to make any money out of this except to cover expenses. What do you think?"

Before she could answer, Nick stopped by to inquire about dessert. They opted to split a tiramisu and each ordered a cappuccino. It was quiet while they waited for it to arrive. Duff could sense that Russo was giving his proposition some serious thought. The dessert arrived. It was placed in the center of the table and each of them was given a fork. They each raked in a chunk of the sumptuous delicacy as their eyes met.

Kelle broke the silence. "I can't do this." Duff's eyes closed and his gut took a punch. "That is, not the way you have described it. We would be taking enormous risk. We can't do this for free. Lawyers charge what, a third plus reimbursement of expenses? We should be compensated fairly. And only from perps or, in this case, their filthy rich families. I mean, I don't want to retire on this stuff, but

I've got a mortgage and car payments. And I'd like to go to Italy someday.

"Just one caveat. You must follow all my directives as to how we communicate. Cyber security is my forte. At this point, you know more about ordering wine, which isn't much. And yes, I can hack with the best of them. But it will only be used against known targets. No one else. No matter what we find out.

"And one final requirement. We share this with no one. Not even our most trusted friends. And especially not with the victims, if we are successful. They must never know their benefactors.

"So, Doc, do we have a deal?"

"Yes, Nurse. We do."

CHAPTER ELEVEN

Leverage

The frequent detours from marital fidelity occasioned by Baron Harold Wilkerson over the years would be nothing more than a mere annoyance for him to address should someone be stupid enough to wave them in his face for a handout. No . . . there had to be something with more depth, more wide-reaching impact, and, above all else, more enticement for the public. As in "breaking news," front page headlines, everybody's talk at the office water cooler.

They found it. Doc and the Nurse hit the jackpot. Twice, actually. The only decision was how to play it. It was an easy choice: money before prison.

★　★　★

It is not uncommon at all in the American legal system for a person who commits a crime to also incur a substantial civil liability, i.e., money. The problem is that most criminals who get caught are poor. Good case but no reward. Although rare, sometimes the criminal also has sufficient wealth to compensate the victim. The best modern-day example of this is the O.J. Simpson case.

The legal system is slow—very, very slow. Typically, the criminal case moves well before any contemplated civil litigation. By the end of Simpson's criminal trial, his assets had been substantially dissipated to the benefit of his lawyers and the detriment of the Goldman and Smith families, who were pursuing a civil action for money damages. Despite their substantial judgment against "the Juice," there was little juice left in the game to squeeze.

This scenario would not repeat itself for Doc. The dirt accumulated against the patriarch of the Wilkerson clan would not be shared with the authorities until such time as sufficient juice had been extracted from "Pops."

DIRT #1
"Show me the money"

At medium or big law firms in the city, an attorney is valued not only by the quality of the work performed in the office or courtroom, but also by the number of well-paying clients that they bring through the doors of their wood-paneled offices. Who you know really does count.

Hal knew Tad McAvoy. He was a member at Hampshire Hills. They had played in some club events together over the years and had shared some embellishments over cocktails at the nineteenth hole club bar. Tad was well off financially and things were about to get considerably better. His father had died recently, and Tad was the sole beneficiary of his will. Hal made a business decision to attend the funeral. It worked. A week later, Tad called Hal at his office.

"Do you do estate work?"

"Oh yes."

Easy money.

But it was so much better than the mundane work of handling an estate, which would have been delegated to a second-year associate, investing more hours than necessary to complete the work and augment the fees. There was a dispute. Litigation. Motions, legal research, depositions, discovery, hearings, investigation, analysis, negotiations. . . billings out the wazoo.

It was Tad's sister, Maggie, whom he despised; she was contesting the will. She had been left out. "I don't give a shit about the money. I just don't want her to get any. She's a bitch of the first water."

A perfect storm. And the beginning of a never-ending one for Harold Wilkerson.

Tad and Maggie McAvoy had never gotten along. He was the compliant "golden boy" four years senior to his rebellious sister, Margaret Marie McAvoy, who never missed an opportunity to tell any stranger how much she hated her name. "Call me Maggie." How she loathed it as a child when her parents would scold her (a frequent occurrence back then . . . and later), as in: "Margaret Marie, you are late for school," or "Margaret Marie McAvoy, that makeup is so unbecoming," or "Margaret Marie, that behavior is not acceptable." *Call me fucking Maggie. I'm not a nun.* That was true.

Tad had learned his sister's soft spot at an early age, and he jabbed at it relentlessly, especially when she'd started dating. "Have a good time, Sister Margaret" was a common refrain. She could never forgive him. Never.

The relationship between Maggie and her family worsened exponentially once she'd reached adulthood. Her first marriage lasted less than a year. Quick divorce. Church expulsion. Embarrassment. Not to Maggie, of course, but to her parents and to her hypocritical and pretentious older fucking brother, Thaddeus Timothy McAvoy.

The biggest blow to the McAvoy clan came when "Margaret Marie" broadened her sexual preferences. She began seeing a black woman who was a client at the River North art gallery where Maggie worked. Her name was Julian; it ended when Julian reconciled with her husband. That relationship was followed by an array of partners from both sides of the menu, all having diverse heritage.

It didn't take long for Maggie to be shunned by her family. This was of little consequence to her; that is, until she reached her fifties and came to the realization that more funds would be needed to support her lifestyle. Her mom had died about two years before. Then Dad (Matthew Milton McAvoy) expired. It came as no surprise that she'd been omitted from his will. But she had a little ace up her sleeve.

"Loose lips sink ships." They can also provide the basis for a lawsuit. Will contest. Undue influence. Incompetency. Or both.

About a year prior to the death of the elder McAvoy, Tad and his wife had attended a fundraising dinner at the Field Museum in Chicago to support underprivileged youth pursuing careers in fine arts. Following the dinner and uninspiring speeches, Tad gravitated to the cash bar with an old acquaintance, Ron McDougal, where they updated each other on the current events of their respective families.

"So, how is your Dad doing?"

Tad responded, "Well, physically he's doing quite well. Still takes his daily walk before breakfast. But he's become disoriented lately. Actually, it's been a gradual thing that started about six months ago. His normal thirty-minute morning stroll took two hours last week because he got lost in his own neighborhood, one he's lived in for the past sixty years."

"So sorry to hear that. And how is Maggie, that 'piss and vinegar' sister of yours?" Now on his third post-dinner martini (not to mention the two *pre*-dinner martinis), "loose lips" took over.

Tad answered, "Actually, I haven't seen her in a couple of years, which is fine by me. She's become an absolute embarrassment to the family, Ron." He went on and on about the details of her abhorrent lifestyle, their mutual hatred for each other, and her lack of compassion for her father during his failing years. He ended by saying, "I can't imagine the old man leaving her a dime. And if I have anything to do with it . . . well."

Amy Kincaid was working the bar that night, having volunteered her services for the evening as a member of the sponsoring organization. She had crafted the martinis for Tad and Ron. She heard every word of the exchange. For whatever reason, she took note of the name badges that were prominently displayed on the two chums. Tad McAvoy and Ron McDougal. *Hmmm*, she thought.

The next day, Amy went to her 7:00 a.m. yoga class. She had befriended another woman in the class who worked at an art gallery about a block away. During their first break, she turned to Maggie and said, "By the way, do you have a brother named Tad?"

One fundraiser, two beneficiaries.

Maggie hired two young lawyers whose Lincoln Park office was close to her condo. Ezio Collins and Webb

Paciorek had been in partnership for about five years. They were both from Chicago. Each had gone to undergraduate and law school in the city. Neither desired a Loop practice with an established firm of any size. They represented a lot of underdogs and relished the idea of battling cases out with the "big boys" downtown. Maggie liked that.

Maggie was by no means poor. And, of course, her motive in the case was not strictly monetary. Truth be known, it was more out of her enmity for "Brother Thaddeus." But a little more change would round things out. She knew the young lawyers could not finance the legal action. She would be able to sustain it and the lawyers' cut would be a contingent one third of the settlement or verdict. She also liked that, as it gave the young legal eagles more incentive to do a good job.

Wilkerson, Clark, and Rowe had been around for slightly longer than five years—more like five generations. Harold's grandfather's name was still on the letterhead. They occupied two full floors in the AON (formerly known as Standard Oil) building on East Randolph Street in the Loop. All the partners' offices faced Lake Michigan from an approximate height of 750 feet. The executive restrooms at the firm had considerably more square footage than the entire office space of Collins and Paciorek. They were royalty.

Their practice specialized in many areas of the law. Corporate. Estates. Big estates. Real estate. Not house closings, but complicated commercial leases, sales, and purchases of skyscrapers and shopping malls. Tax. They saved a lot of money for rich people so they could remain rich people. Insurance. This part of the practice was huge. Insurance companies hire law firms when their insureds get sued. They pay them big bucks on an hourly basis. And in counties like Cook, the cases can be dragged out for years. Bean counters have concluded that it is more profitable to prolong a civil suit and pay lawyers than to settle with the injured party, especially if it a big exposure case.

Accordingly, "WCR" had a very well-oiled litigation division. Senior associate Ben Clarkson, an honors graduate from Georgetown, was assigned to the McAvoy case. He had never heard of Collins and Paciorek. *Piece of cake*, or so he thought.

Six months after the suit was filed, Ben scheduled the deposition of Amy Kincaid, Maggie's yoga buddy, who appeared to be the main witness supporting her claim of incompetency as to Dad and undue influence exerted by her brother. The deposition took place in a conference room at the law firm in the sky.

At this point in the proceedings, Harold was being basically serving as a "hand holder" to Tad. He took his phone calls, explained court procedure, and gave assessments of "how it was going." He had informed Tad of the "bartender witness" whose deposition was forthcoming. Tad decided to attend the deposition and Hal would accompany.

Those present at the deposition: Court Reporter Jamie Phillips; Deponent, Amy Kincaid; Defendant and executor of the estate of Matthew Milton McAvoy, Thaddeus McAvoy; Harold Wilkerson and Benjamin Clarkson, attorneys for the defendant; Ezio Collins, attorney for the plaintiff; and Maggie McAvoy, plaintiff.

Tension filled the room when everyone sat down and identified themselves for the record to the Court Reporter. It had been over three years since Sister Margaret and Brother Thaddeus had seen each other. Hal had never met the plaintiff. He knew her only through the eyes of his client.

Amy proved to be a sound witness. She certainly had no bias at the time she heard the conversation between Tad and Ron. She didn't even know them or their connection to Maggie. What she'd heard was easily corroborated. And although she had been a casual acquaintance of Maggie's at the yoga studio, that had ended abruptly when Amy moved downstate to reunite with her boyfriend.

Ben Clarkson attempted to discredit her testimony by challenging her inexperience as a bartender, her own drinking at the event ("No, sir."), her deflected attention by serving other imbibers (there had only been two other patrons at her section of the bar), and her apparent eavesdropping ("Actually, sir, everybody at the bar could hear Mr. McAvoy. No one needed to eavesdrop."). Amy was telling the truth, and she answered the question without bias, in substance or tone. Difficult to cross-examine the truth. The Hoya scored no points.

The deposition lasted the entire morning. Harold Wilkerson's focus on the deponent's testimony was sporadic. His primary attention was elsewhere. Across the conference table to the left of witness Kincaid sat Sister Maggie. She was far from the image that Hal had conjured. She was composed, confident, alluring, attractive, sexy, and gifted as a non-verbal communicator. She maintained a pleasant facial expression for the entire proceeding, and on those occasions when his glance intersected with her eyes, she turned her head and a subtle smile was arrowed in his direction.

Hal knew better. Oh my God, he knew better. But too often the knowledge in his brain was superseded by organs in his southern hemisphere.

It was about ten days later when he orchestrated a "chance meeting" with Maggie. He had, of course, learned a lot about her from Tad. Like where she worked. Where she had lunch. How she got to work. Where she lived. Where she drank. What she drank. "The more we know about our opponents, the better."

Hal chose Marshall's Landing in the Merchandise Mart, a chic hub for coffee, cocktails, and comfort food with nice views of the river. He situated himself conspicuously with a generous view of people entering for lunch. He had overheard Maggie talking on the phone after the deposition. She'd mentioned something about meeting at the "landing." It was an educated guess on Hal's part that he was at the right place. He also knew she worked a block away.

He ate his lunch at a turtle's pace and was just about to leave when he spotted her walking up the steps from the Mart lobby into the casual cocktail area of the eatery. His heart raced. *Why the fuck am I here?* It was a rhetorical question. He knew why and he suspected that she did, too. She was considerably hotter in this less formal setting; he could see her walk, interact, laugh. She picked up her "to go" lunch from the bartender, glanced to her left, and spotted her prey.

Without hesitation, she walked up to her opposing counsel, his legs slightly quivering, and confidently spoke, "Ah, Mr. Wilkerson. So nice to see you. Slumming it today? All the restaurants on Michigan Avenue booked during the lunch hour?"

He knew it was sarcasm. But he was having difficulty concentrating, so he decided to answer her as if it were a genuine inquiry. "Oh no, I have a client in the Mart. Just

R.A. SIMPSON

got through meeting with him." It was true that he had a
client with offices in the Mart. That he had just met with
him was bullshit.

And she knew it. "Really. What's his name? Maybe
I could meet him some night after work for a drink. The
views of the river are best around sunset." She had no
intention of meeting Wilkerson's client. She was volunteering information.

He replied, "Ah, I don't think that would work. He's
married."

So are you, you stupid ass. She gave him thirty days. It
wouldn't take that long.

So, to recap: Harold was about to start banging Maggie
"Sister Margaret" McAvoy. In no specific order, here is the
leverage that he would create in others to satisfy his libido:

1. His client, Tad McAvoy. "Really, Hal. You're
sleeping with my sister. Do you think that might
be a conflict of interest? I don't think your malpractice insurance will cover this. How much are
you worth?"

2. His law partners. "Really, dickhead. Do you have
any idea what you have exposed us to? Your
name is coming off the door and the letterhead,
and your father's and grandfather's names, too.
How much is your house in Sycamore Pointe
worth?"

3. Illinois Attorney Registration & Disciplinary
Commission (ARDC). "Mr. Wilkerson, I'm sure
you are aware of all the ethical rules that have

been breached by your misfeasance. Please turn in your law license forthwith."

4. His wife, Beatrice. "Jesus Christ, Hal, couldn't you cheat on me with someone else? Who's the best divorce lawyer in Chicago?"
5. Maggie McAvoy. "I'll tell you what, Hal. We can keep fucking. But it's going to cost you. What's your portfolio worth?"
6. And last, but not least: Doc and the Nurse. The Baron didn't even know these people existed. Or where their interests lay. And they were the only ones who knew the secret of Hal and Maggie.

In terms of leverage, they were Numero Uno.

Oh my, Doc and the Nurse had done their homework.

Hal Wilkerson had three email accounts. One was used solely for his legal work. The second was used for communicating with family and friends. The third was used for his private matters. Like setting up trysts with sexual partners, the most recent of whom was Maggie McAvoy. It took the Nurse less than an hour to hack into all three. His life was an open book. And he had no clue.

In conjunction with the information acquired from Harold's emails to Maggie, Doc hired Alex Hightower, a young and upcoming private detective in the city to follow their secret romantic interludes. Initially, hotels in the Loop and its surrounds were visited with frequency. Overnight visits to "consult with out-of-town clients" were better. Checkout time, 11:00 a.m. In due time, they abandoned the hotel module. Hal would leave the office early and take the Brown Line to the Armitage station and walk two blocks to Maggie's condo. Digital photography, still and video, memorialized it all. But it wasn't enough. Albeit convincing, it was all circumstantial—Doc knew it would lack the impact on the "mark" that he needed. Then came Lake Geneva.

Lake Geneva, Wisconsin, about ninety miles north of Chicago, had long been a playground for families from Chicago and the 'burbs. Cottages on the lake, waterskiing, fishing, partying, golf, hunting, and now trysting for Wilk and Maggie at the Grand Geneva Lodge, formerly known as The Playboy Resort. How perfectly ironic.

Of course, the Nurse discovered the lustful plans and relayed the info to Doc, who put the gumshoe Hightower on the road to Wisconsin. His girlfriend Nicole came along, and they rented a room for one night . . . on a Thursday. They requested Suite 1107, as it was the room they had stayed in "five years earlier on their honeymoon." Nicole gave Alex a nudge to the arm, a smile, and a kiss on the cheek. Better than she had rehearsed. It was all a ruse, of course. They'd been dating for three months.

The booking agent was more than glad to oblige. It had a fireplace. And a kitchenette. And a balcony that overlooked the lake and golf course.

"Just one reminder, Mr. Hightower. Checkout is 10:00 a.m. The cleaners need extra time because of the fireplace and kitchen. I hope that won't be too much of an inconvenience. We have guests coming in for the weekend."

Oh yes, he was aware of that. "No problem at all. One additional thing. I'd like to book the same room again for this Sunday. Is it available?"

The agent checked his computer. "That's not a problem. You're all set. Oh, and some good news . . . you get the Sunday discount." Sweet.

It was a beautiful early spring day in Lake Geneva. Alex rented a golf cart with clubs and played a round with Nicole at his side. He shot an eighty-one, which wasn't too bad for having never seen the course before. In addition, Nicole was periodically hindering his concentration. It was an enjoyable round. Golf was followed by some drinks on the veranda and a wonderful dinner of Beef Wellington and lobster. During dinner, Alex took a sip of his red Tuscan wine, looked at Nicole, and said, "So what do you think, Mrs. Hightower? A hundred bucks an hour plus expenses. Can't beat it." She chuckled and gave him a squeeze under the table.

The next morning, Alex arose early and went right to work. Fortunately, there were three ceiling fans in the suite. There was one in the living room above the couch; one in the center of the bathroom; and, of course, for the main attraction, one directly above the king bed in the bedroom.

Alex quickly installed the miniature cameras in the living room and bath. He covered the bedroom while his girlfriend was showering. She was unaware of his handiwork. It was better that way. The cameras were extremely high tech. Controlled by remote. Incredible digital, high definition video. Color. Crisp stereo audio. Great home movies. Should net around ten million . . . without even being released to the theaters.

The detective and his girlfriend returned Sunday afternoon for another day of leisure at Suite 1107 at the Grand Geneva. Another round of golf, another great meal, and a restful night of sleep with just one interruption. Alex turned the lights out and the cameras off before tucking Nicole in. This was not going to be a double feature.

The same routine as the previous Thursday was followed the next morning, except this time it included the removal of the electronic spies. Alex was able to do a small preview of each camera from a covert website.

Oh my! Doc will be pleased.

Doc and the Nurse collaborated on the following let-ter. They enclosed eight-by-ten-inch color photos of the weekend in Suite 1107 of the Grand Geneva, along with a DVD of video highlights of the Baron and Maggie.

Dear Mr. Wilkerson:

You don't know us. And you never will. We, however, know you quite well as the enclosed photos and video can attest. Our demands, as outlined below, will be met. If not, copies of the enclosed will be sent simultaneously to your wife, your law partners, your client Thaddeus McAvoy, his sister Maggie McAvoy, the ARDC, your son Charles, your daughter Jewel, and the President of the Hampshire Hills Country Club. Envelopes to all are currently addressed with postage affixed. Photographs of the same will be sent to your cell phone in ten minutes.

We have estimated your net worth at approximately ten million dollars. We want one third of that within thirty days. We know you are reading this right now. We actually know your every move. Within the next ten minutes, go the southeast corner of your office and raise and lower your window blind as a signal of compliance. Your continuing compliance will be checked daily. Any hint that authorities have been contacted, and the mail goes out.

Until tomorrow.

Harold Wilkerson's office had a small bathroom. He barely made it there before the first hurl expelled into the sink. He finished his work in the toilet, rinsed out the sink, and threw cold water in his face. He looked at himself in the mirror. He gasped for breath. He thought of killing himself. He thought of going on a rampage of killing. He threw up again. His life was over. He went back to his desk. Perhaps it was just a horrific nightmare or an unforgiving practical joke. The manila envelope had been hand delivered to his office by persons unknown. He reread the letter. He looked at the photos again. He rushed to the directed window and raised and lowered his blind three times. He repeated the same action five minutes later.

His phone lit up. It was a text message that read: *Okay. That's enough.*

Doc looked up from his Grant Park location and lowered his binoculars. He texted the Nurse and told her things were looking up.

DIRT #2

Doc and the Nurse never bought the story of the dissenting juror, whose not guilty vote allowed Bryce Wilkerson to walk. They decided to investigate.

Raymond Hopkins was from the south suburbs and had an associate's degree in general studies from South

Suburban Community College. He'd married Peggy at age twenty-four, had two children, and divorced at age thirty. He made frequent trips to Hammond, Indiana. Horseshoe Casino. That was one of the reasons the marriage didn't last . . . and the only one that caused him to be $10,000 in arrears with his child support. His credit cards were maxed out as well.

Towards the end of January, a little over a month after the trial, Doc paid a visit to the child support division of Cook County and discovered that Raymond had brought his account current with one bulk payment of $10,800. The Nurse easily accessed his credit card accounts, which had been paid off in full around the same day. Raymond was now driving a new SUV.

Jackpot in Hammond? Bank loan? Uptick at work . . . selling insurance? The Nurse was able to refute all as sources for his new-found income. His bank records were void of any newly realized income as well. So, what type of instruments had been used to wash away Raymond's debt?

Child support payment came in a cashier's check from a Loop bank; credit card payments the same way from two different Loop banks. The five-thousand-dollar down payment on the new car had come from a bank closer to Raymond's home. All of it had the sweet smell of cash. Wilkerson cash.

The Nurse was able to find an investment account among the records of the patrician of Sheridan Road. A week after the jury had been impaneled in his son's case, a sale of stock was made for $27,537.98. Sale proceeds were transferred to Lakeland State Bank in Oneida Falls, Wisconsin. A wire transfer was made to the order of Jack Lovington and Associates, LTD—a detective agency used from time to time by the Wilkerson law firm and Hal individually. The initial wire had been for $10,000. A sec-

118

ond wire was sent to Lovington a day after it had been announced by the State's Attorney that there would be no retrial in the sexual abuse case. It was for $15,500.

Raymond Hopkins was an easy mark for the Nurse. She was attractive, congenial, and trustworthy. Her stylish and short brunette hairdo was easily and convincingly concealed by a shoulder-length blonde wig with streaks. A set of contacts would switch her green eyes to brown; reading glasses would add to the disguise, which was completed by adult braces on her beautiful teeth. An adjusted set of shoes would elevate her from five-foot-four to five-foot-eight.

"Good afternoon, Mr. Hopkins. My name is Ashley Reed. I'm here to save you some money on your TV service and add channels. Are you interested? Yes! Sure, I'd love to come in."

Raymond had not had a lengthy conversation with an attractive woman for years. It was easy for the Nurse to keep him at ease and off guard. They talked a little TV, some current events, his insurance career, the weather, blah, blah.

Without changing tone, without pause, and without change of posture, the Nurse looked him in the eyes and inquired, "Where did you get the cash, Ray?"

His face turned crimson. "Uh, uh ... I don't know what you mean." She said nothing. The silence was deafening. He spoke again, "What, what do you mean?" More silence.

Then the Nurse said, "We know about the bribe, Ray. So please, no lying. We're not interested in you. Information is what's important. So how did it happen? Who approached you?"

"Who, who are you? Are you a cop?"

"No, I'm not. But I can go to the authorities . . . or you can tell me what happened. You're going to have to pay the money back. But we can help you get probation. Now, what happened?"

Raymond dropped his head in his hands. He was not the criminal type. But he had done a bad thing and he knew it. In a way, he was glad he'd been caught. The burden of guilt he'd been lugging around was beginning to lift.

He gave a complete statement of what had happened. The day following jury selection in Hope's case, ten grand in cash arrived at his house anonymously. Within a week of the case being dismissed, the remaining fifteen thousand appeared.

The Nurse recorded the entire visit. Together with the paper trail of bank records, Harold Wilkerson would become a felon. Prison. Just a matter of how many years. And no more tee times at Hampshire Hills.

CHAPTER TWELVE

───────── ✦ ─────────

Don't "Show Me the Money"

I t had taken a lot of time, analysis, and luck to put the clamps on Harold Wilkerson and his stash of cash. Of course, his own malfeasance was his undoing. Doc and the Nurse, with the help of an up-and-coming young private investigator, had discovered his sins and, when presented with their work product, the Baron folded like a lawn chair at a high school soccer game.

The masterminds of this plan had committed multiple violations of the criminal law, both on the state and federal levels. But they had chosen the perfect victim. One who had failed to take an interest in his "Beamer" since birth. Is it possible that a little investment in his son's life would have made a difference in his future behavior? Did he feel any empathy for young Hope and her parents? Was there any accountability? Absolutely not.

Not until the blinds were flashed from the seventy-fifth floor for Doc, who was waiting by the Buckingham Fountain in Grant Park.

And how did Duff and Russo feel about their new adventure into the business of criminal enterprise? It was the subject of many discussions.

> Doc: "So did you ever see the movie *The Sting*? It won Best Picture in 1972 or '73, I t'hink."

> The Nurse: "No. That was a little before my time. Why?"

> Doc: "Well, there's a character in the movie—his name is Doyle Lonnegan—who is similar to our good friend Mr. Wilkerson."

> The Nurse: "How so?"

> Doc: "Let me explain. So Lonnegan is this big Irish gangster from New York City during the Depression. He has a numbers racket in Chicago. So, one day . . . "

> The Nurse: "What's a numbers racket?"

> Doc: "It's like an illegal private lottery game. Bets were placed with a bookie. Very popular with poor people, especially during the Depression. Today it's legal. I think it's called Powerball."

> The Nurse: "Okay. Go ahead."

> Doc: "So one day, a courier of Lonnegan's with a lot of cash loses it to a threesome of street grifters in

Chicago, one of them by the name of Luther Coleman. Lonnegan is advised of the loss, which is pennies compared to what he makes daily through all of his illegal enterprises, and he has Coleman whacked. One of Coleman's fellow grifters, Johnny Hooker, who was played by Robert Redford, teams up with Henry Gondorf, who was played by Paul Newman. They devise a plan to scam Lonnegan to avenge the loss of their friend Luther and put a little cash in their own pockets. And it succeeds. To the tune of a half million dollars."

The Nurse: "So Wilkerson is Lonnegan?"

Doc: "Absolutely! The best scene in the movie is a card game on a train between New York and Chicago. Gondorf and Lonnegan are in the game. Lonnegan cheats at cards and Gondorf knows it. So, he stacks his own deck to win. His four jacks beat four nines. Lonnegan is furious but loathe to accuse Gondorf of being a better cheater than him in front of the other players in the game.

"That's the position that Big Hal is in. We're cheating him, but he can't blow the whistle on us without implicating himself in a whole slew of transgressions, some of which could land him in jail for years. More importantly, he doesn't know who swindled him.

"And believe me. Wilkerson is a gold medal cheater. On his wife, on his client, on his law partners, on his profession, and—to me, the worst of all—on the justice system by fixing the jury and the outcome of the trial."

In the end, Doc and the Nurse, although not in a legal sense, justified their actions based upon the purity of their motives—accountability for the perpetrator and compensation for the victims. After all, each had been victimized in a similar manner by someone they trusted. And the accountability for such violations had been suppressed by a larger power, an entity that allowed those offenders to offend again. And neither had received a penny of compensation.

Having reached an understanding, if not rationality, as to the relative morality of their conduct, the next challenge was a more practical one. Doc and the Nurse needed a receptacle for a shit pot full of cash that they were about to exert control over. They needed safety, efficiency, trust, and anonymity. Doc had no clue where to start. The Nurse had a resource.

Russo had been contracted by a medium-sized, south side law firm to do a total revamp of their computer system. Although not advertised, the firm of Santos and Associates dedicated the bulk of their practice to the management of funds and specifically to locating hard-to-find offshore accounts for their clients. And not necessarily banks. "Entities" were often more effective. In addition to hiding money, it also appeared the firm was quite adept at cleaning it, if so required. The latter was of no interest to Russo. She and her partner needed a quick "in and out" of funds absent a paper trail.

The Nurse needed two weeks to convert the state-of-the-art system for the firm. In the middle of the second one, she hit pay dirt. The First Mutual Caribbean Bank of Belize won the nod. According to her "research," FMCBB had considerable experience in the field and, of greater relevance, had never been audited. And they spoke very highly of their ongoing business with the law firm in Chicago.

They had a simple but extremely secure system of receiving and disbursing funds. A separate transaction code was assigned for each wire transfer. Doc would write the code on a sticky note and adhere it to one of the potential mailings containing Wilkerson's compromising video from Grand Geneva. Just a little reminder for compliance purposes. A photo text of the note would be sent to Harold using a disposable phone incapable of being traced. The Nurse would receive an encrypted email from the "bank," confirming receipt of the funds. Both confessed to the rush they were experiencing during this part of the process.

It took about a month for the duo to rake an amount slightly north of three million. There was a fee, of course, exacted by the FMCBB. Fairly pricey. Two-and-a-half points per transaction covering arrivals and departures equally. A quarter of a million dollars. Doc and the Nurse thought it was a little steep but worth it. After all, it wasn't their money.

The exclusionary rule of law basically states that the State cannot use evidence against a defendant if it has been obtained illegally. The rule can only be invoked when the *State* violates the rights of the accused. Or when an agent of the State, such as a drug informer working for the police, obtains information unlawfully. The rule does not apply to the actions of private citizens. Duff had learned this from his prosecutor friend, Jack Strohl.

So, Doc and the Nurse, after the Wilkerson money had safely reached its Caribbean destination, compiled all the information that they had gathered, much of which had been obtained illegally, regarding the bribery of juror Raymond Hopkins. They analyzed it, put it in very readable and logical form, and sent it by courier to the Cook County State's Attorney's office.

The Baron was indicted on Good Friday of 2018, about four months following his son's trial. He was arrested on Easter Sunday at Hampshire Hills Country Club in front of about thirty of his fellow members. Needless to say, he missed his tee time.

His arrest made the ten o'clock news. The next morning, his mug was on page three of the *Tribune* with a lengthy accompanying story about his arrest and the history of his son's case. All the Sycamore Pointe Wilkersons mourned and went into hiding. Many banks began to review their accounts receivable. Worst of all, after posting bond, he had to go home and face the fury of Beatrice.

It had been a bad two months for Hal. He thought he had weathered the storm by complying with the financial demands of his unknown blackmailer. His relief had been short-lived. Now he was facing prison.

CHAPTER THIRTEEN

Collateral Damage

Some victims are not on the radar. Gwen Addison was one of these.

Gwen would never make a lot of money working at the Music Institute of Chicago. She didn't care. She was living her dream, teaching young, underprivileged children piano, violin, guitar, and singing.

The Institute was typically beyond the means of lower income families. Gwen disapproved. She'd gone to the board with a plan to fundraise for scholarships. They'd said, "Fine, it's all yours, but it can't interfere with your normal responsibilities."

And to them she'd said, "Fine, I'll do it." And she did.

Without compensation, she worked an additional twenty to thirty hours a week. She recruited kids from the west and south sides, organized transportation, met with parents, held bake sales, supervised raffles, and, oh yeah, taught. Her kids flourished. She gave them attention not previously experienced. She gave them quality instruction unavailable to them at their public schools. More than anything, she gave them hope.

Her program was an unqualified success. She dubbed it "Operating on a String."

Late one Thursday night, her supervisor, Flynn Ditmar, called her into his office. He extended an obligatory and half-baked compliment to Gwen regarding her work and then asked her to substitute for him the next day. He had set up an interview with a prospective adjunct faculty member. Mr. Ditmar had a conflict and the interview had already been rescheduled once. He did not want to cancel again. The applicant was Bryce Wilkerson.

With silent reluctance, Gwen agreed. Interviewing was not her forte. She was a teacher, not an HR person. Bryce was charming, his resume was polished, and his audio tape was impressive. Gwen, of course, gave him a positive review. The rest was history. When things went south, the Institute needed a scapegoat. They let Gwen go. Her program died. Her kids and their parents mourned. Ripple victims. She lost her apartment and was forced to move in with her parents; she spiraled downward.

During the investigation, the police had questioned Gwen about Bryce Wilkerson. Among other things, the circumstances behind the interview were discussed. She broke down. Her guilt gushed. She felt responsible. Hope Emery-Wright had been one of her early students.

Mr. Ditmar was also questioned. He went into protective mode. Never saw anything unusual in Wilkerson's behavior. He got positive reviews from the parents of his students. Regretted not being able to conduct the hiring interview himself, but his mother had been in the hospital. That was true. But that had not been the scheduling conflict. He'd been playing golf with some college buddies who were visiting from out of town. The police discovered that little lie when they'd checked the hospital records for

Mrs. Ditmar's visitors. It had been inconsequential to the investigators. But not to Michael Duff.

He learned of the story through Jack Strohl, his buddy in the State's Attorney's office. It was a gross injustice to Gwen and her students that had to be addressed.

And it was. Doc and the Nurse made a withdrawal from the Caribbean account.

> Dear Ms. Addison:
>
> We have researched your dismissal from the Music Institute of Chicago and have determined it to be entirely without justification. Accordingly, we have enclosed a money order payable to you in the sum of $76,345, representing your lost salary since your unjust termination and further compensation for your "Operating on a String" program.
>
> Additionally, we are enclosing information regarding a trust account which has been opened with you as trustee, to be used to reinitiate your music program for underprivileged children in Chicago. The receipt for the initial deposit of $100,000 is enclosed.
>
> It is not necessary for you to discover the parties responsible for these gifts. Our thanks in advance for your forbearance in that regard. Our satisfaction will be the observance of the continued success of your program and the hope and opportunity you give to children who

would not otherwise experience the same.

All the best to you and your budding musicians.

Gwen broke down with joy when she received the letter. She called her parents, her friends, and the families of her former students with the incredible news. She established a modest location for her studio that was more accessible to her young musicians. She bought some used instruments. A church on the south side donated a piano. She got a new apartment close to her work and a new lease on life, which would bear fruit for years to come.

And most importantly, her students came back in droves. With a new-found hope in a city that had an abundance of despair.

CHAPTER FOURTEEN

─────── ⚜ ───────

Vesuvius

One would have thought that after extracting millions of dollars in cash from the bluebloods on the North Shore, now safely tucked away in a Caribbean hiding place, Michael Duff would be experiencing a sense of calm, satisfaction, and accomplishment. Not so. The rage capable of spiking without notice was still alive and well within him, causing him not to be any of those things.

There were ignitors everywhere.

The daily newspaper was high on the list. Duff read the *Chicago Tribune* most every morning while riding the Brown Line to his Loop workplace. He knew it wasn't a healthy habit given his history, but it was a regimen he could not break. Simply put, he just wanted to know what was going on in the world. And, of course, almost daily it would spark a collision with his own private demons.

The Attorney General of Illinois had jumped on the bandwagon with those who were attacking the Catholic Church, its priests who had with impunity crushed innocent lives for decades, if not centuries, and the powerful structure of its bureaucracy that had for an equal time blocked these perverts, disguised in black robes and high white collars, from being held accountable.

The Church had given the AG, Lisa Madigan, numbers from the six dioceses in Illinois: 185 offending priests. Her investigation revealed that there had been an additional five hundred priests who had committed sexual atrocities. Madigan's investigation was in part motivated by a similar effort by prosecutors from Kelle Russo's home state of Pennsylvania.

The pattern was clear. A priest molests a child. His boss, the Church, learns of the abuse and hides it. The priest is "traded" to another diocese to potentially abuse again. Huge conferences are called in Rome to deal with the problem. Cardinals and the Pope convene. Nothing happens.

Duff always wondered why the solution wasn't as simple as "call the cops." These "wolves in sheep's clothing" were heinous criminals and should have been treated as such. And the "bosses" who covered it up should have been as well. *Throw them all in fucking jail!*

With every article that Duff read, the temperature of his rage elevated rapidly. Fortunately, his meetings with the Nurse had a calming effect. Maybe it was the wine or her nurse-caring quality. Whatever it was, it put a temporary cap on a powder keg that, if unchecked, would someday do some severe damage. It was the type of anger that Doc was himself afraid of. It was the anger of an abused child who screamed for retribution. It was the anger that ended a marriage. It was the anger that halted full-time fatherhood. It was the level of fury that could put Michael Duff in prison for years.

The high tide for this wave of ire would eventually be detonated by the Beamer with a post on social media that got a lot of "likes." It was a picture of him holding up a recently caught Northern Pike with the caption: "One that got away, one that didn't."

And one big dislike.

CHAPTER FIFTEEN

Unbridled Ire

JUNE 3, 2018

Joshua Emery-Wright, father of Hope, was home alone. His wife, daughter, and son had travelled to the St. Louis area to visit relatives for the week. They needed a change of scenery. He was unable to accompany them because of work obligations. More high-rises going up in the city.

Josh had never experienced a rage like the one that overtook him when he'd first learned that his innocent daughter had been sexually violated by her voice instructor. Had it not been for the efforts of his wife in calming him, Bryce Wilkerson's life would have ended well before his trial.

"Don't victimize Hope again," she'd said. "She needs her father."

Those words had remained uppermost in his memory. But over time, even they were getting buried. The suffering of his daughter, his wife, and himself had taken its toll. The legal process had consumed their lives; the decision (or lack of one, at least in unanimity) had been devastating. This creep had molested his daughter, and he'd walked, free to offend again; justice had been denied, not because of a reasonable doubt but because of dollars. And now he was partying up north and posting his shenanigans on his Facebook page.

Josh's anger had reached the volcanic level. He had to do something. With ease he was able to locate the Wilkerson cabin on Google Earth. It was about a six-hour drive. It was raining; work had been cancelled. No lost wages. He secured his Glock 19 and headed north. There was a long gun secured in his truck as well. He touched a family portrait as he exited his apartment. *I won't get caught . . . I promise.*

He drove north out of the city. He was so overwhelmed and consumed in thought by what he was about to embark upon that he blew by two toll booths without noticing them, much less depositing any change in the receptacles. Photographs of these oversights were taken automatically. A letter demanding payment arriving in a month would be the least of his worries.

His route to Gresham Gathering was being memorialized in other ways as well. It gained momentum in Fond du Lac, Wisconsin, when he swiped his credit card at a local gas station; again in Tomahawk, for a late lunch at a diner; and finally, at a mom-and-pop motel on Route 51 south of Oneida Falls, about three miles from the Wilkerson summer retreat. He didn't care. He was on a mission. The consequences to him personally were of no relevance.

He texted his wife good night. He set the alarm on his phone for 5:00 a.m. He put the Glock in the drawer of his nightstand . . . right next to a Gideon Bible. He tried to sleep.

Jed Tucker had been reading up on Bryce Wilkerson. Knew about his criminal charge in Chicago. Followed the trial. Knew it had been dismissed. Knew the fix was in. He had never really liked this poor little rich boy FIB.

His quiet little cove on Gresham Lake had ceased being so upon the Wilkersons' purchase of the Gathering. Lots of ski boats buzzing his dock. Loud music. Late night parties. Drugs. Fireworks. Trash floating in the pristine waters of God's country.

The police seemed to be oblivious to their actions and to his multiple complaints about them. Neighborhood feuds. Not a big priority, they thought.

Well, he had had about enough and was ready to do something about it.

Tomorrow was Monday and he had an appointment with a homeowner on a kitchen rehab. It was scheduled for 8:00 a.m. He had made an earlier commitment for the same day. In preparation for the same, he retrieved his 30.06 rifle, which had been secured in his bedroom closet.

Michael Duff was now harboring feelings that were light years beyond his wildest meanderings. Five years ago, he had been having suicidal ideations stemming from his childhood victimization. The pain had reached incalculable depths. He had survived and was healing.

Now, he was in contemplation of taking not his own life but someone else's. Bryce Wilkerson. Was that possible? Oh yes, it was. He was ready. And he believed that he could pull it off without detection. No one knew he had followed the case. No one knew his background. No one knew his level of anger. Not even Kelle Russo.

It was Sunday evening. Kelle was in New York for a business meeting the next day. Doc knew the location of Gresham Gathering. His rental car was ready. So was Michael Duff.

Bryce Wilkerson had no way of knowing that June 3 would turn out to be the eve of death.

As previously planned, he met his fishing and drinking buddies, Ted and Todd Blanchard, at Wally's Station around 6:00 a.m. Tackle gear in tow, he bought a case of beer and left his truck to be serviced. The three then piled into Ted's SUV, fishing boat in tow, and headed to Little Hidden Lake. Each finished their first beer prior to arrival.

A long hot day in the sun fishing for Northern Pike came to an end, not coincidentally, with the total depletion of the brew. No worries. Oneida Falls had a myriad of watering holes. They chose The Thirsty Pike, situated on the banks of Lake Papoose. The brothers dropped Bryce off at Wally's, where he picked up his truck after paying for the service with his mom's credit card. Ten minutes later, they met up again at the Pike, around 5:36 p.m. That was, at least, the time of their first beer purchase.

Fortunately, for the subsequent murder investigation, the bartender had kept an open tab on the trio of drinkers. Before tax and tip, the final bill was $141 and was presented to the boys at closing time, slightly after midnight.

Itemized, the bill was as follows:

6 buckets of beer @ $12 per = $72.00

9 shots of whiskey @ $5 per = $45.00

2 Large Pizzas, thin @ $12 per = $24.00

Total $141.00

The bartender also remembered that each one of these marathon imbibers had a shot of whiskey "for the road," for which they paid cash.

Through some miracle, Bryce was able to drive to the Blanchard cabin for yet another nightcap and a shared blunt before navigating back to Gresham Gathering. Once inside, he crashed on the family room couch, and at some point during the night, the pizza, beer, and whiskey combo appeared in a different form, on the newly purchased braided rug upon which the sofa rested.

Just another day in the life of the Beamer—his last day, actually. The next morning, it would be lights out.

CHAPTER SIXTEEN

Coleman's Lantern

The vacation brochures and websites for Pinesap County bragged about the safety of the area. Lowest crime rate in the country. And it was true. The last murder had been about thirty years ago. An inexperienced Oneida Falls cop had been the only witness for the State. He'd arrested the offender at the scene, who'd willingly confessed to shooting his wife and handed the shotgun to the officer. It seemed she was cheating on him, and he was drinking when he found out. And that was that.

The gruesome scene at Gresham Lake was decidedly different.

Sheriff Gregory Wallace, although loathe to admit it, was in deep water; in fact, it was way above his head. To his credit, he contacted the Wisconsin Bureau of Investigation (WBI) in Madison, and an agent was dispatched from its Wausau office to take charge of the investigation. His name was Bennett Coleman.

Agent Coleman was no stranger to homicide investigations. He had earned his stripes initially in Milwaukee and was revered for his keen analysis of crime scenes and intuition regarding behavior and motive. He left Milwaukee and joined the State Bureau in Wausau, a mere ninety miles away from Gresham Lake and the Northwoods where, if things went according to plan, he intended to retire within the next five years.

One thing became quite evident to Detective Coleman upon his arrival in Oneida Falls to investigate the death of Bryce Wilkerson. Enlisting a qualified support roster would be key. Although Wausau was a small field office for the WBI, it had ample staff for a murder investigation. Crime scene technicians, experienced investigators, and sophisticated labs were commonplace. Not so in Pinesap County.

Exhibit A: Sheriff Gregory Wallace.

A lifetime resident of Oneida Falls, Wallace was enjoying his third term as Sheriff of Pinesap County. To say the least, he was quite popular and had been so all of his life.

His parents, Fred and Gladys Wallace, owned the local gas station. Oldest business in town. "Wally's Station." Local fishermen and guides would meet there in the early hours for a cup of coffee before buying their live bait. After a "hard" day on the lake, an evening stop would fetch a six pack of beer, or more, accompanied by stories of the "ones that got away." If a big one were landed, the elder "Wally" would bring out the Polaroid and shoot a picture of the angler and his catch with his business sign in the background. It would be published in the weekly newspaper. Wally never paid a dime for advertising.

Young Gregory, of course, had worked at the station since age ten. He advised tourists what types of baits to use and what lakes to cast them in. The locals bought gas, supplies, groceries, and cigarettes, and enjoyed the gossip that flowed daily. He got to know pretty much everyone in the county. Many referred to him as "Little Wally," a nickname he didn't particularly like, but it was good for business. And after all, this business would be his someday.

Wally's Station continued to flourish when Greg took it over from his father. But alas, he got bored with a routine that he had endured since childhood, not to mention his growing intolerance of his moniker "Little Wally." He decided to make a name of his own. So, he ran for Sheriff. With absolutely no previous experience in law enforcement, Little Wally won by a landslide. He hired a manager to run the station; he donned a uniform and a badge.

But Agent Coleman was in charge now. And he knew exactly how the Sheriff would be used. Local information. History. Secrets. Relationships. Gossip. Sheriff Wallace was the perfect man for the task. He'd been training a lifetime for the job. He put up no resistance. After all, if this crazy murder was solved, he could take the credit.

Detective Brian Spurlock was a bit of a different animal. He was decidedly overqualified for his job but loved the pace and aura of the Northwoods. He had training at UW-Madison, followed by experience in the state capital and later in Wausau. Coleman had met him only by reputation, which was favorable. It didn't take long for Agent Coleman to size up Spurlock as a solid professional with the right amount of moxie for detective work. He would be his Chief Deputy.

When Coleman arrived at Gresham Lake, Wilkerson's corpse was about fifty hours old, a fact not readily apparent by the scene. Upon observing the remains, he opined that the killer had a sense of humor, albeit warped. *The Beamer*

sleeps with the fishes! A similar fate dealt to Luca Brasi, muscle man for Vito Corleone of *The Godfather* fame.

Spurlock had secured the scene until Coleman's arrival. There were a number of photographers there who all needed more sophisticated direction. Coleman obliged. "It's the digital age, guys. You can't take too many." He directed that a video be made of the scene and the various routes that could be taken to get to the cabin, something a prosecutor and potential jury would hopefully appreciate; defense counsel, not so much. Spurlock found the boot prints leading from the lake to the body—or was it from the body to the lake? An escape by boat perhaps? Casts were made of the prints. Size twelve. *Hmmm. Big guy. Perhaps.*

Coleman engaged the Sheriff.

"Who is the victim, Sheriff?"

"His name, we believe, is Bryce Wilkerson. His family lives somewhere in the Chicago area. This is their summer home."

"Do you know him?"

"A little bit. We've had some minor run-ins with him. Alcohol related, mostly."

"Like what?"

"A weak DUI about a year ago. Didn't blow. Hired a hotshot lawyer out of Madison. It was eventually dismissed."

"And?"

"Just some rowdiness at some of the local bars. Nothing serious."

"Does he live up here year-round?"

"I don't think so. Just spends time here randomly."

"Married? Kids?"

"No."

"Employed?"

"Don't know."

"Girlfriends?"

"Don't know."

"Prior record?"

"We're checking on it."

"Okay, Sheriff Wallace, here is your assignment." Little Wally took copious notes while listening. "One. Contact the next of kin and inform them of the death of their son. They are going to want to come up here right away to claim the remains. Tell them that will be a waste of time as I am going to have the body taken to Madison for an autopsy. In as discreet a manner as possible, inform them of the condition of their son. Obtain as much information as they are willing to impart about him. Especially if they have a suspicion of who might want him dead. Give them my name and inform them I will be contacting them at a later time.

"Two. Arrange a TV press conference informing the public of this gruesome offense with a genuine request for help and cooperation. My guess is that this will become a statewide story if not even more widespread.

"Three. Gather as many officers as possible and direct them to find anyone who has had contact with the decedent, no matter the time frame.

"Any questions?"

"No, Agent Coleman."

"Sheriff, it's okay to call me Bennett," Coleman said. "Oh, one other thing. Is there a business in town called Wally's Station?"

"Oh my God, yes! I own it. Why?"

Coleman responded, "Whoever owns this pickup truck got the oil changed there very recently. Get the records."

"So, who discovered the body, Spurlock?" Coleman inquired.

"A salesman from Iowa by the name of Wayne Crawford. Appears to have no prior contact with the decedent. Was actually looking for a college buddy who lives one cabin down. Turned down the wrong lane. I'm having him brought back out here so you can interview him. He went to the ER shortly after we got here last night."

"Good work," said Coleman. "These remains are going nowhere until we've fully interviewed him."

Wayne Crawford had partially regained his composure upon his arrival back to the cabin at Gresham Lake. The corpse was now covered with a black body bag. The stench remained.

Wayne had bought some new clothes. He threw his old ones away. How he wished he could do the same with the memory of what he had experienced the previous evening. He was anxious to get back to Iowa.

"Mr. Crawford, my name is Bennett Coleman. I am the investigator who has been assigned to this case. I need to ask you a few questions." Coleman knew from talking to Spurlock that Crawford was not a suspect. This would not be an interrogation. He just needed to know what he knew.

Crawford recounted the events of his day, including a detailed account of his experience at the cabin.

Coleman: "Did you see anyone in the area of the cabin?"

"No."

"Do you know who lives here?"

"No."

"Did you ever get a hold of your college friend?"

"No."

"Did you touch the body in any way?"

"No. I did throw up very close to it, though. And I think I shit my pants. Can I go now?"

"Yes, Mr. Crawford. You have been very helpful. One last thing. Go with Deputy Spurlock and give him your contact information and a DNA swab. Thank you for your cooperation."

It took a brief explanation to convince him of the necessity for his DNA. *No sense in wasting hours of time chasing down the identity of someone's vomit when we can establish it as yours, Wayne.*

Coleman took a deep breath made a quick checklist in his mind.

Okay, we've got a dead man with a bullet hole through the middle of his head who has been half consumed by the uncaged animals of the Northwoods; he was probably drinking prior to his demise, which is a good thing; a skeleton of a dead walleye (the detective knew his fish); a commingling of vomit regurgitated by a hardware salesman from Iowa and a rookie cop from Pinesap County; a cabin with dirty dishes, soiled floors, and puke-encrusted carpets. Looks like a fraternity house after a football weekend. Footprints all over the place. DNA up the yin-yang. And a pickup truck. There will be a wealth of clues inside. Assign that to Spurlock. Please let it be that no one has disturbed the Silverado. I've got to establish the time of death. It's been a while. And where is this guy's cell phone? And why didn't one of the varmints drag the dead walleye back to his den? And where is the bullet's final resting place?

"Back to work."

Sheriff Wallace came through on his first assignment. It seemed the decedent was involved in a criminal trial about six months prior in Chicago. He'd been acquitted of sexually abusing a ten-year-old girl. The girl's father created quite a scene after the trial—out of control and threatening the young Wilkerson. Had to be restrained by the police and his own family and friends. Suspect #1.

One of his deputies found two locals, brothers Todd and Ted Blanchard, that Beamer had partied with the night before. Initial reports were that they had closed a local watering hole, The Thirsty Pike, at midnight after a five-hour celebration of a successful day of fishing on Little Hidden Lake. The three had polished off a case of beer while angling; they'd switched to beer and shots when they reached their favorite watering hole. Upon closing, the three went to the Blanchard cabin for a nightcap and a blunt. The brothers agreed that Bryce had left around 1:30 a.m. Bingo! Coleman would be able to determine with reasonable certainty the time of death.

Coleman, after considerable difficulty, was able to contact Cook County Assistant State's Attorney Elaine Dunning concerning the trial in which Bryce Wilkerson had been acquitted. Well, that wasn't quite true.

The trial had actually ended in a mistrial when the jury became deadlocked at eleven-to-one for conviction. Hope and her family had suffered enough and did not want to endure another trial. The State was left with no option but to dismiss. It was later discovered that the dissenting juror had been bribed by the defendant's father to vote not guilty. The father, a Harold Wilkerson, Esq., had been arrested and was awaiting trial for bribery and obstruction of justice.

It was true that after the presiding judge had declared a mistrial, the victim's father had become incensed and, in the heat of the moment, threatened the defendant. Ms. Dunning opined that she did not believe Mr. Wright would carry through on his threats. She also offered no expression of condolence upon learning of the fate of young Bryce. She did share with Agent Coleman the names of other victims of the lawyer's son.

That latter disclosure broadened the range of suspects, to the dismay of the Wausau detective.

Spurlock conducted a thorough examination of the pickup truck at the scene. A summary of his findings was included in a report to Coleman:

1. There was no alcohol in the cab and no evidence that any had been consumed therein.
2. The driver's side window was open. An oval-shaped rifle slug was found embedded in the arm rest of the passenger's side door, presumably the round that caused the victim's death.
3. The vehicle was a 2017 Chevrolet Silverado, titled to Beatrice Wilkerson. It had no lien. It had been purchased in a northern suburb of Chicago.
4. The oil on the vehicle had been changed on June 3, around 10:00 a.m., at Wally's Station.
5. The bed of the truck contained fishing tackle, a rod and reel, a net, and a bucket and a gaff, as well as an empty foam cooler.
6. The ashtray contained numerous cigarette butts, all but two being Marlboro Reds; the two excep-

tions were Virginia Slims with pink lipstick on the filters.

7.   Multiple sets of fingerprints were lifted from the interior and exterior of the vehicle.

Coleman met with Harold and Bea Wilkerson in Madison two days after their son's corpse was discovered. They presented an interesting contrast in behavior.

As expected, Bea was beyond composure over the death of her son. Every other sentence was accusatory of the molestation victim's father, Mr. Wright. "I was there. I saw the look in his eye. I heard the threat. Why haven't you arrested him?" She was referring to the reaction of Hope's father when the judge had declared a mistrial in Bryce's case. "He was getting his life back in order. I can't believe he's gone." He, of course, was not getting his life "back in order." It had never been in order. "Tell him, Hal. Tell him to arrest Mr. Wright."

The Baron was in complete control of his emotions. He was consoling his wife, albeit superficially, in Coleman's eyes. He did confirm the outburst of Mr. Wright but made no demand of his arrest. Facing criminal charges himself, he was in no position to be making demands to Wisconsin authorities. His lawyers had cautioned him to be lowkey and cooperative during this process. After all, he would be facing trial within the next year for his bribery and obstruction of justice charges in connection with the Cook County case. He had, of course, pled not guilty and his lawyers had deemed the charges preposterous. "Our client has an impeccable reputation, is totally innocent of these charges, and looks forward to proving the same in a court of law. He's never even met the juror, Mr. Hopkins." Defense lawyers trying the case in the media.

The Wilkersons told Coleman that they had both been at home when Sheriff Wallace called them with the devastating news. And they indicated that they had last visited the cabin in Pinesap County in late March. Coleman generally advised the parents of the investigation. He assured them that "no stone will be left unturned." He volunteered that Bryce's blood alcohol percentage was .219. He omitted the THC, or pot, finding.

"What does that mean?" inquired Bea. "Is that high?"

"Well, ma'am, it is rather high. More than twice the legal limit. But it will help us in determining the time of death. Our preliminary opinion is that Bryce was killed during the early daylight hours of June 4. By the way, we have not been able to find Bryce's phone. Do you happen to know what service he used?"

Bea started weeping again. "We are on the same plan. It's AT&T." She told Coleman that she had talked to Bryce a couple nights before his death. He'd told her that he was going fishing with the Blanchard brothers the next day. She broke down again. "I'm the one who told him to go up north. I thought it would be good if he got away for a while. This would never have happened if I had told him to stay at home. But he needed to get as far away from the girl's crazy father as he could. When will you be arresting him? I know in my heart he is guilty."

Agent Coleman gave each parent his business card and expressed his condolence over their loss. He advised that he would endeavor to keep them apprised of the investigation.

After the Wilkersons left the interview, Coleman called Agent Shemansky at his Wausau office.

"Hey, Ted, this is Coleman. I'm in Madison on this Pinesap County homicide. I need a favor. Go to the AT&T store at the Wausau mall and ask one of the staff to do a phone location on Bryce Miles Wilkerson's phone. The number is 312-940-8819. If they are able to locate it, give the info to Detective Spurlock. He's a deputy with Pinesap. Good man. I'll text you his contact information."

"No problem, Ben. Should have it done within the hour."

"Thanks, Ted."

Coleman called Spurlock to give him a heads up.

CHAPTER SEVENTEEN

Lunch at the Village

I t didn't take long for the news of Beamer's demise
to hit the Chicago media. Typically, page three of
the *Chicago Tribune* was dedicated to stories of
local interest. The murder in the Northwoods occupied top
billing. *Son of local attorney found slain at family cabin* was
the headline. The story gave a general account of events
surrounding the homicide. "According to Sheriff Gregory
Wallace, there were no eyewitnesses to the shooting. All
leads are being pursued. Anyone with information should
call the Pinesap County Sheriff's office."

The bulk of the article recapped the jury trial of the
decedent six months earlier. The eleven-to-one jury vote
resulting in a mistrial. The subsequent criminal indict-
ments of Raymond Hopkins, the lone holdout on the jury
charged with accepting a bribe; and, of course, Harold
Wilkerson, the father of the defendant, now decedent, for
bribery and obstructing justice. It mentioned that both had
pled not guilty and were out on bond awaiting trial.

Kelle Russo was having her morning coffee when she
read the article. She nearly choked on it. She immediately

grabbed her phone and called her compatriot, Michael Duff. It took a while for him to answer.

She did not wait for him to say hello. "Have you seen it? Oh my God, Michael, have you seen it?"

"Seen what?" he replied.

"Bryce Wilkerson was killed four days ago in Wisconsin. At their family cabin. Single shot to the head. I can't believe it. Meet me for lunch. Italian Village." She then hung up.

Actually, he'd read the article online about an hour prior to the call.

Italian Village was a classic eatery in the Loop. It had been around since 1926. Kelle Russo had discovered it three days after she'd moved to Chicago. She was waiting for Duff. They hugged and then settled in.

No idle chit-chat. Kelle got right to the point.

"So, what do you think, Michael?"

There was an awkward pause, or so Kelle thought. He looked at her and then away.

"Here's what I think. Anyone who reads that article and knows the history of the case will think that Hope's father did it. As soon as the Wisconsin authorities find out about the trial and its aftermath, the spotlight will be on the dad. You have to remember, Kelle, I was there when the mistrial was announced by the judge. I saw his reaction and his rage outside the Daley Center when he went after the little shit."

"I know. I know." She lowered her voice. "I just thought that, you know . . . with all the money they received from the Caribbean account, it might have calmed things down."

Doc and the Nurse had made a substantial anonymous gift to Hope's family in the neighborhood of seven figures, compensating them for their pain and agony surrounding the abhorrent abuse and the disastrous judicial aftermath. Referrals had been made for the best counselors in Chicago.

"Maybe it did for a while. But the underlying anger is still there. I believe we both can relate to that. Something may have triggered it."

Like a post on social media by Beamer. The one that had caught Duff's eye. Perhaps Mr. Emery-Wright had seen it also. Kelle had obviously not. She did sense, however, that her friend was preoccupied. She was inclined to pursue it but abandoned the quest when her tortellini soup arrived.

The remainder of the lunch was filled with small talk. Another meeting, one charged with considerable urgency, would soon occur, triggered by the investigation unfolding in God's country.

The growing knot in Duff's gut loosened as the friends bid each other good health. He was concerned that the Nurse may have noticed his uneasiness in discussing the matter of the death of Bryce Miles Wilkerson. He was on edge. *Damn*, he thought to himself, *more secrets.*

CHAPTER EIGHTEEN

Breakthroughs

Ted Shemansky entered the AT&T store at the Wausau mall, flashed his badge, and within seconds, two young and attractive sales reps volunteered to assist. Partial to brunettes, a gal named Lori got the nod. He explained the purpose of his visit, and she hustled to her tablet to begin the process. While pounding away on her keys, Lori became chatty with Ted.

"How long have you been a cop? What type of case are you investigating? What types of phones do you guys use? We have a special this month. I think we give law enforcement like a twenty percent discount. If you, like, have time after we locate this phone, I can tell you about it. Your job must be very interesting. Do you do, like, murders and stuff or is it mainly drugs? This could take a while because the reception in the Northwoods can be sketchy at times. You know you could probably do this if you have, like, an app that finds phones. I can show you how to do it when I'm done."

Ted was now convinced he'd made the wrong choice of clerks. He should have gone with the blonde.

"Thanks, but I'm on a tight schedule. Any luck?"

"Not yet. Hey, Sean, can you help me out here?" Sean appeared to be the manager. He excused himself from his current customer to assist Lori.

"Sean, this is Officer, uh, what is your last name again?"

"Shemansky."

"Yeah, Ted, right?" He nodded. "And he is, like, looking for this phone that is somewhere around Gresham Lake in Pinesap County," Lori continued. "I'm having a little trouble. Don't they have, like, really bad reception up there sometimes? I thought I heard that."

Sean fortunately took charge. He discovered that Lori's screen was in the county north of Pinesap, which happened to be in Upper Michigan, and the lake she had pinpointed was Upper Gresham. Wrong lake, wrong county, wrong state. No winning wagers on that trifecta.

Within moments, Sean had discovered the phone's location. Ted took a screenshot of the pulsating green circle and sent it to Detective Spurlock and Agent Coleman. The location appeared to be in the woods between the Wilkerson and Tucker cabins.

Agent Shemansky thanked Sean and Lori for their help. Lori responded, "No problem. Glad we could help you out." The manager rolled his eyes.

Upon receiving the photo from Shemansky, Spurlock organized a search party for the morning, as dusk was settling in.

Following the medical examination in Madison, Bryce Wilkerson's remains were transferred to Lake Shore

Funeral Home. Two days later, a funeral service was held. At the urging of Beatrice, some of his fellow band members spoke and performed some of his favorite songs, one of which was the Rolling Stones classic, "Time is on My Side," which it obviously wasn't. A minister who had never met Bryce gave a eulogy based on his conversations with family members, predominantly Mother Bea, who understandably wept throughout the brief ceremony. "He was a free spirit. He loved to fish. He loved to sing. He lived life on his own terms." His fondness for young girls was omitted. Oh, the irony of funerals.

What was left of Bryce was cremated. His ashes were deposited in Lake Michigan directly east of the Wilkerson estate. The obligatory post-service reception was catered in the family's backyard. It included hors d'oeuvres, wine, punch, and further songs from the band members. Harold Wilkerson threw down a couple shots of bourbon before he joined the grieving crowd on the bricked patio.

Bennett Coleman attended the funeral and reception, keeping a low profile. Nothing remarkable was observed.

A couple of days later, Beatrice called Coleman.

"Hello, Mrs. Wilkerson. How can I help you?"

"Agent Coleman, I was wondering if I could talk to you about a couple things."

"Of course."

"First of all, I was curious about what Mr. Wright has to say about all this. And how long before he is arrested?"

Coleman composed himself and then responded. "Yesterday afternoon, I travelled to Chicago and met with Dan O'Hearn, a homicide detective from the Chicago Police

Department. We attempted to interview Mr. Wright at his job site in the Loop. When we arrived, we located Mr. Wright and he handed me a business card for his attorney, Stewart Martin. He respectfully declined to talk about the case, which of course is his constitutional right. Detective O'Hearn and I then travelled to the office of Mr. Martin. He informed us that, although he fully understands why his client is a suspect, given the history of this case, he has advised him to refrain from giving any statements at this time."

"Well, there you have it," she responded. "Hal always told me that when they start lawyering up and don't cooperate, it's a sign of their guilt. You should have arrested him on the spot!"

"With all due respect, ma'am, it is way too early to be making arrests based on motive alone. Our goal is to amass evidence that will ensure a conviction. I'm sure your husband can tell you about the burden of proof in a criminal case. Beyond a reasonable doubt." He resisted the temptation to tell her that her husband, as a criminal defendant in Cook County, had exactly the same rights as Mr. Wright. *And, oh, by the way, do I recall correctly that when your husband was arrested, he invoked the Fifth?*

"You said there were a couple of things you wanted to discuss. What else?" inquired Coleman.

She responded, "Well, I don't know if this means anything, but when Beamer went up north, I gave him my American Express credit card in case he needed anything that he couldn't afford. I just got the bill and there might be some stuff on it that could be helpful."

"I'm sorry, who is Beamer?"

"Oh, I'm sorry. 'Beamer' has been Bryce's nickname since he was a kid. It comes from his initials, BMW. You know, the car. His early school friends hung it on him. And it stuck. It was so cute. And since he was born, I always bought Beamers." She began to choke up.

Coleman waited for her to regain her composure. "Oh, I see. Actually, the bill could be quite helpful. Are there many entries?"

"Let me see here." She began to count out loud. When she got to fifteen, Coleman interrupted her.

"Do you have the means to get me a copy of the bill? Fax, email, text?"

"I'll do the fax. There is one in my husband's home office."

Coleman gave her his fax number and thanked her for calling. The bill came about an hour later. He was about to study it when he got a call from Spurlock.

Beamer's phone had been found.

"I'll be right there. Don't touch it until I get there."

Coleman had been in Sheriff Wallace's office when he'd gotten the news from Spurlock. He enlisted a Deputy Crookshank to drive him to the scene. He was more familiar with the territory and shortcuts to the lake. They arrived in record time.

Spurlock greeted him.

"Okay. So, here's the deal. One of the people in our search group found the phone. His name is Troy. He's a volunteer who works at Wally's Station. I briefed the entire group before we started this morning that if anyone found the phone, they should contact me immediately and by all means do not touch it or move it. About thirty minutes ago, Troy is behind the garage and lets out this huge whoop. 'I found it! I found it!' I'm about a hundred feet away in the woods but I can see him cheering like he had just won the Super Bowl. His arms are raised up and the phone is in his right hand. Jesus, I thought he was going to spike the damn thing."

"Where's the phone now?" Coleman asked.

"I had him replace it as near as he could to the place where it was found."

"Where is he now?"

"He's alone on the front porch of the cabin with his head down. I dropped a few F-bombs on him."

"Well, let's go talk to him. Damage is done."

So, what was the damage? On its face, very little. But defense attorneys have a way of making little flaws in a case seem like unforgivable errors, especially in front of a jury. A judge would not buy into it.

Here's an example of how it would play out:

> Detective Spurlock has been sworn as a witness. He, among other things, has testified about the facts that led to the discovery of the decedent's phone. On that point he is being cross-examined by a trial attorney who specializes in criminal defense.
>
> Q: Detective Spurlock, correct me if I'm wrong—you have been involved in law enforcement for about fifteen years?
>
> A: That is correct.
>
> Q: You graduated from the University of Wisconsin-Madison in 2003?
>
> A: Yes.

Q: You have been involved in murder investigations for about the last ten years?

A: Yes.

Q: And, am I correct that a number of those cases were in large urban areas such as Milwaukee County?

A: Yes.

Q: And smaller urban areas such as Wausau?

A: Correct.

Q: And in your most recent position, in rural wooded and lake communities like Oneida Falls?

A: Yes, sir.

Q: Would I be correct that when you were at the University of Wisconsin your studies included preservation of crime scenes?

A: Yes.

Q: And is it also true that you have taken continuing education classes that have dealt with that same subject?

A: Yes.

Q: Is it also true that when you first became a detective, you had the opportunity to work with and observe the crime scene techniques and practices of veteran and more experienced detectives than yourself?

A: That is correct.

Q: In fact, your on-the-job experience, as it is in many professions, has probably been your best teacher in this area?

A: I have no argument with that.

Q: As I understand it, through a phone location service, you were informed of the approximate area where the decedent's phone could be located.

A: Correct.

Q: And this area was a typical and natural Northwoods area.

A: Yes.

Q: High density of pine and deciduous trees?

A: Yes.

Q: Tall grasses to wade through. Dead limbs, branches, pinecones, and the like?

A: For sure.

Q: Animal waste to contend with?

A: Yes.

Q: A very tedious and arduous task, would you agree?

A: I would.

Q: For an extremely important piece of evidence, correct?

A: Correct.

Q: Please tell the jury why this piece of evidence was so crucial.

A: Well, at this stage of the investigation, we were looking for any and all information about the decedent's activities and his relationships. The phone has become a reservoir for both of these areas. In addition, the actual phone itself, the instrument, would have potential value by way of physical evidence.

Q: With respect to that later point, you are referring to possible fingerprints or DNA material that could lead to the identity of a guilty party?

A: Yes.

Q: With respect to crime scene preservation issues, what is contamination?

A: Contamination occurs when a crime scene is changed. It can occur when items within the scene are rearranged or removed. In addition, it can occur when something is added to the scene.

Q: So, if a contaminated crime scene is photographed, there is potential that the photograph will not be accurate and could mislead a jury?

A: That is correct.

Q: You were responsible for assembling the group that was used to search for the valuable piece of evidence, namely, the decedent's cell phone.

A: Yes.

Q: Is it correct that there was a total of six individuals who formed this group?

A: Yes.

Q: Three of the group were law enforcement, one of whom was yourself?

A: Yes.

Q: And one of the other three was Troy Mercer?

A: Correct.

Q: Did you approve him as part of the search party?

A: Yes.

Q: Did he have any experience in law enforcement?

A: No.

Q: What, if you know, is his occupation?

A: He is an auto mechanic.

Q: Where is he employed?

A: Wally's Station in Oneida Falls.

Q: And who owns that business?

A: Greg Wallace, the Sheriff of Pinesap County.

Q: And the other volunteers, I assume, had no background in police work?

A: Correct.

Q: Did you give any instructions to the search group, and if so, what were they?

A: I gave each member of the group a specific area to search with instructions that if they discovered the phone or other item of interest to leave it in the position where found and refrain from touching or picking it up.

Q: To avoid contamination.

A: Yes.

Q: But that didn't occur, did it, because
of the jubilation of the auto mechanic,
Troy Mercer?

A: Correct.

Blah, blah, blah. And of course, during final arguments, all of this would be highlighted together with the other perceived weaknesses of the case to raise reasonable doubt in the minds of the jurors, or at least one of them. Emphasis would be placed on the word *contamination*. Sounds like spoiled food. Leaves a bad taste in everybody's mouth.

Agent Coleman had been around long enough to know two things: (1) The error was not as bad as it would be portrayed, but only if the prosecutor was skilled enough (not all were) to keep the issue in the proper perspective, and (2) Whatever damage was done could not be undone. Spilt milk.

He went over to talk to the auto mechanic who was still recovering from his first mistake as a very part-time cop. He kept it light.

"Hey, Troy. I'm Bennett Coleman," he said while extending his right hand. "Thanks for finding the phone."

Troy accepted the handshake, albeit weakly, and said, "Sorry I fucked up."

"Ah, it's okay. We'll work it out. Not that big a deal. Now why don't you show me how this all went down?"

The mechanic and Coleman went to the area behind the garage, which was more of storage facility for boats, a lawn mower, tools, a work bench, boxes, and assorted other stuff that people collect. The back exterior of the garage was overgrown with weeds, leaves, tall grass, pine straw, pine trees, birch trees, and a couple of old, rusty gas barrels that were elevated on metal carpenter horses. It was a mini jungle. Behind some tall grass that was resting against the backside of the garage, there was a space that had been hollowed out and was probably at one time the entranceway of a denizen of the forest: raccoon, possum, squirrel. The phone had been lying there when Troy found it. In the excitement of the moment, he'd picked it up and celebrated as if he had made a hole in one. The odds were about the same for either. Fortunately, he was wearing gloves which mitigated the mistake.

The phone was now in an evidence bag with Spurlock's initials on the tag. Spurlock removed the bag and contents and, at the direction of Coleman, transferred the same to Deputy Crookshank. Coleman instructed the deputy to deliver the evidence to a John Weatherton, forensic scientist at his Wausau office. Coleman then called Weatherton to explain what was on the way and that he needed his analysis ASAP.

He then returned to his desk at the Pinesap Sheriff's office in Oneida Falls. Time to review Mrs. Wilkerson's American Express statement.

CHAPTER NINETEEN

The next morning, Agent Coleman was anxiously awaiting word from his colleague, John Weatherton, regarding his analysis of Beamer's iPhone. He and John had been golfing buddies for years. He'd checked Wausau's weather forecast for the day and it had called for rain. That was a good thing. Nice weather may have a resulted in a delay of his report of findings.

He poured himself a cup of coffee and began his own study of the American Express bill that had been faxed to him by Bea Wilkerson the previous day. It covered the time period of May 10, 2018 through June 9, 2018. There were forty-six entries representing slightly over $7,000 of purchases. Every charge from May 15 and beyond had been made at businesses in the state of Wisconsin. Coleman knew from a previous interview with Bea that May 15 was the day Bryce had left Illinois, arriving at the cabin later that evening.

He started with the most recent charge and worked back in time from there, scribbling notes in parentheses after each entry.

*June 4, the date of Bryce's death, $141.76 to The Thirsty Pike, Oneida Falls (confirms the narrative of the bartender and the brothers Blanchard)

*June 3, $29.95 to Wally's Station for the oil change (Beamer's truck)

*June 3, $57.11 to Wally's Station for groceries (translation: beer, bait, and shore lunch)

*June 2, $23.67 to Pepe's Pizza (sausage, mushroom, and beer)

*June 2, $58.50 to Wally's Station (gas fill-up and beer)

*June 1, $66.45 to Long's Grocery (food, beer)

*June 1, $99.00 to Northland Sports (transport and docking of ski boat)

*June 1, $75.08 to Northland Sports (fishing gear)

*May 31, $112.96 to Dale's Steak House (dinner for two, a girlfriend perhaps?)

*May 31, $87.41 to Ross Jewelers (necklace; okay, girlfriend; who? give to Sheriff)

*May 31, $244.75 to Morton's Men's Clothing (new outfit for dinner?)

> *May 30, $101.00 to Birch Bark Golf
> Course (eighteen holes of golf with cart;
> a dozen beers)

> *May 30, $38.39 to Cozy Cove Café
> (breakfast for the foursome before golf)

> *May 29, $100.00 to Oneida Falls
> Chamber of Commerce (Memorial Day
> Raffle ticket)

> *May 29, $399.00 to Trout Lake Golf
> Shop (new golf clubs)

Coleman conducted a quick review of Wilkerson's last week on earth. Of one thing he was sure. Bryce Wilkerson was living proof (although no longer) that the American Express card's slogan, "Don't leave home without it," was a marketing success.

In one week, Beamer had spent nearly $2,000 buying golf clubs and then playing golf; buying fishing gear and then fishing; and buying jewelry and then draping it around some gal's neck during a romantic dinner while wearing newly purchased attire. Oh, and he drank a lot of beer. Had he lived and spent money at the same weekly rate, his total annual bill would have been just shy of ninety-nine grand. But Mrs. Wilkerson never cared when it came to money for her baby Beamer. To the Baron, perhaps it was a different story, mused Coleman.

Back to the statement.

> May 28, $339.00 to Home Satellite
> TV Service (covered living room and
> bedroom and four bonus channels)

May 28, $79.00 to Oneida Florist (delivery of bouquet to unknown girlfriend)

May 27, $177.36 to The Thirsty Pike (foreshadowing of things to come)

May 26, $899.00 to a company known as HSS, Inc. out of Stevens Point

HSS? Coleman googled it on his phone, and a number of ads appeared for a company that boasted having the cutting-edge technology on home security systems. Motion sensors, light sensors, doorbell cameras, and (oh yes) home security cameras. Coleman was familiar with the costs of these items. He ruled out the sensors as they were less expensive. It had to be a camera purchase.

Oh my God, Coleman thought, *there may be a video of Bryce Wilkerson's murder recorded on a security camera he purchased a week earlier!*

Settle down, Mr. Coleman. Fifteen years ago, a break in a case like this would have sent him to a frenzy. On more than one occasion, however, the breaks didn't bear fruit. A recanting witness, a DNA sample that failed to match, or a nullifying jury. *Stay calm,* he told himself. And he did on the outside. Internally, he was ramping up.

He made a written notation of the phone number of HSS. He quickened his pace of reviewing the remaining charges on the credit card statement, including purchases made by Bryce's mom prior to her imparting it to her son. He missed one that would have otherwise caught his attention had he not been so anxious to contact the security firm. Before he made the call, he got a hold of Sheriff Wallace.

"Greg, it's Bennett Coleman. I've got a job for you. Bryce Wilkerson had dinner with a gal at Dale's Steak House on May 31. I need to know who she is and her particulars. Age, employment, education, priors, et cetera."

"Do you want me to interview her, Agent Coleman?"

He somehow knew he was going to ask that. "No, Sheriff. Just find out who she is. Make no attempt to contact her. Thanks."

"Is there a big rush on this? I'm scheduled to speak at the Rotary luncheon today."

Stay calm, Bennett. "Yes, Sheriff Wallace. This is a murder investigation. Rush. Please." *Jesus.*

"Of course, Agent Coleman."

Coleman hung up, shaking his head, and began dialing the security company in Stevens Point. Before he could hit the send button, his phone lit up with an incoming call from John Weatherton.

"Hi, John. Still raining in Wausau?"

"It is, Ben. However, it may clear up around three. Should be enough time to play eighteen. Want to join me?"

Coleman knew Weatherton was baiting. He was ninety miles away working on a murder case. It wouldn't look kosher if the lead investigator left work early to play a round of golf.

"So, what's the deal with the phone?"

Weatherton was the master of the understatement and creating suspense. Especially if things were really big. And they were.

"Well, there are a couple of things that might help. But first, the 'no news' portion of the report. There is nothing of real interest on the surface of the phone. It's full of junk. Did someone throw up on this thing? No full prints. A partial of the decedent. A lot of organic material. Dirt.

Animal feces. Unless you're looking for deer, well trained in 30.06's, there's nothing of value forensically."

"And . . ." Coleman knew he was drawing this out.

"Well, Ben, as you might have guessed, the phone had no power when it was delivered. So, we powered it up. My able tech assistant, Griff Winters, observed and logged all the steps. Hey, did you know he was a five handicap? Played golf in college at UW-Oshkosh. Maybe he can play with me tonight if you can't make it down."

"Weatherton, would you please shut the fuck up about your golf game tonight and tell me about the phone?"

"Sure, Ben. Point number one. Your murderer or murderers took a video with the phone camera of the decedent very shortly after his death. It lasts about seven seconds. You can see the fresh blood trickling down from his head wound. But his heart has stopped beating. Gravity is causing the blood to drop. Give or take a few minutes, the time of death is 6:40 a.m. Central Daylight time on June 4. You'll never have a more accurate time of death in a case."

Coleman was speechless.

"Point number two. Our decedent had a number of voicemails that he had not erased. The majority of them were from buddies who were wanting to go fishing or play golf. There are a couple from some unidentified females. And then there were two calls from someone who works for HSS, whatever that is. Wanted to set up a time to make some kind of installation. Maybe some sort of satellite TV dish."

Coleman deflated. Shit. It hadn't been installed yet. "What's this person's name? The one from HSS."

"Hold on," said Weatherton. "I've got it here in my notes. His name is Randy Baxter. Number is 715-347-1099."

"Good work, John. Put everything on a flash drive and I'll have someone pick it up."

"Already done, Ben. Don't want anything to delay my tee time this afternoon."

"Right, John. May the shanks be with you."

Coleman was halfway through dialing the HSS number when he received a call from Little Wally.

"What's up, Sheriff?"

"I was able to find out the name of the girl that Wilkerson had been seeing prior to his death." Pause. As if waiting for praise for his efforts. None was forthcoming.

"And?"

"Her name is Reggie Masterson. She's a member of the local water ski club that gives performances during the summer months. I've known the family for years." (*Of course, you have, "Little Wal."*) "Name of the club is the Oneida Skeeters. They met after a show about three weeks ago at one of the downtown bars. She's sixteen. Will be a junior in high school in August. I know her dad really well. He's on the Village Board. I'm sure he'd be willing to talk to me."

"Not quite yet, Sheriff. I'll want to conduct that one myself. But you can come along if you wish."

"That would be great. Just let me know."

"I will. Thanks for the quick turnaround with the information on the girl."

"You bet. Gotta run to Rotary."

Have a great speech. Win lots of votes.

"Good morning. Home Security Systems. This is Hank. How may I help you?'

"Hank, my name is Bennett Coleman. I'm a special agent with the Wisconsin Bureau of Investigation. I'd like to speak with Randy Baxter."

"I'm sorry, Mr. Coleman, Randy is out of the office today. Is there something I can help you with?"

"When do you expect him back?"

"Not for another week. He's on vacation. Is there something I can help you with?"

"Is there any way I can get in touch with him?"

"Maybe. What is this all about?"

"I am investigating a murder in Pinesap County. We believe that Mr. Baxter may have some information that will be helpful to the investigation."

"Is he a suspect? I can't believe it. He wouldn't hurt a flea."

"He is not a suspect. Where is he?"

"He's somewhere in Italy. Vacationing with his wife. Her parents live around Florence. Left about ten days ago."

"What day did he leave? Need the exact date."

"Hold on." Papers being shuffled. Keys on a computer being tapped. "His last day of work was June 1. He told me he was flying out the next day. What's his connection to all this?"

"We have reason to believe that he sold some type of security system to the victim towards the end of May. I'm wondering if you can check your records. He charged it on an American Express card. Date of sale was May 26."

"Are you sure I can do this? How do I know you're a cop? Don't you need a warrant or something?"

Crap. An amateur lawyer. Coleman decided to take the soft approach. "Okay, Hank. Fair enough. Do you have access to a computer and the internet?"

"Of course."

"Google search 'Bryce Wilkerson murder. Pinesap County, Wisconsin.' You should find about fifty articles.

178

Click on the one in the *Wausau Daily Herald*. According to the article, who is in charge of the investigation?"

There was a thirty-second pause. "Bennett Coleman."

"Perfect. That's me. Now I need your cell number. In thirty seconds, I am going to send you a photo of my badge and ID card. And then we can talk further."

About a minute later, Hank said, "Okay. Got it. Can't be too careful these days." Probably a line he used with prospective customers. "So, what was that date again?"

"May 26."

At that point, Hank began to verbalize all of his thoughts in his attempt find the order. Coleman was irritated but remained outwardly calm.

"Okay, so I have to get into Baxter's pending sales file to see his activity for that time period. It looks as if he had a couple deals pending up in Pinesap. One was on Grassy Lake. Client's name was Watson. Is that the one you're looking for? Eli Watson. Wanted four motion sensors and a doorbell camera. They have become very popular recently with all the Amazon deliveries and such."

"WILKERSON, Hank! You just read an article about it. Bryce Wilkerson."

"Oh yes, how stupid of me. You know, I remember reading about this at the time. Some poor kid from Chicago. Took a slug in the head. I had no idea Randy was working with him. Do you have any suspects?"

"I might if you can locate this order."

"Right. Right. Okay. Let's see. Yes, here it is. Wilkerson on Gresham Lake. Hmmm, nice order. Four HD minis with accompanying figurines. Installation included."

"So, were they installed?"

"Let me see. It looks as if only one was installed. Bad weather cancelled the install of the other three. Randy called him twice, but he never got back to him to reschedule. I wonder why." *Death might be an option.*

"Is there an indication of the location of the camera that was installed?"

"No. But there is a diagram of the four locations. I can send it to you."

"Great. I'll text you my email. By the way, what's the deal with the figurines?"

"These are very small cameras. They are often hidden in figurines or other objects to avoid normal detection by intruders and prevent deactivation. For instance, in this order the figurines are in an owl, two eagles, and a raccoon. Usually, the cameras are placed in an eye of the figurine. It's sometimes even difficult to tell the difference between the real eye and the one that has the camera."

"And the camera that has been installed . . . is it functional?"

"It could be, if Mr. Wilkerson activated it with his computer or phone."

"Thank you, Hank. You have been very helpful. Please keep this conversation confidential. You're in the security business. I'm sure you understand the importance of this request. One last thing, and this is very important. I want you to get ahold of Randy and ask him the location of the camera that was installed. Do that ASAP and call me immediately when you get his answer. Okay?"

"Will do, boss."

"By the way, what is your last name?"

"Record. Henry Record. Emphasis on the first syllable with a long E. Great name for a camera salesman, don't you think?"

"Oh my, yes."

That old frenzied feeling was beginning to percolate through the blood of the veteran detective. In one day, he'd learned of a video of the victim pinpointing the time of death *and* of a camera that may be situated in such a way as to memorialize the commission of a murder.

Stay calm, Coleman. He called Spurlock. "You busy?"

"A little. Checking some motel records. What's up?"

"Grab a deputy and go out to Gresham Gathering. See if you can find any figurines that resemble eagles, owls, or raccoons. Wilkerson bought a security camera system about a week prior to his death, and there may be a miniature camera embedded in an eye or other body part of one of these fake animals. If you find anything, let me know immediately."

"I'm on my way."

Coleman called the Sheriff and told him to set up an interview with Reggie Masterson's parents. Have to talk with Mom or Dad first. He complied, and at 3:00 p.m. they arrived at the Masterson Insurance Agency in downtown Oneida Falls, one of the oldest businesses in town.

The current owner was Reggie's father, Richard Masterson. Richard's dad, George, had been the previous owner. He still came around the office periodically and talked to old customers, flirted with the secretaries, and generally irritated his son. George's dad, Roland, had started the company right before World War II. A giant portrait of him graced the wall in the reception area.

Both secretaries were attractive and knew the Sheriff, probably high school classmates. One said, "Hi, Greg. How's it going?"

He said, "Fine, Carrie."

The other said, "Little Wally. What's happening?"

He bristled. "We have an appointment with Mr. Masterson."

She responded, "I know. He's waiting for you, Wall. I'll take you back." More bristling.

The third-generation insurance man was doing quite well for himself, or at least the plushness of his office so indicated.

Northern Wisconsin traditionally went with the knotty pine interiors, whether it be home, private office, or retail business. And this office at one time probably had that look. No longer. Genuine cherrywood half walls had been installed, above which a rich hunter green wallpaper with subtle four-inch black squares rose to the ceiling. The matching green carpet was so thick and soft that a golf ball would disappear if one did a drop. A massive, glass-covered cherrywood desk occupied center stage, behind which a reclining leather chair with brass button edging served as a throne for this most important Northwoods master.

Directly behind the chair, a six-paned window was centered at eye level. It framed a view consisting of majestic virgin pine with the still waters of Lake Manitowish forming the background. The creatures surrounding the window resembled a small taxidermy studio.

In descending order, they were as follows: directly above the window, a giant moose head with wing-like antlers so big it gave the impression of being some kind of prehistoric half-bird, half-mammal monster. It had a slightly unnatural, mean look on its face, perhaps the result of the animal undertaker following the specific directive of his client. Below Marty Moose and occupying each upper corner of the window frame were two beautiful white-tailed bucks, each living in the neighborhood of fourteen points.

Below the deer, one entered the marine life area. The trophy fish of the Northwoods was the mighty musky, where legend had it that anglers got one strike for every 10,000 casts. So, when you got that explosion at your lure, you'd better not screw it up. Well, apparently, Mr. Masterson at the minimum had been twice successful in landing the lunkers, and they were now facing each other on opposite sides of the window in their final resting places beneath the silent stags. A brass plate attached to the wall beneath each muskellunge memorialized the date of the catch, along with the length, weight, bait, and name of the lake from which it had been extracted. And in capital letters, the name of the angler.

Below each musky were trophy size walleyes with similar brass plates. In case anyone might be in doubt as to who had slayed these animals, multiple eight-by-ten photographs adorned the credenza showing the hunter and his dead prey. Absent from this collection was any depiction of Masterson and the moose. Hmmm.

Coleman had spent a career observing environs and drawing inferences from them about the character of those who occupied the same. His initial assessment of Grandson Richard was that he was a rather large fish in a relatively small pond. His office blared it. *No pun intended but a bit of an overkill*, he thought.

Masterson, wearing the trendy casual attire of a white polo shirt and blue-gray suit, stood up from behind his desk and offered his hand to Little Wally, saying, "Good to see you, Sheriff." They shook and he turned likewise to Coleman and said, "Dick Masterson. Good to meet you."

"Bennett Coleman. My pleasure, Mr. Masterson."

"Call me Dick."

Okay. Maybe, thought Coleman. He really didn't like to get chummy while interviewing witnesses or potential suspects in a murder case. *But then again, based on your showy office, perhaps I can call you "Big Dick."*

"So, what brings you gents here?"

Coleman correctly assumed that Masterton knew exactly why the "gents" were there. There was no way he would have allowed a meeting on such short notice without knowing its purpose, despite Coleman's admonition to Wally to abstain from telling him. He also knew that he would attempt to stonewall any contact with his only child, Reggie, a gifted water skier and summertime underage beer drinker, impressed by the older swing set.

Sheriff Wally deferred to Coleman. "As I'm sure you are aware, I am heading the investigation into the murder of Bryce Wilkerson, whose body was found last week at his family's cabin on Gresham Lake."

"Yes. What a tragedy. I'd never met the lad. But I had talked to his father by phone. I wrote the policies on the cabin and boat."

Of course, you did. "Do you know whether your daughter ever met him?"

He paused. "What do you mean?"

"I don't know how to ask it more clearly, Mr. Masterson. Do you know if your daughter ever had contact with Bryce Wilkerson? His nickname was Beamer, if that helps."

"I do not." His guard was rising. "I don't see how she could. I mean, he was what . . . twenty-seven, twenty-eight? Reggie's sixteen. What are you implying?"

"I am not implying anything, sir. Sheriff Wallace has discovered that your daughter had dinner with Mr. Wilkerson at Dale's Steak House on May 31, four days before his death."

A higher level of contention began to set in. "That's preposterous. I'm good friends with the owner, Dale Ricketts. He would have told me. What's this all about, Wally?"

This posed a problem for Little Wally. If he reminded the "Big Dick" of the details of their earlier phone conversation, Coleman would learn of his disobedience of the order to refrain from forewarning Masterson. It would also demonstrate that the question was a lie. He continued the charade for his own self-protection.

"Well, Dick, the bartender at Dale's has a clear recollection of seeing Reggie with Wilkerson on that night. Their server did, too. And the couple sitting next to them. They were all kind of, you know, surprised to see Reggie there because of, well, you know, I guess . . . his age."

"Well, that is just bullfuckingshit." All pretense of civility evaporated. The guard was now fully constructed. "I know my daughter. There is no way she would do this. I'm going to talk to Ricketts and get to the bottom of this obvious conspiracy to disparage her reputation. And most likely mine."

Coleman jumped in. "So I guess you have indirectly answered my original question. This conversation represents the first knowledge of your daughter having contact with Wilkerson, or even the rumor of it occurring?"

"Absolutely."

"Well then, I'm sure you would have no problem, for clarification of the facts, to allow us to speak with your daughter. Will she be home tonight?"

"Actually, I have a huge fucking problem with that. Nobody's going to talk to my daughter until I do. And then she is going to talk to my lawyer, and we'll see after that whether you talk to her, Mr. Coleman." The guard had become a concrete wall reinforced with rebar.

Coleman remained calm. "That's fine, Mr. Masterton. But let me tell you a few more facts that have come to my attention that Sheriff Wallace here is not privy to.

"Earlier this morning, I reviewed a monthly statement of a credit card that Bryce Wilkerson used for about three weeks prior to his unfortunate demise. He used it to pay for dinner at Dale's Steak House on May 31. A few days prior to that, he bought a necklace at a local jeweler and some fresh flowers by phone for delivery to an unknown recipient, unknown at least for right now. Also, prior to the dinner date at Dale's, a young female left two voice messages for Bryce on his cell phone. We haven't yet been able to track down the owner of the phone, but by late tomorrow morning that information should be forthcoming. Determining the recipient of the flowers will also be an easy task.

"I came here today not because the law requires it. Your daughter may have information to assist in a murder investigation. She is not a suspect. I came because I believe it the proper and courteous thing to do, whether the law mandates it or not. I would hope that any cop worth his salt would give me the same courtesy if the roles were reversed.

"You can remain combative. That's your choice. But this much I know. I will eventually find out when you first knew about Beamer and your daughter seeing him. And I would bet my socks that it was before today. All of which means you just lied to me and the Sheriff. And in my business, under these circumstances, lying makes you a suspect in a murder case, not to mention a potential defendant in a felony criminal case for obstructing justice. Make sure you ask your lawyer about that possibility.

"Oh, yeah, another thing." He rose from his seat and went over to a side wall that displayed a framed insurance license. He mockingly stroked his chin with a feigned pondering. "I'm not sure, but I think convicted felons are barred from selling insurance in the state of Wisconsin.

Your father might have to come out of retirement to keep those premiums flowing in."

Following the speech, Coleman dropped his business card on the shiny desk in front of him, next to a family portrait of the Mastersons.

He walked toward the door to leave but stopped to view a cozy sitting area that had escaped his eye when he'd first entered the office. A plaid sofa and a coffee table laden with issues of *Golf* magazine and *GQ* (perhaps for reading but more likely for effect), flanked by two matching leisure chairs, complementary in color to the couch, were all nestled in front of a gas fireplace, above which a fifty-inch flat screen TV was mounted.

Just prior to his exit, Coleman turned and gave his parting shot to Masterson. "Nice office. It would be a shame to lose it . . . Dick."

Ten minutes later, Coleman got a text from Masterson. He was still in his car parked in front of the insurance shop. The message said, "Come back."

CHAPTER TWENTY

Eagle Eye

Coleman paused for about three minutes before responding to the text, allowing Mr. Masterson's anxiety to spike a touch higher. He texted, "I'll be there in a little while." He turned to Sheriff Wally and told him to stay in the car. He would only be about ten or fifteen minutes.

The detective reentered the insurance office as both secretaries, without speaking, waved him back to their boss's office. Closing the door to the plush inner sanctum, Masterson offered him a seat.

"I owe you an apology, Mr. Coleman. I have been under some enormous stress lately, partly business related but more so related to my daughter, Reggie. She has become increasingly rebellious in the last year. Excessive drinking, maybe drugs, cutting out of school, tattoos, piercings. Things have worsened this summer. But this much I know. I can tell you exactly when I discovered that she had been involved with Wilkerson.

"My wife, Beverly, and I were watching the ten o'clock news on June 6. Reggie had come home early, for once, after one of her ski shows. The leading story, of course, was the murder of Wilkerson. When his picture flashed on the TV, Reggie gasped and then immediately broke down. She sobbed for what seemed to be an eternity." Masterson paused and took a deep breath.

"Go ahead, Mr. Masterson. You're doing fine." Coleman could see his previous guard quickly melting.

"When she finally calmed down, we asked her what was going on. She clammed up initially. Tried to escape to her room but we restrained her. Finally, after considerable badgering, she told us . . . although probably not the entire story.

"She and some of her ski buddies went to a local bar after a show about a week to ten days ago. As usual, the place was packed, mostly with college kids and younger. She met this guy who introduced himself as Beamer. Said he was from Chicago and was in a band that did a lot of gigs in the city. And that he owned a cabin up on Gresham Lake. He even showed her pictures of the lake, cabin, and boat. They had some drinks and that was about it."

"Really. That's it?" pressed Coleman.

"Well, she told us that she saw him one more time at the same bar with pretty much the same group. She said he asked her out, but she put him off. And that was pretty much it."

"She didn't mention receiving flowers or a necklace?"

"No."

"Or dinner."

"No."

"Well, Mr. Masterson. Thank you for calling me back. I understand your stress and I have no reason to doubt that you are now telling me the truth regarding this matter. I am, however, going to have to talk to your daughter. If you want your lawyer present, that's fine. I will also need a short, written statement from you that should include two things: a summary of what you just told me and where you were during the early morning hours of June 4. I do not consider you a suspect, but I want to cover all my bases in this investigation. This will also benefit you, as it will tend to quell any rumors that will undoubtedly start flying, suggesting that you may have been involved in his death. Any problem with that?"

"Not at all."

"Now, when would be a good time to talk to Reggie?"

"I will have to call you on that, as she is out of town visiting some cousins down in Stevens Point. I can give you a call in the morning, if that's okay?"

"That will be fine. Thank you, Richard." They shook hands and Coleman began to leave.

Masterson delayed his exit. "Will Reggie be in any trouble?"

"I won't know for sure until I have talked to her. Most likely not, with the obvious exception of underage drinking. Sounds like the court system might be able to give you and your wife a little support, if not muscle, in that area."

"I can't argue with that."

"Good night. We'll talk tomorrow."

Coleman returned to his vehicle and found Sheriff Wally snoring in the passenger seat.

It was a dreamy, late morning on the island of Elba, a short ferry ride from Piombino, a western coastal town in Tuscany. Randy Baxter was having brunch with his wife, Maria, and her parents, who lived in Manarola, a small, touristy village located on a rocky shoreline of Cinque Terre.

Randy spoke little Italian. He had never met his in-laws. Maria's parents spoke no English. By necessity,

Maria was a part of every conversation as interpreter. And the conversation that was about to take place was important. Maria was pregnant with their first child and her parents' first grandchild. They had picked this spot, this quaint little restaurant overlooking the town of Portoferraio nestled on the Tyrrhenian Sea, to break the news to them. They were just about to relate the upcoming event when Baxter's cell phone abruptly intruded upon the moment with its blaring ring tone of "On Wisconsin." One of the few Italian words Randy had learned was *scusami*, or "excuse me" in English. Maria gave him a glare. Her parents looked puzzled. He said "scusami" and left the table, shuffling to a distance out of earshot of the family.

He saw the call was from his obnoxious boss, nerdy Henry "Hank" Record. He did some quick math and computed that it was 4:00 a.m. in Wisconsin. Maybe some emergency?

"Hello, Hank. What's going on?"

"Hey, Baxie." He called everyone by a nickname, one that he had coined. "Hope I'm not interrupting anything important. Got an issue here. Remember that job you had up in Pinesap County for a customer named Wilkerson? Well, it seems he was murdered about a week ago and the cops want to know where you placed the camera. Your notes indicate you only installed one and had to quit because of rain."

Baxter recreated the sale and installation in his mind. He remembered. "Hank. It's in the left eye of the eagle, which is mounted on the peak of the flagpole by the dock, facing the lane into the cabin area."

"Was it activated?"

"Don't know. Left the instructions with Wilkerson. Guess you can't ask him, can you?"

Hank chuckles. "No. That's a good one, Baxie."

"Gotta run, Hank. Ciao." *Click.*

Randy went back to the table. He apologized and told Maria it was an emergency. One of his clients was murdered and the police needed information. That was all true and it got him off the hook for the interruption in disclosing their joyous news. They resumed their script and the news was greeted with hugs and tears. When all resumed their seats, wine-filled glasses were raised, and everyone said, "*Saluti!*" No translation was necessary.

Bennett Coleman's mind was reeling as he headed back to his motel in Oneida Falls after dropping Sheriff Wallace off at his office. A ton of information had rolled in during the day and he was more than anxious to see what developments it would yield. But he had to decompress and slow the RPMs of his mind to a manageable rate. Plus, he was famished, realizing that his only intake of the day had been black coffee. He showered and dressed in casual wear—jeans, plaid shirt, sandals, and his Packers ball cap. He got into his car and was about to put it in gear when he received a text from Detective Spurlock.

"Located animal figurines. Too dark to make a physical examination. Two of them are very elevated. May need cherry picker. Also, motel owner has some interesting information. Call me."

Coleman responded. "Headed to dinner. Spent. Strong work. Will touch base in AM." Spurlock responded with a "thumbs up" emoji.

Coleman drove to a supper club about twenty minutes away. It was located on a county road, secluded in the woods, ten miles from the nearest town. He needed some peace and privacy. Most of all, he did not want to be recognized. Solitude was in order.

He entered the eatery and was greeted by a cheery college-aged gal. Despite it being a weekday, business was brisk. Summer was high season in the Northwoods.

"Welcome to The Fireside. How many this evening?"

"Just one."

"Booth or table?"

"Booth, please." He spotted a couple just leaving one that was relatively secluded, considering the size of the evening crowd. "Perhaps that booth where those folks are now leaving." He pointed in their direction.

"I'm sure we can arrange that if you don't mind waiting a few minutes while it's cleaned and set up."

"Not a problem."

While waiting, he scanned the crowd, hoping that he would recognize no one, and vice versa. He perused left to right, as if reading a page in a book, and was satisfied that no one was present who would pose a potential interruption. He had picked up a menu and begun to check out the seafood selections when he was drawn to two men exiting a table. His view had been blocked by a pine support pole during his just-conducted inventory. They were headed his way.

He immediately recognized one of them as the local insurance mogul, Richard Masterson. He looked disheveled, flushed, and fatigued. No wonder. The other man had "lawyer" written all over him. Charcoal pinstriped suit, shined wingtips, white shirt, red power tie, briefcase in left hand, and suitcoat slung over his right shoulder.

To avoid detection, Coleman lowered the brim of his Packers cap, told the hostess he'd be back, and made a beeline to the restroom. After washing his hands, so as not to draw attention from the man waiting for a stall, he exited and accurately concluded that all was clear. He noticed that his booth was now ready. He motioned to the hostess that he was going to seat himself. She acknowledged.

Coleman positioned himself in the booth facing the entrance, allowing him to spot any possible interlopers. He took a gulp of water and opened the menu. In short time, his server approached, introduced himself as Luke, and inquired as to whether he wanted a drink besides the water.

"Yes, Luke. I'll have a Crown Royal on the rocks, no garnish. But I will have some lemon for my water."

"I'll put that in right away, sir. Would you care to hear our specials for tonight?"

"Thanks, but that won't be necessary." He knew what he was going to have before he'd left the motel.

Nice kid. College age, like the young hostess. Diametrically different than what he was used to seeing on a daily basis. He at least appeared to have goals beyond when and where he was going to get his next fix. Preppy. Dressed in khakis, penny loafers, light green oxford shirt with dark green club tie exhibiting the Fireside logo in gold. Green and gold. Packers colors. Imagine that.

The drink appeared with great dispatch as well as the lemons and freshly baked bread, the crusts of which were lathered with butter.

"Are you ready to order, sir, or do you need a little more time?"

"No, I believe I'm ready. Let's start out with a bowl of the seafood chowder with oyster crackers. For my entrée, I'd like the fresh walleye, blackened. And for sides, uh . . . twice-baked potato and asparagus spears. Oh, and some drawn garlic butter and a glass of Malbec with my dinner."

"Excellent choice on the walleye, sir. I'll get that soup right out to you."

"Thanks."

Coleman took his much-anticipated first sip of the Canadian whisky. It had the instant effect for which he had been hoping. His internal motors were slipping into a lower gear. Relaxation was growing nearer with each successive taste of the time-tested liquor. His mind was still fixated on the "Beamer" investigation but at a pace that gave him more perspective and less chaos. He removed an extra cocktail napkin from beneath his drink and began bullet pointing the next day's agenda. As he was about to make his first entry, Luke arrived with his chowder.

Noticing the status of his drink, he inquired, "Another one, sir?" Coleman looked up and nodded in the affirmative.

Coleman peppered his chowder and emptied the oyster crackers into the bowl, stirring them into the thick offering. Although right-handed, he used his left to scoop the appetizer into his mouth, freeing up his right to start his list for tomorrow.

*Call Spurlock re: fig locations/motel info
*Review Weatherton disc; selfies? Other mat'l?
*Interview Reggie M.
*Call Hank at HSS (He needed more information as to how this particular camera worked, such as access and capacity.)
*Try to locate Baxter

He was taking his final spoonful, pushing the bowl aside, when he thought of one more task, at least for the present.

*Call Bea Wilkerson re: passwords

He put his pen down and looked out the window, staring at the outline of the pine forest, and allowed his thoughts to wander.

Despite what the Chicago prosecutor had said regarding Josh Wright and his incapability of committing this murder, he remained the main suspect. He certainly had the most obvious motive. Bea Wilkerson was correct about that. But the scene was inconsistent with a crime of revenge. One shot. From a distance. And the fish. And the photograph, such an obvious plant. Coleman opined that the aggrieved father would have wanted a close-range conversation before he blew his head off.

His meanderings were halted as Luke approached with his succulent entrée and glass of red wine.

As he removed the empty chowder bowl from the table, he asked, "Anything else, sir?"

"No, Luke. I believe you've got it covered."

"Holler if you need anything. Enjoy your dinner, sir."

"Thank you."

Coleman's mind roamed again, but not about the case. It was about the meal in front of him. Where did it all come from? How many people were involved in getting this plate of food in front of him that would be gone within the next fifteen to twenty minutes? This was who he was and how he kept his mind sharp. The ultimate Curious George.

He began with the fish, which was probably the easiest to decipher. The menu had read "freshly caught," a fact confirmed by his first bite. Most likely Canada, a commercial operation, as none were allowed in the States to protect the recreational fishing industry, especially in the Badger State.

Potato was pretty much a slam dunk. It was all Wisconsin, the number-two potato-producing state behind Idaho. The cheese in the twice baked? They don't call them cheeseheads for nothing. And the cream? Dairy State, for sure. These supper clubs bought local.

Asparagus? A lot grown out West, but his guess was neighboring Michigan. Almost buying local.

The wine, however, was the most intriguing of the lot. Most of the world's Malbec wine was produced in the Mendoza region of western Argentina in the foothills of the Andes, from vines that dated from the early 1800s. God only knew how many handoffs there were for a bottle of this wine crafted nearly six thousand miles to the south.

So, as Coleman was placing the last bite of walleye in his mouth, he did a recap of the geography lesson his meal had provided. Fish and Crown Royal from Canada, green veggie from Michigan, spuds plus cream and cheese from the home state, and wine from Argentina. Peasants, vintners, farmers, truckers, fishermen, bottlers, importers, distributors, pickers, wholesalers, chefs, and finally a server named Luke, all contributed to the serving and consumption of this $14.99 entrée at a restaurant buried deep in the pine forest. Coleman looked at his watch. Seventeen minutes and done.

Coleman passed on dessert and paid his bill, leaving a handsome tip to Luke and wishing him luck at his senior year in college at UW-Stout. He was majoring in Criminal Justice and aspired to be a cop. The detective didn't have time to give him his speech of dissuasion.

Upon arriving back at his motel in Oneida Falls, Coleman turned on the TV and half listened to the ten o'clock news while he readied himself for what he hoped would be a quality night of sleep, something that had not occurred in over a week. He was half listening until he heard the newscaster introduce his "breaking story," a follow up to the Oneida Falls murder investigation.

"A reliable but anonymous source has indicated that the authorities investigating the killing may have a security camera recording of the commission of the crime. This is a developing story. More tomorrow on our morning news at 7:00 a.m." The same story was picked up by a Chicago news station. It was of more than passing interest to a number of Cook County residents from Roscoe Village to the North Shore.

"Jesus H. Christ," exclaimed Coleman aloud. He quickly located his phone and found Spurlock's number and punched it in.

Spurlock did not even say hello. "I just saw it. What the fuck."

"I know. Any suspects on the leak? Did anyone see you at Gresham Lake this afternoon?"

"The only one was Deputy Crookshank. I don't think it was him. He seems like a stand-up guy."

Coleman agreed.

So, who knew about the cameras? The salesman, Randy Baxter. He was in Italy. Not likely.

Henry "Hank" Record, the manager of the Home Security store in Wausau. Likely. Very likely, in fact. Coleman added "calling Hank" to his cocktail napkin agenda. He would actually hear from the security nerd considerably earlier.

It was by then almost 11:00 p.m. and both cops agreed that nothing could be accomplished that night. They bid each other good night.

Whatever peace had been accomplished in Coleman's mind by his Fireside dinner was short-lived. He was full bore back into the fight and frustrated that because of the hour, he was unable to pursue his instincts. His head hit the pillow with thoughts boomeranging for about two hours until fatigue took over, propelling him into a deep sleep around 2:00 a.m. It ended after a mere two hours.

He rarely shut off his phone, an occupational hazard. It blared around 4:00 a.m., awakening a Coleman disoriented as to time and place.

"Agent Coleman, this is Hank."

"Hank who?"

"Hank Record from Home Security in Wausau."

"Hank? Oh yes, Hank. Do you know what time it is, Hank?

"Yes. It's a little after 4:00 in the morning. But you told me to contact you immediately if I found out any information regarding the location of the camera that was installed at the Wilkerson cabin."

Coleman tried to accelerate his wake-up process. He *had* said that but, really, Hank, exercise some discretion. It's 4:00 in the morning. "What did you find out?"

"Well, I got a hold of Randy Baxter in Italy. Actually, he was on an island off the coast of Italy called Elba. I think Napoleon was exiled there. He was there with his wife and in-laws announcing the upcoming birth of their first child." *Hank, spare me the history lesson and travelogue. What the did he say about the location of the camera?* "So anyway, I told him that you had called and that this poor Wilkerson lad had been murdered. I told him because of the death, he would probably lose his commission and . . ."

"HANK! Where the hell is the camera?"

"I was getting to that. It's in the left eye of the eagle on top of the flagpole."

Coleman was now wide awake and exasperated. "Thank you, Hank. Now here is what I want you to do. Send me a text on the number that you have just called me on and indicate the location of the viable camera. Because I am going to try to go back to sleep and I do not trust my memory of the conversation which we have just had. Do you understand, Hank?"

"Yes. I do," he replied. Three minutes later, Coleman heard the alert noise on his phone indicating a text had arrived. He looked at it, rolled over, and tried to go back to sleep.

He gave up two hours later, got up, made himself a cup of coffee, and removed the cocktail napkin agenda. Back to work.

CHAPTER TWENTY-ONE

Reggie's Redemption

I t was 7:00 a.m. and Coleman had just finished securing his tie in the collar of his freshly
starched shirt. He happened to look out the sec-
ond-floor window of his motel room which revealed the
front parking lot of the Northern Highlands Inn. Two
things caught his eye, both of which were quite familiar to
him. Television cameras and two female reporters, both
young and attractive, with pens and little notebooks, anxiously awaiting his departure as they chatted with each
other between sips of their lattes. He recalled last night's
report on the news about the possibility of security cameras recording the killing. It was a "developing story." He
wanted to keep it that way.

Over the years, the veteran cop had developed a love-
hate relationship with the media. At certain times, their
contribution to an investigation was immeasurable, as it
had been in this case. Spreading the initial details of this
murder all over the state of Wisconsin as well as Chicago
had provided an indispensable jump-start to the process
and had led to the discovery of valuable information. But

that stage was over. The investigation was now ongoing, and there were details that could not be disclosed for fear of compromising progress in the case, if not its eventual solution. The camera issue was a prime example. And they, the media, would hound him to get some sort of comment, even a "no comment," about the status of the location of cameras. It would become an inevitable handicap to his work and to the investigation, like an annoying fly constantly buzzing around his head.

However annoying, it had now become a reality that had to be dealt with. Starting now.

Coleman quickly ripped off his tie, shirt, and khakis, replacing them with his wardrobe of the previous evening, including his Packers cap and a new addition, a pair of sunglasses. The front parking lot had been full when he'd returned last night from dinner, forcing him to park on the east side of the building, a good hundred feet from the front door and the waiting media cluster. Last night's inconvenience had become today's benefit for his escape plan.

He considered packing all his stuff, as he'd be making a lodging change that evening. At this point, however, the speed of his departure warranted a higher priority. He could retrieve his belongings later.

Exiting his second-story room, Coleman glanced in both directions and then began walking east towards the stairway which would eventually lead to his parked vehicle, a mid-sized, gray sedan, barren of any police markings. He trundled down the stairs and left through the east door. Rather than using the remote unlocking system on his car, he opted for the quiet method of inserting and turning the key. He fired up the sedan, backed out of his spot, and exited the lot by way of a little-used service entrance, leaving the media huddle in his wake, oblivious to his departure. Later that morning, Coleman called the motel to check out and to make arrangements for picking up his belongings. Upon his inquiry, the clerk indicated to Coleman that the reporters had stayed around for about an hour after he left. He smiled.

Within seconds of "escaping" his motel, Coleman called Spurlock.

"Good morning, Brian. It's Coleman."

"Morning. What's up?" Spurlock could detect by the background noise that Coleman was in his car.

"Well, I just eluded a media stakeout at my motel, and I suspect that I'll encounter a similar reception at the Sheriff's office. I know it's an effort to follow up on the 'camera story' that we both heard on the news last night. But we've got to meet to exchange notes. Any suggestion where?"

Spurlock thought for a while. "Sure. Why don't you just come out to my place? You're not that far and I've seen no sign of anyone sniffing around out here. My wife is gone for the day and I just made a fresh pot of coffee."

"Sounds perfect."

Spurlock gave him his address, which he plugged into his car's GPS navigation system. How did people ever find anything before these were invented? 454 Hemlock Lane, Oneida Falls. So, Spurlock lived on Hemlock. *I'll bet that's not confusing.* The map said it was only 3.7 miles away and arrival would be in approximately six minutes. Simple enough.

Whispering Needle Road to County K. K to County M. M to North Creek Road. North Creek for a mile and a half, left on Princess Pine Lane, then a quick right on Hemlock. Spurlock was waiting for Coleman outside with a cup of coffee in hand and his pet German Shepherd by his side. Coleman approached his fellow cop and canine.

"He won't bite unless I tell him to."

"I believe you, Brian. What's his name?" inquired Coleman.

"Nitschke. Old Packers linebacker. Number 66."

"I remember him well. If he's half as mean as Ray was in his prime, I'm sure he's a helluva guard dog."

Both men entered the two-bedroom cottage, leaving Nitschke outside to stand guard. The abode was warm, orderly, and cozy. Although not on a lake, access to one was readily available, allowing Spurlock to indulge in his true passion of fishing, which one day he hoped could be par-layed into a retirement vocation as a guide.

"So, tell me about the camera situation at the Wilkerson cabin," opened Coleman as he sipped his fresh cup of coffee.

"As the diagram indicates from the salesman, there are four locations for the figurines . . ."

"Stop!" interjected Coleman as he proceeded to remove his phone from his jeans pocket and scroll through his messages. He opened the first one, received at 4:07 a.m., from Hank at HSS. It read: *left eye of eagle on top of flagpole.* In all the commotion of the morning escape and lack of quality sleep, he had temporarily forgotten about the Hank Record 4:00 a.m. wake-up call.

"Well, that should save us some time," said Spurlock. "And the best view of the crime scene. But we will need a cherry picker to access the unit to determine if its opera-tional. Ladders won't work. I'll call Little Wally."

Jesus, Coleman thought, *Wallace's only detective didn't even give him any respect.*

"Also, I will give you the number of this Hank guy in Wausau at the security shop to find out how this system works. I'm already tired of dealing with him. Find out how the recordings can be accessed. DVR? Website? Some private facility? They've got to be stored somewhere. Also, the capacity, timewise. Very important. This may be a race against the clock to make sure nothing relevant has been deleted. If you have to, drive down there to get the full picture. Also, make sure the barricade at the Wilkerson cabin is secure. I don't want any press snooping around. And remember we have a solid time of death. June 4 at 6:40 a.m. Should be easy to remember—6-4 at 6:40."

Coleman paused for a breath. "What's the deal with the motel?"

"So, there is an old mom-and-pop motel about three miles south of town called Redd's Lakeview Motel. Family owned, been there for years. Twelve units, clean, TV, phone. No frills. Nice view through the pine of Spider Lake. Owned by a couple in their sixties named Frank and Louise Drysdale. They live on the premises and do all the work, Louise probably more so. Anyway, during the summer, they take off on weekends and hire local college kids to handle the work while they take short trips in their RV.

"Last week, Louise got a call from one of the part timers. Seems she was reading about the murder and told her about a guy who checked in very late one night that was close in time to the murder. She remembered the guy because of his late arrival and early departure the next day. She had gotten up at 6:30 a.m. and he was already gone. And he drove a white pick-up truck with Illinois plates. Louise is in the process of checking her records. Typically, they save a photocopy of the driver's license in addition to the check-in card. She is supposed to get back to me today."

"What's the name of the part-time employee?"

Spurlock flipped through his notes. "Her name is Lindsey Mitchell. Phone number 715-465-2332. She will be working at the motel this weekend, if we need to interview her."

"Absolutely. Let me know when you hear from Mrs. Drysdale."

Coleman's phone lit up. It was Richard Masterson. "Good morning, Richard." Spurlock noticed the name of the caller. Coleman acknowledged his observation and allowed him to listen to the conversation by putting his phone on speaker.

"Good morning, Agent Coleman. My daughter is due to arrive back at around 10:00 a.m. I want her to spend some time with my lawyer. Would 11:00 a.m. work for you?"

"It would. Your home or office?"

"I think I would prefer home. I will text you my address."

"Works for me. See you later this morning."

"Whoa! Does little Reggie have something to do with this?" Spurlock asked when Coleman ended the call.

"Do you know her?"

"Pretty much every cop in town does. Budding alcoholic, pot smoker, probably harder drugs, regularly truant. And a nasty attitude with the cops, except the cute ones. Big insurance policy. Her dad, or the 'Big Dick' as he is often referred to in hushed tones around the station, is on the Village Board and Chairman of the Law Enforcement Committee. How is she involved?"

"She had involvement with the decedent within a week prior to his death. Drank with him at a couple of bars after ski shows. Likely had dinner together. He probably was grooming her for a visit out to his cabin on Gresham. I won't know the extent of it all until I interview her later this morning."

"And even then you may not. She's a skillful liar."

"Thanks for the tip. I'll let you know how she holds up."

Coleman wanted to hang out at Spurlock's cottage to prepare for his interview with Reggie Masterson. Spurlock was about ready to leave to begin his assignments for the day.

"Stay here as long as you want. There is still a half pot of java." Spurlock departed and Coleman called Sheriff Wallace, who was beside himself. Coleman knew why.

"Morning, Greg. Are you keeping the frenzied reporters at bay?"

"How did you know? When are you coming in?'

"I have work to do, Sheriff. That's the last place I want to be. Are you familiar with the phrase 'No comment'?"

"Yes, but they're very persistent. You probably have more experience dealing with this kind of stuff. Please come in. Besides, you have a package from your office in Wausau."

Awesome. Weatherton had come through before his tee time yesterday.

"Glad to hear that, Greg. Here's what I want you to do ASAP. I am at Brian Spurlock's house. Have one of your deputies deliver the Wausau package to me. It's very important that it get here no later than fifteen minutes from now. Okay?"

"Sure. But what do I do with all these goddamn reporters?"

Come on, Little Wally. Step up. "You tell them nothing. Do you understand? Nothing. No comment. Tell them that discussing the investigation at this stage would severely jeopardize the solving of this heinous crime and deter the capture of the person who committed it. What the fuck? You're the Sheriff. Start acting like one. Now get that package to me." *Click.*

The Wausau package arrived in ten minutes.

Coleman's golfing buddy had done his typical professional job in organizing the data on Beamer's phone. For
right now, his attention would have to remain limited to
that which would be relevant to his interview with Reggie
Masterson. He inserted the flash drive into his laptop. And
there was plenty.

He took a yellow legal pad from his briefcase and
began his outline:

1. Female Phone Messages:
    a) Reggie: 5/31 @ 5:08 p.m. "Hi, Beamer. It's
        me. Really looking forward to tonight. See
        you in a little while."
    b) Reggie: 6/1 @ 1:13 p.m. "My God. Last
        night was, like, fucking awesome! Ski show
        tonight. See you at The Pike afterwards."
        Both calls had been made from a cell phone
        owned by Reggie.
    c) Carrie: 5/31 @ 7:48 p.m. "Hey, dickhead.
        It's Carrie Denton. Remember me? We had a
        date tonight to go to the Pure Prairie League
        concert in Eagle Creek. As you may recall, I
        bought the tickets. I'm home alone without
        wheels. I know that you know where I live.
        You were here last night. Send me seventy
        dollars for the cost of the tickets. And then
        go fuck yourself."

Beamer and Reggie would have been ordering dessert
at Dale's Steak House when this message arrived.

What a dude, thought Coleman. He stood up a gal
who bought tickets to a live concert; instead, he opts to
take a sixteen-year-old to dinner, someone thirteen years
his junior. Six months earlier, he'd escaped being convicted

of molesting a ten-year-old girl because the lone juror had been bribed by his dad to vote not guilty. *If the guilty party is ever caught,* Coleman mused, *some slick lawyer with a keen imagination will use this never-ending list of atrocious facts about the Beamer and his absence of character and morality to argue that his client was doing the public a huge service by ending this slime's life.*

There were multiple calls made without voice messages being left. And texts galore flowing back and forth between the two.

2.   Photographs: "Wow! Selfies of both at the bars. Red cups filled with beer. Reggie and Beamer kissing at the bars. Provocative photos of Reggie in her ski club bikini; another one in sexy lingerie, with the caption, "Waddya think? Want some?" Holy shit! Wait until Daddy sees this stuff. Thank God the lawyer is going to be there. More pictures at the restaurant." (And the one that Coleman had been waiting for.) "A selfie of both at Gresham Gathering, in the cabin, clinking beer bottles in front of the fire, on May 31, 2018, at 10:37 p.m."

Post dinner activity. Well. Agent Coleman had enough ammunition to encourage young Reggie to just tell the truth. And that was all he wanted. He wasn't interested in getting her in any more trouble than she would find herself in after disclosing the contents of the phone to her parents and the family lawyer. He was conducting a homicide investigation, not presiding over Juvenile Court. But he couldn't help but think where this spoiled brat was headed with her permissive behavior.

Coleman would have to look at the remainder of the phone contents later in the day. He was running late, having been caught up in the material opened up by his forensic buddy. He got in his car, entered the Masterson address, and followed the prompts. He arrived at the Masterson mansion ten minutes late.

And a mansion it was. If the office of Richard Masterson was plush, and indeed it was, Coleman was at a loss to describe his cabin in the woods. Extravagant? Check. Ostentatious? Double check. Over the top in every way? Oh my, yes.

The detective was trying his best not to gawk, but his facial muscles and eye contact were just not cooperating. Massive picture windows revealing the north shoreline of the pristine waters of Upper Wildcat Lake. A ski boat and sailboat straddled a one hundred-foot pier that jutted out from a nice sandy beach area, at the end of which was a gazebo that could easily accommodate eight people. Opposite the picture windows, a Wisconsin stone fireplace rose twenty feet to the apex of a magnificent vaulted ceiling. Built-in bookcases flanked the dual fireplace (the other side serviced the dining room), filled with unread classics and multiple family portraits of present and past generations.

Multi-pointed bucks mounted above the bookcases served as sentries over the seating area in front of the fireplace, which consisted of a soft leather couch, matching chairs, and a textured, copper coffee table, bordered in dark pine slats with circles cut out as holders for glasses, cans, or bottles for the beverage of the day.

Masterson introduced Coleman to his wife, Beverly, who appeared to be more anxious to leave for a round of golf than to stick around and witness the legal slaughter of her only child. She had yielded discipline and control over Reggie to her husband a while back.

"My attorney is running a little bit late, Agent Coleman. He should be here in about ten minutes. Can I get you a cup of coffee?"

"That would be fine. I would like to spend a little bit of time with you and your counsel before I meet Reggie. Your wife is free to join us, if she wishes."

Without hesitation, she declined.

The family lawyer arrived as Coleman was finishing his coffee. He recognized him from the previous evening at the Fireside, but of course did not let on. Extending his hand to Coleman, he said, "Ross Pearson."

"Bennett Coleman. My pleasure."

Masterson interceded. "Agent Coleman has suggested we meet privately before Reggie is brought down."

"That's fine." All three went from the fireplace area to the dining room, which had more suitability for the business at hand. Coleman presided.

"Gentlemen, as you know, I am leading the investigation of the Bryce Wilkerson murder up on Gresham Lake, which occurred early last week. We have information that Richard's daughter, Reggie, had contact with the deceased the week prior to his shooting. Until this morning, the nature of that contact was unknown. This morning, however, I have been reviewing material that would indicate that their contact was quite extensive. I have been able to obtain numerous photographs of them drinking at local bars, as well as numerous text messages and photographs exchanged. They had a dinner date at Dale's Steak House.

He purchased jewelry and flowers for her. And she spent time with him alone at his cabin."

By design, Coleman omitted any reference to the bikini and lingerie photos. He could see the effect on Dad. His face was in his hands. The lawyer placed a reassuring palm on his client's shoulder and said, "Go on."

"Obviously, Reggie may have valuable information regarding this investigation. And if she does, I need to access it as soon as possible. Hopefully, today. I would like us all to show a united front when I question her. And, most importantly, whatever comes out must be kept in the strictest of confidence."

"Where did you get this information?" asked the lawyer.

"It was data that we were able to retrieve from phone records. Trust me, it is one hundred percent reliable. In time, I may be able to be more specific and show you the actual texts and photos. As far as Reggie committing any crimes, as I told Mr. Masterson last night, underage drinking appears to be the extent. However, let me be crystal clear about one thing. If Reggie starts lying or shading the truth, she has then obstructed justice, which is a felony. We want to avoid that at all costs."

"So where do we go from here?" asked Pearson.

"Well," responded Coleman, "I would suggest that you and Mr. Masterson have a private conversation with Reggie before I enter the picture. Emphasize the importance of her telling the truth and the consequences for not doing so. She is being interviewed as a witness in a murder investigation and it is imperative that she cooperate. I know she is going to be defensive. She knows she's in deep shit with her parents. Ask her, Mr. Pearson, if she would rather that her parents not be present during the interview. I have no problem with that, as long as Mr. Pearson remains part of the process. Do you have any problem with that, Richard?"

"No. I understand."

"And Beverly?" It was an obligatory question. Coleman already knew the answer.

"No problem."

"Okay. Any questions before we ask Reggie to come down?" Both shook their heads in the negative. "Ask Beverly to go get her. We'll use this dining room."

Masterson left, had a brief moment with his wife, and then asked her to fetch their daughter. A few minutes later, Beverly's voice could be heard from the top of the stairs. "Dick. Reggie does not feel well. She doesn't want to come down."

There was a slight pause. Then Dad responded, "She didn't look sick when she got home a half hour ago. Get her down here. She's got no choice."

Now all below could hear Reggie's combative and whiny voice. "I'm not going. I don't know anything."

The cop, lawyer, and insurance mogul exchanged glances. Coleman knew what it was going to take. He looked at Dad and motioned his head and eyes in an upward direction. He read the cue and left to make the trek upstairs. Coleman wondered how many times this scenario had repeated itself.

After about three minutes, Beverly descended the stairs, undoubtedly at the direction of her husband. She entered the dining room and just shook her head. Things were quiet upstairs. Sounded like a Mexican standoff. Coleman had an idea that might speed things up.

He picked up his phone and asked Beverly if her husband had his.

"Are you kidding me? He sleeps with it."

Coleman sent a text to Masterson. "Tell your daughter that if she is not down here in the next two minutes, I will be coming upstairs to arrest her. Not a bluff."

He then started the stopwatch on his phone. Two sets of footsteps came rumbling down the stairway. Father and daughter entered the dining room and Coleman hit the "stop" button like an official at a high school track meet. It read fifty-six seconds. Ahh. The threat of loss of freedom. Usually a sound bet.

After Coleman introduced himself to the young incorrigible, he vacated the dining room along with Mom, allowing the lawyer to prepare the witness. It was accomplished in about ten minutes. Pearson and Masterson retrieved Coleman. Dad said, "I'm out. I'll only piss her off more than she is now." Lawyer Pearson told Coleman, "She's as ready as she'll ever be."

Secretly, Coleman was glad that Dad had eliminated himself from the game. It was the best possible combination. Beverly wasn't even asked to be present, which was just fine with her. She called her golfing partner and cancelled.

Coleman placed himself at the head of the dining table, a position of superiority and command. He invited, no, *directed* Reggie to sit to his immediate left with the attorney Pearson to her left. That formation would preclude her from looking at her attorney if she felt some anxiety when answering a delicate question. And it would allow Coleman to maintain eye contact and nonverbal communication with Pearson. At this point, the cop and the lawyer were allies, not opponents.

Coleman was no stranger to interviewing, interrogating, or whatever you wanted to call it. Reggie Masterson, no matter how cool, no matter how many beers she could chug or how many tattoos she sported, was only sixteen years old. She was a child. She was vulnerable. The situation called for a kid-glove approach until some other style became necessary. And the veteran detective knew he still had his ace in the hole: arrest the little rebel.

"Reggie, again, I am Bennett Coleman. I am from Wausau. I am the lead detective in this case. And you know what case I am referring to. Would that be correct?"

"Yes." She was not looking at him. She was sitting crosswise on the dining room chair with her arms encircling her elevated knees.

"I have only two rules. Answer my questions and tell the truth. Do you understand?"

"I don't know anything."

"No, do you understand, Reggie?"

"Yeah."

"Thank you." He paused. "Let me ask you something, Reggie. Look at me." She complied. "Do you know why I am here?"

"Yeah. Kinda."

"Why? Look at me, Reggie." Again, she did. A good sign.

"You're trying to find out who killed Beamer."

"Correct. And why am I talking to you?"

"I don't know. Like, you must think I know who did it or something. But I don't. I don't know anything. I told my mom and dad upstairs that I know nothing. Why doesn't anybody believe me?"

"Well, you are correct about one thing. You don't know who did it. Because if you did, you would have come forward, right?"

"Right."

"But Reggie, without even knowing it, you may have information that is helpful to our investigation. Do you understand that?"

"Yeah. I think so."

"So, let's explore. Together. You can be part of our team. You're on a ski team, right? And you do more than shows—you compete, right?" She nodded yes. "And your specialty is trick skis? Right?" Her eyes lit up. He didn't wait for an answer. He knew he was right. Homework. "So, everybody does their best, including you, so that you can bring home some hardware. So, I want to bring home some hardware. I want to arrest the person who killed the guy that you liked quite a bit." He could see her suppress some tears. "So, my question now is: are you on my team?"

"Yes, I am, Mr. Coleman."

"Good. Welcome aboard." She made eye contact. She sat up. Let's get started. *And that is called "building rapport."*

"Okay. When was the last time you saw Bryce?"

"It was June 1. After one of the water ski shows."

"And that would have been the night after you and he went to dinner at Dale's Steak House?"

She paused, looked down and then at Mr. Pearson. "It's okay, Reggie. Answer his question."

She resumed eye contact and said, "Yes."

"And where were you when you last saw him?"

"The Thirsty Pike."

"Were you with him alone or part of a group?"

"No, it was a group. Like most of the times after ski shows."

"Did you hear from him after that night?"

"Yes. We were supposed to go to a movie two nights after that, but it didn't happen."

"What happened?"

"I don't know. I called him but he never got back to me. I tried calling him the next two days but . . ." The immature young girl broke down like a baby. Pearson consoled her until she regained her composure. "And then I found out."

"And how did you find out?"

"It was here. At home. On the ten o'clock news. I had just gotten home from the ski show."

"Is that when your folks found out for the first time that you knew Bryce?"

"Yes."

"Are you sure?"

"Absolutely." She continued sniffling. "I broke down because it was such a shock. I mean, I had just gone out with this guy and now he was dead. Shot in the head outside his own cabin. They were shocked when I told them I knew him."

"Were you ever at his cabin?"

Pause. "Yes. But only once, after our dinner at Dale's." It had been a while since Reggie had told the truth to her parents. Telling it to a stranger, even a cop, was beginning to reduce the baggage of guilt that she had been carrying around.

"Did Bryce ever talk about any enemies that he had?"

"Well, he did talk quite a bit about a case that he had in Chicago, especially when he had been drinking too much. He didn't tell me what kind of case it was, other than he had won it and the other side was pretty pissed at him. His lawyer had told him to put security cameras at his cabin just in case."

"And did he, if you know?"

"Oh yeah. He was constantly checking his phone and looking at the cabin. He would show a lot of people."

"Did he ever show you?"

"Sure."

Coleman paused. "This is important, Reggie. When he showed you his cabin on the phone, tell me what you saw."

"Well, their cabin is on Gresham. And it seemed that the camera was, like, high on the lake looking towards the lane entrance. You could see part of the garage and part of the cabin. And the woods, of course."

"Was there any other view that he showed you from the phone?"

"No. Actually, he said he was getting other cameras installed later that would cover, like, different areas."

"Did you ever see any people who had been recorded on the camera?"

"I never did, no."

"During the time you knew Bryce, to your knowledge, did he date anyone else?"

"Not really. I mean, I only knew him for about ten days. Actually, the night we went to dinner, he told me he broke a date with a girl for some concert. Said he much preferred to be with me." She looked down and began to tear up.

Coleman said it was time to take a break. He went outside to call Spurlock. He picked up on the second ring.

"What's going on?"

"Where are you?"

"Headed south. About an hour from Wausau."

"Great. Call Hank at the security store. Tell him the camera from the eagle on the lake is active. And you want to see what's on it when you get there. Call me when you do. We may have an electronic eyewitness to this murder."

"It will probably be encrypted if... hold on, I'm getting a call."

It was Louise Drysdale at Redd's Lakeview Motel. She'd found the registration card on the guy from Illinois but no photocopy of his driver's license. Spurlock told her that Agent Coleman would be in touch. He relayed the information to Coleman.

"I'll see her this afternoon. Stay in touch."

Coleman was anxious to move on to the mom-and-pop motel down the road. He asked a few more questions of Reggie and then thanked her for her cooperation and told her that if she thought of something later on to give him a call. He then gathered the group together and sternly lectured them about keeping everything confidential. Very important. Any violations would result in an arrest for obstructing justice. "Oh my," Beverly sighed. He also gave his little speech to Reggie that she had an opportunity to convert this otherwise negative experience into a positive step in her life. Knock off the drinking. At her current rate, she would need a liver transplant before she was forty.

He thanked the group for their help, especially attorney Pearson and then departed.

He had a date with a gal named Louise.

CHAPTER TWENTY-TWO

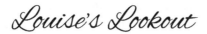

Louise's Lookout

Coleman did not need GPS to find Redd's Lakeview Motel. He had driven by the establishment numerous times since his assignment to uncover the mystery at Oneida Falls. Motels like these were vestiges of a previous era in American life— when two-lane highways ruled and chain hotels had yet to be invented. There were still many of these mom-and-pop motels around the state of Wisconsin, with a higher concentration in the smaller tourist villages in God's country.

Redd's was situated on Route 45 about three miles south of the Falls and was set a good distance from the road to minimize traffic noise. It was, of course, a one-story frame building painted in white with shutters and doors accented in green. The number of each room was designated by brass numerals attached to the door. A corresponding parking space was provided with the same number painted between the lines. There were twelve units. Each had a flower box in full bloom, resting beneath the front window. Two picnic tables and a swing set rested in a common area in front of the motel. The grounds were meticulously maintained. There was no pool. There were no amenities.

The original neon sign stood next to the office bearing the name *Redd's* (scripted in red color) *Lakeview Motel* (in a bluish-green color in block style) with a *(No) Vacancy* sign in white. If there were rooms available, the "Vacancy" part of the sign would blink on and off. If all rooms were taken, the "No" portion of the sign would light up without the blink. From June through September, "No" dominated.

The interior of each room was identical. Knotty pine walls (of course), two queen-size beds, separated by a nightstand and a small flat-screen TV resting on a dresser. At the rear, there was a half-size fridge, a small toaster oven, and two electric coiled burners resting on a countertop. The bathrooms were of Lilliputian dimensions.

A back door led to a well-worn path, winding through mature Norway pines and ending at a dock on Spider Lake suitable for small tackle casting with the hope of landing lunch or dinner.

Everything about this place evoked a slower, more peaceful era in American culture that had all but vanished.

Coleman had called Louise Drysdale after leaving the Mastersons, so she was expecting him when he pulled into the driveway of her home and business. She gregariously invited him into the living quarters, passing through the motel office on the way, and immediately offered him a slice of apple pie. He politely declined. She ignored him and promptly served him up with a fresh slice of the homemade offering, topped with a scoop of vanilla ice cream. He wolfed it down and wanted to give her a hug.

"That was wonderful, Mrs. Drysdale. Thank you so much."

"You're very welcome and, please, call me Louise and we'll get along much better. Hearing someone call me

'Mrs. Drysdale' make me feel ten years older and closer to 'Jell-o hour' at the home for the aged."

"That will be fine, Louise. And you may feel free to call me Bennett."

"Okay, Ben. So where do you want to start?"

"Well. Deputy Spurlock informed me that he had spoken to you about finding a registration card that may be of interest to our investigation. Do you recall that?'

"Oh my, yes. You know I have known Brian since he was a kid. Hadn't seen him for a while. Actually, I thought he was still down in Madison. When he showed up the other day, I didn't recognize him at first and then he said his name, 'Spurlock,' and I remembered. Frank used to be his Little League coach. Very handsome boy and in good shape. Send him out here anytime."

"Frank?"

"That's my husband."

"Oh, I thought your husband was Redd."

"No, no. Redd was Frank's grandfather. He built this place back in the forties. No reason to change the name. Would have to buy a new sign."

"Sure," he nodded. "About that card."

"Oh yeah, I found it late last night. Now where did I put that thing?" Louise shuffled through a little basket that appeared to contain old bills, photographs, coupons, newspaper articles, and finally, a registration card for Redd's. "Here it is. Sometimes I set things down without remembering where."

"Don't worry about it, Louise. It happens to the best of us."

She handed the card to Coleman. The name on it was Joshua Wright. The address was listed as 4528 N. Ravenswood, Chicago, Illinois. The vehicle was described as a 2014 Chevy pickup. Illinois plates. No tag number was listed. Signature: J. Wright. Rather scribbled. Time of registration was hand written as "10:46 p.m., June 3, 2018," with the initials *L.M.* written to the right thereof. Length of stay: one night.

Louise explained that the initials "L.M." belonged to Lindsey Mitchell. "Sweet gal. Lives down the road a piece in Hazelton. Works at Debbie's Diner. She covers for us on weekends when Jack and I take off in our RV to the hinterlands. Normally, we make a photocopy of the driver's license of the guest. I couldn't find one though. She probably overlooked doing it because it was so late."

Coleman removed his phone and accessed his photos, scrolling down until he found a picture of Josh Wright's driver's license. The address was the same as on the card. The signature appeared the same, but of course, forensics would provide the only opinion that counted.

"Louise, I would like to look at room number seven. Am I correct that that was the room Mr. Wright stayed in on June 3? At least according to this card."

"Yes, but it has been cleaned and scrubbed numerous times since then. You probably won't find much."

"I know, Louise, but I have to see the layout of the room and take some photographs."

Coleman's mood turned somber. It was becoming more probable that the victim's father had exacted his revenge against the molester of his beautiful and talented daughter. The veteran cop understood, and it saddened him. The pain of a parent, like that of the child, defied measurement. It was compounded by the guilt that the abuse could have been prevented. The anger and frustration mounted to a level where one no longer cared about any consequence that would flow from avenging the monstrous violation that had befallen them and their loved ones.

Louise led him down to unit seven, unlocked the door, and ushered him in. She sensed his mood change, and she adjusted hers accordingly, abandoning her typically funny and quirky self.

He photographed the general layout of the room and then donned latex gloves in the event something of value was discovered. He aimlessly paced around the spotless room. He opened the dresser drawers. He walked back to the kitchenette and looked in the cabinets. More drawers opened and closed. What the hell was he looking for? He hadn't a clue.

He opened the back door and inhaled the fresh pine-scented air that greeted his nostrils. He marveled at the density of the majestic trees, which sloped towards the crystal blue lake that glistened in the early afternoon sun.

Coleman reentered room seven and continued his pursuit of the unknown to the tiny bathroom. Nothing remarkable there.

He returned to the center of the room and sat down on one of the two beds with the nightstand to his right. He looked out the window and saw flowers, a swing set, and picnic tables. He wondered if Hope's father had observed the same setting on the morning of June 4 when he awoke.

Coleman looked at the nightstand. It was highly polished. He opened the drawer. There was one item inside. A Gideon Bible. Based on its condition, it was reasonable to conclude that the book had been there since the forties when Redd's had first opened. He picked it up and fanned the pages with his left thumb. While doing so, he noticed a small cardboard-like rectangle buried between two pages in the book of Psalms. It appeared to be about two-by-three inches. He removed it from the book. One side was solid and cream colored. He turned it over. It appeared to be a school picture—third or fourth grade. The smiling face on the picture was unmistakable. It was Hope Emery-Wright.

Coleman turned back to the Bible, to the point where the picture had been buried. At the top of the page on the right, it read "Psalm Twenty-Three."

He felt like he'd been punched in the gut. He photographed the picture of Hope and the spot in the Bible where it had been found. He told Louise that he would have to take these items with him, as they were evidence. She, of course, understood. They went back to the office. The registration card would also have to be taken as evidence. She made a photocopy of it and handed the original to Coleman, who placed it in an evidence bag.

One further thing. "Louise, I noticed that the registration card indicates that Mr. Wright used a credit card to pay for his room. I need to find out his account number. Could you tell me where you bank, so that I can run that down?"

"Sure. It's North Lakeland Bank. There's a branch in town. I'll call one of the officers there. He's my cousin. It'll give you a head start. His name is Jimmy Bryan."

"Thanks, Louise. You've been a tremendous help."

She instinctively gave him a hug. He needed it. "All the best to you, Bennett."

Coleman left Redd's and headed back into town. He pulled over into a bank parking lot, took a couple deep breaths, and called Sheriff Wallace.

"Hello, Agent Coleman." Sounded as if the Sheriff was being a little officious since his ass chewing of this morning regarding the press.

"Hi, Greg. Hey, I need a photo array of four men, Caucasian, between the ages of thirty-five and forty-five. Make them all eight-by-ten, black and white. How long will it take you to get that done?"

Pause. Longer than usual.

"Sheriff?"

"Yes. You say an array?"

Educated guess: he had no clue what that meant. "Yes. An array. A group of four individual photographs, most likely taken from mug shots, converted to eight-by-ten size, black and white. No captions or writing on any of the prints. All Caucasian men between the ages of thirty-five and forty-five. Call your jailer for assistance. I'll be by in a half an hour to pick them up." *Click.*

He then called Lindsey Mitchell, the weekend worker who'd checked in Josh Wright at the motel on June 3 at 10:46 p.m. Or was it someone else trying to set Josh up? In any event, he should know in about an hour whether Lindsey could pick him out from a photo lineup.

Coleman searched his phone for the nearest drug store. There was one downtown. He called, checking to if see if they did photo developing from cell phones. They did, but there might be a slight wait. No problem.

He drove to the store, parked in the lot, and noticed a Pinesap County Squad conspicuously positioned next to the front door, a good thirty feet from the nearest parking space. Coleman put two and two together.

Coleman spotted the photo section and the two uniformed officers anxiously awaiting the development of their photos. One, of course, was Sheriff Wallace and the other appeared to be a correctional officer who likely had dug out the mug shots. Coleman positioned himself behind them without announcing his presence. The Sheriff was being very impatient with the photo machine operator.

"Ma'am, this is very urgent. Please, let's just speed up the process."

"Wally, the machine can only go so fast. So just cool your jets."

Coleman chuckled. He thought he noticed a subtle grin from the correctional officer. The Sheriff was seething, having just been called out by a drug store employee. He was about to strike back at her when Coleman preempted the counterattack.

"Excuse me, ma'am, are these guys giving you a hard time?"

Little Wally did an abrupt about face and blurted out, "Look, pal, this is official police business, so you better . . ."

Coleman lifted the bill of his Packers cap. "Better *what*, Sheriff?"

Wallace was now in full retreat mode. "Agent Coleman. I'm sorry. I didn't realize it was you. We were just getting those photos ready that you had requested."

"Lighten up, Sheriff. I was just messing with you. Let's see what you got." Three of the four photos had already been developed. He reviewed them. They would be acceptable. He had briefly considered showing Ms. Mitchell the one photo he had of Josh Wright but thought better of it to avoid a future argument that such a procedure would be too suggestive. A photo lineup was the better practice.

The remaining photos were processed. Coleman considered sending Wally to the bank to retrieve Josh Wright's credit card account from Jimmy Bryan, Louise's cousin. He thought better of it, knowing that the news would circulate before sundown, creating another "late breaking developing story" for ten o'clock viewers.

The cops exited the drug store. Coleman couldn't help himself as he passed the county squad. "Nice park job, Wall."

★ ★ ★

Coleman sailed past Redd's Lakeview Motel on his way to meet Lindsey Mitchell in Hazelton. The parking lot was beginning to reach capacity. Louise was watering the flowers.

A weary-looking Lindsey Mitchell was waiting for Coleman, having just finished her long workday that had begun at 6:00 a.m. She was seated at a picnic table resting on a bed of pine straw to the north side of the diner entrance. They introduced themselves. The detective took a seat opposite the waitress and part-time motel clerk. Cute gal despite her sad and dejected countenance. As was his practice, he gathered some background information.

Lindsey was a single parent of a two-year-old daughter named Jasmine. She had dropped out of high school her senior year when she became pregnant. The father was not in the picture. Nor was hers. Buck Mitchell was a part-time laborer and full-time alcoholic. Without regret, she had not seen him in five years. Had no idea where he lived. Her mother, Dawn Mitchell, lived with her boyfriend about an hour away. She worked at a local tavern. Boyfriend did not work but did visit Dawn daily at her workplace. A week ago, Dawn had paid a visit to see her only granddaughter. She had made a valiant effort to cover up a shiner on her left eye with excess Maybelline. Lindsey asked what happened. A door slammed into her at work. *Right.* Lindsey had one older brother who had escaped the daily routine of dysfunction by joining the Army.

She had worked at the diner for about a year. The last two summers she'd supplemented her income by filling in on weekends at Redd's. She loved working there. Coleman gleaned that it wasn't so much the actual work that appealed to her. It was Louise and Frank. Her eyes lit up at the sound of their names. "They are so good to me. I don't know what I would do without them."

Prior to displaying the photos, Coleman asked Lindsey what she could recall of the events of June 3. She recalled that her mom had been in town to watch Jasmine while she worked at the motel. She'd arrived around 7:00 a.m. with her pet cocker spaniel, Harvey, a real yapper, especially late at night when unexpected travelers arrived seeking a room. And that was the situation that night. She had nodded off watching TV when she was awakened by Harvey's incessant barking. She looked out the window, saw a white pickup and a man waiting at the office door that had a sign that read, "Ring for Service." Lindsey remembered that earlier in the evening a prospective guest had called to cancel a reservation. She remembered flipping on the blinking "Vacancy" sign. Unit seven was the only room left.

"I'm sure I can identify him. He seemed, ah, like, pre-occupied. Talked very little. Just wanted to get to his room. I understood. It was late. And he probably had driven a long way. Card said Chicago. He wasn't rude—more like short. I didn't make a copy of his driver's license. Our copy machine is ancient and takes forever to warm up. I didn't want him to have to wait. The next morning, I got up around 6:15 and made the coffee, which is free to guests. I went outside to start watering the flowers and noticed that his truck was already gone. Checkout time is 11:00 a.m. He never came back."

Coleman displayed the eight-by-ten photos. Josh Wright's was second from the left. She pointed to it immediately. She then chuckled. Coleman asked to be let in on the joke.

She directed his attention to the photo on the far right. "Do you know him?"

"Oh yeah. His name is Freddie Burton. He's my mom's boyfriend."

He thanked her and requested her confidentiality regarding the case. She nodded. He told her to stick with Louise and Frank. Smiling, she replied, "Oh yeah. For sure."

Coleman had left his phone in the car while interviewing Lindsey Mitchell. She was a key witness. He wanted to avoid interruptions while interviewing her. He had made the right call. His phone was lighting up. Voicemail from Bea Wilkerson. Another from Brian Spurlock. Another from Louise Drysdale. And last and most recent, one from Little Wally.

He decided to listen to all of them in order received and then prioritize his return calls.

Call number one, from Bea Wilkerson: "Mr. Coleman, this is Bea Wilkerson. I have just returned from the beauty salon where I was getting my nails done. There was a gal next to me getting her nails done also. I don't know her name, but I can get it if you think that's important. Anyway, she was telling her nail tech that she was watching the Channel 9 news last night and she heard that there was an actual video of that boy being murdered earlier this month in Wisconsin. I am assuming 'that boy' is my Beamer. Well, I left the salon crying my heart out . . . again . . . and came home to call you to see what the hell is going on up there. Please call me right away. I'll be at home." There was a pause in the message. "Well, wait a minute. Actually, I will be at Rosie's Salon. You can call me there. She only did my left hand. Goodbye." Extremely low priority. Lower than the belly of a snake in a wagon rut.

Call number two, from Deputy Spurlock: "Spurlock here. I'm at the security store in Wausau talking to Mr. Record about the security cams at the Wilkerson cabin. The system is wireless, and the images are sent to a cloud. They can be accessed through the company's website, but we need a username and password to access the recordings. He says the storage capacity is huge so there should be no issue with deleting prior recordings. The cameras are motion activated. The company that makes the cameras is out of New York. KT Security. I called them but they are unable to help without a warrant. Need decedent's username, which is probably his email address, and password. He probably has an app on his phone. Call me."

He sent a text instead. "Got your voicemail. Stay in Wausau. Go to my office and ask for John Weatherton. Text me back when you get there."

Coleman looked at his watch. It was 5:30 p.m. His forensic buddy was on the golf course for sure. The only question was whether he had his phone with him. He called it. Straight to voicemail. *Shit*. Coleman left a message to call him back immediately. Extremely urgent. He'd give him five minutes, tops.

Time's up. Okay. Where is he playing? If he stayed in Wausau, probably Towering Pines. They played there often. He had the number in his phone. Priorities.

"Good afternoon. Towering Pines Golf Course. This is Ray."

"Ray, this is Bennett Coleman. I'm trying to locate John Weatherton. Is he out there playing by any chance?"

"Ben, there's nobody playing today. Greens and tee boxes are being aerated."

"Oh. Okay. Thanks, Ray."

He got a text from Spurlock. "Office is closed."

Response: "Hang tight. Call you in 10."

Where is he playing? Then it dawned on him. *He plays in a city league at the muni. He's always complaining about the condition of the course. What's the name of that goat ranch? Wausau Royal Links, that's it.* It wasn't a links course and there was nothing about it that resembled "Royal." But it was in Wausau. A quick search yielded the number.

"Wausau Royal Links. How can I help you?'

"Hi. My name is Bennett Coleman and I am a detective with the Wisconsin Bureau of Investigation. I'm looking for a colleague of mine by the name of John Weatherton. I'm wondering if you could find out if he is playing there today? It's very important."

"I'll sure try. Can you hold?"

"Sure." A couple minutes went by.

"Okay. Are you still there?"

"Yes."

"There is a Weatherton playing here today. He teed off about two hours ago. He's playing in a singles match. They should be making the turn very shortly. Do you want me to give him a message?"

"Yes. This is very important. Have him call Bennett Coleman."

"Will do, Mr. Coleman. Does he have your number?"

"Yes, he does. Thank you so much."

Waiting for the call back, Coleman dialed up Spurlock. He told him that he was trying to run down his forensic chief so they could all meet at his office to check out the decedent's phone and potential access to his security recordings. The conversation was cut short when the call from Weatherton came in.

"Hi, John. This is huge."

"It better be. I was down two after six. I've won three holes in a row to go one up at the turn. But I am very fearful that this fucking call is going to bring all my momentum to a screeching halt."

"Actually, it's going to bring your entire match to a screeching halt. I need you to meet me at the office ASAP so we can further examine the Wilkerson phone."

"What the fuck for?"

"To see if he has an app that can be used to check security cameras at his cabin. John, there may be a video of this shooting!"

"Well, that's great, Bennett. But why can't this wait until the morning? I mean, who else knows?"

"Not that many. Probably no more than two million people."

"What?!"

"Yeah. Last night it was reported on the news that there may be a video involved in the investigation. It's already reached Rosie's Salon in Sycamore Pointe, Illinois."

"What the hell is that all about?"

"Nothing. I'll tell you later. I'm leaving for the office now."

"Wait a minute. Where are you?"

"I'm just south of Oneida Falls."

"What the hell. I thought you were at the office. I'm going to finish this match. I'll see you in an hour and a half. Bring some beer." *Click.*

Coleman called Spurlock and told him the plan. By the end of the night, all three might be watching a video of the events of June 4 at 6:40 at Gresham Gathering, Wisconsin. Beer included. And cheese, of course.

CHAPTER TWENTY-THREE

Pet Names and Passwords

Coleman was about an hour from his Wausau office when he realized that he had not listened to the remaining two voice messages on his phone. He punched them in his radio speakers.

Call number three, from Louise Drysdale: "Agent Coleman, this is Louise Drysdale at the motel. I went ahead and called my cousin at the bank and got that information about the credit card used by Mr. Wright when he checked in on June 3. I'll text it to you. Knowing my cousin and the people he works with at the bank, if you had gone in there to get it, the rumor mill would have gone into full throttle. Didn't think you would want that. Hope that's okay. Call me if you have any questions."

Okay?! It's perfect, Coleman thought. It saved him a good hour of work and, moreover, avoided the hassle that would ensue if the press discovered the name of the prime suspect. Louise should run for sheriff.

He called her back and expressed his gratitude in a voice message. She was probably checking in guests and telling them why their motel had "Lakeview" in its name.

Call number four, from Sheriff Wallace: "Agent Coleman, Sheriff Wallace here. When I got back from getting those photos enlarged, a reporter asked me what was going on at the drug store. I told her 'No comment.' But then I thought, maybe one of those guys is a suspect and on the loose and the press could help us. What do you think? Give me a call."

Here is what I think, Little Wally. If the people of Pinesap County knew your lack of law enforcement acumen, you would lose the next election and revert back to pumping gas and selling beer and minnows.

To avoid a long-winded conversation, Coleman texted back: "Got your phone message. Your 'no comment' response was perfect. Keep it up." He immediately replied with the "thumbs up" emoji.

Coleman began collecting his thoughts during the ride to his Wausau office. He needed to get a hold of Detective O'Hearn in Chicago for assistance in getting a search warrant for Josh Wright's credit card account. There very well could be other charges that were used during his trek to the vintage motel. He assumed this could be accomplished with more dispatch and less notice than requesting the same procedure in Oneida Falls. He was correct on both counts.

He also needed to be on alert in the event the security video conclusively identified Wright as the killer. O'Hearn would have to make the arrest.

Bea Wilkerson's call had to be answered and he was the only one who could do it. He decided to get it out of the way.

"Hello."

Ah, perfect. It was Mr. Wilkerson. He would be short and so would Coleman.

"Mr. Wilkerson?"

"Yes."

"Mr. Wilkerson, this is Agent Bennett Coleman calling from Wisconsin. Your wife left a message on my voicemail and I was returning her call."

"Yes, she told me you might be calling. She's actually out right now. Is there a message I can take? Have there been new developments in the case?"

"Well, in her message, she mentioned hearing something at her hair salon about a news report indicating that there may have been a video of the shooting. As usual, that report was slightly exaggerated but know that as we speak, we are following up on that possibility and will keep you informed if anything materializes."

"Thank you, Mr. Coleman. I'll make sure to pass on that information to my wife."

"Thank you, sir. Goodbye."

Well, that was easy, thought Coleman. Such an interesting contrast between husband and wife, one he had observed upon first meeting them. She, so impulsive, raw, and demanding. He, so reticent, measured, and seemingly complacent.

Of course, he at all costs wanted to avoid telling the Wilkersons about the guest record of Josh Wright at Redd's Lakeview Motel and the positive ID of him by the weekend clerk, Lindsey Mitchell. In fact, at this point in the investigation there would be no updates to anyone except Spurlock, Weatherton, and O'Hearn. If Wright was arrested, it would not be based on probable cause. He had already hit that standard. It would be a "proof beyond a reasonable doubt" arrest. Ironically, the deceased's security camera video would likely be the linchpin.

★ ★ ★

Spurlock was outside Coleman's office when he arrived, wolfing down a double cheeseburger and fries. Coleman exited his car and waved him up to the entrance of the office building that housed the Wisconsin Bureau of Investigation, Wausau unit. The building was quite modest, a two-story brick structure adorned with government signs, photos of elected officials, the usual. There was a reception window centered inside the entrance with a waiting area that had matching seats for people having business with the cops inside. Angling out from each side of the reception area were locked doors leading to hallways where employee offices were situated.

Coleman unlocked the door to the right and went to his office three doors down. They entered, Coleman sitting behind his desk, Spurlock opposite. The environs of this office were a considerable downgrade from the Masterson suite that he had visited yesterday.

Off-white painted walls, steel desk with unmatching chair on rollers, file cabinet to the right, next to a window with a parking lot view. Two modest wooden chairs for guests, one of which was occupied by Spurlock as he finished his fast food fare. In the upper left-hand corner of the room, a video screen was mounted, allowing Coleman to view anyone entering the building or his hallway. The office felt cramped. There were stacks of files on his desk, no doubt future work awaiting his return from the Pinesap investigation.

There were no knotty pine walls, no fireplace, and no taxidermy. There was a single photograph of Coleman and his two young adult sons, Vaughn and Dane. They were on the first tee of Erin Hills Golf Course. No spousal pictures. Coleman had been divorced for years. Occupational hazard.

John Weatherton had yet to arrive. Coleman placed a paper sack on his desk. It contained a six pack of Stella Artois and a brick of sharp cheddar. Coleman had stopped at a food mart to purchase his buddy's consolation prize. "No way he wins his match."

Five minutes later, his prediction was confirmed as the forensics expert entered the building looking disheveled, sweaty, and pissed off. Weatherton was rather tall, probably six-foot-two, overweight around the midsection, and sporting a blue visor with his dark blond, wavy hair poking out the top. He still had his golf shoes on, ankle socks as well as blue Bermuda shorts and a light yellow polo shirt, untucked.

He went straight to Coleman's door and entered without knocking. No greeting. Coleman waited for the barrage.

"This better be good, you son of a bitch. I'm one up after nine. Then you call. We halve the next hole and then I proceed to lose the next five holes in a row and the match four and three. I shank two into the woods on the final hole and just pick up and concede the match. God, I hate this fucking game."

Without saying a word, Coleman reached into his desk and pulled out a church key, cracking open a cold bottle of the brew and handing it to Weatherton, who accepted readily. He then pulled out a sharp paring knife and stabbed the unwrapped cheese right in the center.

Weatherton took two gulps of beer before he even noticed that there was someone else in the room.

"I'm sorry. I'm John Weatherton." He extended his hand.

"Brian Spurlock. Pleasure. Sorry about your game."

"Don't be. Happens all the time. Do you play golf?"

"No. I fish."

"Smart. Golf sucks. It will drive you crazy. I mean, just look at Coleman here, if you want proof."

"You're right, John," Coleman said. "Just drink your beer." And he did. He sliced up some cheese and inhaled the same.

"We have to wait for my assistant. I think he was having dinner with his girlfriend. You're making a lot of friends around here, Coleman."

"You know you're probably right, John. It's just a murder investigation. Maybe we should wait until next week. Don't you get new microscopes in then? Or new DNA kits? Perhaps I have jumped the gun. Let's just all go bowling. Whaddya say?"

"I say 'fuck you, Coleman.' Next match you're giving me extra strokes." He grabbed another beer.

Spurlock was enjoying the banter. There was a knock on the door. It was Weatherton's assistant, Griff Winters. More introductions and then the foursome headed down the hall to the lab and location of Beamer's phone.

Weatherton went to an evidence cabinet, donned some purple latex gloves, and removed a plastic bag that contained the decedent's smartphone. He looked at his watch and then the calendar on the wall and made a notation on a label affixed to the bag. Winters was silently making notations in a journal as to the protocol of his superior. The jocular and sarcastic mood of the previous ten minutes was now abandoned, replaced by an informal professionalism.

Weatherton was in charge. He announced, "I will be the only one to touch this phone. Trust me. It will make it much easier if testimony is needed later in court. Now, someone tell me what we're looking for."

Coleman nodded and deferred to Spurlock. "We are looking for an app from a company that calls itself KT Security. Their icon looks like this." He removed a printed copy of their logo with white lettering on a royal blue field. Weatherton had already activated the phone. He began swiping the phone, searching for the app, which finally appeared on the fifth screen with two other icons. He tapped on it. The window showed fields for both a user-name and a password.

Weatherton knew the username. It was BEAMER96@ yahoo.com. Coleman explained the origin of "Beamer." 1996 was the year of his birth. Everybody rolled their eyes.

Weatherton entered the username. "Okay, now what? Do you have the password, Ben?"

"No, but I think Brian has a suggestion."

"We can enter some passwords that will not work. Then it will ask us 'Forget password?' and if we want to change our password. A code will be sent by text to the phone, which we will use during the procedure of chang-ing the password. We get a new one, and it's Wednesday night at the movies."

"Question," said Weatherton. "Are we running the risk of tampering with this piece of evidence if we change the password?" There was a significant pause.

Coleman finally said, "Well, I don't see that as an issue. We are not tampering with the mechanism. We're not deleting or adding information to the phone. We are merely changing our ability to access information. If this were a safe and we didn't have the combination to it and absolutely had to discover the contents to investigate a murder . . ."

"We would probably get a search warrant!" inter-rupted Weatherton.

A more significant pause.

Coleman, having pondered the circumstances, coun-tered. "We would only need a warrant if the contents con-tained evidence against a defendant in a criminal case and if *he* owned the safe. This phone is the property of a dead man. Who is going to challenge that? Besides, for all I know, thanks to the ten o'clock news, there are hackers out there now, trying to access this video for their own amusement or to delete it or for whatever purpose, while we sit here and ponder whether we need to wake up some judge in the middle of the night to sign a warrant. I'll take the heat if I'm wrong."

Spurlock and Winters were silent. This debate was between the two veterans.

It was Weatherton's turn. "I agree with your reasoning. I think we should go ahead. I also agree that, if you are wrong, you will take the heat."

"Fuck you very much, John."

The suggested procedure was followed. A text message was sent to the phone. An unexpected obstacle arose.

Before a new password could be suggested, a security question had to be answered.

"What was the name of your favorite pet?"

They all looked at each other in puzzlement. Spurlock, who seemed to have the greatest cyber knowledge in the group, spoke up.

"We've got to answer this question correctly. If we answer it incorrectly, we'll get shut down."

So, who would know the answer to this question? Coleman knew. Beatrice Wilkerson. Surely, she would know the name of her little Beamer's favorite pet. And he would have to make the call. He checked his watch. It was 10:10 p.m. He found her cell number. He punched it in and put the phone on speaker.

Surprisingly, she answered right away. "Hello, Mr. Coleman. Good timing. I was just watching the news on WGN to see if they had any updates since I can't get any from you." The group winced.

"Did your husband give you the message that I called?"

"Yeah, he did. Said you were working on it. Sounds like you're giving me the runaround."

"I assure you, ma'am, that we are not. In fact, as we speak, I am in the lab with three of my associates analyzing the contents of your son's phone. And we need your help."

"Oh really. And how is that?"

"We are attempting to access the photo file of his phone, but we need an answer to a security question."

"And what is the question, Mr. Coleman?"

"The question is: 'What was the name of your favorite pet?'"

There was a prolonged silence on the other end. The group exchanged worried glances, as if she might not know.

"Mrs. Wilkerson? Are you there?"

Another pause and then the sound of a muted sniffle. "Yes. I am here. I'm sorry. I wasn't expecting that question. Of course, I know the answer. It's just so upsetting."

Coleman whispered to the group, "Storytime."

"It was his thirteenth birthday and I sensed that Beamer was feeling a little left out. Many of his classmates at school were Jewish and they were celebrating their bar mitzvahs. We are not Jewish, so I wanted to do something very special for him. I bought him a puppy. It was a Doberman Pinscher. We were discussing a name for the dog when I came up with Benzie. It was close to 'Benji,' which was a popular movie at the time. But it was also a variation of the second part of Mercedes Benz. And since his nickname came from a German car, you know— Beamer, I thought it was cute that his dog's name would have the same kind of twist to it. He liked it. And so, it was Beamer and his dog Benzie. He really loved that dog." More sniffling.

Nausea was quickly settling in on the group of cops in Wausau, Wisconsin. Coleman thought it would have been nice for Mommy Beatrice to tell little Beamer that Dobermans had been used by the Nazis during World War II as guard dogs while they were massacring millions of his classmates' ancestors. Another nice twist.

"So, the dog's name was Benzie, spelled B-e-n-z-i-e. Correct?"

"Yes. That's it."

"Thanks so much, Mrs. Wilkerson. You've been a great help."

No response other than the click from her phone.

The men looked at each other incredulously. Beamer and Benzie. *Are you shitting me?*

Coleman broke the silence. "Well, boys, let's find out if Mommy is correct."

The screen came up with the security question. Weatherton typed in "Benzie." It responded, "Correct! Please enter new password."

The group had predetermined to use a password that had relevance to the investigation with no hidden meaning or humor. PinesapCounty. Simple. It was entered twice, deemed successful by some cyber decoder chip. The screen to the KT website appeared. It showed multiple squares, similar to jumbo TVs in some sports bars. Weatherton was able to interface the phone to a high definition computer screen so that all present could view the video with ease.

He clicked on the first square.

Showtime.

CHAPTER TWENTY-FOUR

Home Movies

The website was a storage receptacle for all activity that had been recorded from the first (and only) activated camera. The camera in question faced north and was mounted on top of a flagpole approximately fifteen feet high and close to the beginning of the dock. It basically showed activity between the cabin to the left and garage to the right. Traffic entering and exiting was also covered.

There was some discussion about going straight to the June 4 segment. In the end, it was agreed by all that a sequential viewing would be utilized. Weatherton made sure that an exact copy of each video segment was downloaded to one of his lab's computers.

The initial recording showed Randy Baxter, the salesman now vacationing in Italy, doing a test recording of the camera. It was late in the afternoon a week before the murder and showed him waving to the camera midway between the garage and cabin, while saying "Test. This is a test. Testing one, two." The clarity of both the sound and video was off-the-charts amazing.

Fortunately, this was not a "24/7" camera. Its recording system was triggered by motion. The majority of the first three days compared favorably to a wildlife documentary film starring white-tailed deer. The only human activity recorded was Bryce Wilkerson's comings and goings, until May 31 when he and Reggie Masterson arrived following their dinner at Dale's Steak House. He pulled his truck straight towards the dock, presumably to better view the moonlight glistening on the smooth waters of Gresham Lake. The camera was unable to pick up the in-cab activity. Same with the in-cabin activity, which lasted about three hours. Perhaps young Reggie could fill in the details later.

Around midnight, the couple left.

It was now midnight in Wausau. Coleman was having trouble staying awake. He had been up since 4:00 a.m. He called a timeout and went to his office, sat down on his chair, leaned back, and took a forty-five-minute nap. The other three continued to review the recording of events at the Wilkerson cabin and took notes to brief Coleman when he returned from his battery charge.

Nothing of significance happened until 10:15 a.m. the morning of June 2. Beamer departed to playgrounds unknown. Thirty minutes later, a Cadillac SUV was seen entering the property and pulling up to the back door of the cabin. The driver and passengers, if any, were unidentifiable because of tinted windows. No one got out of the vehicle. It stayed about ten minutes and then departed. Spurlock recognized the car and made a notation.

Coleman woke up from his nap and headed to a restroom down the hall where he threw cold water into his face multiple times. He returned to the lab. The activities of June 3 were up next.

Around 6:00 a.m., Wilkerson was seen throwing fishing tackle and coolers into the bed of his pickup. He was off to his day of fishing and drinking with the Blanchard brothers. Bambi and his cousins and fellow wildlife friends occupied the remainder of the day intermittently until around 1:40 a.m. on June 4.

The white pickup appeared from the drive and parked after making a left turn facing the garage. Beamer exited the vehicle and stumbled to the back door of the cabin. His movements inside the cabin were outside the purview of the camera. It did, however, pick up that an interior light was activated. It stayed on all night.

Around 5:30 a.m., a figure dressed in all black appeared on the lane and walked toward the pickup truck. He was carrying what appeared to be some sort of bucket. The cops agreed that the person was male. Coleman's initial assessment was that he was the approximate height of Josh Wright but more slender in build. Perhaps the effect of the all-black clothing.

The figure approached the truck and lowered himself by the door, which blocked his activity from the eagle eye lens. He stayed in that low position for about three minutes and then departed, disappearing on the same path that had brought him to the scene. Coleman had seen that walk before but could not place it. It would gnaw at him.

The back door of the cabin opened around 6:30 a.m. and Beamer exited and could be seen urinating on the combination of sand and grass about ten feet from the cabin. He finished and dragged himself back inside.

About ten minutes later, he reappeared and walked toward his truck, opened the door, and retrieved his cigarettes from the interior. He looked down and reached over to lift objects unknown to the camera at the time but later discovered to be a dead walleye and a family photo Hope Emery-Wright. He turned to the direction of the camera and then back to the direction of the woods.

It was about 1:30 a.m. in the forensic lab. All present were about to witness something for the first time in their respective careers. A recording of a murder.

The audio component of the camera clearly captured the unmistakable sound of a single rifle discharge. Concurrently, the high definition lens recorded the final moment of Bryce Miles Wilkerson's life as he was struck by the round and then slumped beneath the view of the camera. The recording was paused, and Weatherton noted the time of death: 6:41.07 a.m.

In less than a minute, the black-clad figure reemerged from the woods and approached the expired figure. He leaned down and moments later stood and headed to the cabin. He entered, removing himself from the eyes of the camera and the four men glued to the screen. He reentered the sphere of the lens and returned to the lifeless body. Again, he lowered himself and spent some final moments with the deceased.

He stood and walked around the truck and headed towards the camera and the lake, as if to take a bow for his murderous act. He was in total black from head to toe. His face was completely covered in a black nylon; no eyes, no nose, no mouth, no hair was visible. He was deliberate in his walk. His black boots imprinted the sand as he took his loop from the lake back to the truck and then disappeared into his green forested haven. The time imprint on the video was 7:01.11 a.m.

Coleman: "I don't know about you guys, but I think we should adjourn tonight and come back tomorrow morning, say about 10:00. I want to study this recording again. There is no doubt that we have missed something."

There were no dissenting votes.

★　★　★

Bennett Coleman lived in a two-bedroom condo in Wausau. He invited Spurlock to stay with him rather than drive back to his cottage in the woods ninety miles to the north. The next morning, they shared information over coffee. Of particular note was the visit of the Cadillac SUV to the Wilkerson cabin two days prior to the murder. Spurlock knew the owner. Dick Masterson, the insurance mogul.

"That's interesting," said Coleman. "The Mastersons told me they didn't find out about their daughter being with him until two days afterwards, when it was reported on the ten o'clock news. And no ID on the driver?"

"Nope. Heavy tint on the windows."

"Could have been Reggie. I'll check it out when we get back up north."

"What about the father, Josh Wright?" asked Spurlock. "Do we have enough to get an arrest warrant?"

"Probably. But there's something really bothersome about pinning this crime on him. You watched the footage last night. The guy is in all black. He went to great lengths to conceal his identity, yet he left the family photo at the scene. It's got to be a plant. Wright made no effort at all to hide his actions getting up to Wisconsin. He used his own name and credit card to pay for his motel room only three miles away. No disguise when he checked in. And he does so at a late hour when there was no way of him being confused with another guest. And then this elaborate and calculated shooting. It doesn't make sense."

Coleman contacted Detective O'Hearn in Chicago and spent about a half an hour updating him on the status of the case. He gave him the information on Josh Wright's credit card and requested a search warrant for a history of the account. The wily Chicago veteran indicated he would be able to get that done by the following morning. He also passed on to Coleman that suspect Wright was keeping to his routine and showing no signs of leaving the city. Coleman was not surprised.

Coleman and Spurlock took separate vehicles to the office and met the forensic team of Weatherton and Winters in the lab. They picked up their review of the security footage with post-mortem activity. Not much was learned other than that apparently not all white-tail deer are total vegetarians. The same for raccoons and buzzards. The discovery of the body by Wayne Crawford from Iowa was memorialized, as well as the first involvement by law enforcement, Deputy Hallie Hogan. Their respective regurgitations brought eye rolls and head shakes from the group. Easy for them. They weren't there to smell it.

And, of course, the entire investigation at the scene had been recorded. Defense attorneys would have a field day. They would be entitled to have access to everything as part of the discovery process once this case was charged. Every little mistake would be magnified.

The morning of June 4 was revisited. The assassin had made two appearances. One before death with the bucket. It was played over and over. With multiple pauses. Nothing remarkable that had not been observed during the initial viewing. No defining markings on his clothing or the bucket. Just that walk, which Coleman found to be distinctive but not yet identifiable.

The second appearance was longer. The shooting, followed by the short visit to the body; then the breach of the cabin; back to the body and, finally, the saunter to the lake and back to his invisible perch. Each segment was replayed repeatedly for dissection.

Nothing noted during his entry to check on the condition of his prey except that he did not have the bucket. And then he went to the cabin. Why on earth would Wright, if he were the killer, go into the cabin? It made no sense. Why did the assassin go into the cabin at all? And then back to the body? It must have been for the phone.

His walk to the lake and back. Pause. Study. Pause again. Study. There was something different. What was it? The collar on his black coat had been turned up. Pause it. There was a design under the collar.

"John, can you enlarge that design? Do you see it?"

"Not really, Coleman. Where is it?" responded Weatherton.

He directed Weatherton to back up the recording a frame. There was an extremely small patch of embroidery under the collar. It was a dull gold in color and only visible within that frame because of the angle of the rising sun hitting it.

"There it is, John. Can you enlarge it?"

"Hold on." Weatherton enlarged the frame to the point where the design was evident though somewhat blurry. He printed it.

It looked like some sort of four-legged animal being suspended by a belt-like object around the belly of the beast.

It would appear that the assassin, while awaiting his prey to make his final appearance in life, kept warm by the simple act of lifting his coat collar around his neck. He had no idea that there was an animal underneath. Was it an albatross?

There was also a slight tear in the fabric directly below the suspended creature. Weatherton printed a photo of that as well.

Ten minutes later, Coleman had determined the origin of the design. Thanks, Google. Since 1850, the golden fleece has been the logo of Brooks Brothers clothiers, signifying their heritage, quality, and service in the apparel industry. The killer of Bryce Wilkerson was wearing one of their jackets.

Coleman also did some online window shopping on the Brooks Brothers website. Very pricey. Very upscale. Very white collar. A bit of a stretch that Josh Wright would be outfitted there. Maybe the jacket was on sale? Or a gift? *Wait a minute.* Brooks Brothers? Where had he seen that before?

He had to get back to his makeshift office at the Pinesap County Sheriff's office.

Three hundred and fifty miles south, in a town called the Windy City, a female hacker was conducting an urgent cyber search. A request had been made from an unknown, but ample paying client, to delete the scenes just viewed by the Wisconsin lawmen.

The race to erase was on.

CHAPTER TWENTY-FIVE

The Hacker Unhinged

About a week after Bryce Wilkerson's demise, the Nurse was returning home to her condo in the Little Italy neighborhood on the near south side of the city. It was a Sunday afternoon. She carried a box containing six bottles of Italian reds from various regions of the boot country, compliments of a friend whose computer needed a cleanup.

Approaching her front door, she noticed a small box with the Amazon logo affixed. Interesting. She had not ordered anything recently. A gift, perhaps? She grabbed the package and went inside.

After securing the wine in her rack, she sat down and opened the box. It was not from Amazon. But it was a gift. Actually, fifty of them, all bearing a framed likeness of Benjamin Franklin. Five grand in a plain five-by-seven manila envelope.

Included in the envelope was a typed note bearing a cryptic message. "Within the next 24 hours, please empty the clouds that appear at the enclosed address and a like gift from the Franklin Mint will arrive soon thereafter." An email address and password were included in the note.

Russo read the note again. She recounted the money. She examined the address label on the box. Typewritten. No return address. No postage. It had been hand delivered. A dark, nervous feeling entered her stomach. She'd been found out.

The Nurse took a deep breath and then opened one of the bottles from the rack. She turned her computer on and, upon entering the provided address and password, accessed the site. Her screen depicted various activities at a deeply wooded cabin retreat by a pristine lake. Late May and June of 2018. The June 4 video came on. It showed a young man in boxers and a t-shirt taking a leak outside a cabin. Ten minutes later, the same young man was shot in the head.

Kelle went into a state of semi-shock. She began to hyperventilate. Panic set in immediately. She started pacing around her condo. She had just witnessed a murder. Its impact on her was in no way abated because it was on a recording. She knew who it was.

The attractive hacker sat down, poured herself another glass of wine, and called Michael Duff.

"Michael. You've got to come here right away. I've just witnessed a murder and I'm pretty sure it was the Wilkerson kid."

"Whoa. Whoa. What do you mean you 'just witnessed a murder'?"

"Well, not literally. I saw it on my computer. Somebody sent me this website and five thousand dollars to erase a recording of a murder floating around in cyber space. Michael, you've got to get here immediately. I'm losing it."

"Okay, look. I'll be there as fast as I can. In the meantime, settle down and have a glass of wine. Whatever is going on, I'm sure it's not as bad as you think."

"Easy for you to say. You haven't seen what I have. And, by the way, I'm on my third glass."

"I'm ordering an Uber as we speak. Take deep breaths. I should be there in no later than a half an hour."

"Thank you. Please hurry."

The Sunday night traffic in the city was light. Duff made it to Little Italy in less than the anticipated time. He called the Nurse along the way to check on his friend's emotional status. She was a wreck.

As soon as he entered, she started her rant. "Michael. They've found me. They know I'm a professional hacker. They want me to cover up a murder. They're gonna find out what we've done. We'll both go to jail. Michael, what the fuck are we going to do?"

He'd never seen her this out of control. First F-bomb ever. "Well, the first thing we're going to do is at least try to relax so I can figure out what is going on. Who is 'they'?"

"That's the problem. I don't know."

The Nurse related what had occurred since she'd arrived home about an hour and a half earlier. Duff examined the box, the note, and the cash. She then started to play the video from the computer. Before she hit the play button, he interrupted.

"Wait a second. Can your computer be identified as going on this site?"

"I don't think so. It would take a very sophisticated program to break through my security. This is a site for a home security camera. Not that sophisticated. We'll be safe." Duff was impressed by the answer. More so by the relative calm of its delivery.

"Okay. Go ahead. Let's watch it."

They went straight to the of events of June 4. They sat mesmerized, watching in clear digital color the final moments of Bryce Miles Wilkerson's life. And all that followed. The unidentifiable man in black methodically adjusting the scene of his crime. The animals loping in to feast on the corpse. (The gal from Pittsburgh shielded her eyes as if watching a Freddie Krueger horror movie.) The sound of a grown man regurgitating as he discovered what was left of the boy from Chicago's North Shore. Followed by a female cop with a similar reaction.

Duff had seen enough. He turned to Kelle. "Pack for two days. We're getting out of here."

"What are you talking about?"

"Trust me. You're not safe here. Go pack. We'll take your car to my place. I'll drive."

Ten minutes later, they were headed north to Roscoe Village.

★ ★ ★

Duff needed some time to process the events of the last hour. He decided against the Kennedy Expressway and opted for Damen Avenue, a north-south thoroughfare that intersected a variety of neighborhoods and districts, including the UI-Chicago campus, hospital district, United Center, Wicker Park, Buck Town, and Roscoe Village.

The Nurse broke the silence as they passed the home of the Bulls and Blackhawks.

"What are you thinking?"

Doc collected his thoughts before responding. "Well, I'm sure you have concluded, as have I, that whoever dropped off that cash and requested your services is either the killer or someone who is wanting to protect the killer. And, of course, we have no idea who that is. But whoever it is, he or she knows of you. And that is a little scary on a number of levels."

"Well, that makes me feel a whole lot better."

"Hey, look, I know, I know. But we have to deal with the facts as they present themselves. This is not rosy. Let me ask you some questions. Where were you when the package was delivered?"

"I was at a friend's working on her computer."

"And how long were you gone?"

"About an hour and a half," she answered.

"Where does your friend live and how did you get there?"

"She lives about a half mile away. I walked."

"Are you positive that the box was not there when you left?"

"Yes. Why?" asked Kelle.

"Well, a couple of things. I'm trying to pinpoint as closely as possible when it arrived. The note says 'in the next 24 hours.' Also, was someone waiting for you to leave before the package was delivered? Or was someone just lucky to have delivered it while you were gone? Which would also mean they had to find a way to access the locked building."

Duff was thinking out loud. He was trying to remain calm and rational despite all the dark scenarios that were bombarding his mind. It wasn't that long ago that he had convinced the Nurse to use her illegal hacking skills to extract millions of dollars from Harold Wilkerson, father of a sexual predator. The predator was now dead, murdered by a rifle round to the head, and she was being asked to destroy evidence of that crime. He felt guilty and responsible. He had put his friend and confidant in harm's way. Hopefully, he could rectify the situation.

They arrived at Duff's condo.

"Can you do it?" he asked.

"Do what?"

"Delete the video. Erase it. Make it go away."

She pondered the question, knowing the limited cyber knowledge of the one who asked it.

"Oh, it can probably be deleted. But with a sophisticated program and operator, it could be restored. No permanency."

"Delay?"

"For sure."

Doc and the Nurse were generally aware of the ongoing investigation in Wisconsin. Neither, however, had looked for daily updates . . . until now. The Nurse did a search. She found an article and video on a Milwaukee TV station that indicated that the police may have a video of the murder scene. There was no official word from the investigators to confirm this matter. It was "a developing story."

At Duff's request, she identified the lead investigator on the case, a Bennett Coleman with the Wisconsin Bureau of Investigation. She also located the fax number of the *Wausau Daily Herald*.

Duff presented his plan to Russo. It would be subject to further discussion and her approval. "Obviously, you cannot do anything to this video. I think we can both agree on that. It would constitute all sorts of serious criminal behavior. Capeesh?"

"For sure."

"But let's face it. We have some incredibly valuable information here that the police may not have. I think we have a duty to advise them of it as soon as possible. The question is how. We can't call them. No email. No text. What's the safest way? Whether we like it or not, both of us are involved in this investigation. Which means . . ." Duff saw Russo shake her head and then put her face in her hands. He did not have to finish his speech for her benefit. But he did. ". . . we may become exposed."

Duff had been pacing. She was sitting on his couch. He sat beside her and placed a consoling hand on her shoulder. Here they were again. They looked in each other's eyes. Hers had fear. He was still strategizing.

"I give up. What should we do?" she asked.

He stood. "How about this? There are a number of Kinko's stores in the Loop. I go to one and have them fax this website address and password to the Wausau paper with directions to deliver it to Detective Coleman ASAP. I pay cash. I alter my appearance. I believe it would minimize our risk. Reaction?"

She hesitated. "I guess it's okay. But what about all this damn money? It just creeps me out having it around and knowing what it's for."

He got it. Somebody had delivered a ton of cash to her home. To cover up a murder. She would probably have to move from the quaint condo in her ethnic neighborhood.

"I'll take care of it."

Duff had no time to waste. His destination was a west Loop Kinko's store set to close in forty-five minutes. He hopped on the Kennedy Expressway and in fifteen minutes parked a block from the store on North Wacker.

Anticipating security cameras inside the store, he'd dressed accordingly. Jeans, an old pair of running shoes, a long-sleeved t-shirt with an old school Cubs logo and an old Cubs cap would be the uniform of the day. During the summer, probably no more than a half million Chicagoans would be clad in some variety of that fashionwear. A passable long-haired dark brown wig and reading glasses completed the deception. The brim of the ball cap stayed down during the entirety of the transaction. Later on, when it was merely academic, a superficial effort would be undertaken to discover the sender of the fax. The security video was low quality. The only reasonable conclusion after viewing the same was that the sender was a Cubs fan. Nothing further.

During the last five years, Doc and the Nurse had had numerous occasions to hug. The first had occurred two hours after they'd met at the William Penn Hotel in Pittsburgh following his initial disclosure of his childhood sexual abuse. They had both been in tears. Another was when she'd moved to Chicago. Again, following the successful launch of their anonymous group therapies for victims. A huge celebratory embrace upon scamming the North Shore royalty out of millions. Meet for dinner or lunch, a hug.

They were all "A-frame" hugs. Sibling hugs. All genuine, all authentic. But never intimate.

Until tonight.

Kelle was waiting for him when he arrived back at his home. She had changed into her pajamas. Black sweats and a Pittsburgh Steelers t-shirt. She appeared to have been crying. She quickened her pace to him, exclaiming, "Oh, Michael, I am so afraid." There was no time to avoid the embrace, not that he would have. She wrapped her arms around his waist, pressed her breasts to his lower chest while nestling her right cheek on his right shoulder. She pulled him into her, and he reciprocated.

He caressed her hair and neck and back. He kissed her forehead. With each endearing moment, she responded with a further tug. Was this the start of a new level in their relationship? A prelude to intimacy? Or was this the involuntary response of a woman who was inescapably vulnerable and in need of protection from her fears? Or both, perhaps?

Whatever it meant, there was no denying the effect it had on Duff. He was aroused. He attempted to kiss her on the lips. But she would not budge her face from his chest. He did not press the matter but continued to hold her until she broke free. She kissed him on the cheek. "Thank you, Michael. I'm going to try and get some rest." Her left hand brushed his arm as she drifted to the guest bedroom.

Michael had to work the next day. And it was Monday. By far the busiest day of the week in pharmacy land. Lots of traffic from people getting prescriptions that were unavailable during weekend hours. He needed rest.

It wasn't going to happen. The stimulus from the events of the last five hours made sleep elusive. Actually, downright impossible. Kelle was in peril and they were both facing major legal repercussions if their scheme against Wilkerson was exposed. After all, theirs had been a major heist. Over three million dollars. Prison, perhaps. Financial ruin. Future plans destroyed. The mitigation of their past abuse would be just that: mitigation. Instead of ten years in the slammer, maybe only seven. It was dark. In his mind, in his soul, and in his room. He looked at his phone. It was 2:00 a.m.

It was his turn to feel vulnerable. He got up and walked down the hall to where Kelle was. He pushed open the door. She was in a semi-fetal position facing away from where Duff stood. He sat down on her bed. She rolled over on her back. There was enough light for them to see each other's eyes. His heart pounded like a kettle drum. He leaned over. Their lips drew nearer.

Three hours ago, Duff had been denied a kiss. It would not happen again.

CHAPTER TWENTY-SIX

Taking Him to the Cleaners

Things were clicking with Agent Coleman. And with each new click, he was ramping up emotionally. He left his car in Wausau and rode with Brian Spurlock, filling him in on his hunches and conclusions along the way. Back in Oneida Falls, Coleman went straight to the Sheriff's office. He dispatched Spurlock to the Mastersons to reconcile their version of when they discovered Reggie's connection to the Beamer. Someone was not telling the truth. Notwithstanding, it wasn't Richard Masterson in the all-black suit on June 4. He was just not that lean and agile.

Coleman pulled a file from his desk, the one that contained the May/June American Express statement of Beatrice Wilkerson. There it was. May 11; $699.00; Brooks Bros Mich. Ave.

Coleman looked up the number of the Brooks Brothers shop on the Magnificent Mile in Chicago. He started to call but realized the shop would not give him the information over the phone. Instead, he called his Chicago counterpart, Detective O'Hearn, whom he had just spoken to that morning regarding a warrant for Josh Wright's credit card.

"Good morning again, Bennett. Hey, I don't work that fast."

"I know. I know. I've got something else. Do you know where the Brooks Brothers store is on Michigan Avenue in your city?"

"I'm sure I can find it. I don't shop there regularly, mind you. A little too rich for my blood."

"Well, if you can, I need some information ASAP. I am going to send you a snapshot of a transaction on Beatrice Wilkerson's American Express card statement. I'm fairly certain it's for some type of men's jacket. Probably black in color. It may be the one that was worn by the killer of her son. I need the size of the jacket and, most importantly, whether there is a small logo embroidered beneath the back collar."

"I am only about ten minutes from there. Will call you back as soon as I've got it."

Coleman took a photo of the transaction in question and sent it to O'Hearn's phone. Sheriff Wallace popped his head in and asked how things were going.

"Kind of slow," Coleman lied.

"What's the latest on the cameras?"

"Still working on it, Walls," he lied again.

"Well, let me know if I can help. Things have kind of slowed down here."

"You bet, Sheriff." Coleman completed his trifecta of lies.

As Wallace was leaving, his phone lit up. It was O'Hearn. That was quick.

"Okay, I've got the salesman who actually handled the sale with Mrs. Wilkerson. He remembers it. Or shall I say, he remembers it because he remembers her. A bit of a spoiled ditz. It was actually a birthday present for her husband, who is a bit of a sharp shooter. Size was extra-large. Has the company logo under the collar. He also has the garment number, whatever that is. Another way of identifying the jacket, I believe. Do you want to talk to him? He's right here."

"Yeah, put him on."

"Hello. This is Roland."

"Hi, Roland. My name is Bennett Coleman. I'm sure Detective O'Hearn has briefed you about this jacket issue and its importance to our investigation. It's very crucial that you keep this matter confidential. Just a couple of follow-up questions. Tell me about this sharp shooting."

"Well, Mrs. Wilkerson, she is a regular customer, was getting this item for her husband's birthday. Said he belongs to a gun club somewhere up on the North Shore, and he's defending club champion so she wanted something special. She spotted this black hunting jacket and it was on sale. Normally $899. She got it for $699. Saved two bills. Charged it on her American Express. Apparently, she forgot her Brooks Brothers charge so she didn't get her points."

"Anything else you can remember about the sale, Roland?"

"No, that's about it."

"Thanks so much. Make sure you give your contact information to Detective O'Hearn. Oh, one last thing. The embroidered logo under the back collar. What color is it?"

"You mean the Golden Fleece? It's called old gold. It's not real bright."

"Thanks again. Hand me back to the officer there."

"Will do." He handed the phone back to the detective.

"Dan, we've got to find this jacket. I'm going to need some help in Sycamore Pointe. You know anybody there worth their weight?"

"Not off hand. I'll check it out and get back to you. What's the plan?"

"I'm going to call Bea Wilkerson and try to lay a little trap for her sharp shooting husband. I'll keep you apprised."

Coleman found Bea's number and punched it in.

"Hello."

"Mrs. Wilkerson, this is Agent Coleman calling from Wisconsin."

"Oh, hello, Mr. Coleman. What can I do for you?"

"We're trying to account for all of your son's possessions. I can't seem to find the jacket you bought for him at Brooks Brothers. I was wondering if he actually brought it up with him to Wisconsin."

"What are you talking about? I don't understand."

"Well, you remember the American Express statement you sent? It shows a black hunting jacket from Brooks Brothers in Chicago. Let's see here . . . yes, it was purchased at the Michigan Avenue store."

"Oh that. That wasn't for Beamer. It was for my husband for his birthday. Hunting jacket. He's a very accomplished marksman."

"No kidding. I do a little shooting myself. Small world."

"I should say so. Funny you should ask me about it. I found it in the garage yesterday. All crumpled up. Took it to the cleaners. Filthy. Also had a tear in the back. One wearing and the thing is almost ruined. Glad I bought it on sale."

"Oh my, yes. We guys can be hard on things. Well, Mrs. Wilkerson, sorry to have bothered you. We'll be in touch."

"Right."

★　★　★

Hal Wilkerson entered the kitchen just as his wife was hanging up the phone. He had been listening just outside the room.

"Who was that?" he asked.

"Oh, that Coleman guy from Wisconsin. Stupid call. Thought the hunting jacket I bought for your birthday was Bryce's. What difference does it make?"

"Precisely. What possible difference could it make? Where is that jacket, anyway? I was looking for it the other day."

"Took it to the cleaners, Hal. You trashed it. Found it all wadded up in the garage. You must have really liked it."

"Which cleaners?"

"Zigler's on Green Bay. Why?"

"Just curious."

★　★　★

Coleman immediately googled dry cleaners in Sycamore Pointe, Illinois. There were three. He chose the one that was closest to the Wilkerson estate and gave them a call.

"Good morning. Zigler's."

"Good morning. May I please speak to the owner?"

"I'm sorry. The owner is on vacation. How may I help you?"

"My name is Bennett Coleman. I'm an investigator with the Wisconsin Bureau of Investigation. I am in charge of the investigation of the murder of Bryce Wilkerson.

He was from Sycamore Pointe. I need your cooperation regarding an important issue that has come up in this matter. What is your name?"

"My name is Emma Zigler. I am a niece of the owners. I heard about that case on the news."

"Perfect. Then you know how important this is. Where are the owners vacationing?"

"They are on the road in their RV. Headed to Yellowstone."

"Are you able to contact them?" inquired Coleman.

"Well, that depends on where they are. A lot of places don't have a signal. Can you hold for a second? I have to wait on a customer."

"Sure." Coleman could feel his heartrate increasing. He was 350 miles away from a piece of evidence that could solve this murder case. A father killing his adult son. How could that be? He'd never heard of such darkness in a criminal act.

"Okay. I'm back."

"Emma. This is crucial. Has anyone in the Wilkerson family brought in any clothes in the last couple of days?"

"Let me check. No offense, Mr. Coleman, but are you sure I can do this?"

"Emma, I understand your reluctance. But I am very close to solving this horrible crime. And you can help."

"Okay." There was a pause. "Yes. Mrs. Wilkerson brought in five items. Two shirts, two pairs of slacks, one jacket."

"When did she bring them in?"

"Yesterday."

"And when will they be ready for pick up?"

"Tomorrow after three. Normally they would be ready today but there was a repair."

"So, it takes longer?"

"Yes. We send repairs out."

"Oh really. Where?" asked the detective.

"To a Mrs. Biondi up in Highwood."

Emma gave Coleman Mrs. Biondi's contact information.

"Emma, you have been a great help. Are you in school?"

"Yes, I'll be a senior at Loyola in Chicago."

"And what are you studying?"

"Criminal justice. I'm hoping to go to law school next year."

"Wow! That's fantastic. This will be some early training for you. I will be in touch with you. Let me know if anyone asks about the clothes. I am going to fly down this afternoon and will stop by and we will talk further. I can't tell you how grateful I am."

"Oh, you're welcome. Glad I can help."

Coleman called Sheriff Wallace. He needed a private plane and pilot to fly him to Chicago. He got a return text in fifteen minutes. "Plane departs at noon from Oneida Falls airport. Arrives Chicago Executive airport at 2:15 p.m. Pilot is Craig Billings." Little Wally came through.

The detective then called Spurlock.

"Brian. Two things. Number one. Go home and pack. We're headed to Chicago. Number two. Stop by the Northern Highlands Hotel and pick up my bags. Then pick me up at the Sheriff's office. We leave at noon. By plane." *Click.*

Coleman called the Irish cop O'Hearn in Chicago.

"Hey, Dan. Things are moving pretty rapidly. I'm wondering if you have been able to pinpoint a cop in

Sycamore Pointe who can help us out. I've located the jacket. It's probably at the home of a Rosa Biondi in Highwood, Illinois. She does clothing repair for dry cleaners in the area, including a Zigler's in Sycamore Pointe. Mrs. Wilkerson took the jacket there yesterday."

"I'm waiting for a call from their PD. I think you need to get down here."

"Agreed. I'm on my way. Due to arrive at the Chicago Exec around 2:15. Can you pick me up? And get me a vehicle with GPS? I don't know Chicago."

"I'll be there, Bennett, with a car. Also, if I can't find anyone out of Sycamore PD, I'll check with the Cook County Sheriff to see if they can get me a warm body. Seems like we should have a tail on Wilkerson or a stakeout on the cleaners. Do you think he's aware of our interest in the jacket?"

"I would bet on it," said Coleman. "His wife will inadvertently tell him everything. She has no clue what is going on, and that's fine with her. I think he'll pick it up tomorrow. We've got to be ready when he does. I believe he will try to destroy it. Need cameras and as many bodies as possible."

"Why don't we just seize it now, if we know where it is? This seems too risky."

"Trust me, I have thought of that. He'll say it was someone trying to set him up. Plus, his wife does not have to testify. Spousal privilege. She's the one with the most valuable information. But she also has the most to lose. No cooperation there. No, I believe we have got to get the jacket in his possession so he can try to destroy it. That will be the most telling proof. How is he or his lawyer going to explain destroying the only piece of evidence that links him to the crime?"

"Okay. You're the boss. See you at the airport."

Spurlock arrived at the Sheriff's office.

"What did the Mastersons have to say?"

"You're gonna love this. It was Beverly Masterson in the car. Her husband and Reggie were at work. She had been to the hair salon and overheard two ladies talking about Reggie being at the restaurant with someone named Bryce. One of them said he was twenty years older than she was. She drove out to his cabin to check him out, but he wasn't there. She was afraid to tell you earlier because her husband was there. She apologized. Asked me not to tell Big Dick."

Coleman shook his head and chuckled. They both got their bags and headed to the airport.

The two-hour flight from the forests of Northern Wisconsin to the third largest metropolis in the country was precisely what Agent Coleman needed. For the past two days, he had been going non-stop in his pursuit of the facts that would lead him to the assassin of Bryce Wilkerson. He needed to decompress and allow those facts alone, and not his subjective thoughts, to weigh in on what had happened on the shores of Gresham Lake.

His inner voice had always been rooting for some other suspect to emerge rather than the obvious one, Josh Wright, the father of the victim, and a victim himself. There was ample evidence that pointed in his direction. Motive. Motive. And, oh yes, motive. His outburst following the trial. His presence three miles from the cabin. His early departure from Redd's Lakeview Motel within an hour of the shooting. And perhaps, most compelling, the picture of his beautiful daughter left in a telling chapter of the Bible.

Yet with all this mounting evidence, it did not square with the scene. The motive and the journey were inconsistent with the act of assassination. The video was not conclusive. There had to be another version of the killing.

Enter Harold Wilkerson and his Brooks Brothers black hunting jacket. But he was the father of the decedent. His own flesh and blood. What twisted and distorted thinking would allow a father to take the life of his own son? The answer to that question would have to wait. Coleman had not had time to process that unthinkable scenario.

But this much he did know: the murderer wore a jacket identical to the one purchased by Beatrice Wilkerson for her husband, marksman champion of the North Shore of Chicago. She'd found the jacket and had taken it to the cleaners. It had a tear. And now he was going to find out if Mr. Wilkerson had as much interest in destroying the jacket as Coleman hoped he would.

Rosa Biondi was eighty-two years old and lived alone in a modest two-bedroom home in Highwood, Illinois. She'd moved to the United States when she was a teenager from a small town outside of Modena in northern Italy. She was widowed. Filippo, her husband of forty-eight years, had died two years earlier. He, too, had come from the same town in Italy. She still mostly spoke Italian, her English being fairly broken.

She was kept quite busy by cooking weekend meals for her three sons and their families. She had nine grandchildren who all lived within a fifteen-minute drive from her home. Her oldest was named Marco.

Rosa's father was a tailor and she'd picked up many of his talents during her younger years. About ten years ago, after all her sons had left home, she'd started a small business out of her home doing clothing alterations and repairs for individual customers as well as dry-cleaning establishments in the area. Zigler's Cleaners was one of her long-standing clients. Rosa was dependable and did quality work for a fair price.

About the time that Bennett Coleman's flight was taking off from Oneida Falls, Rosa was staring down at a black jacket that had a tear in the upper back of the garment below a company embroidered logo. It was a simple repair. She would charge her minimum of three dollars. Attached to the item was a tag upon which the name "Wilkerson" had been handwritten. As was her custom in cases of repair, she took a picture of the garment, the area of repair, and the tag with her cell phone. She wasn't entirely old school.

Rosa, of course, had no idea of the importance of the black jacket that she was going to mend nor the danger she was in for having it in her brief possession. Fortunately for her, Marco broke up with his girlfriend that night.

★ ★ ★

The remainder of the flight to Chicago was taken up by planning. Coleman somehow had to get the black jacket to its rightful owner. And its rightful owner had to demonstrate to Coleman an urgent interest in it. Each step along the way would confirm or negate Coleman's factual theory of the solution to the crime. He had a plan. It would take the cooperation of a lot of cops and one senior criminal justice major who, during the summer months, managed a dry-cleaning business.

A very pleasant surprise greeted Coleman and Spurlock when they landed at the Chicago Executive Airport in the northwest suburb of Wheeling. Chicago police detective Dan O'Hearn had enlisted police officers from Sycamore Pointe, Lake County, and the Illinois State Police. All were plain clothes detectives, with the exception of Sycamore Pointe officer James Clancy. He was in blue uniform. Tara Gardner was from the Lake County Sheriff's Department. Randal Carlos was a special agent with the ISP. Everybody went through the introductions and handshakes. Coleman and Spurlock rode with O'Hearn and followed the other three to the Sycamore Pointe Police Department.

Coleman felt like a fish out of water. Ditto Spurlock. They were no longer in the Northwoods. Lots of traffic. Lots of highways, some six lanes . . . in one direction. Stoplights. Lots of them. And rush hours, the great oxymoron.

But above all, the Wisconsin cops were outsiders. They were out of their element. Visitors. They were going to have to adapt instantaneously. Especially Coleman. This was his case. He was in charge. He had been to Chicago a few times, but they were vacations. This was work, and he wasn't familiar with the territory. It was one thing going from Wausau to Oneida Falls. But Oneida Falls to Chicago was like going from your backyard above-ground pool to the Atlantic Ocean . . . or at least Lake Michigan.

Coleman felt he was up to the task. He had worked cases in big cities. Milwaukee for one. The challenge was to get a feel for the area, especially the transportation, which would be a key to the success of his plan. Planes, trains, and automobiles were all in the picture. Boats, too, maybe.

All six law enforcement officers convened in a conference room at the SPPD. He gave them an outline of his plan. Coleman had met Wilkerson on two occasions so he would have to stay behind the scenes and give direction. Officer Clancy had an idea for keeping watch over the Wilkerson estate. The three locals were assigned to the job of gumshoeing Wilkerson; that is, if everything worked according to plan.

A main component of the scheme would inevitably include the cooperation of Emma Zigler at the cleaners. Coleman was headed her way.

Zigler's Cleaners was a family business and had been in operation for over thirty years. The founders of the business (who were currently out west in their RV at a location unknown) had selected a strategic location, less than a block from the train station that transported thousands of commuters monthly into the Loop, the main business area in downtown Chicago. Drop your slacks and shirts on the way to the train in the morning; pick them up on the way home.

The location also proved beneficial for the detective from the Badger State. His homework on Wilkerson indicated that he had ridden the train into the city for the last three decades. If he took the bait (and the train), Detectives O'Hearn and Gardner would become North Shore commuters for the day. Carlos, Spurlock, and Coleman would travel by car.

Coleman brought Officer Clancy with him to visit Emma Zigler at the cleaners. The young woman would be more relaxed with a local officer present. Emma was waiting for them, eager to help in what would be her first involvement in a murder case. It was a little after 7:00 p.m. and the cleaners was shutting down for the day. Before Coleman was able to share his plan, Emma initiated the conversation.

"I need to tell you something. About fifteen minutes ago, Shane got a call from Mr. Wilkerson asking about his jacket."

"Wait a minute. Who is Shane?" interrupted Coleman.

"He works here. He's still up front closing out the register. I told him to stick around, thinking you probably would want to talk to him." She'd thought correctly. "Anyway, he was wanting to know if his jacket was ready to pick up. Shane looked it up and saw that it was at repair and would not be ready until tomorrow after 3:00 p.m. He asked who did the repair and he gave him the name and number of our repair lady. Said he was rather pushy about finding his jacket. Something about leaving a credit card in one of the pockets. I've already checked the notations on the order. Nothing was in any of the pockets."

Wilkerson's call to the cleaners spiked Coleman's confidence meter. He got the contact information for the elderly Mrs. Biondi and gave her a call. No answer. He then called Spurlock and had him put Tara Gardner on the phone.

"I have a feeling Wilkerson or someone at his direction is headed for Highwood to retrieve the jacket. Are you okay going up there to check things out?"

"Absolutely," she replied. "They don't have any local cops, so Lake County gives them coverage. I'll keep you posted along the way."

"Take one of the warm bodies there to ride shotgun."

She chose the State Agent Carlos.

Back to Emma Zigler.

"Sometime tomorrow morning, at my direction, I want you to call Mr. Wilkerson and tell him that his jacket arrived early and can be picked up at his convenience. Hopefully, he will pick it up with the other items shortly after the call. Put the jacket in the same plastic bag as the blouses. Put the slacks in a separate bag and then a final bag around the whole set of clothes. Just treat it like any other transaction. We'll pick him up when he leaves. Got it?"

"You bet."

"You have my number, so if anything happens that you think I should know about, give me a call but only after he leaves the store and is out of sight. I'll be here when you make the call so if there is any change, I can fill you in then. Any questions?

"No, I think I got it."

"Awesome, Emma. You'll be fine. I can't thank you enough."

"Oh, you're welcome, Officer Coleman. Glad I can help."

Coleman talked to Shane, the employee who had spoken with Wilkerson. He indicated that the Baron had been polite in asking about his garment until Shane balked on giving him the name of Rosa Biondi. He'd then pulled rank, telling the young lad that he was an attorney and if anyone used the credit card that he thought was in the jacket, he would hold him responsible in a court of law. *Whoa, Hal. And to make sure you win the lawsuit, you could bribe the jurors.*

Shane had caved in, as any eighteen-year-old would under the circumstances, and gave Wilkerson Rosa's name and phone number. He didn't have her address. That would be no problem in today's Google world. Seriously, how many Rosa Biondis are there in Highwood, Illinois? Coleman and Clancy left the dry cleaners and were headed back to the station by foot when a call came in from Detective Gardner. She was in Highwood talking to Marco Biondi, Rosa's oldest grandson.

Marco Biondi was seventeen years old and had just completed his junior year at Carmel High School, a private parochial school in the northern suburbs of Chicago. He was a good student and an accomplished soccer player on his school's varsity team. When soccer was not in season, he helped his grandmother out with her modest clothing repair business. During summer vacation, he made the rounds of the local dry cleaners and picked up the items that needed repair and delivered them to Rosa at her home in Highwood. While there, he picked up the items that had been altered or repaired for delivery back to the stores the next day.

Marco was Rosa's oldest grandchild. They had a special bond. They typically had a short visit each night during the delivery routine. She often made a fresh batch of cannoli for him to take home to his family. Tonight, Rosa had sensed something was troubling her *nipote*.

"*Che c'e'*, Marco?"

Normally very talkative, Marco made no response. Rosa persisted.

"It's my girlfriend, Claire. She called me last night. She wants to break up." He put his head down. She put her hand on his shoulder. In a while, he lifted up, revealing his red, teary eyes. She gave him a hug. "*Cuore spezzato.*"

Marco was able to open up to his grandmother. She was touched that he could confide in her. She listened to his heartbreak and comforted him when the need arose. Their intimate interchange was halted by a sharp rap on the door. Marco responded.

As he approached the door, he noticed through the living room window a black Mercedes sedan parked on the street that was not there when he'd arrived a half hour ago. It made an interesting contrast with his old, beat up, light blue Volkswagen bug.

The man at the door was in his sixties, well-groomed and dressed casually in a pair of neatly pressed khakis and a blue oxford shirt. He wore shiny cordovan penny loafers. As Marco would tell Detective Gardner, "He wore a blue shirt, but he definitely was not blue collar."

"May I help you?"

"Hello. I was wondering if this is the home of Rosa Biondi."

"Yes, it is," Marco responded through the screen door.

"May I have a word with her please? It's very important."

"She's retired for the evening." That was a lie. But a protective one. "Perhaps I can help you. I am her grandson."

"I believe she has a jacket of mine that she is repairing for Zigler's Cleaners in Sycamore Pointe. I think I may have left a credit card in one of the pockets. I need to check."

"Hold on. What did you say your name is?" He hadn't.

"Wilkerson."

"Stay here. I'll check." Marco went to the kitchen where he and Rosa had been talking prior to the interruption. He had placed the clothing pickups for that day on a cabinet knob. He easily found the repaired jacket with the Wilkerson tag and carefully checked the pockets. They were empty, of course. Plus, Emma at Zigler's would have found it. *What's the deal with this guy driving up here at 7:30 at night to look for a credit card?* Marco's intuition kicked into gear.

He went back to the door.

"I found the jacket. Pockets are all empty. You probably should check with Zigler's in the morning. They would have kept anything that had been accidentally left."

Wilkerson paused, contemplating his response. "Well then, I'm wondering if I could just pick up the jacket now. I'll pay your grandmother and the cleaning fee all at once."

"I'm afraid that's not going to work, sir."

"Why not? I can make it worth your while with an extra twenty." He opened his wallet.

"That's very generous but I can't do it. I'd have to wake up my Grandma. She's in her late eighties." Okay. A slight exaggeration. "She would say 'no' anyway. Because then she would have to call Emma at the cleaners, who would have to call her aunt and uncle who own the place. And if anything happened to the jacket, she could not live with herself. So really, Mr. Wilkerson, it's not going to happen. You can pick it up tomorrow at Zigler's. After three."

Wilkerson put the twenty back in his wallet and gave Marco a disgusted glare as he walked back to his car.

Marco gave him a parting shot. "Nice ride. *Ciao.*"

After Gardner's briefing, Coleman spoke directly to Marco. He gave him as much information as he could about the case to persuade him to give the jacket up to the officers who were present. Apparently, they'd arrived within minutes of Wilkerson leaving. During the conversation, Marco related the procedure that his grandmother used when she received an item for repair or alteration, including the photography step. He sent him a picture in a text. There it was. The back of the jacket, the Golden Fleece, the tear, and the tag bearing the name *Wilkerson*. In the future, "PEOPLE'S EXHIBIT #1." He thanked the young soccer player who may have saved the day.

The internal light in Coleman's lantern had just become considerably brighter.

Coleman had no sooner ended his call with Marco Biondi when his phone illuminated with the number of Gregory Wallace, Sheriff of Pinesap County. The recent spike in his confidence was about to be dulled.

"Hello, Sheriff. What's up?"

"Agent Coleman. This is Sheriff Wallace. I have some news to pass along."

"Okay. What is it?"

"Well, this afternoon an old buddy of mine came to my office and wanted to speak to me. I was out at the time, checking on some junk cars that the judge had ordered be removed from a property. Some zoning violations. Seems like we've been after this guy for years to clean it up. Anyway, I got back to the office around 5:15 or so, and this guy is still here. He doesn't want to talk to anyone but me. He wants to speak privately and 'not on the record'."

"Go ahead, Sheriff. What does he say?" Coleman was reaching the perturbed level with Little Wally more quickly than usual.

"So, he tells me about a week ago, he's at a rest stop and boat landing south of town on Spider Lake. He sees this white pickup pull in and the driver gets out and throws something as far as he can into the middle of the lake. He couldn't see what the object was. But he thought it was fairly heavy because of the clunk it made when it hit the water. And it didn't float. After this, the driver dropped to his knees and put his hands to his face as if he were crying or something. He stayed there for about a minute and then got back into his truck and drove away going south. He said the truck had Illinois plates. That same day, he leaves for vacation to Mount Rushmore in his camper. He got back last night and heard about the murder for the first time. Thought there might be a connection."

Indeed, thought Coleman as his enthusiasm plummeted. *Wake up,* he told himself. *You've put all your eggs in one basket—or, in this case, one jacket. You don't want it to be the father, Josh Wright. It has shaded your judgment and objectivity. So what if Wilkerson made a big deal about finding his jacket to retrieve his credit card? Maybe he thought he had left one in the pocket. He's getting up there in years and doesn't want some thief maxing it out on a year full of booze and tattoos. What a wonderful argument to make before a jury, especially to the seniors. You're only seeing what you want to see.*

He knew the answer to the next question before he asked it. "Does he know what day it was?"

"Yes. He's pretty sure it was the morning of June 4 because that was the first day of his vacation. Around 7:00 a.m."

"Who is this guy? And what was he doing at a boat landing at seven in the morning on the day he's leaving for vacation?"

"Well, that's where it gets kinda tricky."

"What do you mean, 'kinda tricky'?" asked Coleman.

"Ah, well . . . this rest stop has a really pretty view of the lake. It's very secluded from the road and, well, he was out there with his girlfriend and they were out there in his truck and well, ah . . . they were um . . ."

"Fucking! Is that it, Wally? They were fucking, weren't they? Go ahead, Wally, you can say it." Coleman had totally lost his filter.

"Yes."

"Well, terrific. What does it matter? Did it affect his vision?"

"No, I don't think so. I didn't ask. But this is why he wanted it 'off the record.' They're both married. But not to each other."

Coleman let that sink in. How would that fact play out before a jury, should this cheater become a witness for the State?

"*So, what were you doing at seven in the morning at this romantic rest stop in your pickup truck?*"

"*I was having sex with my girlfriend.*"

"*And what did you do later in the day around noon?*"

"*Left for Mount Rushmore with the wife and kids.*"

"*So, you mounted your girlfriend and then a few hours later you left for the Mount? No further questions, Your Honor.*"

"Okay. I give up, Wally, who is this guy? Some old fishing buddy?"

There was a pause. "Well, we used to go fishing when we were kids. But not much anymore."

It was Coleman's turn to pause. "Sheriff, what is his name?" The teapot was about to whistle.

"His name is Keg. Keg Wallace. He's my first cousin."

Coleman was literally shaking his head. The day was getting worse at rapid-fire speed.

"So, did you record his statement?"

"Well, I didn't really because I wanted to check with you first about this 'off the record' stuff and everything."

Bennett Coleman was now summoning all the self-control he could muster before he verbally lashed out at this person who imitated, albeit poorly, a law enforcement officer. It was not enough. He couldn't hold back. The dam broke.

"Sheriff Fucking Wallace. This is a murder case. Not a zoning violation. Your cousin Keg is a potential eyewitness to the behavior of someone who may have just committed a murder. I don't care if he was getting it on with the whole Oneida Falls ski club, he's a fucking eyewitness. And by the way, nothing is ever off the record. The air is out of the balloon. It can't be put back in. You can't unhear what he told you. Now get his ass back in and have everything put on tape. Tonight. And tell him when I get back, I will review the tape and pick up where your incompetent ass left off. And another thing. Call my office in Wausau first thing in the morning and have them contact the diving team we use. And when they arrive, have your cheating cousin, to the best of his ability, point out where the thing went 'clunk.' You might want to tell them that it's probably some kind of weapon. Do you understand?"

"Yes."

Click.

Officer Clancy had heard the entire conversation. He didn't know whether to laugh or keep his mouth shut. Coleman sensed his indecision and said, "It's okay. You can let it out." At which point Clancy guffawed and Coleman just shook his head and smiled. Wait until he told Spurlock.

The six cops met back at the police station late evening to go over the plan for the following day. Everyone was given their assignments. They were to meet in the morning at 7:00 a.m. sharp. O'Hearn had gotten the information on Josh Wright's credit card activity. He had used it at a gas station and restaurant before checking in at Redd's Lakeview Motel. He'd also blown through two toll booths before leaving Illinois. Pictures were on their way. Coleman was not surprised. It added to his exhaustion and sinking attitude.

While leaving the station, Coleman was handed a package previously delivered by special courier. Roland at Brooks Brothers had come through.

He and Spurlock went to their hotel ten minutes away. Tomorrow would be huge. Coleman hoped he could sleep. One could always hope.

CHAPTER TWENTY-SEVEN

Coleman got to his hotel room around 11:00 p.m. Another long day on minimal sleep. His outburst at Sheriff Wallace was a clear indication that the stress of the investigation and lack of rest was taking its toll. He knew he would, and indeed should, apologize. He sent him an email.

> Sheriff Wallace,
>
> I want to apologize for losing my temper at you earlier this evening. It was uncalled for and inexcusable. You have been a great help to me during this investigation and in no way were you deserving of that verbal abuse. I am genuinely sorry.
>
> Agent Bennett Coleman

In his next election, Sheriff Wallace would make much of the words "You have been a great help to me in this investigation." They would be repeated ad nauseum at campaign rallies.

Deep down inside, Coleman was a softie. He actually despised the macho-type cop and rarely adopted that persona. He knew he could catch more flies with honey than with vinegar.

He set his alarm for 5:30 a.m., fully aware his awakening would occur considerably sooner. He had obtained some Chicago maps at the police station and began studying them. The process was overwhelming. He decided to concentrate on the main routes, expressways, major arteries in the city, and, most importantly, the train lines. Wilkerson had spent years using public transportation, including suburban commuter trains and the CTA (Chicago Transit Authority) which operated the iconic "L."

There was also the possibility that if Wilkerson took the bait, he would turn around, evidence in hand, and go home. Probably not, though, as wife Beatrice would be there. She would undoubtedly ask about the jacket to see if the repair was done correctly. In either event, contingency plans were in effect.

With the nightstand lamp still burning and his Chicago CTA map turned to stops on the Red Line, Coleman finally passed out. It was 12:45 a.m. About three hours later, he awoke, disoriented as to time and place. He threw on some jeans and a t-shirt and hobbled down to the lobby hoping to find a source of coffee. The hotel clerk looked up from his *People* magazine, indicating that the coffee wouldn't get brewed until 6:00 a.m. "An all-night diner is two blocks away," the clerk grunted.

The clock on the wall said 4:07. *What the hell*, thought Coleman, *I'm not going back to sleep*. He set out seeking his first dose of caffeine for the day.

Twenty minutes later, Coleman was back in his room with forty ounces of black coffee. He settled in at the desk, pen and paper in hand. Time to crystallize the game plan and lineup for the day.

First of all, there had to be a set of eyes on the Wilkerson mansion. Officer Clancy had told Coleman the previous day that a patrol car would typically monitor speed on Sheridan Road during the morning rush hour. There was a location on the shoulder of the road that would allow full view of all comings and goings at the Wilkersons' place without arousing suspicion. Clancy would man the patrol car.

The previous day Coleman had called John Weatherton, his forensic colleague in Wausau. Fortunately, he was not on the golf course. He needed a still photograph of the Cadillac SUV owned by the Mastersons parked in front of the Wilkerson cabin. They had viewed it on the video. It arrived ten minutes later and was currently at the Sycamore Pointe Police Department. The photo would lure Beatrice Wilkerson out of her house. A desk man on the morning shift would make the call. Coleman just knew she would show up.

Provided Bea left her home, the next call would go to the Baron. It would be placed by Emma at Zigler's Cleaners, and she would tell him that the cleaning order had come in early and could be picked up anytime. Given his urgency and desperation to retrieve the jacket, exemplified by his trip to the Biondi residence the previous evening, he should bolt out of his Sheridan Road castle like a sprinter out of the blocks. At least that was Coleman's prediction.

Officer Clancy would keep everyone apprised of the Wilkerson traffic on Sheridan Road.

Assuming Harold picked up his items at the cleaners, jacket included, the remainder of the day would be spent keeping track of him and the key piece of evidence in his possession. A total of five cops would be on the surveillance team. Two from Wisconsin, Coleman and Spurlock. One from the CPD, O'Hearn; one from the Lake County Sheriff, Gardner; and one from the Illinois State Police, Carlos. All would wear body cams, covertly placed and operable. All cell phones fully charged. Some would be dressed casually, some with suits, some disheveled. Hopefully, none of them would look like cops.

Upon completing his notes, Coleman showered and put on his uniform of the day. It consisted of jeans, a blue-and-white striped polo shirt, sunglasses, and a Chicago Cubs ball cap that had been borrowed from one of the officers. He was actually a Milwaukee Brewers fan, but the last thing he wanted to do was drop a clue that he was from Wisconsin. Especially to the parents of the deceased.

Upon leaving his room, his phone lit up. Not recognizing the number, he ignored it. The phone rang again. Same number.

"Coleman."

"Is this Detective Bennett with the Wisconsin Bureau of Investigation?"

"It is. Who's calling?"

"Sir, my name is Renee Jablonski, and I work in the news bureau of the *Wausau Daily Herald*. Late last night, our paper received a faxed message from a Kinko's store in Chicago containing a rather interesting message." Renee proceeded to relay the information anonymously sent by Cubs fan Michael Duff the previous evening. Coleman shook his head and whispered to himself, "I can't deal with this right now."

"Renee, thank you for the call. Please do me a favor. Take a snapshot of the document that your paper received and send it to the phone number you just reached me on. Also include the number of the Kinko's store. Can you do that?"

"For sure. You'll have it in the next five minutes."

"Thank you."

He proceeded to the lobby and met Spurlock. He told him about the phone call and directed him get ahold of Weatherton when he had a chance. They helped themselves to some freshly brewed java and left for what would prove to be a most interesting and adventurous day.

Coleman dropped Spurlock off at the train station and headed for Zigler's to meet with Emma. He handed her the package that had been delivered to him the previous evening. She knew what to do with it.

They went over the plan. Coleman would give her the signal when to call the Wilkerson house. If he showed up, she was just to handle it like any other routine transaction. Once he left, her job was over. Emma had no questions. She was looking forward to it.

Back to the station and a final meeting with the assembled law enforcement officers. The Chicago detective O'Hearn and Lake County officer Gardner were the most knowledgeable about Chicago's transportation system, especially the railways. Both had purchased tickets for the commuter train ride into the city in the event that it was the route that Wilkerson chose.

State detective Randal Carlos and Spurlock were in a vehicle prepared to follow Wilkerson if he opted to drive. Coleman would eventually occupy a separate car being driven by retired Sycamore Pointe police officer Paul Riley. He had grown up in the city and was accustomed to negotiating Chicago traffic. Clancy was on Sheridan Road monitoring the mansion.

Officer Russell was manning the desk at the Sycamore Pointe police station. Coleman had briefed him on the set up to induce Beatrice to come to the station. He was right next to him when he called.

"Hello." It was Beatrice who answered.

"Is this Mrs. Wilkerson?"

"Yes, it is. Who's calling?"

"Ma'am, this is Officer Russell at the Sycamore Pointe Police Department. I've just gotten off the phone with an Agent Bennett Coleman in Wisconsin. I believe he is investigating your son's death. Do you know him, ma'am?"

She sighed. "Yes. I do."

"Well, Mr. Coleman has sent me a picture of a vehicle parked outside your cabin in Wisconsin. He was wondering if you could look at the photo to see if you recognized it. He sounded like it was pretty important."

"Well, I suppose I can. When will you be stopping by to show it to me?"

"Well, ma'am, I'm afraid I can't do that. I'm the only one manning the office at the present. I'm unable to leave. I was wondering if you could just come to the station. It won't take but a second. I know Agent Coleman would appreciate it."

There was hesitation. She put the phone down. Both Russell and Coleman could hear the ensuing conversation.

"Hal. It's the police station. They've got some photo from up north that they want me to look at. Is it okay for me to do that? Or do you want to go?"

Coleman was wincing. He could hear Hal faintly reply. "No, that's okay, Bea. You can go. If it's something important, I'll catch up on it later." Hal was drinking his morning coffee and working a crossword puzzle. Coleman exhaled. Bea went back to the duty cop.

"Okay, officer. I'll come down. Give me fifteen minutes."

"Thank you, ma'am."

Coleman gave Russell a high five. He texted all the other officers the good news. Told Clancy to be on the lookout. Twenty minutes later, Clancy called Coleman, informing him that Beatrice had just left her house. She was driving a white Mercedes 450 SL. It was about a five-minute drive to the police station.

Coleman immediately left the station and headed for the dry cleaners. Emma was waiting for him. The store was busy and Shane hadn't arrived yet. She looked a little panicked. He told her it was time to make the call. The customer line was growing.

"Go to the back and make the call. I'll handle the crowd." She left as directed.

He addressed the impatient customers. "Folks, bear with us. I'm an uncle of Emma's. There was a bit of an emergency with one of her relatives and she has to make a few phone calls. She shouldn't be more than a few minutes. Thank you for your patience."

He then headed to the back room as Emma dialed the Wilkerson number. There was no answer. She left a message. "Hi, this Emma from the cleaners. Your order came back early from repair. You can pick it up any time. Thanks. Bye." That wasn't good enough for Coleman. Wilkerson might not check the messages. Bea would do it when she got back, and it would screw up the plan.

"Okay, look, Emma. I've got Mr. Wilkerson's cell phone number. I want you to call him on that. Same routine. If he asks you how you got his number, just say, 'I don't know. It was on the order slip.' Are you good with that?"

"I guess but look at the crowd out there." The words were no sooner out of her mouth when Shane busted through the back door and said "sorry" and headed straight to the counter. That eased Emma. She took a deep breath and dialed the number. It was answered after three rings.

"Hal Wilkerson here."

"Mr. Wilkerson, this is Emma at Zigler's Dry Cleaners. The item that had to be sent out for repair—it was a jacket, I believe—came back first thing this morning. So, you can pick it up at your convenience. You don't have to wait until three."

"Well, what a nice surprise and how good of you to call. By the way, how did you have my number? I don't believe I've ever given it to your uncle."

"Mr. Wilkerson. I really don't know. I didn't do the intake on this, but it was on the order slip. As well as your home number. I called that first and left a message."

"I see. Well, thank you again. "

"You're welcome, sir."

She hung up and Coleman gave her a big smile. "By the way, if anyone asks, I'm your other uncle and you had an emergency to take care of. You did a great job."

"Thanks, Uncle Coleman."

As Coleman departed the cleaners, he saw the white Mercedes headed to the station a couple of blocks away. He pulled the brim of his Cubs cap down a skosh and sent a group text to his colleagues. "The Baron has been informed that his jacket is ready for pickup."

Harold Wilkerson put down his pencil and puzzle and took a last sip from his coffee. Apparently, the little confrontation with young Marco Biondi the previous evening had hastened the delivery of the inculpatory piece of clothing. Like Coleman, the Baron had mapped out a plan and its execution had just been accelerated; and that should work to his benefit, or so he thought.

He left a terse note for his wife: "B- Headed to the city to meet with my lawyers. Should be back for dinner. H."

He grabbed his briefcase, shoved the unfinished crossword puzzle in it, and headed to the garage for his trip to the cleaners. Officer Clancy saw him leave and offered the friendly police-officer wave. It was not lost on Wilkerson. His strategy assumed that he was being surveilled. Coleman's thinking was the same. He, too, assumed that that the sly Loop lawyer was aware that all eyes were on him. Hopefully, he would remain unaware as to whom those eyes belonged.

Clancy immediately sent a text to his teammates. Coleman's heart rate elevated as he read it. In a couple minutes, it would experience another uptick, as he saw the black Mercedes sedan pull into one of the parking lots reserved for commuters travelling south to the Loop. Mrs. Wilkerson was two blocks away, having responded to Officer Russell's request.

"I have no idea who owns that car," she said as she looked at the photo of the Cadillac SUV owned by the Masterson insurance mogul of the Northwoods. "I've never seen it before. What the hell is this Coleman guy doing up there? This case should have been solved a week ago. The culprit lives somewhere on the north side of Chicago. They should be down here looking for him." *How ominous of you to say so, Mrs. Wilkerson.*

As Beatrice Wilkerson was bickering with Officer Russell, her husband entered Zigler's Dry Cleaners a couple of blocks away. The crowd had thinned out. Emma greeted Harold, who identified himself and apologized for not having the claim ticket. She politely told him, "No problem," reminding him that they had talked on the phone within the last ten minutes. The clothes had been arranged per Agent Coleman's previous instructions. She hung them on a bar and gave Wilkerson change for his fifty. He inspected the cluster of clothes, assuring himself that the Golden Fleece jacket was present.

"Would you like a receipt with that, sir?"

"No. That won't be necessary. Thank you."

Not for him perhaps. But she would hold on to it, momentarily handing it off to the Wisconsin detective Brian Spurlock who, unknown to the Baron, was next in line at the cleaners. The entire transaction had been recorded.

An hour later, Mrs. Wilkerson, having listened to the original message left by Emma, showed up at the cleaners to claim the clothes. She was informed, of course, that her husband had already picked them up. She thought that was rather strange. Hal never engaged in such routine chores. Never.

A lightbulb had finally gone off in Coleman's head. He had positioned himself so that he could observe Wilkerson leaving the dry cleaners and heading to his car in the train parking lot. It was the walk. It was that same walk of the man dressed in all black at Gresham Gathering that he had seen in the video two nights previously. Tall, erect, deliberate, purposeful. The walk of a Baron. Coleman's confidence buoyed, as did his pulse rate.

With the dry-cleaned items slung over his shoulder, he went back to his car and retrieved his briefcase. For a moment, it looked as if he were leaving all the clothes in the car. As it turned out, he was just lightening his load by leaving two blouses. The jacket and two pairs of slacks remained. From the parking lot, he went to the platform to await the 9:09 train to the city. Detectives O'Hearn and Gardner occupied the same platform along with about fifteen other commuters.

In Chicago, there were two basic rail services. One was a suburban commuter line called The Metra. The other was the CTA. Wilkerson was about to board the Metra North Line, which originated in Kenosha, Wisconsin and had as its final destination the Ogilvie Transportation Center in downtown Chicago, named for one of the rare Illinois governors who'd avoided prison. The cars were double decker, and the first level contained seats that could easily accommodate two people. The upper level had individual seating after climbing a short set of winding steps. Some riders preferred the upper deck, as it allowed for more privacy. On this day, that was Wilkerson's choice.

O'Hearn, dressed in a business suit, sat in the lower deck, which allowed his peripheral version to keep track of today's commuter of interest. Gardner was also downstairs and had a similar view of Wilkerson, albeit from a different angle. She wore jeans, a sleeveless white blouse, and a red Blackhawks cap. She was reading the latest issue of *Time*.

If Hal exited the train prior to the depot, Gardner would get off at the same stop and O'Hearn would stay on the train. That did not occur. All three exited at the Ogilvie Center. Things would begin to get a little bit dicey from there.

First of all, there were lots of people exiting their trains from the sixteen sets of tracks. There were also riders boarding trains headed out of the city. All of which created a high density of pedestrians and made following just one a daunting task.

Fortunately, Wilkerson was tall, so he stood out. And he appeared to be the only person with dry cleaning slung over his shoulder.

He turned left out of the Ogilvie Center onto Madison Street. He was heading east when he took another quick left just before the Madison Street bridge, which crossed the south branch of the Chicago River. He quickly descended the steps leading to the river, where a Chicago water taxi was waiting. Gardner followed.

Detective O'Hearn, however, was unable to keep up, having been enmeshed in a wave of humanity landing him on the other side of the bridge. He stopped and could see Wilkerson board one of the taxis that read "Goose Island." Having purchased a ticket in advance, he easily boarded the vessel by merely showing his phone. O'Hearn texted Gardner to get on the boat, but it was too late. The line to buy a ticket was lengthy. And Gardner did not want to pull rank by flashing her badge. It would have alerted the mark.

There were no contingencies in Coleman's plan for a water taxi diversion. Fortunately for the team, the ISP detective, Randal Carlos, was well acquainted with the Goose Island stop. He had just been there with his wife and young children about a month before. He was about a mile away in lunch hour traffic on the north side. Spurlock was with him. It was going to be close.

Gardner took the next water taxi to Goose Island. She was about ten minutes behind Wilkerson. O'Hearn flagged the first patrol car he saw, flashed his detective's badge, and directed the uniformed officer to head to the Goose Island taxi stop.

Coleman and his driver Paul Riley were cruising the north side in the Lakeview neighborhood, home of Wrigley Field. The Cubs were not in town, a benefit that resulted in considerably lighter traffic.

It was nearing 12:30 p.m. when Hal's water taxi reached its destination at Goose Island. He was getting hungry. Confident he had eluded any of his pursuers on the train, he ordered an Uber. He knew a great bar in the Southport area where he could enjoy lunch. It was also close to a Brown Line CTA stop. His plan was still well intact.

He climbed the steps leading from the docking area on North Avenue and waited for his ride. It was a late model Honda Civic, silver in color. He entered using the rear passenger side door. The plastic covering over the jacket and slacks caught a gust of wind, almost causing Wilkerson to lose control of the valuable property. He grabbed it with his left hand and forced it into the interior of the vehicle. Southport Lanes was his destination, address 3325 North Southport.

So, let's see here. He was going west on North Avenue headed to a location on north Southport. And the bar was on the east side of the street. No wonder people got confused when travelling around the Windy City.

"There he is!" yelled Spurlock. He and Carlos were headed in the opposite direction when the Northwoods cop caught sight of the flapping plastic being shoved inside the silver Honda. Carlos did an immediate U-turn, narrowly avoiding a head-on collision with a car headed west, causing the driver to throttle up to a level-five road rage. Sitting in the back seat of his Uber ride, Wilkerson was oblivious to the commotion behind him. He heard lots of honking horns and tires screeching. Routine background noises in the city. No reason to turn around. By contrast, Spurlock felt like he was on a roller coaster ride. He was enjoying every minute of it.

Spurlock alerted everyone that they were back on point with the Baron. They were two cars behind the Honda but not in a position to determine a license plate number. O'Hearn was about a half mile away in the marked squad car with two uniformed police. Not close, given the time it took to navigate during lunch-time city traffic. However, he had the advantage to alert other patrol cars in the area by radio, which is exactly what he did.

They got a positive hit from Officer Shannon at the intersection of North Avenue and Ashland. The Uber Honda had just turned north onto Ashland as the light turned red. Carlos and Spurlock were left waiting at the light, unable to pursue their prey. Officer Shannon took up the pursuit in his marked car, keeping everyone alert as to the location of Mr. Wilkerson and his dry cleaning.

Traffic was heavy on Ashland but moving at a fairly even clip. Shannon's patrol car was two behind the Honda, strategically a favorable position so as not to alarm the driver of the Honda or his passenger. Nobody, even innocent people, liked to be tailed by a cop.

The Honda reached Belmont Avenue, a main east-west artery, and turned left just as the light turned red. Officer Shannon, still two cars behind, had to make a snap decision. It turned out to be the correct one. He gave a short burst to his siren and turned on his red flashing overheads. All east-west traffic came to an abrupt halt as Shannon pulled out of his lane of traffic and negotiated the left turn onto Belmont, regaining visibility of the Uber vehicle a short city block ahead. He immediately turned his overheads off.

The driver of the Uber was Luiz Santana. He was from Mexico and his green card had expired six months earlier. He had seen the maneuver of the Chicago cop in his rearview mirror but said nothing. Although Chicago was a sanctuary city, his fear of deportation had skyrocketed since 2016. *Surely, I won't be stopped for the red-light violation*, he thought. And he was correct.

In a matter of minutes, Wilkerson was delivered to 3325 North Southport, the home of Southport Lanes. Shannon's patrol car drove by the Honda as he gave all interested parties the Baron's new location.

Southport Lanes used to be known as The Nook, having been established in the early 1900s by the Schlitz Brewing Company, back in the day when brewers could own taverns. The giant Schlitz Globe logo still emblazoned the façade of the bar.

During Prohibition, it had been a speakeasy and its name was changed to its current one. Legend (more likely historical fact) had it that the activity inside the bar also changed. In addition to the alcohol that flowed upon giving the correct password, prostitution and illegal gambling took hold. An early mayor of Chicago, Anton Cermak, was said to have had a weekly poker game in one of the secret rooms of the establishment.

Over the years, the building had been renovated without losing the feel and vibe of the past. And it still had a bowling alley. Four beautiful lanes adorned by a beautiful, classic Schlitz mural and, best of all, human pin setters. No automatic machines. Old school at its best.

During favorable weather, meals were served outside. Wilkerson waited for an outside table to become available and when it did, he ordered a burger and a pint of Schlitz. He removed the crossword from his briefcase and draped his slacks and jacket on the vacant chair opposite him.

The place was abuzz with yuppies having an extended lunch hour and young moms walking by with strollers, the infants inside getting their first taste of street life in the big city. The windows to the bar were open, allowing jukebox music to fill the air as well as the unmistakable sounds of bowling balls crushing pins and billiards balls whacking each other.

Harold's lunch break allowed the cops to regroup.

After her water taxi ride to Goose Island, Gardner rented a blue Divvy bike, typically used by tourists wanting to experience the city sights from a more intimate vantage point. It gave her greater flexibility and maneuverability in the traffic. She pedaled enthusiastically, arriving at Southport Lanes about fifteen minutes after Wilkerson was seated. She had exchanged her Blackhawks cap for one with a Cubs logo (Wrigley Field was a mere five blocks away) and breezed by the "Lanes," where she saw Harold munching on his burger while finishing his crossword puzzle and taking intermittent sips on his Schlitz. She blended in perfectly.

Meanwhile, ISP Carlos and Spurlock had brought themselves up to speed in their pursuit of Wilkerson. Carlos double-parked his vehicle at the entrance to the Southport CTA station, went to the lobby, and bought two five-ride passes. He came back to the car and handed one to Spurlock, asking him if he had ever ridden on the "L." Of course, he hadn't.

"Why?" he asked Carlos.

"Well, I have a pretty good feeling that within the next half hour or so, we're going to be taking a ride on the Brown Line. We'll either board here or at the Addison station about four blocks north of here. Just stick with me and do what I do and act like a dumb out-of-towner."

"Trust me, Randal. It won't be an act."

Carlos decided to park his car midway between the two stations. He found a place on Cornelia Street about a block from the former speakeasy where Wilkerson was lunching. He and Spurlock walked to the bar area and each ordered a beer. Spurlock was impressed. Drinking on the job. Fitting in. Carlos texted their new location to Coleman and the rest of the crew.

O'Hearn decided he was better off cruising in the marked squad car. He was currently parked about a block from the Addison CTA stop, a potential boarding option for Harold.

And that left Coleman and his chauffeur, Paul Riley. When Coleman got the text from Carlos, they were driving west on Addison along the south side of Wrigley Field. He asked Riley how far they were from 4825 North Ravenswood.

"Not far," Riley replied. "Why?"

"Take me there." There was a sense of urgency in his voice.

Bennett Coleman was destined to become an investigator. As a child, he'd always been asking where things came from, how things worked, with the most-used inquiry being *why*. He was a "why" child. Drove his parents nuts.

He was now fifty-seven years old and he was still asking "Why?" What was the motivation behind someone's behavior? Why was Harold Wilkerson leading all these cops on a wild goose chase carrying around two pairs of slacks and a black hunting jacket in a plastic covering? Why not just ditch the items in the nearest Dumpster? Or take them home and burn them in one of your three fireplaces? Coleman settled on this as an answer to his own self inquiries. Wilkerson did not want to destroy the jacket. He wanted to permanently relinquish it and, at the same time, further implicate the number one suspect in the case, Joshua Wright.

"How far is 'not far'?" Coleman asked Riley.

"My guess is that he'll get on at the Southport station. From there he can be at that address in about fifteen minutes. Probably the Montrose stop. Could be longer depending how long he has to wait for the train."

Coleman texted everyone with his prediction.

Riley directed his car north on Ashland Avenue. It wouldn't take long to reach the neighborhood in Chicago known as Ravenswood, so named by the developers a century and a half ago because of the vibrant population of ravens that had inhabited the then-wooded area of the city. The neighborhood had long been known for its many three-story courtyard apartment buildings. Joshua Wright, his wife Amaya, and their two children Hope and Will lived on the second floor of one at 4825 North Ravenswood.

Coleman didn't have much time. If he was correct in his thinking, Wilkerson could be there within the hour. Riley let him out in front of the apartment building, the grounds of which were well maintained. Professionally trimmed shrubbery, ornamental trees, well-defined flower beds, and a beautiful lawn void of weeds. He entered the foyer of the building and found the number for the Wrights' apartment. 2B. He rang the buzzer. As expected, there was no answer.

He then walked to the alley behind the apartment. There were garages all in a row, four units to each with corresponding apartment numbers clearly marked above each door. Outside garage number 2B was an oversized garbage can with the same number conspicuously painted on both the lid and body of the disposal container.

The garage and garbage area were midway between Montrose Avenue to the south and Sunnyside Street to the north. Montrose had lots of commercial traffic; Sunnyside not so much, being mostly residential. Coleman studied the scene from every angle. The previous evening, the same scene had been studied on Google Earth by the man who was having a solitary lunch at Southport Lanes. He'd just asked for the check.

Whether by design or not, Carlos and Spurlock finished their beers as Wilkerson was leaving a tip for his server. He left his newspaper at the table, picked up his dry-cleaned items, and headed south along the sidewalk that ran parallel to the outside tables at the vintage bar. He was two-and-a-half blocks from the Southport CTA station. The two cops exited the bar and followed him from a distance of half a block. The pedestrian traffic was heavy, which allowed the tail to be accomplished without detection.

Within minutes, Wilkerson entered the station, scanned his CTA pass, and headed for the set of stairs clearly marked with the words "To Kimball." The Kimball Station was the last stop to the northwest on the Brown Line, formerly known as the "Ravenswood" prior to the CTA color coding their routes. The two cops followed suit, Carlos going first with Spurlock at his heels. The Badger was going on his first "L" ride in pursuit of a murder suspect. He was struggling to hide his excitement.

There were seven people on the platform waiting for the next train, scheduled to arrive in four minutes. Wilkerson, the two cops, three women who had been partying it up at one of the local watering holes on Southport, and Robert Swiderski.

Randal Carlos, the ISP detective, had started his law enforcement career with the Chicago Police Department. He'd graduated from the police academy with a kid from the south side, a rather rotund and fun-loving guy of Polish descent by the name of Robert Swiderski, known affectionately as "Big Bobbie." Big Bobbie had earned his nickname legitimately, with a playing weight north of three hundred pounds. He was now standing directly to the north of

Harold Wilkerson as everyone waited for the next train. Carlos had not seen him for about five years.

Carlos knew if Swiderski recognized him, his cover could be blown. Big Bobbie was naturally loud. Would probably bellow out something like, "Hey, Carlos, how's it like being a dick for State boys?" And, of course, if he did, the ball game would be over.

Detective Carlos became proactive.

"Hey, Big Bobbie, how's it going? Where ya been, buddy?" Carlos moved directly towards him and the suspect they had been following since 8:00 that morning. They met and embraced as Carlos led his old friend to his previous spot on the platform.

He dominated the conversation until he was a safe distance away from Wilkerson, at which point in time he whispered two words in his ear, "I'm undercover." Swiderski picked up on the cue. Pretense entered their conversation until the train arrived. As had been planned, the two working cops, and now Big Bobbie, entered a car directly behind the one selected by the Baron. He remained in their view.

Carlos sent another text to update the ground forces.

While the mark was having lunch and making his way to the "L," Bennett Coleman was getting acquainted with Isaac Jackson. Isaac could be seen most days ambling along Montrose Avenue in the Ravenswood neighborhood on the north side of Chicago. He was homeless, a fate that was pretty much sealed at birth, if not at conception.

Isaac was black, having been born on the west side of Chicago in the Garfield Park neighborhood. His mother was seventeen at his birth, unmarried, and addicted to the street drug of the day, crack cocaine. He had never met his father; he was not even sure of his name.

His mother knew early on that she would not be able to tackle the responsibility of parenting Isaac. When he was four, she'd chosen an "Auntie" of hers who lived in the same neighborhood to undertake the task of raising her son. Auntie Leticia had three children of her own and another niece and nephew when Isaac joined the household. She was a strong and loving woman and no doubt tried her best to discipline all of her children, a monumental challenge in light of the environment that she was embedded in, marked by extreme poverty, gun violence, open air drug dealing, and the gangs that ruled the streets. Kids didn't have the opportunity to mature on the west side of the city; they were too busy surviving.

As so often happens, the gangs had become the family for Isaac. He'd dropped out of school in the ninth grade and joined the Black Souls. It was then that he began to experience a series of juvenile arrests for shoplifting, car burglaries, and drug possession. Police diversion programs didn't work. Probation failed also. Time in juvenile detention had no impact on the tough street kid. Eventually, there'd been only one option left for the court system: the Illinois Department of Juvenile Justice. Translation: prison for kids. He was seventeen when the bus arrived at the Cook County Detention Center for a short trip west.

Isaac had been sent to St. Charles, Illinois, about thirty miles west of the city, for an indeterminate time to last no longer than his reaching the age of twenty-one. While in prison, he'd been given a chance by the authorities to cooperate and accelerate his discharge date by disclosing some key gang members who managed the Garfield Park drug activity. Not happening. They were his family, his brothers. Motivated by loyalty and survival, he would not be a rat. They would smell him, even from thirty miles away.

He'd been released from juvie prison after about eighteen months and paroled back to Auntie Leticia's home. He lived there sporadically. He showed up when his parole officer scheduled a visit, when he needed to crash and recover from a drug overdose, or when he was in need of a homecooked meal. Leticia was angered by his behavior and wanted to kick him out the door, but she knew he would have a better chance of surviving at her home. She thought that someday, if he lived to reach a certain age, he would wake up and abandon the path he had taken. Or had it been chosen for him by culture and history?

Although surrounded by violence on a daily basis, Isaac had never taken anyone's life or inflicted any major injury. It was not that he hadn't had the opportunity. He had easy access to guns and often carried one. It would eventually lead to more time behind bars, this time as an adult.

It was a botched armed robbery of a liquor store on the west side. It was one of those places that was barred up when closed and still looked barred up when open. People always hanging out, smoking, drinking, waiting for some action. Well, it came.

Sam's Liquors had occupied a corner location on West Madison Street for about fifteen years. It was Saturday night at closing time and Sam was securing the barred door to his business when Isaac and one of his Black Soul brothers muscled themselves in the door with guns drawn. They shoved the owner back to the register and demanded that he empty it, using colorful street talk. The two thugs were unaware of Sam Jr.'s presence in the stock room. He heard what was going down as he grabbed his loaded .357 Magnum. He appeared and immediately opened fire, killing Isaac's co-conspirator. Isaac turned to run while trying to shoot his weapon for some brief cover. It jammed and he fell. Sam Jr. arrived before he could get up, penetrated his knee to Isaac's stomach, and pointed the handgun directly at his nose. He cocked the weapon. Isaac closed his eyes, believing his life was about to end. Sam Jr. moved the barrel to his right and fired. The powerful round obliterated Isaac's left elbow.

Dad called the cops. Isaac didn't move until they and an ambulance had arrived. His arm would later be amputated above the shattered joint. Isaac was arrested and charged with armed robbery and first-degree murder.

In Illinois, as in many other states, if a death occurred during the commission of a forcible felony, anyone involved with the commission of that crime could be charged with murder. The dead person did not have to be the victim. And in this case, it wasn't. It was Isaac's gang buddy.

Isaac sat in the Cook County Jail for more than a year before the state and his public defender had finally reached a deal. Ten years on the armed robbery with a dismissal of the murder charge. His lack of a prior record of violence was the only card his PD could play. Well, that, and the fact that the dead person here was a gangbanger.

Isaac was twenty the day he was sentenced. He would be out in seven years. His Auntie would pass six months before his release.

When Agent Coleman first saw Isaac, he was sitting against a lamppost at the northeast corner of Montrose and Ravenswood, about a half block from the apartment of the Josh Wright family. He was horribly overdressed for the warm summer day. He had not shaved or bathed for weeks. He was dirty, filthy dirty. A large plastic garbage bag was at his side, presumably filled with all his earthly possessions, and leaning against the bag was a crude cardboard sign that read "Homeless. Please help. Thank you." He wore an old Chicago Bulls cap. His right hand held a large Styrofoam cup containing coins. It was being shaken constantly, producing a sound common to the many panhandlers in the city.

Coleman leaned down so he could look him in the eye. Riley sat in the 7-Eleven parking lot across the street, keeping track of everyone's whereabouts.

"What's your name?"

"Why? Are you a cop or something?"

"Actually, I am. But you're not in any trouble. I need your help. How would you like to make a quick hondo?"

"Are you shittin' me, man?"

"No, I am not. But I need to know your name please."

"Okay. It's Isaac. But I'm not the violent type. I won't fuckin' take anyone out for you."

"Nor would I ask you to. No, this is a very simple job. Come here. I want to show you something."

Coleman helped Isaac to his feet. They walked a half block east to the alley that ran behind the Wrights' apartment building. They stopped at the garage marked 2B. Coleman pointed to the garbage can with the same marking. He showed him a picture of Harold Wilkerson.

"It's my guess that within the next half hour or so, this man is going to place a black jacket in this garbage can. All you have to do is remove it after he does and make enough noise to alert him as to what you have done. He's going to want it back. And he'll pay you for it. Dicker with him. Whatever he gives you is yours to keep. But you have to sell it back to him. Okay?"

"You sure the guy is not packin' heat?" inquired Isaac.

312

"Absolutely positive. Here's half your salary." Coleman handed him a fifty-dollar bill.

"Oh, and what about my stuff, man?"

"We'll take care of it for you, Isaac. If this guy does not show up, we'll bring your stuff back to you and you can keep the fifty. If he shows up and our plan works, your money will be doubled."

"Oh, it'll work." Isaac was shaking his head as Coleman went back to the street. *Shit, man. A hundred bucks for something I do every day of the week.* It had been a while since Isaac Jackson had felt this good.

★ ★ ★

While Coleman was awaiting anxiously for events to unfold in the Ravenswood neighborhood, he got another call from the Wausau newspaper.

"Detective Coleman, this is Renee again from the *Wausau Daily Herald.* Five minutes ago, I received a phone call from an unidentified man. He wanted to give you a message that a Harold Wilkerson should be considered a major suspect in the case you are currently working on. I asked him his name and he hung up immediately."

"Thank you for the call, Renee. Please make a memo of the time and content of the call."

"Will do, Detective."

What the hell is going on? mused Coleman. *Some other party is conducting a similar investigation, perhaps?* Whatever was going on, he had no choice but to let it pass. Obviously, he was not going to deal with it right now.

As Coleman was leaving his newly recruited under-cover panhandler, Lake County detective Tara Gardner, having heard the news of Wilkerson boarding the Brown

Line at the Southport Station, put her Divvy bike into overdrive. She was weaving in and out of traffic, going on sidewalks, blowing stop signs and red lights, and making considerably better time than if travelling by car. Her destination was the Wright residence on Ravenswood. She estimated she was about ten minutes away.

O'Hearn directed his uniformed driver to step on it to Ravenswood. They would arrive within minutes.

That left the contingent of officers riding on the Brown Line CTA car directly behind the lawyer.

Wilkerson had boarded at the Southport Station. If, in fact, he was headed to the Ravenswood apartment of the Wright family, his two logical options for departure would be Montrose or Damen. Montrose was the more likely of the two and was a mere four stops from where he had boarded. The next stop was announced by the recorded voice over the speakers of the car. "Montrose Avenue will be next. Montrose." Wilkerson did not move. Neither did the three cops in the trailing car. Carlos so advised the officers on the street. Coleman was worried. He'd thought that the Baron would exit the train at Montrose, as it was closest to the apartment.

The train turned west after the Montrose Station and travelled about four city blocks to the next stop. The same voice travelled through the speakers, alerting passengers what was coming next. "Damen Avenue will be next. Damen."

Carlos had anticipated that Wilkerson would be getting off at the Damen stop. He was correct and he likewise exited. He instructed Spurlock to go to the next exit, Western Avenue, cross to the platform on the other side, and get on a train headed back to the Loop.

"Get off at Montrose. Lay low and wait for instructions. Big Bobbie here will show you the way."

Big Bobbie was now part of the team. Spurlock was having a ball. He swore someday he'd write a book.

★　★　★

Exiting the Damen Station puts one on Lawrence Avenue, perhaps the most diverse commercial street in America, if not the world. It was like walking the halls of the United Nations building in east Manhattan but with a lot more grit and soul and honesty.

From Lake Michigan on the east to the western border of the city in the Jefferson Park area, there was an abundance of shops, open markets, diners, bars, theaters, and a plethora of other businesses that could be experienced, representing at least thirty different cultures. In a day, one could travel from Korea and Japan, south to the Philippines, then west and north to Vietnam and Cambodia, enter Africa and travel to Nigeria, head north for a stop in Iraq, and then go to European villages in Greece, Sicily, Bosnia, Serbia, Poland, Germany, and Scandinavia. After that, one might cross the Atlantic and enjoy seven to eight more stops in Central and South America. It was better than Epcot, and a lot easier on the pocketbook.

It was this burst of diversity that greeted both the Baron and ISP Randal Carlos upon exiting the Damen Avenue Station. Carlos had been the first to hit the street as Wilkerson had hesitated getting off the train and just made it before the doors automatically closed. Carlos immediately crossed the busy street and ducked into a Sears store, out of sight of the filicide suspect but positioned so as to allow an unfettered view of him. He texted everyone the location of Harold and the Golden Fleece jacket.

It took Wilkerson a while to vacate the station. And when he did, he appeared somewhat confused as to which way to travel, a common experience for those who are not accustomed to riding the "L." Eventually he turned right, which was the correct direction for him as well as those who were waiting for him. Coleman was trying desperately to remain calm inside and was failing miserably.

It actually was a bit of a hike for Wilkerson to the Ravenswood destination. He walked briskly on the south side of the busy international street while Carlos safely lagged behind him on the north side, keeping his teammates updated as to their progress. The length of the walk gave the cops some much needed preparation time.

Somewhat laboring, Gardner arrived by bike at their temporary headquarters, at an art supply shop on Montrose, a half block from the garbage can marked 2B in bold font. The owners felt like they were in an episode of *Chicago PD*. O'Hearn was dropped off by the two patrolmen, who were directed to cruise the area and stay in touch in the event they observed something relevant to the task ahead.

There was a neighborhood pizzeria with outdoor seating. It allowed Coleman to have a clear view of the alley. A furniture repair store to the north gave O'Hearn easy access to the alley. Gardner stayed at the art supply store. Isaac Jackson played the role of roaming undercover panhandler. Nobody could currently see him, but his eye was glued to garage 2B and he was out of sight to anyone who might have an interest in the corrugated metal garbage can with the same number.

Big Bob Swiderski and Brian Spurlock were waiting for an inbound train to the Loop. They were currently not in the field of play.

The Baron continued his saunter east on Lawrence Avenue. He exuded confidence in his mission even as a patrol car passed him going the opposite direction. His appearance to the casual eye was totally innocuous. A city commuter coming home from a day in the Loop after picking up his dry cleaning. No one would notice that the lettering on the plastic wrap said "Zigler's Dry Cleaners, Sycamore Pointe, Illinois." Likewise, the briefcase, which on closer inspection had a Baker Brief tag, was made in Italy, and sold for $2,195, would not give anyone cause for suspicion.

Wilkerson stopped at the intersection of Lawrence and Ashland, an extremely busy area for both vehicular and pedestrian traffic. Where in the hell was he going? He had overshot the turn onto Ravenswood by three blocks.

No doubt he was out of his element in this area of the city. From his shirt pocket, he pulled out a map of the area that he had printed the previous evening. There was a yellow highlight of the Ravenswood district and the general location of the apartment he was seeking. What a nice exhibit that would make for the prosecutor at trial.

Upon review of his map, he regained his bearings, did an about face, and headed west. He reached Ravenswood in about three minutes. Carlos maintained his visual contact without being noticed by Harold. He was able to see him turn south on Ravenswood and reported his observations to the trio who had surrounded the point of interest outside garage number 2B.

His gait was not as sure as it had been before. There was a hint of tentativeness. It wasn't like he was lost, but more like he was in an away ballpark and it affected his confidence. And he was getting closer to his destination and his nerves were beginning to take their toll.

He approached the first cross street, slowed down, and searched for the street sign. Leland Avenue. He didn't remember that on his map. He pulled it out again. Okay . . . next was Wilson and then Sunnyside. That was the one he was looking for. Sunnyside.

There was a bit of a wait at Wilson with traffic being fairly busy at this time of the afternoon. Upon it passing, the blue blood from the North Shore regained his strut heading south, briefcase in his left hand and the wind-blown, plastic-covered clothing slung over his right shoulder.

Upon reaching West Sunnyside Avenue, Harold Wilkerson stopped, took a deep breath, and convinced himself that he was just doing a routine chore that was done a million times daily by everyone in America. Taking out the trash. It would take ten seconds, tops. Remove jacket from plastic wrap, lift trash can lid, drop jacket in, replace lid. A quick anonymous call to the Chicago Police Department would lead to its discovery and seal the verdict against Joshua Wright for murdering his son. Piece of cake.

He turned left on Sunnyside, walked about ten steps, and took an immediate right into the alley that ran behind the apartments of the Wright family. He passed the furniture refinishing store and the eyesight of faux patron, Dan O'Hearn, who signaled Coleman that he was headed his way. As he strolled down the alley, Wilkerson was checking the numbers on the garage buildings. The first set of units was numbered "4." Two more to go. His breathing became labored, his heart pumped more so. It was so quiet. Eerily quiet.

Coleman took a swig of his Old Style and a bite of his pizza from the patio area of Michelinni's. He was a big believer that in times of stress one should do something that came naturally. It would have a calming effect.

The Baron came into his field of vision from the right. He stopped at the garbage can clearly marked 2B. The alley was deserted. Nonetheless, Wilkerson set down his briefcase to take a look around to make sure. Satisfied that he was alone, he reached into the plastic wrap and ripped out the jacket that his loving wife had given him a month ago as a birthday gift. He removed the cleaner's identifying tab intertwined into the lowest buttonhole. Coleman hoped that he would fail to notice that this jacket was a size large as indicated by the letter L imprinted inside the center of the collar. It appeared as if he didn't notice.

He proceeded to lift the lid of the trash container, thrusting the incriminating jacket as deeply as the contents would allow. He replaced the lid, did a right face, and began his walk back to the north end of the alley where Sunnyside Avenue waited for his departure. He took a sigh of relief. He was reaching for his cell phone when he heard a loud clang behind him. He turned and met Isaac Jackson.

You would have to search high and low to find two people more diverse in their socio-economic backgrounds. Wilkerson, a waspy blue blood from the North Shore born into a family with mega wealth and never given the opportunity to fail. And then there was Isaac, a black kid from the west side who never had a family nor the opportunity to succeed.

"Hey, what are you doing there?" asked Wilkerson as he stared down Isaac holding the jacket that he had just retrieved from trash can 2B.

"What the fuck does it look like I'm doing?" he replied. "I'm doing my shopping at the trash can mall. What's it to ya?"

"Well, listen, that, that jacket is not yours. It doesn't belong to you."

"No, you listen. I just saw you stuff this jacket in the can and walk away. You must not have wanted it. But I do. Looks like a nice jacket. Brooks Brothers, if I'm reading the label correctly. Probably cost you a pretty piece. Mine now."

Wilkerson was panicking. He'd devoted the entire day in an attempt to frame the father of his son's victim and was now being thwarted by a homeless panhandler. He resorted to the usual.

"Okay, okay. How much do you want for it?" He proceeded to flash a wad of bills.

"What did you pay for it?" responded Jackson.

"I don't know. It was a gift from my wife. I'll tell you what, I'll give you a hundred bucks for it."

"Whoa, wait a minute. Your bitch gave you this beautiful motherfuckin' jacket and you threw it away. What's wrong with it? You been cheatin' on her? Is there fuckin' lipstick on here that won't come out?" He did a mock search of the jacket.

"No, dammit! Now give me that fucking thing and here's a C-note." Wilkerson attempted to grab it away from Isaac but he was too quick.

"Five hundred clams," bluffed Isaac. He would have taken two.

Wilkerson conceded. He pulled five crisp hundreds from his pocket and fanned them in front of Jackson. "Now give me the goddamn jacket and stay away from this place or I'll have one of my thug friends blow you away." It was, of course, a veiled threat from the Baron and Isaac knew it. He also knew he had played him long enough. He relented.

He threw the Golden Fleece at Harold's shiny penny loafers and snatched the bills from Wilkerson before he had a chance to renege. Isaac tipped his raggedy old Bulls cap as he spoke his parting words, "Nice doin' business with you, bitch."

Isaac turned and began his slow gait south, feeling a sense of pride for a job well done in his inaugural role as undercover panhandle cop. He had just earned six hundred bucks for about one hour of work. And, thanks to the mini camera pinned to the inside of an airhole of his beloved Bulls cap, his performance was memorialized for future viewings. His smile could not have been broader as he turned right at the end of the alley onto Montrose Avenue on his way back to his "home corner."

Wilkerson watched him disappear down row of garage units before he once again stuffed the jacket down into the garbage can. He retraced his steps north towards Sunnyside and punched in a number that he had saved the night before. It was to the 14th Precinct of the Chicago Police Department, located three blocks from his current location. As he was waiting for the precinct to answer, he noticed a middle-aged guy walking towards him in an awkward way, his left hand raised, holding something unidentifiable and his right arm straight at his side. It was Detective Dan O'Hearn. Coleman had given the instruction "Go" seconds before, causing him to exit the furniture store, badge raised and service revolver cocked.

The Baron, feigning as if he had forgotten something, did a 180 in the alley and started back to the area of the 2B garage. He immediately noticed a blue bike emerge from Montrose Avenue. As it drew nearer, he observed that the person pedaling it was wearing a Cubs cap.

Still in avoidance mode, he attempted to enter the backyard area of the apartments through a gate next to the garage. It was locked and too high for a man in his mid-sixties to leap. As biker and pedestrian closed, a man from behind called out his name.

"Excuse me, Mr. Wilkerson." The voice sounded vaguely familiar. He turned and walking toward him was Coleman, now sporting his Green Bay Packers cap. He removed his sunglasses.

"Perhaps you may remember me. We met in Madison, Wisconsin about two weeks ago. I also attended your son's funeral. My name is Bennett Coleman, Special Agent with the Wisconsin Bureau of Investigation and you, sir, are under arrest for the murder of your son, Bryce Miles Wilkerson."

It was difficult to determine which reaction occurred more quickly. Was it the blood draining from Wilkerson's face, or the closing of his eyes concurrent with the drooping of his head? It didn't matter, of course. His nonverbal responses to the words of the Badger detective reeked with guilt and were recorded for posterity by the body cams of the converging trio of cops.

Coleman immediately advised the Baron of his constitutional rights pursuant the Supreme Court case of *Miranda vs. Arizona*. Deputy Gardner alit from her blue bike at the garbage can marked 2B and removed the incriminating jacket.

Feigning surprise, Wilkerson quizzed, "What the hell is that?"

"Spare us the amateur acting job, Harold," answered Coleman. "That's the jacket you picked up this morning at Zigler's. Birthday gift from Beatrice, if I'm not mistaken. Ring a bell? About five minutes ago, you bought it from Isaac Jackson for $500 and then stuffed it back into the trash can. For a second time. You remember Isaac, don't you, Hal? Young black kid, no left arm, wearing a Bulls cap with a mini camera in the logo. Hey, don't worry if your memory is a little bit sketchy. We can sit down later at the Cook County Jail and review all the movies. You'll be a star."

Chicago Detective O'Hearn cuffed Wilkerson and volunteered to take him to the Cook County Jail. The threesome of cops who had gumshoed the murder suspect on the Brown Line appeared at the arrest scene in the alley. So did Isaac, who, unbeknownst to anyone, had watched the whole thing go down while hiding between two garages about a hundred feet away from the action. Turning to Coleman, he spoke first.

"Hey, man, can I keep the five Bennies?" he asked, referring to the five one-hundred-dollar bills Wilkerson had given him for the jacket.

"After some photography, I don't see why not. Looked like a fair transaction to me. Oh, by the way, here's the remainder of your salary for today's performance." He handed him another fifty-dollar bill. "Not a bad day's work, Isaac. Six hundred bucks for about an hour's worth of work. Hell, lawyers don't even charge that much. Do they, Hal?"

Wilkerson just sneered.

CHAPTER TWENTY-EIGHT

Relief . . . at Last

Ation of the cops left the scene. Some perhaps would
begin their report writing that night. Most
would wait until the next day, preferring to
visit any one of a number of watering holes on the north
side of the city to celebrate the events of the day. Detective
Coleman did neither. He had a more urgent task.

He told Paul Riley, his chauffeur for the day, to pick
him up in about a half hour in front of the apartment
building opposite their current location in the alley. He
was paying a visit to the family in unit 2B.

As he made his way to the front of the apartment
building, Coleman recapped the events that had shaped
the life of Josh and Amaya Emery-Wright during the last
two years. The immeasurable pain of it all. Discovering
that their beautiful and talented Hope had been sexually
violated. Their own guilt for not protecting her. The utter
failure of the legal system. And the experience of Josh
being the prime suspect in the murder of his daughter's
predator. Coleman could not comprehend the depth of
their anguish.

He entered the foyer for the second time that day and hit the buzzer to 2B. He heard Amaya's voice.

"Who is it, please?"

"Ma'am, it's Bennett Coleman, the lead detective on the Bryce Wilkerson death investigation. I'm wondering if I could speak to you and your husband."

"Oh, um, just a moment." She consulted her husband, who made his way to the intercom.

"What is it, Coleman? What do you want? You know I have a lawyer."

"I do indeed," Coleman responded. "But I have some positive news that I would prefer to tell you in person. In no way do I want ask you any questions. If you feel more comfortable, I am willing to wait until your lawyer arrives."

There was a pause before Josh answered. "Okay. I'm going to buzz you in."

Coleman could feel his emotions peaking as he ascended the steps to apartment 2B. The door opened as he hit the landing. Josh and Amaya were waiting for him. They appeared fatigued and fragile but not beaten. He was invited into the living room. He heard melodic singing coming from a distant bedroom. It provided a perfect and fitting background for the moment.

The couples' expressions asked why he was there. They did not need to speak.

"I am pleased to inform you both that Josh is no longer a suspect in the murder of Bryce Wilkerson."

Amaya gasped and began to sob as she wilted to her knees. Her husband embraced her at her level as tears gushed from him. They held on to each other, as they had during this entire ordeal. Coleman subtly retreated a few steps to minimize his intrusion on this poignant moment.

Upon gaining composure, the couple offered the detective a chair as they remained glued together on an adjoining couch.

"What . . . what happened?" inquired Josh.

"About an hour ago, Harold Wilkerson was arrested for the murder of his son, Bryce Wilkerson. He is on his way to the Cook County Jail as we speak. I am confident that the arrest is solid, and the evidence will support a successful prosecution." He then looked directly into the eyes of Hope's father. "Professionally and personally, I am quite pleased that no further efforts in this investigation will be directed towards you."

Coleman would undoubtedly have to speak with Mr. Emery-Wright to clarify his activities on the days he had ventured into Wisconsin. Now was not the time. His presence there was to give a wounded family uplifting information. A ray of hope, if not a beam, that their lives could now return to some level of normalcy. The singing in the background was an indication that the healing process had begun.

About a week after Wilkerson's arrest, Coleman contacted Stewart Martin, Josh Wright's attorney. He briefed the lawyer on the information that had been gathered on his client prior to Wilkerson's arrest. A meeting was scheduled to fill in the details.

Hope's dad would be present. Amaya, his wife, would not attend. Coleman had no way of knowing whether Josh had confided to his wife how close he had gotten to Gresham Gathering on the day of Bryce's demise. The meeting was to gain facts, not ignite a marital quarrel.

327

As it turned out, leaving Amaya at home was the right call. Josh had not yet told her. He did, however, come clean with his attorney and Coleman present.

Coleman recited the evidence that had been gathered regarding Josh's travels to Wisconsin. The blown toll booths, gas in Oshkosh, late lunch in Tomahawk, and his lodging at Redd's Lakeview Motel south of Oneida Falls. He confirmed everything. Some of his activities on the morning of June 4 were already known by Coleman. Now the picture was complete.

The plan to kill Bryce was simple. Josh was going to drive to the Wilkerson cabin at daybreak, knock on the door, and shoot him in the chest, waiting long enough before the trigger was pulled for Bryce to recognize that he was Hope's father. He didn't know or care if there were witnesses. He was oblivious to the trail he had left to the Northwoods cabin. Or that he would be the prime suspect in a murder case. It just didn't matter to him.

But he was stopped in his tracks about thirty minutes before the execution of his plan.

On the way to the cabin, a video had arrived on his phone. It was from Amaya. They were at a birthday party in St. Louis for her niece. She entitled the video "Hope Sings." It depicted Hope singing with elation on her face and a perfect pitch in her voice. No one had seen or heard that in over a year.

Amaya, of course, thought Josh was in Chicago. She had no inkling of his six-hour trek to northern Wisconsin. She delayed sending the video late at night for fear of waking him up. She'd waited until the following morning, musing that it would be a memorable wake-up call. It had arrived in the nick of time.

Josh had watched the video while driving. He pulled into a wayside, stopped his truck, and viewed it again.

Twice actually, before breaking down. He sobbed profusely with his hands in his face and forehead against the steering wheel. He watched it one last time. The Glock pistol was beside him underneath a sweatshirt. The aggrieved dad grabbed the weapon, exited his truck, and ran down the corrugated concrete boat landing. He threw the handgun with all his might into the calm waters of Little Spider Lake. He'd thought it would never be found. For his sake, it was, providing final confirmation to his account.

Josh then returned to his truck. About ten feet short, he dropped to his knees and sobbed again. He realized that his daughter had saved his life. He texted Amaya, "Absolutely beautiful. I love you both."

He turned south and headed home. Someday he would tell them both how Hope had saved the day.

CHAPTER TWENTY-NINE

The Baron's Post-Mortem

F ollowing his arrest, Hal Wilkerson was taken to the Cook County Jail, located on the near south-west side of Chicago at 2700 South California. Veteran Chicago Detective Dan O'Hearn did the honors.

It was the largest single-site jail in the country. Over the years, it had been referred to as "Crook County Jail" and "Hotel California." It housed about 6,500 prisoners, although still inadequate as the county rented space at other facilities throughout the state. Some experts opined that it was one of the nation's most dangerous facilities. To say the least, the North Shore Baron was out of his element and scared shitless.

Many of the inmates were awaiting trial for murder, sexual assault, armed violence, aggravated battery, various drug-related charges, and the like. For some, the jail represented home, having been incarcerated there longer than any residence maintained on the outside.

All arrestees went to Division 8 of the jail for intake and booking. An electronic monitoring system was implemented to ensure that no weapons or contraband were brought into the jail. Hal passed. The next step was to draw a line on the forearm of the inmate, from elbow to wrist, with a magic marker. The booking number was then written on the line, visible to both the inmates and the staff processing them.

A brief photography session followed with frontals and profiles, more commonly known as mug shots. On high-profile cases like Wilkerson's, the mugs made the newspaper. Very flattering. Harold's likeness would make all the dailies in Chicago and one in Northern Wisconsin.

He was housed at the "hotel" with the worst of the worst. Mostly murderers and rapists and child sex offenders. Hal had never experienced such fear. He called his lawyer. Setting bond was out of the question. He had just been arrested for murder at a time when he was out on bond for obstruction of justice and bribery. And the murder had been committed in the state of Wisconsin. There would be no pretrial release this time.

During his brief stay at 27th and California, the blue blood from the North Shore learned that holding on to your soap in the shower was more than mere anecdotal advice for inmates.

Four days after his arrest, Wilkerson appeared before Associate Judge Duncan Piersall at the Leighton Justice Center, the criminal courthouse adjacent to the jail. He enthusiastically waived extradition and anxiously awaited the Wisconsin authorities to arrive and transport him to Pinesap County. It took a week for them to make the trip south. Even with GPS, Sheriff Gregory Wallace, with Spurlock riding shotgun, got lost on the south side of Chicago trying to find the jail. They were an hour and a half late.

Wilkerson had never been happier to see a squad car.

Sheriff Wally white-knuckled it all the way to the Wisconsin border, after enduring his first (and most likely last) Chicago rush hour. They arrived in Oneida Falls around midnight.

Compared to the Hotel California in Chitown, the Pinesap County Jail was the Ritz.

Bennett Coleman had never seen or heard of a case the likes of the one that had brought him to God's country. When Harold Wilkerson became a suspect upon discovering the Golden Fleece logo on his black hunting jacket, the Wausau detective was awestruck and bewildered, to say the least. A father shooting his son. And by no means impulsively, in a fit of rage, but on the contrary—meticulously orchestrated with the utmost of premeditation. After the arrest, Coleman would learn that the Baron, a man born into this world with wealth and status, had no more than a sliver of character and a vaporizing soul.

The proper investigation of a case does not end with the arrest. There is always more information to gather. In the Pinesap County murder case, there was a veritable harvest.

Various detectives from Wisconsin and Illinois unveiled the following relevant information, which further inculpated the Baron in the murder of his spoiled-brat son.

1. Shortly after the mistrial and dismissal of Bryce's sexual abuse case, his dad had purchased a one-million-dollar life insurance policy on his son, naming himself as sole beneficiary.

2. Bryce, as well as his siblings, all had trusts that had been established by their grandparents. The First Bank of Chicago was trustee. After some maneuvering, Hal had become the trustee, giving himself control over funds exceeding a quarter of a million dollars.

3. To establish an alibi for the early morning hours of June 4, 2018, he had staged a fake video-taped deposition of a doctor in a medical malpractice case at the office of a law firm in Milwaukee. At the beginning of the deposition, Wilkerson stated the following: "Let the record show that this is the discovery deposition of Dr. Gilbert Ross of Milwaukee, Wisconsin, in the case of *Henkel v. Weiss Hospital et al.*, case number 17-L-876, in the Circuit Court of Cook County, Illinois. Present are Dr. Ross; John Ramsey, attorney for the plaintiff; and Harold Wilkerson, attorney for the defendant, Weiss Hospital. The date is June 1, 2018, and the deposition is being held at the law offices of Hall and McFetridge, Milwaukee, Wisconsin."

All of that was true. There was such a case pending. And it was June 1. And it was not uncommon for video tapes to be made at depositions, especially of doctors, with the anticipation that it may be used later at trial to avoid the expense of him appearing for live testimony. Nor was it unusual for the lawyers to go to the doctor's location rather than the opposite. In addition, there was a very small digital clock, in a location that was barely visible on a bookshelf. At the beginning of the recording it said, June 4, 9:02 a.m. It caught the lens of the video recorder.

It, of course, was a plant. No one in the room noticed it except the person who had put it there fifteen minutes prior to the beginning of the deposition. Embroidered on the cuffs of that person's starched white dress shirt were the initials HEW.

And to further create the illusion to the untrained detective that it was in fact June 4, a slight tinkering of the sound portion of the recording was effectuated changing the Baron's voice, which now told us that the date was June 4, 2018. One syllable. First to fourth. A forensic examination of the tape, however, read lips. And while the court reporter, now retired and living in South Carolina, had no recollection of the exact date, her work calendar and invoice did.

Bad alibis enhanced the state's case. Nothing smells worse than a bad coverup.

4.   To say the least, the killer had also "muddied up" the crime scene. Oversized boots. The photograph of Hope and her family. Footprints to the lake and back. And, of course, the dead fish, as in a mob hit. All of which could be argued raised reasonable doubt in the event his malicious deed was uncovered.

But in the end, it was Wilkerson's own greed that did him in more than anything else. Had he just destroyed the only piece of evidence that linked him to the crime, he may well have avoided detection as the culprit of this unthinkable murderous act.

But then again, how would he know that the jacket, this obligatory birthday gift from his unloved spouse, would prove to be his downfall? How would he know that the chill in the air on the morning of June 4 would cause him to naturally, without thought, tuck the collar around his neck to provide a modicum of warmth and comfort? And how would he know that his son had purchased a security system that would memorialize his actions forever from the only installed camera that could have detected the miniscule Brooks Brothers logo? And lastly, how would he know that the angle of the early morning sun was so precise that its rays touched upon the gold thread of the Golden Fleece to the extent that it was barely observed by Coleman's lantern?

Ah, but once Wilkerson knew what Coleman knew, another plan was hatched. Another pawn on the chess board was moved. Another plant of evidence was sought to be effectuated. Another seed of reasonable doubt was attempted to be sewn. Place the incriminating jacket in trashcan number 2B belonging to the individual with the greatest motive to kill his son: Joshua Wright.

The Baron was, however, was unaware of Bennett Coleman's acumen to move chess pieces around the sixty-four squares. Once he'd learned that Wilkerson had expressed an interest in the whereabouts of the hunting jacket, he'd called Roland at the Brooks Brothers store on the "Mag Mile." He inquired if there were any jackets left of the same size and color. Unfortunately, there were no XLs. The best he could do was a size large. Coleman had no choice. He had to take a chance. He'd dispatched a courier to the store where the duplicate jacket (but one size smaller) was delivered by Roland and brought back to the Sycamore Pointe Police Department.

The next morning, Agent Coleman delivered the new jacket to Emma Zigler at the dry cleaners and secured the one that had been worn by the assassin and repaired by Rosa Biondi. He could not risk losing custody of the genuine article. It was her grandson, Marco, who had saved the day when he'd stoned Wilkerson's attempts to retrieve the evidence at his grandma's home in Highwood. Perhaps Marco should consider changing his soccer position from mid-fielder to goaltender.

The entire next day, Coleman had to sweat it out that Harold would somehow notice that the jacket he was carrying around all over Chicago in a plastic covering was a size "L" instead of "XL." It didn't happen.

At trial, the two jackets would be marked as exhibits. One was stuffed down a trash can on the northwest side of Chicago. The other was worn by the defendant when he shot his son in God's country.

CHAPTER THIRTY

The Wilkersons Uprooted

I
t was all but over for Beatrice Wilkerson. She had little to live for. Her baby was dead, murdered horrifically by her blue blood husband of more than thirty-five years, who was now languishing in a jail somewhere in northern Wisconsin. The cabin on Gresham Lake would be sold for less than its encumbered debt. The mansion on Sheridan Road was being foreclosed; it would likely be purchased by a member of the Wilkerson clan at a Sheriff's auction. None of them would bother to ask Bea if she would like to continue living there. Her life was changing considerably more rapidly than it had back in the days when she and Hal had frequented the sand traps of Hampshire Hills to satisfy their mutual carnal yearnings.

Those days were gone, as well as the attendant superficial lifestyle. No more Wednesday morning women's golf league followed by lunch on the veranda. Bridge group on Thursdays evaporated. Shopping on Oak Street in Chicago was nothing more than a faint memory of where she had once been and a grave reminder of what she was returning to. Invites to gala dinners for special causes abruptly ended. One came by mistake. *Sorry, can't make it.* No new dress, no right arm by which to be escorted, and no money left to give to a cause that had more appeal as a tax write-off. The show was over.

No calls of condolence were forthcoming from any of her "friends," all of whom knew enough to keep their distance from the foul odor of scandal and crime. Her surviving children, Jewel and Charlie, had provided comfort for over a week, but they had their lives to lead far from the disaster zone they once called home. Remaining members of the Wilkerson clan disappeared like an April dusting of snow in Kentucky. Her two gardeners, brothers Juan and Luis Rodriguez, on their final workday extended Mrs. Wilkerson fresh fruit from their mother's south side produce stand and in broken English said, "Sorry." Bea broke down and sobbed in their arms.

There was, however, one remaining bit of business.

To visit her husband in Northern Wisconsin was logistically challenging for Beatrice. Taking her personal car was out of the question. She literally had never driven her pretty white Mercedes convertible more than ten miles from home. There were no train or bus routes to Oneida Falls. In any event, the thought of riding on either mode of transportation "with those people" for such a long distance was repulsive.

She settled on flying. The airport in Rhinelander, Wisconsin was about an hour from her husband's new lodgings. Upon arrival, she rented a car with GPS and made the trip, albeit with major trepidation.

Obviously, she could not stay at the cabin on Gresham Lake. Seeing the exact location of where her

Beamer had died would be beyond devastating. Prior to leaving home, she had made a reservation at the Northern Highlands Inn. Ironically, Detective Coleman had stayed there earlier that summer.

Beatrice did not sleep well the night before visiting her husband. Her mind was hopelessly incapable of relaxation. It raced chaotically, jumping decades at a time recounting her history, her relationships, but most of all the sorrow that now had its unbreakable grip on her existence. Her short-burst screams quickly morphed to extended and profound weeping. Exhaustion led to brief periods of sleep followed by quick awakenings and another round of mental and emotional torture.

Her jail visit was scheduled for 10:00 a.m. She finally dragged herself out of bed at 8:30 feeling considerably more fatigued than when she had retired the previous evening. After showering, she began the task of making herself attractive, a process that would at least attempt to hide her pain, sorrow, age, and anger. She talked out loud as she applied her makeup, looking into the mirror: "You son of a bitch, Harold. How could you do it? How could you shoot our son? Your own flesh and blood."

It was a question that people at all levels had been asking themselves. From the cops who'd busted the case to the casual observer listening to the ten o'clock news, the reaction had been the same: *How could a father kill his son?* In about an hour, Beatrice would get her answer.

The Pinesap County Jail was new and had a more modern look and feel than most. It made the visit a little more palatable for Beatrice. Shortly after her arrival, she was led into the visiting room. It contained five visiting stations. Each contained a metal stool, a counter, a phone, and an unbreakable glass partition. Mrs. Wilkerson's presence was not lost on the jail personnel. It was a topic of great interest and conversation, in hushed tones while she was present and upon her departure with relaxed openness. Along with Harold, she was a bit of a celebrity.

Five minutes later, her husband was ushered into the prisoners' side of the visiting room. He wore an orange jumpsuit with the words *Pinesap County* imprinted in black across the chest area. Same lettering on the back, only larger. It had been well over a month since Bea had last seen him at his extradition hearing in Chicago. To her disappointment, his appearance had improved. He seemed to have gained some weight. He was relaxed. And despite his current environment, he maintained an aura of smugness and superiority.

They lifted their phones simultaneously. Their eyes were no more than two feet apart. There were no other people in the room. Jail policy dictated that their conversation be monitored. Bea didn't care; for legal reasons, Harold did.

Bea spoke first. Despite her attempts at crafting a script, she was lost. "Uh, Hal . . . I, uh, really don't know what to say. I am still in shock as to what has happened to my . . . our life. But I knew I had to come to see you. For the last time, perhaps." This last expression was pleasing to the prisoner, though he chose not to reveal it.

There was a pause. Harold said nothing. He continued to look at his wife without expression. He sensed her frustration at his silence. Years of experience had taught him to recognize the coming of her meteoric rises to rage. It wasn't far away. He would say nothing until the explosion. His preparation had been flawless.

"You sonofabitch. You rotten sonofabitch. How can you sit there and say nothing? You high and mighty sonofabitch. You murdered our son. You shot him in the head with your fucking deer rifle. How could you do that? How could you kill your own flesh and blood?" She was no longer talking on the phone but screaming through the partition. Her nose was touching the glass as she pounded the phone against it. The Baron remained silent until Bea regained a modicum of composure. It was then that he broke his silence.

"Excuse me, Beatrice. Did you say 'our child'? Really. 'Our child'? And my 'flesh and blood'? What do you take me for?"

"Of course, I said 'our child.' What the fuck is wrong with you, Harold?"

He responded, "Oh, Bea. You sad soul. I will tell you."

"Tell me what?"

With great deliberation, he extracted a folded letter from the left breast pocket of his jumpsuit. He put it on his counter without opening it. He then told his story.

"I'm sure you will remember an incident that occurred about ten years ago. Bryce was in high school and still living at home, unfortunately, when he developed a severe nosebleed after one of his jam sessions in the garage. You sat him down in the family room and applied pressure to his nose with a newly purchased guest hand towel. Every ten seconds, you would direct him to sit up to see if the bleeding had stopped. It did not, of course, because the pressure needed to be applied for a more extended period time. Does any of this ring a bell, Beatrice?"

"Well, of course it does. I remember it well. I ended up taking the poor kid to the emergency room while you stayed home, you worthless piece of shit. And if I'm not mistaken, I lost the brand-new guest towel in the process."

"Ah, my darling Beatrice, I just knew you would remember." Each time he called her Beatrice, her anger ramped up. It really spiked when he said "darling Beatrice."

He continued. "So, while you and Beamer, as you loved to call him, were at the ER, I was left holding this towel with his blood all over it. It was then that I decided to finally discover whether my previous suspicions about him were in fact true. The next morning, I went to the office and consulted with one of our criminal attorneys about DNA testing. He provided me with a list of labs. The towel was now secure in my desk, awaiting dispatch to Lab Centers, Inc., Charlotte, North Carolina, together with a sample of my own blood and a sizeable check to cover expedited service. In less than thirty days, I received this."

Wilkerson meticulously unfolded the letter in front of him, read it to himself, and then with both hands plastered the same on the glass partition, allowing his wife the opportunity to examine the exhibit. She fumbled retrieving her reading glasses from her purse. She leaned towards the glass and read the letter. The last sentence in the report said it all. "It is the finding of the undersigned that there is no DNA match between Exhibit One (blood of BMW) and Exhibit Two (blood of HEW)."

She feigned shock. "What? What? What does this mean?"

"Quite simply, it means two things, my dear. One. Bryce was not *our* child. And two, Bryce was not my FLESH and BLOOD! If you like, you may pick up a copy of this letter at the front desk where you entered. Oh, and by the way, sorry about the towel."

That last comment ignited another barrage of profanity from Bea. Wilkerson rose and began his exit. He stopped at the door, turning for one last look at his wife. She was feral. Her fusillade of obscenities inundated both sides of the partitioned room. She called him a "slimy bastard." She wanted to "fucking kill him." Her fists were pounding the glass. "Rot in hell" were the last words Hal heard.

He smirked and waved. "Goodbye, Beatrice." He then shuffled back to his cell.

Beatrice could not hear the last words of her husband. Actually, nothing was audible over the din of her fury. But she knew what he had said.

It took two correctional officers to restore the peace. Bea eventually ran out of energy, calling a halt to her tirade. Incessant sobbing ensued as she was escorted to the jail's lobby. About fifteen minutes elapsed before a minimal level of composure was established. She eventually left the jail, rejecting any further assistance or consolation from the officers.

For a time, Beatrice wandered aimlessly around the streets of Oneida Falls, her mind and emotions seemingly separated from her body. Her secret was out. It genuinely surprised her. The lie had been uncovered. It was a lie that had endured for nearly three decades—one that she had grown to accept as the truth.

She made it back to the jail and located her rental car. She opened the door and stared at the edifice which now held a prisoner who was her husband of three-and-a-half decades. She whispered, "Goodbye, Hal."

She then drove to the airport.

In the coming days, Jewel made an obligatory offer to her mom to come live with her family, knowing in advance that she would decline. Charlie gave her sufficient funds to pack and transport her furniture and other personal items to her new location. She left her golf clubs and many of her once-worn dresses. There would be no need for either at her new destination.

A distant cousin had reached out to Beatrice. She had found a modest apartment and part-time job that could hold her over until something better came along. She accepted knowing that, at this point in her life, nothing better would ever come along.

She ordered a taxi to take her to the Metra Station on Green Bay Road. When the cab arrived, she turned for one last look at the Sheridan Road dwelling. Her mind was a whirlwind of random thoughts. The unexpected wealth, the status, the pretension, the superficiality, the fakery of happiness, stability and trust, the betrayals, the secrets, all culminating in the horrific death of her youngest child. She entered the cab, departing the edifice that she had always had trouble calling home. More accurately put, it was where she had lived.

She boarded the train for Chicago, wondering if anyone saw her or cared. She wore sunglasses despite the overcast skies, a feeble disguise necessary for protection of her vanity.

In forty minutes, she arrived at the Ogilvie station. She embarked on the three-block walk to Union Station where she bought a one-way Amtrak ticket on the Zephyr Line. Destination: Galesburg.

The Carl Sandburg Museum awaited its newest employee.

The multiple ironies surrounding his apprehension had not escaped Harold Wilkerson's notice. They had merely gained more scrutiny and focus given the fallen Baron's current custodial environment.

High on the list, of course, was the birthday gift from his wife. The jacket. Not just any jacket but a hunting jacket. One to be worn while shooting deer or pheasant or clay pigeons. But not human beings. And certainly not her beloved Beamer.

He had chosen to wear it because it was black. But it also passed his mind, while donning it the morning of the shooting, how ironically callous it would appear to end the life of Bea's illegitimate son while dressed in her birthday gift to him. As it turned out, due to Detective Coleman's keen eye, the final irony landed on Hal.

And then there was the security camera. Ordered by Bryce, having been suggested by Beatrice and paid for by . . . drum roll: Harold Wilkerson himself! Of course, through one form or another, Hal had always taken care of the bills. Even the one that paid for the technology resulting in his arrest.

Not since the early 1930s had Pinesap County experienced a more nefarious figure than Harold Wilkerson. John Dillinger was his name. Unlike their current resident, Public Enemy Number One had managed to escape.

Mr. Dillinger and his gang, Baby Face Nelson included, were enjoying a little rest and recreation from their career of crime at Little Bohemia, a secluded lodge fifteen miles from the Pinesap County Jail. The feds had been given a tip of their whereabouts. The ensuing raid and shootout were foiled, and the gang escaped by boat on Spider Lake. The lodge and restaurant were still in existence, together with a small museum, bullet holes intact. In fact, Mr. Wilkerson and his family had dined there about a year ago. Bea had given it rave reviews on Facebook.

The case of *The People of the State of Wisconsin vs. Harold E. Wilkerson* became a cause celebre for the citizens of Oneida Falls and the surrounding area. TV stations covered all court proceedings. The spectator section in the main courtroom was standing room only for all hearings. Sheriff Gregory Wallace—Little Wally—stood behind the local prosecutor with a squad of his deputies. From time to time, he granted interviews to the media.

The main attraction, however, was the defendant. People rubbernecked to catch a glimpse of the high-priced Chicago lawyer who had offed his own son. Harold liked the attention. His spirits were beginning to buoy. Bea was gone, along with her out-of-wedlock son. Both had been albatrosses around his neck. He was getting his second wind.

His lawyers had contacted some expert witnesses in the field of psychology. At the very least, an insanity defense would be assessed. The public now knew that the victim in this case was not the blood son of the defendant. They also knew that the victim had a proclivity for improperly touching little girls prior to his demise. The defense lawyers believed that was huge. It would increase the chances of getting a hung jury. They only had to convince one of the twelve that the victim "had it coming."

Let the adversarial battle begin.

It was fortuitous that Hal had been assigned a cell with a two-foot square window having a western exposure. The Cook County Jail offered no such amenities. The scenery, like the room and board, bore no added expense. Had it been required, the inmate would have gladly covered the option. As long as the sun shone each day, it gave him a sense of consolation.

The break of dawn saw the Norway pines glistening as their dew-infested needles were bombarded by the sun's first outpouring of energy. By mid-morning, the droplets had evaporated, revealing a rich hunter green hue to the majestic towers swaying effortlessly in the breeze. At dusk, Wilkerson's cell was enveloped with the glow of the sun's setting rays filtering through the pine branches. A distant lake's reflection, exhibiting shades of pink and gold, culminated his daily view of the outside world. And if he listened very closely, he could hear the distant song of a loon. He'd gone full circle.

The final irony. It had taken a jail cell for him to finally appreciate the meaning of the old adage "the best things in life are free." And it occurred at a time when he was not.

About a mile from the jail, turmoil was lurking in an ostentatious cabin with a lakeside view, deeply embedded in the conifers. The Mastersons.

Apparently, young Reggie had shoplifted an item from a local drug store. She had been caught, not by the store, but by her parents. It was causing them both extreme anguish. It was not, however, the petty criminal infraction that was the source of their distress. It was the item she took.

Reggie trusted no one to buy the pregnancy test for her, nor could she do it herself. The rumor mill would kick into overdrive. And so, she stole it.

Things had begun to improve in the Masterson house-hold since Detective Coleman's interview of their daughter. Reggie had begun counseling. She was complying with curfew. She had quit drinking. Now, all hell was breaking loose. The torn test package had been found by mom while changing the sheets on Reggie's bed. The young girl was confronted. The test was positive.

Reggie wanted to have the baby. Dad wanted to send her as far away as possible to have the fetus aborted. Mom wanted to bury her head in the sand and go play golf.

Richard Masterson had served as a Village trustee for over ten years. He was a staunch Republican in a dominantly conservative area. He was pro-life. Or so claimed to be. His Lexus SUV had a bumper sticker that read, "Abortion Stops a Beating Heart." He attended church every Sunday and was extremely vocal in his opposition to abortion.

Oh my, the gossip that would be generated if she gave birth. He could hear it already. "You know who the father is, don't you? It's that child molester who was murdered by his father, only I don't think he really was his father. I can't even imagine what Dick and Beverly are going through. I hardly see them anymore. I understand that he's not going to run for reelection to the Village Board. And I'm sure it's hurt his insurance business. I'm told the baby looks just like the dad. Let's hope he doesn't turn out like him." And so on and so on.

Mr. Masterson became adamant. Reggie, however, was not to be denied. He couldn't make her get an abortion. But she was getting damn tired of his incessant daily pressure to do so, not to mention his blatant hypocrisy on the subject. One day, she made a sign out of bright yellow poster board. It read: "BAN ABORTION (unless it's the baby of your 16-year-old daughter)!!!" She threatened to put it in the front window of his insurance office. She eventually found a better way.

Reggie had stopped going to church with her parents a few years back. She did, however, know the associate pastor, a younger guy by the name of Glenn Solokowski. Nice guy. Easy to approach. So, Reggie did.

She related her situation and, with much detail, her father's attitude and actions about the whole ordeal. "Pastor Glenn, he's making my life miserable. It's affecting my health. I feel as if it's also hurting my baby. Can you please help me?"

"Yes, I can." And he did.

He called the insurance man at his office. After summarizing his consultation with Reggie, he let into him. "Mr. Masterson, it's time you began to celebrate the coming of your grandchild and cease your efforts to murder this miracle that is growing in your daughter's womb. And if you don't, please know that I will personally go to the Council of Ministries and you will be stripped of your deaconship in this church. The reasons for this action will spread like wildfire among the congregation and the hypocrisy of your ways will become common knowledge in the community. I will be meeting with Reggie this time next week. She will give me a report of your response to this matter. I trust that it will be positive. Have a blessed day." *Click.*

Miles George Masterson was born seven months later. How about that. Initials MGM. A Hollywood actor, perhaps? The maternal grandparents would never know.

CHAPTER THIRTY-ONE

A Goalie's Vindication

S
o often we learn from the news media about unsolved crimes. The police are looking for suspects, or they are interviewing suspects or "persons of interest" as we now call them in our politically correct world. We think nothing of it. But if you are a suspect, it's all you think of.

Jed Tucker was a suspect. He had motive. He was open to the police about his hatred for the Wilkerson family who lived a dock down from his cabin, especially the young "Beamer." He knew about the criminal case in the Chicago and had been openly hoping that Bryce would be convicted and sent away for years. It didn't happen. And then the "young FIB punk" was back at the lake "throwing his fucking money around" and lying about his innocence. "Fucking perv. Got what he deserved." Diplomacy had never been one of Jed's strong suits.

Opportunity was no problem. He could access the Gathering (by land or lake) by riding his bike or paddling his canoe or kayak. He was familiar with the woods, knew the secret paths and all sorts of perches from which to test his marksmanship.

And Jed's temper was well reputed. Just ask anyone on his hockey team, past or current. Never hesitated to drop the gloves. And he'd had his share of scrapes in many of the local watering holes, defending himself or the honor of some attractive local. After all, he was a hockey player.

And, of course, like many Northwoodsmen, he was a hunter and owned multiple long guns.

Notwithstanding all of the circumstantial evidence pointing to Tucker, Agent Coleman had never bought into his guilt, contrary to the voice of local public opinion. He fully recognized all the motive and opportunity that the goalie had, but he also was impressed with his openness and his cooperation with his investigation, however crude his manner. "Sure, come on in. Search all you want. You want to test all my guns? Test away."

There was only one apparent detail that had needed some verification. The projectile that had killed Bryce was a bullet from a 30.06 rifle. Jed owned such a weapon, but it wasn't at his home. He indicated to Detective Coleman that a good friend of his had entered into a shooting contest and wanted to use his Winchester rifle. Jed had delivered the gun to him during the early morning hours of June 4 before he went to his job site.

There would have been plenty of time for Jed to secretly position himself at the Wilkerson cabin, pick off the Beamer, travel across town, and deliver the rifle to his friend and then head to his kitchen remodel job. Believable alibis . . . but perhaps created. Coleman had Spurlock check out the story. And it checked out.

The final confirmation was in the science. Jed's friend, Rob Gentry, after receiving phone permission from Jed, turned the weapon over to Spurlock. It was taken to Madison for testing. Jed was exonerated. No match in the rifling.

Being a prime suspect in a small-town murder case was nothing to be taken lightly. The rumors were rampant. Turned heads and whispers often occurred as Jed entered any of the local banks, grocery stores, or bars. Jed felt it.

Another ripple effect victim, to be anonymously compensated by the Doc and the Nurse duo.

Learning of his passion for ice hockey, they formulated a gift list for Tucker.

a)   Glenn Hall was a retired goalie who'd played fifteen years in the National Hockey League and was a member of the Hall of Fame. During one stretch with the Chicago Blackhawks, he'd played in 512 consecutive games with skimpy equipment and no mask. He'd earned the nickname "Mr. Goalie," a well-deserved moniker. Doc wrote Mr. Hall at his home in Alberta, Canada, requesting a signed goalie stick. It arrived in a short turnaround time for a modest price and was forwarded to Tucker on Gresham Lake. The inscription on the blade of the stick read:

Dear Jed,
The puck stops here.
Best wishes, Glenn Hall, Mr. Goalie, #1

It occupied a prominent space on the wall of his cabin above the fireplace.

b)   Jed's fishing boat had seen better days. It was retired when a new one appeared at his dock one morning with attached Minnesota Wild decals framing the words *Tucker's Troll.*

c)   The rink at Oneida Falls was used by all levels of hockey players from Pee Wee to over-fifty leagues. It needed new goalposts and nets. They arrived at the rink the same week as the boat and goalie stick.

As was always the plan, the gifts were sent by Doc and the Nurse with anonymity. They had discussed the possibility of giving Jed a clue that these tokens were paid for by Wilkerson money, as that would have given him added satisfaction. In the end, they opted against the idea.

Actually, Jed's best gift was not from the generous duo in Chicago. His lakeside cabin was restored to tranquility when the new owners of Gresham Gathering removed all signs with the exception of the one that led to their retirement home: "Peaceful Waters."

Jed would welcome them with open arms. Allen and Wilma Waters.

CHAPTER THIRTY-TWO

Doc and the Nurse Reconciled

M ichael Duff got up later than usual but not by much. It was 7:07 a.m. He may have gotten a few hours of sleep, but no more. Kelle was sound asleep facing the window, or so she appeared. She did not stir. He did not touch her.

Upon finishing his bathroom routine, he went to the kitchen, made coffee, and called his assistant manager at the drug store. "Congratulations," he told him. "You have been promoted to store manager for one day. Call if an emergency comes up." No way he could handle work, especially on a Monday. Too much to process. Too many layers of conflict. He took deep breaths . . . five in a row.

Duff was not well. What was that old song? "What a difference a day makes." Only in the song, the "twenty-four little hours" brought sunshine, not darkness.

Yesterday at this time, he'd been on his third cup of coffee, half watching his Sunday morning news shows. He'd been mentally planning the week ahead, especially the Indiana weekend visit with his girls. It would include their annual visit to the Indiana Dunes. Maybe Kate would join them for one of the days.

He'd had a late lunch at D'Agostino's, a local pub and pizzeria at Southport and Addison with a standing room only crowd of Cubs fans who either didn't have tickets to the game or couldn't afford them. It was considerably cheaper to celebrate the games with friends at a bar where the beers were a third of Wrigley's price. Everyone left chagrined as the Cubs bullpen failed to protect a three-run lead against the Cardinals.

Michael enjoyed the six-block walk back to his home in Roscoe Village amid the horn-honking traffic and well-oiled baseball fans. Upon arrival, he turned on his flat screen and settled in to watch the final round of the weekend golf tournament. Ironically, during the sudden death overtime match, the call came in.

The fear in Kelle's voice was palpable, the chaos in her thinking rampant. Doc had never seen her in this condition. She was always so grounded, logical, and dependable. It was he who had the short fuse, whose mood and behavior could turn on a dime. Now they were both a mess.

And it was his doing. His overhyped plan to con the rich and bring a level of the justice to the abused. A whole new network of secrets and schemes hatched by two people who were still recovering from the effects of suppressed events from their dark pasts.

And now, the fear of being caught. The consequences, the conflicts, futures scuttled, relationships fractured, hopes doused. The serenity of dozing while watching TV golf was supplanted by an immediate, downward spiraling feeling of peril. Like a nightmare. Falling, then falling again with no safety net.

But wait. *Let's add to the tumult of the moment,* Duff now thought. More than a consoling hug. More than a peck on the cheek. Two bodies had connected, battling the terror that could not be defeated individually. A kiss, an open-mouthed, tongue-exploring kiss, dripping with passion. But the context, the timing? But most of all, the meaning.

All these thoughts were bombarding the cranium of M.D. when Kelle entered the kitchen, still wearing her white Steelers jersey with a black #32 on the back. Franco Harris. The immaculate reception. Most memorable play in NFL history. Doc and the Nurse needed a play of similar magnitude. An immaculate deception, perhaps?

"Michael, I've got to go back to my place," she said.

"Kelle, I don't think it's safe there."

"I know. Not to stay there. I have to get some things that I forgot to pack. Some work files and some meds. It'll only take me a few minutes. Can't we just drive down there? Or are you going to work?"

"No. I'm taking the day off. Sure. We can drive down. When do you want to leave?"

"Ten minutes." She turned around and headed to the bathroom.

The drive to Russo's condo was eerily quiet. Duff kept a news radio station on to mitigate the silence. He commented about the heavy traffic. He mentioned the way the Cubs had blown the game yesterday. Kelle wasn't buying into any of his canned conversation. Fortunately for both of them, her phone rang. The number was familiar, but she couldn't place it.

"Hello."

"Hi. Is this Kelle Russo?"

"Yes, it is. Who's calling?"

"Kelle, this is Nick Santos. You did some computer work for our law firm last spring."

She remembered her Caribbean connection well. "Oh, Nick. Hi. How are you? Something wrong with the system?"

"No. Not at all. It's been great. I was actually calling to give you a heads up. I got a call from a law firm downtown that I've done some business for. They were wanting a referral for a new security system for their office. Seems they had some fire walls go down recently. I told him you were the best. It all came about rather strangely, though, because he called me at home on a Saturday. Anyway, I gave him your number. Could be a lucrative account."

"That's very nice of you, Nick. What's the name of the firm?"

"Wilkerson, Clark, and Rowe. Old established firm. They have a couple floors of space high in the Aon building."

There was a pregnant pause during which Kelle begged for composure.

"Are you still there?" asked Santos.

"Yeah. I'm fine. In traffic. You broke up a little. Do you remember who made the call?"

"I don't. He told me his name, but I can't remember it. Said he was in their tech department. Sounded like he had some age to him. Thought that was strange, too. Old people are usually not tech savvy. Anyway, I'll text you the contact number."

"Okay, Nick. Thanks again. Have a good week."

Kelle looked at Duff. "You're not going to believe this."

"You have got to be shitting me!" Duff was in disbelief. The news from attorney Santos broke the ice in the vehicle. They processed it in dialogue.

Michael began, "If it was Wilkerson who called Santos, on a Saturday at his house, mind you, does it not follow that it was he who delivered the cash and cyber assignment to your condo yesterday? And that means that he is the killer of his son. Or is protecting the killer. Actually, his general description definitely resembles the man in black that we viewed last night on the Northwoods video."

"I'm freaked out that he called the same law firm I had the job at. I mean, how many other lawyers are there in Chicago and he chooses Santos," responded Kelle.

"Well, I think you have to remember the type of work these guys do. They hide money. They launder it. They did some work for Wilkerson's clients. Their scruples are aligned, or rather their lack of them. Bottom feeders. Wilkerson was looking for someone who could bend the rules for a price. It's damn near identical to his bribing of the juror in Hope's case. I mean, he dropped off five K in cash yesterday with the promise of more if you succeeded. He's on the run in a murder case, not going after you for revenge."

"Maybe he wants both. You know, kill two birds with one stone. Use me long enough to delete the incriminating evidence and then hit the delete key on me. If you're right, and he killed his own son, doing away with me will be like a walk in the park." Kelle was nowhere near a comfort zone yet, thought Michael.

"If that were the case, he would have to show his hand. Confront you personally or have someone else do it. You're going to be fine." She wasn't buying his assurance. And he knew it.

He cut it off there. They were in Little Italy. He parked in front of her condo while she ran in to retrieve her items. It took longer than expected. When she came back to the car, there was new information.

"I just had a talk with Luca."

"Who is Luca?" asked Michael.

"Luca is one of Leona's kids. He is eleven, I think. They live down the hall from me, above their Italian deli. He wanted to make sure that I got the package yesterday."

"Oh really."

"Yes. Yesterday afternoon, he was sweeping the entrance and sidewalk to their deli when a man approached him. He was very polite and asked whether he lived in the condo here. He said he did. He then asked Luca if he would deliver the Amazon labeled package to me. Said he was a close friend and it was a surprise. Offered him ten bucks, which Luca refused. Told me the man was older, rather tall, slender, and drove a black car that he thought was a Mercedes. He was alone. Luca said he took the box upstairs and left it outside my door when no one answered his knock."

"Well, that certainly fits Hal Wilkerson's description. Apparently, he knows where you live. Probably easy after he got your name from Santos. Google or White Pages."

"Let's get out of here," was her only reply.

★ ★ ★

"I feel like we should go the police. We have information as to who the murderer is. And he knows who I am. I don't feel safe as long as he is at large."

"I totally agree," Michael responded. He took a slight detour and stopped at a Walgreens on Halstead and Monroe in the west Loop. He purchased a burner phone.

"Get me the number for that Wausau paper that I sent the fax to last night."

Kelle found it and he called the number. There was an automated menu. Fortunately, the first option was "news desk." He punched one.

"News desk. Renee speaking."

"Renee, please inform Detective Bennett Coleman that Harold Wilkerson is a main suspect in the case he is currently investigating." He spoke slowly and deliberately.

"And who is calling please?"

Click. Duff stopped and exited the car, dropped the phone, crushed it with his foot, and dumped it in a city garbage can.

On the ride back to his condo, Duff further attempted to allay the fears of his friend.

"Kelle, hear me out. After giving it more thought, I'm convinced that Wilkerson has no idea you were involved in the scam. Because if he did, he would not have asked Luca to deliver the Amazon box. He would have done it himself. He would have found a way to enter your building. And no need for cash. He would have just coerced you to delete the video.

"But he didn't do that. And why? Because he wants to protect his identity. I'm telling you, it was a desperate move on his part. A Hail Mary."

She responded, "I don't know. You may be right. I can't think straight. My mind is all jumbled. Let's go have lunch somewhere."

"Good idea."

Duff was familiar with all the eateries in his neighborhood. He chose John's Place, a quaint corner shop with an easy menu and outdoor seating. And privacy.

Kelle ordered lemonade; Duff, a beer. He had a feeling the upcoming conversation would require some liquid courage.

She started. He knew she would. "Michael, we have got to talk about last night."

"What part of last night?"

"Don't be stupid, Michael. You know exactly what I'm talking about."

Of course, he did. "You're right. Why don't you start? I'm not very good at this."

"Well, I'm not sure I am, either. But we've got to deal with this. At least it's something within our control. I think."

She took a deep breath. So did he. "Michael, I was scared to death last night. I haven't felt such panic since I was a kid. I needed to be held. I'm sorry. But I needed to be held." She began to break up.

"Kelle, it's okay. You need not apologize for being human. We were both vulnerable. I obviously needed to be held also. The kiss was something, I don't know, it just happened. And I'm not sorry about it. By the same token, I'm not sure it was the right thing to do. Somehow, I'm feeling the weight of it."

"Of course, you do. I do, too. Michael, we have been through a world of shit and stress and we are still recovering from it. We're making progress. But we can only deal with so much. Especially in our current situation. Whether we like it or not, we have intertwined ourselves in a murder investigation. We may be exposed. But you know what. Even if that mess were to go away, be thankful that we both intuitively knew that the kiss is where it had to stop last night. This is going to sound weird but thank you for holding me last night while we slept. I was a wounded child.

"But there is another thing, Michael. And you know it better than I do." She grabbed his hands and looked directly into his eyes. "You have a more important relationship to reconcile. Kate. Your beautiful daughters. We've talked about it. Endlessly. Maybe now is the time that *we* stopped talking about it and *you* started doing something about it."

My, oh my, how she knows me well, mused Duff. He loved her directness. A quality he lacked when it came to issues of intimacy. Old habits die hard.

"Thanks, Kel. You know, I feel the same way about last night. I just didn't know how to say it. Or perhaps I lacked the courage. Same with Kate and the girls. Too much fear to overcome. Afraid of the reaction if I shared my secret. Damn. Maybe this weekend."

Lunch came. She had a chef's salad. He a Reuben sandwich. The heavy stuff was out of the way. The Nurse had done most of the lifting. They clinked glasses and enjoyed their meal. Eight hours later, their stress level would experience another drastic reduction.

★   ★   ★

The leading local TV station in Chicago was WGN, channel 9. The call letters stood for "World's Greatest Newspaper." *The Chicago Tribune* used to own WGN TV and radio.

Duff was a faithful viewer of WGN's late evening news, which came on at 9:00 p.m. He was watching it now on the couch, his feet propped up on a coffee table. The Nurse was in the kitchen, working on her laptop within earshot of the TV.

Prior to the sports segment, the anchor advised viewers: "This just in. The Chicago Police Department has reported that Harold Wilkerson, a prominent attorney from Sycamore Pointe, was arrested this evening in the Ravenswood neighborhood of Chicago and is being charged with the murder of his son, Bryce Wilkerson, who was found slain earlier this month in Pinesap County, Wisconsin. Tune in to our 6:00 a.m. news for further details on this breaking story. And now, let's turn to Dan Roan with today's sports."

It was one of those times in life that one would always remember where they were when it happened. Or in this case for Doc and the Nurse, when they had heard it.

There was a moment of silence, as if the two were trying to convince themselves they had accurately heard the words spoken. Duff had one of those TVs that had replay capabilities. He backed it up thirty seconds. They listened again. They had heard right. The remote control went flying in the air as Duff ran to the Nurse in the kitchen, where they engaged in a celebratory hug, one totally different than the one twenty-four hours prior. This was a World Series hug, a Stanley Cup embrace, a "one moment in time" moment.

Duff knew that Kelle was unaware of the locale of the Ravenswood neighborhood. They were only about a mile away. He did not volunteer that tidbit, and he was relieved she didn't ask.

It took a while for their ebullience to decline. The heightened stress and fear that had spiked yesterday was also on the wane. They both wondered whether the two communications to the police via the Wausau paper had played a part in the arrest. The follow-up media reports on the case made no mention of an anonymous tip.

Bennett Coleman had mentioned it to his team of officers. No one had a clue.

EPILOGUE

Shortly following the arrest of Harold Wilkerson, Doc made an overdue confession to the Nurse.

The day prior to the murder in Wisconsin, he'd spent the day in Zion, Illinois. That had not been his plan; his intended destination was Gresham Lake outside of Oneida Falls, Wisconsin. The cabin owned by the Wilkerson family of Sycamore Pointe fame.

He had a gun and he'd had enough. The young sexual predator had posted some ugly and provocative photos that had ignited yet another of his untapped reservoirs of rage. In the first photo, he was shown pointing to himself. He titled it, "The One that Got Away." In the second photo, he was pointing at a fish that he had just reeled in. Its title was, "The One that Didn't."

Kelle had been out of town. He'd secured a vehicle that would be difficult to trace and headed north. About an hour out of the city and not yet in Wisconsin, he'd hit a pothole. The front right tire was shredded. The car had no spare. He and the disabled vehicle were towed to Zion. No one had the tire in stock.

Christian literature at times has referred to "Zion" as a heavenly place. It was where Michael Duff had spent the day, his trip to God's country having been nullified. As well as his act of vengeance.

About three months later, Michael Duff needed another car. He had a 155-mile drive ahead of him. As was his custom, he rented one at a local rental agency in the city. Paperwork was done. It was a Ford Fusion. Foreshadowing, perhaps, considering the reasons for the journey. One that would include more than his biweekly visits with Gabby and Hannah. One that would end a vicious cycle of procrastination.

He and Kelle had completed the process of distributing the money to Hope and her family as well as the other ancillary victims that stemmed from the young lady's abuse. He knew, as did his cohort, that multiple laws had been violated in the process; notwithstanding, he felt a sense of satisfaction that superseded any regrets for his legal transgressions. Moreover, the entire experience had been tonic for his own malady.

His anger was now in recession. The guilt and shame stemming from his childhood trauma was in full remission. He was ready to move on.

It was a beautiful fall day as he headed south and then east out of Chicago. The splendor of the autumn palette was at its peak. For the first time in years, Duff felt a certain calm as he neared his destination in north central Indiana. A year ago, he would have pulled the car over somewhere in the country to rid himself of his lower GI conflict.

As he pulled into the driveway of this rural subdivision home, he saw children outside playing in their yards. Some were throwing footballs and running pass patterns. Not his girls. They were doing flips on a backyard trampoline.

His heart was doing flips as he knocked on the front door. Kate came to the door and smiled.

It was the same smile that he had fallen in love with his junior year in high school. The same smile she wore when she'd visited him in the hospital following his drunken crash. And the same smile she'd given him on their wedding day.

"Hello, Michael."

"Hello, Kate. Can I come in? There's something I've been wanting to tell you."

There would be no more secrets. Only hope.

It had been years since the two-story dilapidated building on North Halstead Street in Chicago had enjoyed a purpose. The location was great, but the owner lacked vision, imagination, and oh yes, everybody's favorite, money. It was destined for demolition and then to become a parking lot. Out of nowhere, a civic theater group came up with the funds to buy and renovate the building, converting it into a theater in the round. They were preparing to hold rehearsals for their inaugural production, a rather bold undertaking . . . *The Sound of Music.*

Anonymous donors had made the purchase of the structure and its conversion to a modest fine arts venue a reality. A dream come true, actually.

It seems that there was a final residue of funds in a Caribbean account that needed to travel north. In addition, another $5,000 was awkwardly hanging around with nowhere to go. It, too, contributed to the stage construction fund.

One of benefactors would be attending the opening night performance. He would be watching and listening with eager anticipation to the solo "Climb Every Mountain" sung by Mother Abbess, the Mother Superior of the Austrian Abbey. His name: Michael Duff. Seated to his left was his date for the evening. Her name was Kate.

The name of the actress, singer, and fellow anonymous donor: Kelle Russo.

She nailed it. It moved Michael and Kate to tears.

So, the young girl from Pittsburgh who'd stopped singing as a child upon being molested by a Catholic priest was singing again while playing the part of a Catholic nun. The irony of the moment was too painful to dwell on; her climb of the mountain was not.

Pain. How do we measure it? For decades, doctors and nurses have questioned patients about their level of pain. "On a scale of one to ten (ten highest, one lowest), what is your pain level?" A subjective test of a pain that will likely have a finite life. A laceration that has been stitched, a broken bone that has been set and cast, a sciatic back pain relieved by a steroid shot. Physical pain is usually short lived and can be addressed readily by drugs, thread, splints, tape, red wine, ultrasound, Irish whiskey, x-rays, more drugs, blah, blah, blah.

Hope Emery-Wright's pain could not be seen. There was no blood. No broken bones. No pulled muscles. No physical pain in her head, arms, legs, hands, or feet. A pain that could not be rated on the "one to ten scale." It was a pain unique to the victims of sexual abuse.

But it was always there. It followed her everywhere, ebbing and flowing in her daily routine, abruptly spiking when she heard a certain song on the radio, a made-for-TV movie, or a newspaper article narrating the "alleged" facts behind a teacher being arrested for sexual abuse.

It was ugly. It could not be described by a girl of her tender age. It was shame. It ended dreams. It disturbed her sleep. It created chaos where there had previously been routine. Structure was demolished. Joy vanished. Confusion reigned. Smiles were feigned. Walls erected. Remaining silent always the default option.

The parents' pain was different, albeit equally disturbing. Coupled with uncompromising guilt, Josh fluctuated between melancholy and hot anger, the latter maturing to a rage which very nearly netted him a long prison sentence. Praise to his daughter for Dad escaping that criminality.

Amaya. A mother's pain. *How could I allow this to happen to the baby I labored to bring into this world? Where did I fall short? I cannot sleep until she heals.* But she may never heal! How is it that this ugly act of a dysfunctional man could cause such pain for so many people for so long? People would never know the toll.

The many counselors that the Emery-Wright family engaged over the years were consistent in their message. Hope would benefit from the early revelations of her abuse. Some victims took it to their graves. It would be a long process . . . for all of them. Months, perhaps years, of therapy. Constant reminders of the experience; years of emotional pain and adjustment and expenditure.

Money would not be an issue. The dollars squeezed from Baron Wilkerson prior to his arrest would compensate the family for all their counseling, medical, and musical needs.

As far as the pain? Pain can never be effectively compensated. Money can only mitigate it. Doc and the Nurse did what they could. Amaya, Josh, Hope, and her little brother would never want for anything financially. They were already rich in more important ways.

Hope found her voice again. She found her smile. After a near-disastrous detour, she rebounded. Goals reappeared. Laughter returned for all. There would always be mountains to scale, valleys to endure. But they were going to make it. And they would be stronger for it.

Hope springs eternal; and Hope would sing eternally.

Bennett Coleman turned west off Highway 51 heading to Trout Lake Golf Course for a 2:30 tee time with John Weatherton, his able crime lab tech from Wausau. His two sons, Vaughn and Dane, would complete the foursome. As he approached the entrance to the course, he noticed a campaign sign referencing an election that was to be held in about two months. It read: RE-ELECT GREG WALLACE SHERIFF OF PINESAP COUNTY. Below that bold lettering, it said: "You've been a great help. - Agent Bennett Coleman."

Coleman smiled to himself and wondered what the voters would think if they knew the context of those words.

Over the years, the veteran Wisconsin sleuth had spent vacations in the Northwoods at old time resorts in the area. In more recent times, he and his boys had rented condos. Really? Condos in the Northwoods? Perhaps his sons, both millennials, had an influence in that decision. He remembers them mentioning something about a pool, wide screen TVs, and a spa. Whatever the reason, following his successful investigation of the murder in Pinesap County, Redd's Lakeview Motel became his "go to" place.

With a little arm twisting, he was able to convince his sons to join him. They occupied a room next to Coleman's. They would play golf one day, fish the next, and then a day off with no agenda. The last of those were the best. Each night, they had an aroma contest to see who could guess the type of pie Louise Drysdale was making for dessert.

Those times with his boys were so peaceful and pure, each one adding another chapter to Coleman's fond memory bank as their father. And by contrast, an ironic reminder of his recently solved case.

He loved the old school rooms. He relished his morning coffee as he descended the steps to the wooden dock, overlooking the pristine waters of Spider Lake framed by majestic Norway conifers. He reveled in inhaling the fresh, pine-scented air. The water sparkled in the early morning sun. The white-tailed doe bounding unscathed through the dense forest piqued his amazement. The loon's morning song in perfect pitch brought a pensive smile to his face.

And it was all natural. The water, the trees, the air, the birds, the animals. Nothing from man had augmented the beauty. Over the years, quite the contrary.

No cost, either. Just lean back, relax, and let your senses do the rest. Free. Priceless. Spiritual.

God's Country.